Critical Care

Critical Care

Richard Dooling

William Morrow and Company, Inc.
New York

It is the policy of William Morrow and Company, Inc., and its imprints and affiliates, recognizing the importance of preserving what has been written, to print the books we publish on acid-free paper, and we exert our best efforts to that end.

Library of Congress Cataloging-in-Publication Data

Dooling, Richard.
    Critical care / by Richard Dooling.
        p.   cm.
    ISBN 0-688-10926-8
    I. Title.
    PS3554.0583S77   1991   91-12520
    813'.54—dc20   CIP

Printed in the United States of America

First Edition

1 2 3 4 5 6 7 8 9 10

BOOK DESIGN BY LISA STOKES

A.M.D.G.

For Kristy Kay and for Bob Shaddy

The book owes Frank Majka, Paul Johnson, M.D., and Paul Gilmore, M.D., for their careful reading and editorial assistance.

Thanks to Bryan Cave for the generous support, and to Lisa D. McLaughlin for her trusts and estates expertise.

Thanks to Jean Naggar and Adrian Zackheim for taking the manuscript in off the streets and bringing it up right.

The meaning of life is that it stops.
—Franz Kafka

We sometimes congratulate ourselves at the moment of waking
from a troubled dream: it may be so the moment after death.
—Nathaniel Hawthorne

Death is the poor man's doctor.
—German Proverb

Chapter

1

D_{r.} Peter Werner Ernst was the Internal Medicine resident on call and in charge of deaths occurring at night. Every third night, Werner went without sleep, presiding over the Ninth-Floor Intensive Care Unit from a circular console stacked high with computer terminals and cardiac monitors. At dawn, he worked another regular twelve-hour day, then staggered home to bed.

During the wee hours of his nights on call, Werner liked to think of the console as the bridge of the *Starship Enterprise,* and himself as . . . well, not Mr. Sulu. Instead of peering out into deep space or faraway galaxies, Werner was surrounded by eight windowed pods arranged in an octagon around the console, with a set of automatic glass doors that led to the fire escape and the Visitors' Lounge.

The space fantasy usually wore off about 2:00 or 3:00 A.M., and he became just another mad scientist, growing hair on the palms of his hands and the soles of his feet, wearing a white lab coat, surgical scrubs, and running shoes, with a stethoscope around his neck and a beeper tucked inside the drawstring of his surgical pants.

He swiveled in his chair at the console and surveyed his mad
laboratory of glass pods, where the stainless steel railings of hospital beds shone in the gloaming of color TVs.

Each pod in the octagonal Death Lab contained a naked, dying person, whose wrists and ankles were strapped to the bed
rails with four-point cotton restraints. Buzzing gadgets, beeping
machines, and flashing monitors were strapped, wired, or attached by tubes to the bodies. Fluorescent blips zigzagged across
oscilloscopes; ventilators hissed; electronic IVs clicked out dosages. High in the corner of each pod, a color TV was mounted
on ceiling brackets, tipped forward to provide a perfect angle for
viewing from the bed. The hanging televisions were obviously
designed by an architect or a hospital administrator who knew
almost nothing about ICU patients. When was the last time
somebody had seen one of these stiffs sitting up in bed watching
a ball game? Instead of their lives flashing before their eyes, these
patients died slow deaths listening to American car commercials,
the 2.9 percent financing, the unbelievable buyer protection
plans. . . .

Werner peered intently at the monitor marked "Bed 1" and
yawned a gaping, teary-eyed yawn. "Coffee," he shouted to no
one in particular, and thirty seconds later no one in particular set
a Styrofoam cup at his elbow.

More than anything else, Werner wanted sleep. If sleep were
a beverage, he thought, he would sling a jug of it over the back
of his hand and guzzle away until he aspirated on deep draughts
and died; if sleep were a dangerous, illegal drug, he would risk
prison and degradation just to wallow in it for eight hours;
if sleep were a woman, Werner would sleep with her, but he
would be too tired to please her; a pond, and Werner would dive
into sleep and drown. If sleep were anything but downtime for
Werner's information processing systems, he would sleep to
excess.

After the twenty-fourth hour in the Ninth-Floor ICU, a portion
of his brain, possibly a gland, did nothing but scream for sleep.
Once out of medical school, all he wanted out of life was twelve
hours of deep, throbless, uninterrupted slumber. As an undergraduate, he once thought he understood "Ode to a Nightingale," by
John Keats. As a medical resident, he realized the poem was about
a physician overcome with sleep lust.

Fade far away, dissolve, and quite forget
  What thou among the leaves hast never known,
The weariness, the fever, and the fret
  Here, where men sit and hear each other groan;
Where palsy shakes a few, sad, last gray hairs,
  Where youth grows pale, and spectre-thin, and dies;
    Where but to think is to be full of sorrow
    And leaden-eyed despairs,
  Where Beauty cannot keep her lustrous eyes,
    Or new Love pine at them beyond to-morrow.

Werner punched a button on the console and nervously clicked the clicker of a drug company fountain pen in and out a dozen times, while Bed One's cardiac monitor unspooled strips of EKG readings. He pored over the results, fighting brain fatigue and caffeine-induced intestinal distress. An audio monitor picked up some interference and piped a tinny rendition of a beer commercial over the hisses, clicks, and beeps of the life support systems.

A nurse approached Werner bearing a sheet of paper, which she wanted to give to him without disturbing him.

"I have Bed One's blood gases, Dr. Ernst," she said shyly.

As a rule, Werner acknowledged only older, veteran nurses who knew their medicine inside and out, or younger nubile ones who made his penis hard. The rest were nondescript wombats, like the creature at his elbow. Feeling sorry for them only distracted him from his work.

"Shall I call Respiratory Therapy and ask them to increase the oxygen?" she asked, blushing in four or five shades of pink.

Werner used to squander countless hours every workweek just being nice and friendly to the nurses and hospital staff. Before long, he realized that, while he was busy being nice and friendly, patients were busy dying all around him. More important, while he was busy being nice and friendly, other young residents were busy poring over journal articles and searching for clues in volumes of the patients' charts from previous admissions. Being nice and friendly to people who were not sick kept Werner from getting the upper hand on a particularly troublesome case of Legionnaires' disease; some third-year medical student got there ahead of him. Another time, being nice and friendly to people who were not sick resulted in a radiology resident's nailing down a diagnosis of

Goodpasture's syndrome, after Werner had told the entire medical hierarchy during grand rounds that it was idiopathic pulmonary hemosiderosis.

Early in his residency, Werner saw that to be a supernova, to ride the cutting edge in a place like the University Medical Center, an Internal Medicine resident had to conserve every possible increment of time and energy for the study and conquest of disease. Lower-order tasks, such as being nice and friendly, had to be delegated to lower-order personnel. If a resident wanted a future at the Medical Center, he judiciously had to avoid getting into a conversation with someone, like the baggage at his elbow, who could stand in front of a blue patient, hand you lab results confirming your suspicion that every cell in the patient's body was screaming for oxygen, and ask you if you wanted her to call a respiratory therapist to turn up the oxygen.

"No," Werner said, without looking at her. "Let's not turn up the oxygen. Let's call down to Housekeeping and requisition a big trash bag."

"A trash bag?" Marie Something whispered hoarsely, her face now burnished crimson by engorged capillaries.

"Yeah," Werner said, "so we can wrap it around Bed One's head and see how long it takes for those funny little squiggles on his cardiac monitor to stop."

Werner drained half the cold coffee from the Styrofoam cup and tried to stomach the unbearable realization that he would not even be able to steal a nap before his day started over, three hours from now, at 6:30 A.M. He leaned over his paper work and closed his eyes: an experience more terrifying than falling asleep at the wheel because, when his eyes closed, his subconscious burst at the seams, a circus of dream imagery exploding on the back of his eyelids, replaying the day's terrors and emergencies back so vividly that he jolted upright and scanned the monitors to see if he had veered off the road and killed somebody in the ICU. What if the nightmares that were crackling like fireworks on the back of his eyelids started leaking over into his waking moments? Experiments have shown that sleep-deprived subjects eventually start acting out their dreams in real life. What if one sleepless night Werner acted out one of his fondest dreams in the middle of the ICU? Perhaps the dream in which he executes a nurse with a semiautomatic pistol each time she makes a mistake, or how about the one in which he strangles a patient to death in an effort to save the patient's life? There was no lack of nurses and patients crying out to be strangled and beaten with stainless steel surgical tools. Would the Head Resident, Dr. Marlowe, believe him if Werner's story was that he could not remember any of it? That it had all occurred during a fugue state or a sleepwalk? A sleep rampage? Would the mugwumps in hospital administration swallow that one? "Murder?" Werner could protest. "She woke me up. Isn't that more like justifiable homicide?" Would the Med Center's insurance still cover him?

A different nurse startled Werner out of his chin nap. This one had yellow hair and square, copper-tinted glasses and freckled flab where her boobs belonged.

"Marie is crying," the nurse said.

"Who's Marie?" Werner asked, thinking instantly of the female liver patient in Bed Six. "You mean, the liver in Bed Six?"

"No," the nurse said. "Marie. Bed One's nurse."

"Bed One's nurse is crying," Werner said, as if someone had just told him that trash was blowing across the highway in Waco, Texas. "Where's Stella Stanley? Have you seen her?"

Apprehending that Werner was not about to inquire after the cause of Marie's tears, the nurse with the square glasses offered, "She's crying because she doesn't like to get yelled at."

Werner dumped the last of the cold coffee into his mouth and swished it around to keep the grounds from sticking to his teeth.

"Oh," Werner said, "I see. Someone who doesn't like to get yelled at went to nursing school of all places. Is this important information? And where is Stella Stanley?"

"Stella!" Werner called.

A voice came from the half-light in Bed Three. "I already upped Bed One's oxygen to sixty percent."

"Oh," Werner said. "Thank you."

"Yeah," Stella said. "Write the order now, before you drop off again."

Werner listened to Stella Stanley, R.N., doing cranial checks on a semialert, eighty-three-year-old bowel obstruction in Bed Three.

"Hi, there," Stella said, "do you know where you are?"

"Yes," the patient assured her.

"Good," Stella said. "'Now, can you tell me where you are?"

"I'm not at home," the patient said. "I'm somewhere else."

"Do you know where you are?" Stella continued.

"I'm with you," the woman said.

Stella pumped up a blood pressure cuff. "OK," she said. "Do you know what day it is?"

"Friday," the patient informed her, "or Saturday. My egg man always comes on Friday," Bed Three said, "and he was just here. But he told me earlier in the week that he wouldn't be able to come until Saturday. It must be Saturday."

"It's Tuesday," Stella said, "but that's OK, don't worry about it. I have trouble remembering what day it is myself. Try this one on for size: Who's the President of the United States?"

"I like Ike," Bed Three said, "and so do you. Didn't you tell me that yesterday?"

"I may have," Stella chirruped, "but I'm like you, I can't remember." Stella pulled a sheet up to Bed Three's chin. "The important thing is that you and I both are playing with a full deck, the cards are shuffled and dealt, and we're ready to bet. I'll be back in with some medication for you in just a little bit."

"Thank you, honey," Bed Three called after her.

Werner spread out the graphs and charts and lab results that together summed up Bed One's condition and tried to rally to the task at hand.

Bed One was spraddled, belly up, under the bright lights. His skin was cyanotic blue and shriveled with age, his torso swabbed and stained orange by disinfectants. A well-ventilated corpse festooned with skin tags and moles and mottled with age spots. Wires, tubes, and lines ran into his remaining accessible veins; a couple of external valves gave easy access to his arteries; a seam of stainless steel staples held his chest together.

Most of the space in Bed One's pod was taken up by an intra-aortic balloon pump, bigger than a rolltop desk, with a panoply of dials, switches, screens, and meters that only the intra-aortic balloon pump technician knew how to operate. From the pump's console, large plastic tubes went into the femoral artery on the inner aspect of Bed One's thigh and snaked up below his heart, where an inflatable balloon served as an extra valve. The bellows in the pump beat softly, like the drums of a warlike tribe throbbing in the distance.

A few hours ago, the surgeons had had Bed One downstairs. They sawed his sternum open and pried his rib cage apart. Well-paid personnel peered into him from all sides. Their rubber hands and steel instruments rooted around inside him, redid the upholstery inside Bed One's thorax, and shoved his lungs around like piles of cheap pork livers. When the surgeons finished with him, Bed One looked like something out of Mary Shelley's nightmares, blue all over, except for the watercolor disinfectant stains.

Bed One bucked the ventilator, a sign that he needed suctioning and pulmonary toilet. A woman in a white lab coat put on rubber gloves. She disconnected Bed One from his ventilator and squirted 5 cc of half-normal saline down his endotracheal tube. Bed One gagged and coughed, while the woman suctioned secretions from his lungs into a liter sputum trap.

"Thataboy," she said. "Now we're gettin' that nasty stuff outta there."

The chart said the doctors went in two months ago to replace a valve in Bed One's heart. A routine procedure, which meant Bed One was supposed to wake up afterward. Bed One did not wake up, resulting in a statistical aberration.

When patients did not wake up afterward, someone had to console the family by telling them that, although the risks of complications associated with the procedure were low, every procedure carries risks. Pretty soon, nobody talked about the case without calling their attorney first.

The cardiologists speculated that the surgeons shook a clot loose when they were in there, that the clot then went up and lodged somewhere in Bed One's brainstem, effectively squeezing off the supply of blood and oxygen to all points north, making mush out of everything above the neck. The surgeons hypothesized that the cardiologists had failed to prescribe enough blood thinners after surgery, causing a clot that would have formed whether Bed One had been in surgery or not. The surgeons and the cardiologists agreed that the Internal Medicine people were at fault for allowing such a high-risk candidate to undergo surgery.

Bed One was the thin slice of a pie diagram showing risk and complication in aortic valve replacements.

The busy young staff members in the Ninth-Floor ICU did not give an environmental technician's damn about Bed One, because they knew enough about medicine and rudimentary physiology to know that Bed One was a slab of warm lunch meat with reflexes and poor vital signs—a life-size figure carved out of Spam instead of wax. But they all also had a healthy respect for the kind of assault Bed One could mount against them. Bed One could make the next four hours of their lives miserable, just by changing the electrical conduction of his heart and going into a Code Blue. By simply perishing, he could send the nurses into a shrieking panic worthy of the weird sisters.

Resignation was the order of the day. Everybody from the nurses on down to the respiratory therapists and the lab techs had already privately agreed that Bed One would "code" sometime tonight, "code" being short for Code Blue. Bed One's heart would stop beating, or he would stop breathing, or both; the hospital operator would then announce, "Code Blue, Ninth-Floor Intensive Care Unit," three times over the hospital's public-address system, and a dozen or so specially trained personnel would then descend on Bed One, snap Bed One's head back, pump Bed One's lungs full of oxygen with an ambu bag, inject massive doses of expensive drugs in some of Bed One's veins, draw blood for expensive tests from other veins, shock Bed One with electricity, beat on Bed One's chest, and generally do everything possible to jumpstart Bed One, as if Bed One were a '57 Chevy that should have been taken to the junkyard twenty years ago, and the doctors and nurses were a bunch of drunk teenagers whose car had broken down on the way to a pig roast.

It would go on for hours. It would require more blood, lab, stool, and sputum specimens to be drawn and sent to the lab. Worse yet, everything would have to be scrupulously documented for the Legal Department. Afterward there would be witness interviews, probably depositions, just like the ones after the craniotomy in Bed Seven had been struck by lightning that came in through the TV set.

Bed One had no business dying from a simple valve replacement. The lawyers knew that.

Because it was 3:30 A.M., Werner was solely responsible for the likes of Bed One. All the real doctors and primary physicians had gone home, had barbecued steaks, had watched a few hours of cable TV, and had gone to bed. In his capacity as House Officer, Werner had to respond to every medical emergency occurring outside the normal hours of the medical workday: like Bed One's dying too soon.

"This is what makes it all worthwhile," he said to a wombat at his elbow. "Being able to help people. This is where training pays off."

Werner looked the impending medical crisis squarely in the eye and measured himself against it, his self-confidence barely surmounting sleepless anxiety. As usual, he fought the urge to panic by silently reminding himself of his credentials: *I am Dr. Peter Werner Ernst. I graduated at the top of my medical school class. I was Editor in Chief of the University's* Journal of Medicine. *I am qualified and capable of practicing medicine. I will not panic or succumb to stress and make the wrong decision. That would be irrational and inconsistent with my past performance.*

Given the hopelessness of Bed One's situation, another medical resident might have thrown up his hands and accepted the inevitable descent of the patient. Another resident might have been discouraged by the resignation on the faces of the Intensive Care Unit nurses—faces that said, "Bed One is about to code, creating shitloads of pointless labor and paper work for us all." Yes, another resident might have allowed the normal course of human events to degenerate into chaos, death, and a Code Blue. But not Werner Ernst. Werner was blessed with a superior medical mind, trained in the healing arts.

Werner's rigorous training had prepared him for this moment, when he, the House Officer in charge of the Medical Center and the resident physician immediately responsible for the welfare of Bed One, would come up with the right combination of medications to drip into Bed One, just the right mix of dosages given at just the right intervals, to keep blood pressure up, keep CO_2 down, keep heartbeats passably even, and urine flowing . . . keep everything just so, for six or seven hours at least . . . so that Bed One would go down the tubes and croak on the day shift, not the night shift. So that Werner could eat and possibly nap tonight, instead of presiding over the death of a corpse. So that the ICU nursing staff could embroider or read romance novels through the wee hours. So that Bed One could sleep one, last, peaceful, vegetable sleep before being assaulted by a Code Blue wrecking crew trying to save his life. And above all, so that all the wicked, ridiculous shit concerning the demise of Bed One (who only two months ago was a grandpa, a loving husband, and a dad to the people who had brought him here) would come down on Bed One's primary physician and the day shift. The day shift had advised Bed One and

Bed One's family that eighty was not too old to try for another valve replacement. Eighty? Bed One's primary physician, Bed One's chest surgeon, and Bed One's family made Bed One's bed of slaughter and anguish. Why should Werner and the night shift sleep in it?

"Hey, Wiener," a male nurse shouted from Bed One's pod, "Bed One's pulmonary wedge pressure is dropping again."

Werner's eyes shifted to phosphorescent green lines squiggling across the screen marked "Bed 1."

"Do we have the first volume of his chart?" Werner asked. "Are there three volumes, or four?"

"The bottom's falling out of his wedge again," the nurse repeated.

"Right. Give him the same thing we gave him the last time he pulled that stunt. And tell him he can't die until he sees the smiling faces of the day shift."

Werner paused to reflect that, if the Medical Center were a closed system governed by Reason (instead of a wide-open delusional system governed by humans), Bed One's primary physician might have declared Bed One a "No Code," in which case, Bed One could have died without being molested in his final hour. But as bad luck would have it, Bed One's primary physician was Randolph Hiram Butz (better known as Buttface after he had left the room). Buttface was a hopelessly senile alcoholic, incapable of even basic intellectual and motor skills after lunch. At high noon each day Butz broke out a hip flask of Johnnie Walker Black Label, and by one o'clock or so he could be seen cheerfully roaming the hospital corridors, confining himself mainly to the Intensive Care Units, where the patients were so gorked out they would never have noticed the odor of scotch on their attending physician's breath.

The state medical licensing board had come after Butz at least twice, but he had outmaneuvered them both times. Before he became a raging drunk, Butz had amassed an impregnable set of credentials and enough political connections to deep-six the board's investigations. Forty years ago, Butz had graduated magna cum laude from the Yale Medical School. Twenty years ago, before he met Johnnie Walker, he had coauthored a book called *The Fundamentals of Internal Medicine*, which had been updated every five years by teams of assistant editors. The text was still used in two thirds of the nation's medical schools, and it still had Butz's name on it, even though he could no longer balance a checkbook or write a complete sentence. His inability to write also insulated him from medical malpractice suits, because he was the only one who could read his own Physician's Orders. It meant that the orders he wrote in his patients' charts said whatever his lawyers told him they should say.

The more vicious hospital gossips circulated the rumor that Buttface used to wear only Brooks Brothers wing tips, that these days he wore only tasseled slip-ons, and that Mona Washburn, the Head Nurse over in Coronary Care, had made him start wearing tasseled slip-ons because she was sick and tired of tying his shoes for him whenever he was too hammered to tie them himself.

"Hey, Wienerhead," said another nurse, this one a short, pushy health care commando with a helmet of clipped wire for a hairdo. She slapped a computer printout down at Werner's elbow. "Bed Two's electrolytes, Dr. Wienerschnitzel, and pretty fucking nasty-looking, if you want my opinion."

Stella Stanley, R.N., better known around the ICU as Stan, was a critical care nurse with twenty years of death, disease, and excretions behind her. The Army had had her in San Francisco for four years and had trained her on amputees and burn victims in the Vietnam era. Then she had done five years working night shift on a burn unit in Chicago, scrubbing dead skin out of raw third-degree wounds. After five years of that, she began to have trouble with her hearing. First, she saw an Ear, Nose, and Throat man. Then she brought suit against the hospital where she worked, claiming that it was the infernal screaming of burn victims that had caused her hearing to deteriorate. She testified in court that, when she used to go home in the mornings and try to sleep, her ears would go on ringing for hours with the screams of her patients until, finally, she was forced to clamber out of bed and drown out the sound with a twelve-pack of Budweiser, making the hospital responsible for her hearing loss, as well as her alcoholism. Ultimately, she lost the civil suit for damages and had to make do with a workers' compensation award. Shortly thereafter, she came to the Medical Center and the Ninth-Floor Intensive Care Unit, which, she insisted, was a Holiday Inn compared with the burn

unit. Somewhere along the line (probably Chicago), she had acquired the bedside manner of a mobster, the sound of her voice
having all the tenderness of a saw-toothed rectal probe.

"How's his potassium, Stan?" Werner asked, referring to one of
Bed Two's electrolytes, though his head was still buried in the
enigma of Bed One's chart.

"WHAT?" Stella yelled, cupping an ear. "MY HEARING AID'S ON
THE FRITZ."

"I say, HOW'S BED TWO'S POTASSIUM?"

"Oh." Stan took another look at the computer printout of Bed
Two's electrolytes. "It depends," she said, in a voice so loud that
any one of four comatose patients might have heard her every word,
if they could have only risen for a moment from the dead. She
snapped a wad of gum way back in her molars. "It depends on what
you wanna be when you grow up, Wiener. If you wanna be a mortician when you grow up, then I'd say Bed Two's potassium looks
pretty good. On the other hand, if you wanna be a doctor . . ."

"Thank you, Stanley," Werner said. "That will be all."

"WHAT?"

"I SAY THANK YOU."

"Sure thing, chum,"said Stella. "By the by, is it still OK with
you if I slam ten milligrams of morphine into Bed Seven every time
he wakes up and starts messing around with his tubes?"

"YES, Stanley."

"And would you write that in the Physician's Orders before you
leave for your nap?"

Bed Two had a skin color that would take any other twenty-
three-year-old white male a solid three weeks of rotisserie tanning
in the Bahamas to achieve. Bed Two's solarless tan was caused by
toxic waste products, which his kidneys used to filter out of his
blood and drip into his bladder, whence the orange poison could
be jettisoned at his and his bladder's convenience. Now, all that
piss and vinegar was oozing out of Bed Two's skin because his
kidneys no longer functioned. His was a deep, dark, all-over tan,
which would be the envy of the ICU, except that it meant impending physiological doom.

"Nothing more depressing than a young kidney patient," someone in the Report Room said.

"Oh, yes, there is," Stella Stanley retorted. "Cleaning up the loose stools of a young kidney patient is more depressing than a young kidney patient."

Calling Bed Two a kidney patient was something of a misnomer, because like most kidney patients, Bed Two did not have any kidneys.

Any doctor devoted to Nephrology (the study of kidneys) will tell you that the human body is really nothing but a primitive go-cart containing a simple pump, wires, tubes, cables, a blob of gray matter functioning as a rudimentary battery, two gas bags, various units concerned with food processing and reproduction— all nothing but a transport and reproduction mechanism for two highly sophisticated little electrochemical miracles called kidneys, organs that make the most advanced computers look like clumsy racks of on-off switches.

There have been reports of kidney doctors who, as medical residents, were religious nonbelievers or agnostics until they went into Nephrology and began to get an idea of what really goes on inside a kidney, at which point they had mystical experiences and realized that only a divine, all-knowing intelligence could design a kidney. The hair-trigger balance of electrolytes, hormones, poisons, fluids, gases in solution, sugars, and particles trafficking back and forth across membranes in the kidney is beyond mortal comprehension. It has been said that if St. Paul were alive today, he would not have been knocked off his horse by a lightning bolt on his way to Damascus; he would have been a Nephrology resident struck speechless by the awesome complexity of a kidney. Some kidney doctors have gone so far as to leave their practices altogether, becoming TV evangelists who go on the air with anatomical models of kidneys, preaching their message that the Way to Eternal Life is through an understanding of the kidney.

Because Bed Two had no kidneys of his own, every two or three days, a dialysis technician wheeled a machine into Bed Two's room—a machine that approximated the myriad functions of Bed Two's kidneys about as closely as a crystal radio approximated a Bang and Olufsen stereo system. Through a nylon tube that had been permanently installed in Bed Two's forearm, the dialysis technician siphoned Bed Two's blood through the man-made, Model T kidney, doing the best he could with all the poisons, hormones, and electrolytes. The dialysis machine had not done much for Bed

Two's skin color; neither had the machine done much for Bed Two's self-esteem or his bridge game.

Though one would never know it by looking at him, Bed Two had recently received his degree in missile systems engineering from the University. He had just been out to Seattle, where he had landed a job with a major aerospace contractor. Bed Two had flown back home to announce his engagement to the nicest woman anybody in the ICU had ever met. He went to a party and got trashed on piña coladas; he played nine holes of golf with his best friend. Two days later, Bed Two started coughing up blood; one day later his kidneys gave out, and he was shipped to the Ninth-Floor ICU with a diagnosis of idiopathic pulmonary hemosiderosis, later changed to Goodpasture's syndrome, a disease that must have received its name from somebody who believed that we all are headed for greener pastures in the next life, because Goodpasture's syndrome is almost always fatal. The most extreme cure is removal of both kidneys and a life of dialysis three times a week. Usually even that does not work.

No one knows what causes Goodpasture's syndrome, or why it strikes mainly young, healthy males who are inevitably bright, popular, and talented and who have promising futures. No one knows why a missile systems engineer and groom-to-be should be turned into a kidney patient overnight. It just happens, and when something bad happens—no matter how bad it is—the best thing to do is to make the best of the situation, right? The fact that Bed Two was a terminal, orange, kidney patient, out of his gourd and tied down in bed with four-point restraints was a foregone conclusion. Water under the bridge. Spilled milk. Werner could have sat around, wringing his hands over the legacy of random misfortune for weeks or months. Instead, he was pragmatic. Although every medical person has heard of Goodpasture's syndrome, precious few of them have actually seen it. Bed Two was a rare opportunity to follow a case of clinical, end-stage Goodpasture's syndrome, and Werner vowed to learn everything he could from Bed Two, before Bed Two took the far turn in life and headed for the cliff.

Besides turning his skin orange, the toxic wastes accumulating in Bed Two's blood also made him crazier than a bedbug in a jar of laughing gas. He had been "confused," as is said in chart talk, and in a wild-eyed daze for three or four days now, and dialysis had not helped any.

"Good morning," Stella said, pulling a plastic cap off a large syringe with her teeth and stringing up another IV bottle on a hook over Bed Two's head.

"The doctor says that you have to be NPO," Stella explained, without looking at him. "That means you can't have any fluids, understand? You can't have any fluids because you don't have any kidneys, so you can't pee. Follow me? But if you'd like, I can give you some ice chips every so often. Would you like some ice chips now?"

Bed Two's mouth opened in dismay at Stella's question. "I don't believe in God anymore," he advised her.

Stella spit the plastic syringe cap into the nearest wastebasket. "Hey, Poindexter," she yelled, without turning her head in the direction of the other seven pods.

"What?" came a male nurse's reply from the general vicinity of Beds Seven and Eight.

"Bed Two doesn't believe in God anymore."

"I know," the voice said. "He told me that yesterday when I was doing cranial checks on him."

Stella grabbed an orange rubber tube that was sticking out of Bed Two's nose. "I'm going to flush your NG tube," she said, using her right hand to fill a 20 cc bulb syringe with normal saline, simultaneously slipping the rubber-tipped prongs of her stethoscope into her ears. "You might feel some gurgling in your stomach."

"God was murdered," Bed Two said. "And I know who did it."

"So this God thing," Stella said, "that's pretty offbeat, ain't it? People like you usually turn into believers, not unbelievers."

Stella squirted the bulb syringe into the orange tube in Bed Two's nose and listened to the normal saline gurgle deep in the reeds and bulrushes of Bed Two's organs.

"God would not answer my prayers with suffering like this," Bed Two said.

Stella clamped off the orange tube and tossed the syringe in the wastebasket.

"I don't know," she said. "I've always felt that Trouble means that somewhere there is a Troublemaker."

Chapter

2

Seven years ago, Peter Werner Ernst gradu
ated from the University with a liberal arts degree and went home
to read all the books he never had time to read in college. He got
a part-time job loading trucks for an overnight mail service and
rented a cheap apartment. Convinced that the best things in this
world, including sleeping and reading, happened lying down, he
furnished the apartment with a bed and a couch. He set out to
discover whether it was possible to make a life out of chasing
women and reading great books.

The significant others in Werner's life had significant, other
plans. Beautiful women, parents, even his best friend told Werner
to get a job. It was a question of diet and shelter, they argued.

Werner found their entreaties objectionable. Every profound
sage Werner had read about in college had done a considerable
amount of reading and womanizing before doing anything else in
life. Socrates, St. Augustine, Voltaire, Ignatius Loyola, James
Boswell, Samuel Johnson, Rimbaud, Valéry, Nietzsche—all those
guys spent years reading or debauching before they lifted a finger
to feed themselves or take out the trash. Furthermore, Werner had
majored in linguistics and the philosophy of language, which

meant that whenever somebody said something, Werner had to pause and reflect on the nature of words.

Werner tried to get a job as a nice guy with a good education who liked to lie around and read. The liberal arts had thoroughly trained him in the rigors of lying around and reading. His qualifications were in order, and he had a résumé to back them up. He beat the pavements and diagrammed the want ads. He chased down every maybe and trod the razor's edge that separated being confidently assertive about one's superior qualifications from being pitifully desperate for some income.

The truth was disconcerting: There were no openings for a nice guy with a good education who liked to lie around and read. Those positions all had been filled by other nice guys who had been lying around and reading for so long they had master's degrees and Ph.D.'s. Western civilization had degenerated to such an extent that there were absolutely no openings for a Renaissance man with a major in linguistics and a lot of loose science courses lying around.

Under increasing pressure from beautiful women who said they would not sleep with him unless he found a job and talked about marriage first, Werner thought out loud about becoming a hunter-gatherer or a Kurdish tribesman. No, the beautiful women said. Not a job, a good job.

Freud's bones chuckled in his grave when Werner, the Renaissance man, consulted a job counselor, at his father's expense, to assist him in distinguishing good jobs from jobs.

"A good job is one that matches your preferences with your abilities," the counselor said. "First, you must list your skills and achievements, and then we will make a list of all the jobs that comprise those skills and achievements. Then we will simply rank those jobs according to your preferences."

"How much do people pay for this kind of advice?" Werner asked.

Werner couched his achievements in the negative: He was not an alcoholic; he did not take drugs; he was not violent. He listed two skills: (1) falling in love with beautiful women; (2) reading.

The session ended when Werner applied for the counselor's job, and the counselor returned half his fee to Werner's father.

For a while, beautiful women slept with Werner because he was looking for a good job, and because he swore he was not averse to marriage. Werner rose to the occasion of looking for a good job, but winced in the execution: He did not actually find a good job.

Werner's parents had perceived an underlying pattern in the checkerboard of Werner's academic pursuits and were quick to make helpful career suggestions. After all, there were any number of challenging, respectable fields open to a bright, ambitious, young college graduate. How about law or medicine, they had suggested, professions anyone would be proud to wear around? And if neither of those appealed to him, they consoled him with the idea of becoming a doctor or a lawyer. Not wanting to wear out their credibility, they had gone on to suggest that Werner might do worse than becoming a medical specialist or a tax attorney. How about a physician or a barrister? Two perfectly good occupations. In lieu of any of those, Werner's father suggested Werner might try looking into something in the legal field or the medical profession, by applying to law school or medical school.

Werner selected Medicine from the vocational horn of plenty. That September, he became seriously ill, then died and went to medical school. After four years of lying around reading thick science books and taking multiple-choice tests, Werner had begun to think that Medicine might not be all that bad. The material was not something he would have chosen to read, but after being force-fed on the stuff, he found it mildly interesting. It had a certain internal consistency, as long as one refrained from examining its major premises. And after all, he reasoned, it was a profession for which one was paid well to help relieve the sufferings of others.

That was before Werner had spent his first night in the ICU. After a few nights on call, Werner became an unearthly being in suspended animation, a well-trained intellect doomed to walk the linoleum floors of the Death Labs.

Werner's nose flared and quivered slightly, not because any interesting females had arrived on the scene, but because he had just touched a lighted panel switch that opened the automatic doors to the Ninth-Floor ICU; he was preparing himself for the odor.

The first time Werner smelled a hospital, his nose told him he was traversing a place of pestilence and evil. That was on the first floor, where even the lobby smells of floor wax, vinyl upholstery, and the Gift Shop's floral displays could not hide the warring, hospital odors of antiseptics and decaying human flesh. What was true for the rest of the hospital increased to the power of at least ten in the Ninth-Floor Intensive Care Unit. The Death Lab was a clearinghouse for all the odors found everywhere else in the hospital.

Werner took a deep breath and tried to make it last as long as possible, before he would be forced to inhale Intensive Care air. After thirty seconds or so, he took his first breath through the nose, hoping the nasal hairs, turbinates, and mucosae of the nasal fossae would filter out any airborne bacteria before they got to his lungs. The nasal architecture is designed so that a sniff will draw noxious environmental gases only so far as the olfactory region, where the odious fumes may be sampled and expelled before passing farther into the respiratory tract. This assumes, of course, that the organism will have enough common sense to flee the source of the miasma and forever shun the place. But the brain of civilized man has "evolved" much faster than his nose. Society promised to pay Werner a lot of money someday for cultivating self-discipline and for teaching his brain to suppress the flight stimulus caused by the swamp gas wafting out of these corpses. Werner the organism stayed and inhaled the smell of Death, day in and day out, even though the same smell would have prompted his male ancestors to gather the women and the livestock and migrate to another savanna.

Within moments, Werner was acting like a doctor: reading the charts and pulling EKG strips out of the cardiac monitor. He took in the eight windowed cubicles and observed once again that, although each window had venetian blinds, to the best of Werner's recollection, the blinds had never been drawn, probably because the half-naked stiffs inside the pods had never regained enough consciousness to request privacy. The staff members preferred to keep the flesh chambers brightly lit twenty-four hours a day, so the specters within could be viewed at a glance from the central console.

"Dr. Salami, how's it going?"

Werner was not unhappy to see Stella Stanley, R.N. Even though she was only a nurse, she had a lot going for her. For instance, Stella did not have diabetes, heart disease, rheumatoid arthritis, or emphysema. She was not a senior medical officer, nor was she refusing to put out urine.

"An abysmal day," Werner confessed. "Death and chaos, with no sex to round it all out. Furthermore, a critical error has come to my attention."

Stella took the death and chaos business with a grain of salt. If Werner was still complaining, it meant he was still capable of judgment. Calling the day abysmal also meant the young doctor was still distinguishing one day from the next; not bad for somebody who never saw the sun rise or set from one day to the next and went without sleep every third night.

"You mean, Bed One?" Stella asked.

"Precisely," Werner said, showing her the most recent volume of the chart with a big red "1" emblazoned on the front and surrounded by allergy warning stickers. "What happened?"

"Maybe we gave him too much dopamine," she said. "Don't look at me. I thought he was going to cash his chips in before noon."

"Somebody on day shift did this"—Werner scowled—"and I'm going to find out who. Aren't they much better staffed to handle this sort of thing on days?"

"I concur, Dr. Frankurter," Stella said. "The day shift is more qualified to process deaths. They are also much better at explaining precisely why someone died. On our shift, patients just up and get it over with, unceremoniously, and we don't bother with why."

"Family here again tonight?" Werner asked.

"The place is crawling with them," said Stella, "and they are mad as hell about only being let in for ten minutes on the hour."

"Family" was a collective noun used by ICU staff members to designate persons visiting the unit who were neither patients nor health care personnel. "Family" was a euphemism for intruders who had a medically useless, highly emotional concern for patients. They had a tendency to stand underfoot, moping, grieving, and asking inane questions, especially at night.

On day shift the Pastoral Care program staffed the Units with clergymen and clergywomen of all faiths, who in turn enlisted the support of seminarians, deacons, nuns, and chaplains to spend time with sick people and Family. The program generated revenue almost instantly, because it allowed doctors to spend more time performing billable procedures. Instead of comforting distraught family members in the Visitors' Lounge, the doctors could go back to work in the ICUs. But at night, Pastoral Care shut down, and Family sought out the medical residents and nurses.

Werner looked at his watch and peered down the hallway toward the Visitors' Lounge. It was time. He could see Family coming, moving slowly in stunned clusters, like drought-stricken animals on a march to find water.

"Here they come," Werner said. "I'll give them your home phone number."

Bed One's family showed up at the automatic doors of the ICU: the wife, a squat, round, feeble woman with silver hair and a game leg; the son a beef-bellied old farmer in cowboy boots, Osh-Kosh overalls, and a NAPA auto parts cap. The two of them were old and fat enough for someone to sneak up behind them with stretchers and roll them into their own private pods.

Werner hid his head in the charts of Bed One. He had told these people a dozen times exactly what they did not want to hear.

"How's he doing?" the old woman asked with a sniffle.

Stella went into Bed One's pod and removed a thermometer from the patient's armpit. "A little better," she said. "He took a bad spin there for a while; but we got his blood pressure back up with some medication, and the doctor has ordered his ventilator set to give him more breaths per minute. He's getting more oxygen than he was before. His color's still not good, though. He put out a tiny bit of urine, which is more than he's put out in days."

"There's hope then," the son said, shuffling from one boot to the other and clearing his throat.

"He ain't woke up yet?" the old woman asked, rolling with a gimp toward the bed, chapped whorls of red flab wobbling at the posterior of her elbows.

"No," Stella said. "He's completely unresponsive." She reached over the bed rails. "HEY, MELVIN! SQUEEZE MY HAND. CAN YOU HEAR ME! SQUEEZE MY HAND!" She showed them Bed One's flaccid hand.

The old woman started in on a quiet cry. "Name's Elvin," she said, "not Melvin."

The son tried to make himself useful by saying, "Dad, this is Earl. Squeeze the nurse's hand if you can hear us."

Stella went to work, jabbing buttons and setting dials on one of

Bed One's IV pumps. Bed One's wife and son lined up on either side of the bed, staring at his chest as it rose and fell with the bellows of the ventilator, wondering why he still had his eyes open if he was in a coma.

"How's he doing, Doc?" the son hollered at Werner.

Werner looked up from his charting. "His potassium is better," he said. "Say, may we offer you some coffee?"

Offering coffee to the family was a well-established signal for the nurses to get Family out from underfoot and out of the doctor's hair.

Marie Something promptly answered the bell and led Bed One's family back out to the Visitors' Lounge.

If the coffee gambit failed, Werner had a private backup arrangement with Stella Stanley. If Werner ever said, "I'm expecting a phone call," when he was talking with Family, Stella promptly went to the med room, activated his beeper, and paged him to the Emergency Room.

Werner wrote the date in the Physician's Orders of Bed One's chart. He knew the date but was unsure of the day. Just the reverse of the way things are for the nonmedical world. In the business world, most people know the day, but are unsure of the exact date. Furthermore, most people think of themselves as torture victims stretched on a rack with five notches known as weekdays, and they are always acutely aware of just how far the wheel and pinion have to go before they hit the weekend release. What else serves to mark the passage of time, if not a weekend? For Werner, there was no such thing as a weekend, so he never knew what day it was. But the exact date stared him in the face every time he opened a patient's chart and wrote his orders.

Werner knew that it was 0200 hours (2:00 A.M.), and that he would probably be here in the University Medical Center for the next sixteen hours without sleep; that, in addition to Bed One and Bed Two, there were six other train wrecks to be looked after; that Bed Eight's blood sugar was going through the ceiling; that Bed Three was throwing ominous ventricular beats all over the green-grid cardiac monitor marked "Bed 3"; that if Bed Seven's condition deteriorated any further, the kidney foundation would be removing Bed Seven's kidneys and giving them to Bed Two; that Bed Five was in severe respiratory distress; that Bed Six was in severe respiratory distress; that he, Dr. Peter Werner Ernst, was, for the moment at least, solely responsible for their immediate welfare; and that he wished only to go home, crack open a frosty Budweiser, and watch a rerun of *Star Trek*.

"Are Bed Four's lungs still clear?" Werner asked, clinging to the only good piece of news.

"Light rales," Stan replied. "I think you should up her Lasix and take some fluid out of her. Her wedge pressure is too high."

Stan rolled her eyes, as Werner went into the Bed Four's pod to have a listen for himself.

Bed Four contained an eighty-seven-year-old white female, on the rebound from heart failure and a host of other maladies that once were considered "normal" for someone pushing ninety. She was supine, with pillows wedged under her torso to keep her from rolling around on her curved spine. Her hands were drawn up in front of her like the claws of a dead bird. Her eyes had rolled back halfway into their sockets. Her mouth, which had fallen open, remained permanently ajar. Every now and again, she hyperventilated, and the dark hole of her mouth got bigger and smaller. She also groaned every so often, sounding like an exhausted athlete or an abandoned lover.

The groans startled Werner because he was not used to sounds coming out of his patients. Most of his patients were on ventilators, and the tube that took oxygen from the breathing machine to the patient went in the mouth, down the throat, through the vocal cords, and into the lungs. Once intubated, patients could only mouth silent words with their lips, gesture, or scrawl messages on pads. Even gesturing was usually out of the question for these patients, because their hands were almost always tied to the bed rails with cotton restraints, to keep them from yanking their tubes. Any half-awake mammal with a gag reflex and a tube the size of a fat cigar in its throat will instinctively rip the foreign object out of its airway at the first opportunity. An unplanned extubation meant calling a team from Anesthesia to reintubate the patient and lots of charting explaining how the patient had managed to get the tube out in the first place, not to mention the mess that had to be cleaned up if the vocal cords came out with the tube.

Early in his training, Werner noted that ventilator patients often thrashed about in bed, gesticulating and mouthing silent words at him. Because he was naive, he took pity on them and their desperate inability to communicate. He untied their hands, handed them notebooks, and patiently waited for them to scrawl out messages. He watched them tediously mouth words, syllable by silent syllable, exaggerating every vowel and consonant for emphasis. More experienced residents stood at the door to the cubicle, looking at their watches and jerking their heads at Werner to move along to the next patient. But Werner's compassion was not so easily unseated.

He spent at least forty-five minutes attempting to communicate with his first vent patient, a bloated youngster (late sixties) with cirrhosis of the liver from drinking a quart of Jim Beam every day for forty years. The patient had tugged frantically at Werner's sleeve, motioning for a pad and paper to write on and mouthing emphatic, silent words around his endotracheal tube. Werner was absolutely certain that the man had a message of the utmost importance, if someone would only take the time. At long last, Werner deciphered the man's scrawl with the help of the patient's primary ICU nurse. In tall, wobbly script, with long trails between the letters and words, where the patient had been unable to lift the pencil from the paper, it said: "Dad is not home."

After a few more sessions of this kind, during which dying people clawed at Werner's elbow and beckoned urgently for Werner to lean closer to their ET tubes so he could hear the sibilance of lips and tongues making soundless vowels and consonants, Werner deciphered a few more urgent messages of absolute importance. A seventy-five-year-old aortic aneurysm repair wanted to know where his dead sister had put his pants. A seventy-nine-year-old heart on his third bypass said simply: "Weapons." After Werner repeated, "Weapons?," the heart nodded his head vigorously and made an OK circle with his thumb and forefinger.

The diminishing returns of lipreading and semiotics quickly became apparent, even to Werner, the novice. He seldom received a communication that made any sense, and when he did, it was inevitably a request for something a nurse could provide.

Bed Four groaned again, giving Werner an eerie, happy sensation. He decided to take advantage of her loquaciousness.

"Hello," he said. "How are we doing?"

Bed Four stared at the same spot on the ceiling, eyes atilt and mouth ajar. She was definitely not a member of the consumer group targeted by the silent cereal commercial playing on the TV hanging from the ceiling.

Werner gently took one of her claws and moved one arm aside, feeling it shudder like the wings of the dying baby birds he had found as a boy. He lifted Bed Four's gown and moved his stethoscope methodically, attentively, up and down her rib cage, pausing in a blank stare during moments of intense aural concentration, reaching around and temporarily turning off any machines that interfered with his ability to hear. He went to the foot of the bed and threw the covers back from her yellow feet. He took the metal handle of his reflex hammer and scratched the sole of her foot to check her Babinski reflex.

She groaned again, and without taking her tilted eyes off their ceiling focal point, she said quite plainly, "Doctor."

Werner strode quickly to the head of the bed and looked into her vacant eyes.

"Yes," he said. "I am your doctor."

Bed Four curled her hands and did not take her eyes off the ceiling.

"Can you hear me?" Werner asked, touching one of the claws.

Werner shone his penlight into Bed Four's eyes, and she blinked.

"Hey, Stella," Werner called.

Stella appeared instantly and hit a switch, flooding the room in a blaze of noon from the bright heat lamps overhead.

"What's wrong?" Stella asked. "Her pressure was fine ten minutes ago."

"This is unbelievable," Werner said, pocketing his stethoscope and bopping Stella on the head with his rubber hammer.

"What's wrong?" Stella asked again, impatiently checking Bed Four for any sign of a new neurological deficit or a loss of color. "She's pink and breathing."

"Exactly," Werner said. "I can't tell you what this means to me," he said, leaving the pod and heading for the chart racks.

"Her lungs are clear," Werner said. "She called me Doctor."

"She did not," Stella said, looking back into the pod in disbelief.

"She did," Werner said. "I think this woman is going to make it out of the ICU. I am going to be instrumental in delivering medical care to a patient who will make it out of the ICU and onto one of the medical-surgical floors! This is very big. If all goes well, she may even make it out of the hospital!"

An alarm sounded in Bed Seven, and Stella crooked her head around to make sure that somebody else was answering it.

"Well," Stella said, "I wouldn't get myself too excited. If she called you a doctor, she's still pretty damn confused."

Werner threw open a chart and motioned Stella toward the coffeepot, producing a small, thin calculator with a flick of his wrist.

Stella prepared two Styrofoam cups of black, tarry-smelling coffee, adding powdered creamer and sugar to hers and giving Werner his neat.

"Have you had a gander at Family in Bed Five?" Stella asked, punching a button and getting an EKG strip of some ectopic beats that zigzagged across the screen marked "Bed 1."

"No," Werner said, preoccupied with reviewing Bed Four's Physician's Orders. "Why? Is it the fat, stupid one who's always anxious to talk to a doctor?"

"I don't know whether she's stupid," Stella said, "but she ain't fat by a mile."

Werner looked through the glass of Bed Five's pod and saw the usual landscape of a sheet-draped, supine patient. Just above and beyond the horizon of the patient a young woman perched on a low shelf, next to a stack of clean linens. She tilted her head in rapt concentration on the color TV set suspended from Bed Five's ceiling, the greens and blues and roses of the commercials airbrushing her smooth face. Without lowering her eyes from the tube, she sipped on a straw in a can of diet soda. Her hair was swept back in lustrous braids that met at the nape of her neck in some kind of bun, except for a few sprays of ringlets in skillful disarray at each temple. A gold earring glinted in the soft light below one tanned earlobe. She brought a foil wrapper to her lips and removed a piece of gum, her fingernail polish perfectly matching her lipstick.

Werner's limbic system generated synaptic energy and caused a tingle of peripheral vascular congestion in the instrument he used for recreational pelvic examinations. One of the monitors emitted a droning beep and spit some strips of arrhythmias at Stella and Werner.

"It's Bed Seven throwing PVCs again," Stella advised.

Dr. Werner Ernst stared at the focal point of the tableau framed by the window of Bed Five. She dominated the composition in a skirt, jacket, and pink camisole that looked completely out of place in the Death Lab, as if some mad Flemish master had painted over one of the winged angels in the "Portinari Altarpiece" and left a pinup girl in lace and lingerie instead of swirling robes. Death . . . and the Playboy Bunny, tucked in the background and hovering, just off-center, where the angel belonged in the "Allegory of Bed Five's Death."

Stella drew up a 10 cc syringe of normal saline and squirted it into a vial of dopamine, shaking it and watching the chamber refill. "Quite a package, aye, Wiener?" she said arching her eyebrows toward Bed Five.

"Give me Bed Five's chart," Werner said, preparing to learn more about the medical history of Bed Five and to revisit what he already knew with gusto.

A cursory review of volume six of Bed Five's chart confirmed Werner's suspicion: Bed Five was a classic Death Lab specimen. A sixty-nine-year-old white male in multiple systems failure. It would be fruitless to inquire after an admitting diagnosis, because the first five volumes of his chart had been sent to medical records long ago. Werner did not need the chart to know that Bed Five's biggest disorder was his physician, the esteemed Randolph Hiram Butz. The alcoholic author of *The Fundamentals of Internal Medicine* was Bed Five's primary physician, although Werner did most of the legwork.

Stella could personally recall Bed Five's having a pacemaker put in, gallbladder surgery, several bowel obstructions ultimately resulting in a colostomy, an amputation of the left leg below the knee to remedy gas gangrene, renal dialysis, exploratory surgery of the abdomen, and cataract surgery. Those procedures all had occurred during Bed Five's tenure in the Ninth-Floor ICU. Before that, he had been in the Seventh-Floor ICU, and for all Werner knew, some of the same procedures may have been done down there.

At least half of Bed Five's disorders were what used to be called iatrogenic, meaning they were disorders caused by his doctors. Most of his infections were what used to be called nosocomial, meaning he had been inoculated with strains of bacteria that grew only in hospitals, brought to him by dozens of nurses, technicians, and other modern-day Typhoid Marys, who went from pod to pod performing procedures and spreading pseudomonas bacteria. (As one of Werner's instructors had put it, "The only germs that grow in Intensive Care Units are those that can't be killed, and these supergerms flourish, because antibiotics and disinfectants have killed all their competitors.")

Time was, doctors could safely communicate among themselves by leaving messages written in Greek and Latin in the patient's charts, and iatrogenic—doctor-produced—disorders and nosocomial—hospital-produced—infections were very common. One procedure sometimes created another unanticipated, iatrogenic disorder, and most seriously ill patients eventually became petri dishes for the supergerms that flourished in Intensive Care Units. But when patient charts began falling into the hands of lawyers, who also knew Greek and Latin, modern medicine suddenly conquered most iatrogenic disorders and nosocomial infections, or so it would appear from an analysis of the patients' charts.

The sudden ebb and flow of diseases and disorders afforded physicians no time to rest on their laurels. New afflictions sprang up in the patient population as soon as the old ones were vanquished, and the demise of iatrogenic disorders and nosocomial infections gave way to an epidemic of "idiopathic disorders," or disorders of unknown or spontaneous origin.

Bed Five was a showcase of the new idiopathic disorders and infections. Because he had developed several spontaneous infections of unknown origin, the number of visiting technicians had doubled, for now they had to take blood, urine, and sputum samples from him to culture and to monitor the mysterious strains of bacteria. And after more new procedures, idiopathic side effects appeared, complicated by Bed Five's age and by his compromised immunity.

Werner followed Stella into Bed Five's pod and tried to keep his eyes on the patient.

Bed Five looked to be all of seventy-five pounds, minus whatever the missing leg had weighed. The skull was plainly visible beneath a death mask of dry skin. Instead of an endotracheal tube, Bed Five had a tracheostomy tube. A surgeon had cut a hole in Bed Five's throat so that a tube could be inserted directly into his lungs. The short white tube was held in place by a cloth collar and was hooked up to a couple of larger, flexible plastic tubes, which were in turn rigged up to a square black ventilator, with dials, gauges, lights, and liquid crystal displays. The ventilator made Bed Five's chest rise and fall with a rhythmic, pneumatic hiss. A bellows mounted in a spirometer rose and fell with each machine breath. Clear, delicate tendrils of IV tubing hung from bottles and nosed in with needles at his wrists. An orange rubber nasogastric tube trailed out of one of his nostrils, ducked under the bed rails, and dripped into a large glass bottle on the floor, where pooled a swirling mass of vomit, snot, drugs, clotted blood, and whatever else was being siphoned out of him. At the foot of the bed, a pliant flesh-colored catheter snaked out from between the sheets and emptied into a large plastic cassette that said "Urometer" on it, where cloudy dark brown urine dripped, one drop at a time, into a detachable plastic bag. On a small shelf over his bed, a green phosphor screen traced the blips of Bed Five's heartbeats. Three EKG electrodes descended like wiry tentacles from the screen and fastened themselves at strategic points on his bare, sutured chest, holding themselves in place with the adhesive pads of tree-climbing reptiles, waiting patiently, listening with their little suction ears for the exact moment of death.

"I'm Felicia Potter," the beautiful woman said.

"I'm Dr. Ernst," Werner replied. "Good to meet you."

"Can my father hear me when I talk to him?" she asked.

Werner walked around the foot of Bed Five's bed and saw a meager 2 cc of subfusc urine in the Urometer. He watched a school of ventricular beats break across the portable green screen of the cardiac monitor.

Bed Five's white head shuddered against the pillow. The bloody cracks in his lips had been swabbed with ointment. The long bones of his leg were skinnier than Werner's arms, widening at the knee-cap and tapering again, down a calveless shin, to his yellow claw foot.

Werner did not need the history or the chart to know that if Bed Five was hearing anything, it was trumpets blowing and the tempest howling in the black holes of eternity.

Werner fought off the impulse to sit next to the angel by sitting farther away than he had ever sat from Family before. He gave a speech he had given many times before. "Medical science cannot measure what your father hears or doesn't hear. We can measure his brain waves with an electroencephalogram, an EEG, and he does still have certain types of brain waves."

Werner did not elaborate by explaining that even seawater produces electrical activity, and probably more electrical activity than the ions fermenting in Bed Five's brain. The long and short of it was an attempt to convey to her the mystery of life and the profound complexity of Modern Medicine, which only exceptional people like Werner could grasp.

"I sit here waiting and waiting," she said, her voice cracking and her pretty eyes misting with tears, "because I want to be here if anything happens. But sometimes, it feels like he's already gone."

Werner eyed Bed Five's heart rhythm again and watched the bellows of the ventilator rise and fall. This was not a woman with whom Werner wished to disagree.

A florid, moon-faced woman wearing dark clothes and a shawl to hide her obesity appeared at the door of the pod.

"Hi, Connie," the beautiful woman said.

"Is this the doctor on call?" the big one asked.

"Dr. Ernst," Werner said, shaking the big one's hand, suddenly realizing he had not shaken the hand of the angel in lingerie, probably because he had been afraid to touch it. "Good evening. Or, I guess, good morning," he added, shrugging and looking at his watch.

"I'm Constance Potter," the woman said.

Werner instantly recognized her as the woman he had previously found praying over Bed Five with a Bible.

"How's Daddy?" Connie asked, glancing from the angel to Werner.

Werner paused and stuck out his lower lip. "His potassium is better."

The angel sniffled into a tissue. "I can't stand to see him suffering like this."

"Don't worry," offered the moon-faced one, "he's getting better. He squeezed my hand again this afternoon. I know he can hear me," she said, turning toward Bed Five, "can't you, Dad?"

The big woman made her way around the bed rails. After getting a better look at Constance Potter's face, Werner decided her facial puffiness was not mere obesity, but Cushing's syndrome, most likely caused by steroids.

She took Bed Five's skeletal hand in her chubby paw. "I know Daddy can hear me."

Bed Five's arm twitched, and his fingers momentarily closed around the woman's hand.

"See," she said, showing Werner Bed Five's right metacarpus and phalanges.

"You may be right," Werner politely admitted, "but when you feel your father grasp your hand, it may be nothing more than a tremor, or what we call a fasciculation. A reflex spasm. You may have noticed that he tremors or fasciculates quite a lot, so it's hard to tell whether he is grasping your hand in response to your questions, or just . . . fasciculating."

"I know he can hear me," the woman insisted. "I've been coming in here every day for months and talking to him. One squeeze is yes. No squeeze means no. That's how we did it when he had his first surgery. Now you want to tell me that it's just some kind of a seizure?"

Werner could not bring himself to tell her she had created a language without enough words.

Chapter

3

Seventy-two hours later, Werner sat forward in the hot seat of his control tower in the middle of the Ninth-Floor ICU—an air traffic controller with eight planes in holding patterns, the flight manuals and individual patient charts at his elbow. The EKG monitors spat arrhythmias at him. Technicians in white lab coats handed him computer printouts. Nurses shouted lab values and pressure readings at him from each of the eight cubicles. Instead of his 2:00 A.M. lunch break, he was having dinner served at the console: a vending machine pastry with a dried rubber glob of jelly in the middle, barbecued corn chips, and a cola.

Yesterday, the day shift yanked out all of Bed One's stainless steel staples and took him down to surgery for another cardiac overhaul. They went in and stopped the bleeding, touched up the interiors, took out the spleen for good luck, and stapled him back up. Probably fifteen or twenty thousand dollars' worth of new surgical procedures. Afterward, Bed One managed to produce vital signs for another thirty-six hours, until he left the Ninth-Floor ICU, feet-first, with ID tags on his right arm, his left toe, and his torso.

For Bed One, it was a day like any other, only shorter.

"Harold took Bed One out of here on evening shift," Stella said, referring to Harold, the orderly from the hospital morgue.

"Oh," Werner said. "Bed One died? That means we'll have to give Bed One's family a refund."

"Refund?" Stella laughed.

"Sure," said Werner. "It's a new, money-back guarantee. If you don't get better and go home, you don't have to pay your bill."

"That's fair," Stella said. "We could have Harold bring Family a refund check when he comes for the body."

"Harold will come for us all one day," Werner replied, "grinning horrible a ghastly smile and riding on a pale horse. The fell sergeant is strict in his arrest."

Harold was a disabled construction worker who hated his job as an orderly in the morgue. He had an old-style crew cut with a little waxed widow's peak standing straight up in front. He chewed tobacco constantly and spit into a standard-issue Styrofoam coffee cup, which he carried in his shirt pocket. He usually did not bother to take the cup out of the pocket; he just tucked his chin down, scrunched his left shoulder forward, and spit into the shirt-mounted cup. If anyone made a face or a remark, Harold would pat the cup and say, "Handier than a pocket on a shirt." Then he typically swore and asked who had died and why. "Where's the patient with no pulse?" he asked, or, "Who needs to be put to bed with a shovel?" The only pleasure he took in his work was finding out why somebody had died, so he could remark that he had no history of any such malady in his family, and that he did not smoke or drink.

When a patient died, the nurses called the morgue, and Harold appeared with a scowl on his face and a special gurney with a removable top and a false bottom. Harold and the nurses then placed the body in the rectangular compartment, slid the top in place, and draped it in vinyl upholstery, so that the gurney looked like nothing more than an innocent laundry cart.

Harold hated the special gurney. In the old days, he had pushed a plain, stretcher-type gurney with bodies draped in nothing more than white sheets; sometimes their feet even stuck out, tagged toes and all. In those days, hospital visitors had stepped aside in a reverent hush and had stared when Harold and his cargo appeared in the hospital corridors. Harold had gone out of his way to whistle or chew or hum, eager to show the spectators how dead bodies did not faze him in the least.

Then the Med Center bought the special gurney, and instead of seeing a fearless health care professional pushing a shrouded corpse down the hallway, visitors saw only a working-class stiff pushing a laundry cart. Sometimes, Harold ended up with his special gurney in an elevator crowded with Family. It annoyed him to see them chewing gum, or looking at the numbers, or making small talk. He wanted to open the gurney, or at least announce to the group: "There's a cadaver in here, and it doesn't bother me one bit. Does it bother you?"

To Werner, Harold meant only work. When Harold did show up on Werner's watch, Werner called him the pale priest of the mute people or the grim ferryman that poets write of. Harold resented people who talked over his crew cut and wondered if he could get away with putting some of these wise-ass interns into his gurney with nobody the wiser.

Werner was especially keen on keeping Harold away from the old man in Bed Five. Even though he was not on duty last night, Werner had called Stella several times and asked for a status report on Bed Five. There had been some arrhythmias earlier in the shift, and the thought of Bed Five's dying before Werner got to know the angel better had given Werner sympathetic arrhythmias. Werner had not trusted the House Officer on call to pay enough attention to the patient in Bed Five, so he kept Stella Stanley on the case and left her with strict orders to wake him up at the first sign of trouble.

Once Werner was back at the controls again, he assigned the male nurse known only as Poindexter to watch over Bed Five for the entire night shift.

Poindexter was a wan, bespectacled homunculus who often wore at least half of his surgical scrubs inside out. His face was tufted with wisps of hair that fell short of forming a beard, and his glasses were so thick he looked like an exophthalmic creature from the deep, a moray eel, or Tolkien's Gollum. He was chronically morose, perking up only when he came to work and went into a roomful of machines hooked up to a patient. He was living proof that quality patient care depended primarily on the collection and analysis of pertinent data, because he was renowned for never having had a patient die while in his care. Sometimes one died ten minutes after he walked out the door, but never when he was in attendance. With the proper equipment, he could keep a corpse alive for days.

A few years back, a patient of Poindexter's had coded during Poindexter's lunch break. The code and near death had posed such a threat to his reputation that he had brown-bagged it ever since and took his breaks in the ICU coffee room, so he could run out and check the monitors every five minutes.

Every hour or two, Poindexter emerged from Bed Five with computerized printouts superimposing graphs of the patient's cardiac output, fluid balance, urine output, central venous pressure, pulmonary wedge pressure, and assorted lab work. The numbers were typed into the laptop computer Poindexter kept with him, and printed on tractor feed paper, any relevant strips of EKG tracings or pressure waves were neatly attached.

"I'm getting some bizarre wave forms on the Swan," Poindexter said, handing Werner a paper strip of tracings.

"Wait an hour and get me another strip after you turn up his dopamine, OK?" Werner advised.

Werner's assignment of Poindexter did not sit well with Martha Henderson, the Head Nurse on nights. She, not some snot-nosed intern, made the assignments on her unit. She heaved out of the med room and homed in on Werner, spying an opportunity to get a straight story out of the House Officer before he fell asleep in a room somewhere with his beeper off.

Werner tried to climb inside Bed Five's chart and hide from the approaching, shapeless, pink rotunda of flesh in whites, known far and wide (especially wide) as Martha Henderson, the Head Nurse. Werner avoided her accusatory stare and tried not to remember that the rest of the ICU staff called her the Hippoblimp.

Martha lumbered into his personal space like a repo van pulling into the driveway. Arms crossed, she hovered over him as he wrote in Bed Five's chart. She tapped first one foot, then the other, setting up a ludicrous oscillation that radiated from her ponderous haunches all the way up to the twin bulbous amorphs of her bosom. A pair of Pierre Cardin frames depended from a chain around her neck and bobbled about in the expanses of her billowing cleavage, until she fished them out and gnawed on them.

"Have you seen Bed Eight's blood sugar?" she asked in basso profundo.

"Yes, I've seen Bed Eight's blood sugar," Werner muttered. "Have you?"

"Of course, I have," Martha snapped. "Otherwise I wouldn't be asking you if you had."

"Well," Werner replied, "of course I had, otherwise I wouldn't have been asking you if you had. Now then, if I were you, I'd give him forty units of insulin and send another blood sample to the lab. On the other hand, if I were you, I'd be a nurse, not a doctor, and I wouldn't be giving any orders unless I was asked for my opinion, would I?"

"Have you had a look at Bed Six lately?" she asked venomously.

"Park the crash cart in her room and hope she holds out until we can dump her on the day shift."

"Bed Seven?"

"Corpse," Werner declared. "No Code."

"Have you OK'd that with Dr. Butz?" she demanded.

"Dr. Butz isn't here right now," said Werner. "Perhaps you'd care to reach him on the phone?" An obvious bait, because Dr. Butz was notorious for giving drunken, raving orders over the phone, prescribing medication in doses lethal to the patient, then denying he ever spoke to anyone when he came in the next morning. Stella never called Butz at home without a witness listening in on another line.

"Lab results for Bed Five," Martha yammered, handing Werner a printout. "I think we need to be a little more aggressive at this point, before we lose control of the situation completely."

"Yes, Dr. Henderson," Werner said. "Let there be aggression and let us direct it toward the patient."

Martha did her best to turn smartly on a heel and stomp off in the direction of the med room, but the effect fell short of her intended brusqueness and ended up looking more like a pirouette in a polar bear ballet.

While Poindexter watched Bed Five, Werner kept a weather eye on the automatic glass doors, waiting for the return of Felicia Potter. Each time the doors cycled and it was not the angel, Werner's metabolic rate increased, producing heat, which those with no medical training often mistook for desire. He was on the verge of going out to the Visitors' Lounge, an act of sheer folly for an on-call House Officer, for he would be instantly besieged by the desperate Hydra of Family, a chorus of distraught heads pleading for information about their loved ones.

From his console, Werner could see through the glass doors and down the dim hallways of the ninth floor, out to where a broad shaft of light fell out of the Visitors' Lounge. Werner scrutinized every family member who staggered out of the lounge in search of cigarettes and coffee, every stunned and grief-stricken son and daughter, lost in prayers and fears and searching for a vending machine or a pay phone. At last, a figure emerged from a shadowy cluster of Family, and Werner saw the silhouette that had been haunting him for the last two days, breasts in full bloom and asway over a trim, belted waist and curved hips.

Werner studied her gait, almost hearing the primitive rhythms of her pelvic girdle muscles in motion, the movements of her draped body parts, the alluring strains of her passage, the central theme of the hips, the leitmotiv from the *Symphonie Fantastique* ... and Werner was the infatuated, sleepless poet who just caught sight of her across the crowded ballroom. Hearing the music was not enough; Werner wanted to play the instrument.

If he had met her somewhere else, at a wedding or a party, it might have been different. Here she exposed the terrible discord between what he did and what he had been called to do. Medicine was his profession; romance was his vocation.

Alas, the history of Western civilization had brought Werner to this wretched decade, in which romance was not a financially remunerative occupation. Society's values were completely out of whack. The economy amply rewarded lawyers, doctors, accountants, missile systems experts, stockbrokers, chemical engineers, and athletes, but had nothing to offer a lovesick swain.

The automatic doors cycled open, and Werner abruptly turned back to the console and the monitors, pretending to puzzle over a cardiac rhythm that had not changed in weeks.

"Dr. Ernst?"

"Yes," he replied, not quite feigning surprise. "How may I help you?"

"It's my father," she said, nodding toward Bed Five. "I ... just ..." A tear slipped out of the corner of one eye.

Her complexion defied clinical description, so smooth and so flawless it could have been molded or cast in wax and cocoa butter. Werner feared the tear would dissolve her cheek and leave a permanent streak.

She opened her handbag and took out a tissue, shifting her weight and restating the central motif of the hips, bound in a snug maroon body sheath. A tanned knee wrapped in sheer silver nylon shimmered and slid through a slit in the skirt, just far enough to reveal what he would normally call the vastus lateralis, or in her case a warm piece of thigh, down dimpled knee and curve of calf to matching maroon high heels. On the way back up to her face, his eyes lingered perforce at the center of gravity. All he needed was a fulcrum, and he could tip her slowly onto her back. . . .

Werner felt the eyes of several staff members upon them. Minor weepiness of this kind was usually lateraled off to a nurse or somebody from Pastoral Care. Doctors were reserved for deaths, sudden revelations of terminal illness, or utter hysteria. It probably would not look quite right if he took her to a conference room or the coffee room just because she sniffled a little bit and pulled out a hankie.

"I can't go in there anymore," she said, tilting her head toward Bed Five. "I can't look at him anymore. Who knows what he's feeling in there? He could be suffering pain, and I would have no way of knowing."

More tears appeared, trailing faint gray rivulets of mascara behind them. She began shaking and sobbing in a manner that could arguably be the early stages of something that might develop into hysteria. He could probably hustle her off to a coffee room without arousing any suspicions.

"Would you like a cup of coffee?" Werner asked.

At this, the Hippoblimp perked right up and, taking it as her cue to dispose of another family member, closed in on Felicia. Werner emphatically waved her off.

"I'd like that very much," said Felicia, daubing at a few more droplets with the balled-up tissue.

"I'll be in the coffee room," Werner announced, leading the way.

The Hippoblimp and the nurse with the square tinted glasses exchanged significant glances.

By the time he got her into the coffee room, she had a good cry on. He felt the vestiges of pity stirring within him. He had seen so much of crying that it had become just another reflex, like hiccuping or yawning, coughing or swallowing. Public grief now struck him as bad manners, as if the weeper were engaging in personal hygiene before an unwilling audience.

The coffee room was a kitchenette off the med room with vinyl countertops and stuffed vinyl barstools arranged around a breakfast bar. Werner held her stool for her, had an episode of delirium induced by her perfume, then sat across from her. Under these circumstances, it would probably be acceptable for a particularly compassionate physician to touch the family member and console her in her despair. But the air around her was thick with rays, or orgone energy, or some damn thing, and she looked dangerous to the touch, like a downed power line.

"I feel stupid," she said, dribbling more tears.

"Don't," Werner said, touching her elbow and living to tell about it. "Something terrible happens and people get upset. I've seen it a million times."

More secretions from the lacrimal ducts. Werner made for the tissue box.

"I can't sleep," she blubbered. "I can't relax. I am exhausted. I'm exhausted, but I can't sleep," she said. "Does that make any sense?"

Werner could have chimed right in. *No sleep? Exhaustion? You and I could have quite a conversation.*

"I have a lot of health problems anyway, and this thing is making them all come back, because I'm not sleeping or eating right." Stunning, moist eyes met his. "You're a doctor; you know how important it is to sleep and eat right."

"Of course," Werner said, deciding not to tell her about the dried jelly pastry and the barbecued corn chips.

More crying, the tasteless, shuddering kind that often made Werner think about going to lunch, because by the time he got back, Family was usually just finishing up and ready to ask medical questions again.

"What are my father's chances of getting better?" she asked.

It was his practice to deal with these questions in their literal sense. There was always a chance of getting better, no matter how small. But unless there was an important treatment decision to be made, it was best to be no more precise than to say that his chances were good, or his chances were not good.

"Statistics have meaning only when one is speaking about groups," Werner explained. "What if I were to tell you that your father had a ninety-nine percent chance of a total recovery? You would be happy and relieved, at least for a while. But what if it ultimately turned out that your father was among the one percent who failed to recover? Would you feel any better about his original prognosis?"

"Yeah," she said, a straggle tear dissolving in a dimple on her chin. "What if his chances of getting better are one percent?"

"His odds are not good," Werner said, "but they are certainly better than one percent," then thought: *How does two percent sound?*

"OK," she said. "Could you explain to me about this tube they want to put in him?"

"The gastrostomy," Werner surmised, certain that Bed Five already had every other kind of tube in him. "That's to provide food, nutrition. As you know, we've been feeding him through the orange rubber nasogastric tube that you've seen in his nose. The problem is that the tube passes down the throat and into the stomach, and therefore, it allows reflux to the lungs. When that feeding solution gets into the lungs, it causes infections of the lung, or pneumonia."

"Yes," she said. "He had that for a while."

"We've also been giving him total parenteral nutrition, TPN, which is concentrated nutrition given by IV. But it is extremely expensive, over three hundred dollars for a single vial, and it can't be used indefinitely.

"A gastrostomy is a small incision here, in the abdomen," Werner explained, indicating his own left-upper quadrant. "That allows us to put the regular tube feeding solutions directly into his stomach without compromising his airway or getting any of the solution into his lungs."

"So," she said with a sniffle, "he can't eat, right? He can't drink, can he? He can't breathe, the machine's doing that, right? He can't walk, right? He can't see, right, because his eyes are closed, right? He can't talk because of the breathing tube." More tears appeared at the rims of her color-crafted eyes. "What's left? He used to be an athlete."

Images of a young Bed Five flashed in Werner's mind. The young hairy-chested Bed Five and his wife on a king-size bed making the sweaty beast with two backs, his skin flushed and well perfused, his blood bright red with oxygen, nail beds pink, good muscle tone; alert, oriented, pupils equal and reactive to light, bowel sounds audible, chest clear to auscultation and percussion, external genitalia erect and within normal limits, normal sphincter tone . . . The young Bed Five and his wife climax while staring into each other's eyes. Afterward Bed Five pours chilled chardonnay into two glasses that sparkle in the spring sunlight. The room is white, with a white ceiling fan beating softly overhead. Two sets of French doors open onto balconies; a May breeze stirs billows in the curtains. Bed Five and his wife giggle and wipe themselves with the sheets, filling their lungs with air and laughing. . . .

"In reviewing the chart, I noticed that there is some disagreement among the family members about whether to proceed with the gastrostomy," Werner offered.

"Yeah," she said. "My half sister, Connie, has trouble accepting reality, so she wants to draw the whole thing out as long as possible, even if it only means more suffering for my father."

She had remarkable medical instincts for an immediate family member.

"But it's not that simple," Werner explained. "The odds are against your father's recovery. But many physicians, including Dr. Butz, as you know, would continue to treat your father aggressively because a recovery is not yet out of the question. Doctors have seen patients in worse shape than your father get better and go home."

Werner believed just enough of this to say it with a straight face. It all was technically true.

"That's Dr. Butz," she said. "What do you think?"

"Well." Werner thought: *I think we should call Harold and have him tag and transport Bed Five. I'll perform a recreational pelvic examination, and you and I can put the bed to good use.* "Dr. Butz and I are a team," he explained. "We confer with each other and the family members and then arrive at a common plan about how to proceed."

"You're not listening," she interrupted, showing him her face, all wet and puffy like a bruised flower petal. I said, 'What do you think?' "

"About the gastrostomy?" Werner asked.

"About my father."

"Your father has a life-threatening illness," Werner said. "We have to take things one step at a time. Right now, a decision must be made about whether to proceed with the gastrostomy. Some physicians would argue that the tube feedings will only keep your father alive indefinitely and prolong the process of dying; others would argue equally well that nutrition is not medical treatment and that getting nutrients into your father's system could give him the strength he needs to get well again. The body can't fight off infections or heal itself unless it has fuel, nutrients, building blocks. But I don't know the answer. We just have to make our decision based on the information we have."

She sucked back some of the tears and smeared some of the colors around her eyelids with the tissue. "Somebody told me," she said, "that once you get one of these tubes in, if you decide later you want to take it out, you can't, unless you go to court. Is that true?"

Caution yellow. Red flag. There was a lawyer involved. A good one from the look of her wardrobe. He kicked himself for leaving his mouth running. Here he had been pattering along, coming closer and closer to telling her what he really thought, almost becoming her ally, only to find out she had consulted a lawyer.

"When it's a question of food and water," Werner said, an abundance of caution directing him back to standard hospital policies, "we err on the side of providing it rather than withholding it. Going to court would be unnecessary, unless there was total disagreement about how to proceed with the patient's care. It's best worked out among the physicians and the family members."

"What if one of the family members is a jerk?" she said, reaching into her purse and pulling out a cigarette case.

"People often disagree in the beginning," Werner said encouragingly, "but as time goes on, they come to a mutual decision."

"In the meantime," she said, pulling a long decorated cigarette from the case, "I'm just supposed to walk around all day knowing my father is in there . . . suffering." She held off on lighting the cigarette when another case of the weepies broke out red and wet all over her face.

"He's been in the Intensive Care Unit for six months. He's been half comatose ever since he had his stroke. We camped out in that Visitors' Lounge for the first two weeks, and we've been coming to visit every day since. How much longer can this go on? I stay up all night thinking: Can I do something to help him? Should I have stayed with him at the hospital? Should I try to talk to him, or is he already dead? Should I visit him? Does he even know I'm there when I come to see him? Is that still him inside there? Or is he already in heaven?"

She lit the cigarette and puffed, leaving maroon lipstick on the snow-white filter. "I need sleep," she said vacantly, dribbling more tears on the countertop. "If this keeps up much longer, I'm going to get sick again."

Listen, Werner thought, *we both need sleep. Well? Maybe if we worked at it* together. *That's it, we can sleep* together.

Werner's beeper sounded and announced that Bed Five's family wanted to meet with him.

"That's Connie," Felicia said. She pulled out a compact and assessed the flood damage. "I'm outta here."

"Wait," Werner said. "Why don't we all talk this thing out together?"

"Right." She stabbed the pretty cigarette out in the glass ashtray. "Catch ya."

Werner stayed put so he could study her departure, the muscles of her haunch rippling under the maroon sheath.

"Will you be here again tomorrow?" she asked, her hand on the doorknob of the coffee room.

"All night, all day, until six," Werner said. "Forget about trying to reach me before noon. Mornings are chaos."

The Hippoblimp delivered Bed Five's other daughter, and Werner went for the coffeepot.

"How can I help you?" Werner asked.

Connie had made up her moon face since yesterday, and Werner could see where the taupe streaks ended and the white flab began. She was dressed in a different black dress and loaded with jewelry, including thick gold bracelets, which failed to make her hands appear any smaller.

"I thought my sister was in here with you," she said.

"She was," Werner replied. "She had to leave."

"Were you discussing my father's care?"

"We discussed the gastrostomy," Werner said.

"She has no business participating in decisions about my father's care," she said. "I'm the one who fed him when he was too sick to sit up. I'm the one who took care of him. Where was she then?"

Werner poured himself a cup. "Her only concern is that your father's suffering not be prolonged," Werner said, "unless there is a real chance for a cure."

"Funny, she was never concerned until he started dying," Connie snapped. "Before that she wouldn't have anything to do with him. I think that's the reason he got sick in the first place. She broke his heart. One year she didn't even show up for Christmas."

"Sometimes a tragedy mends the differences between people," Werner said. "Sometimes it makes people realize how little time they have together." He lifted his eyebrows suggestively.

Constance gave him a humorless, searching look. "I'd watch myself around her, Dr. Ernst," she said. "My sister usually gets what she wants from men, because she's attractive, and because she's good at pretending she's dumber than they are."

"Really?" Werner said agreeably. He had a good laugh inside at the thought of what life would look like if he were even half as soft in the head as either of these sister marshmallows.

"Really," Connie said evenly. "But she's not why I'm here," she continued, hoisting her girth up onto the stool. "I'm here because I've spoken to Dr. Butz about a number of things without getting any results."

Werner instantly knew that she must have addressed her concerns to Butz after his liquid lunch.

"I know you are skeptical, but I am absolutely certain that my father hears every word I say. I believe it with my heart. Furthermore, I have discussed his care with him, and he wants us to put the feeding tube in. He also wants to be treated more like a person. I have noticed that the nurses do not converse with him when they are going about their chores, nor do they show respect for him or his privacy when they are in his room. I don't think it's appropriate for nurses to be watching sporting events on the TV in his room when they are attending him. I have also heard technicians and therapists telling one another jokes, laughing, and talking about their personal lives when they are in my father's room, as if he weren't there. As if there weren't another living person in the room. I want those things stopped."

Werner graciously bowed his head in an effort to do penance

for his staff. "Let me offer at least a partial explanation," he said. "These people work under tremendous stress and pressure. Sometimes they giggle or tell a joke, purely in self-defense, because the sickness and suffering are just too much."

"I see where your priorities lie," she said. "You're worried that some nurse might have an unpleasant eight-hour shift. You forget that my father is strapped down in bed on a ventilator for twenty-four hours a day. He can't tell any jokes in self-defense, can he?"

"I will convey your wishes to Dr. Butz and to the entire staff," Werner said, making a mental note to get with Butz before noon and formulate a plan for caging this shrew.

"One more thing," she said, rearranging her handbag on her lap and settling in for a long bitch session. "Since my sister doesn't believe my father should be receiving any life support, I don't think it would be appropriate to allow her to be alone with him in his room."

Werner heard Stella rummaging through a supply cabinet in the med room.

"I'm expecting a call from Dr. Butz regarding another matter," he said as loudly as he dared.

The rummaging stopped.

"And I will tell him about our conversation," he added. "You may also want to take advantage of our Pastoral Care program. It is staffed with religious people of all faiths, counselors, and psychologists who are dedicated to helping our patients and their families—"

Werner's beeper signaled, paging him stat. "I am sorry," he said, rising quickly and shaking Constance Potter's hand. "I was glad for our chance to talk, but I must take this call."

Stella met Werner at the console.

"We've got a new one in Bed Six," she said. "She's an old friend of yours."

Werner mentally reviewed the short list of patients who had made it out of the Ninth-Floor Intensive Care Unit during his tenure as a resident and tried to think of one that would match the nasty look on Stella's face. Miracles of modern medicine made it out of the Ninth-Floor Intensive Care Unit in three or four days; they did not stay long enough to acquire a *nom de bed*. Left behind were the likes of Bed Five and Bed Seven, who persisted vegetatively for months, sometimes years, until they turned into mush-rooms, molds, and fungi. But Stella was apparently referring to a repeat admission. Most unusual.

"Not Orca," he said.

"None other," said Stella.

"We shipped her to Seven ICU," he protested.

"They shipped her back," Stella said.

Orca was one of those rare patients who made it in and out of the hospital so many times that they actually became known by name, instead of bed number, disease process, or last performed surgical procedure.

The new occupant of Bed Six was a fifty-nine-year-old Caucasian female known variously as Orca, or Orca the Beached Female. Along with her weight—just over 350 pounds—she was also young, fifty-nine, a teenager by ICU standards.

Every two or three months, Orca had what staff members came to refer to as a fat attack. Usually, her initial complaint upon admission was that she could no longer get out of bed and go to the kitchen. The early stages of the fat attack were also characterized by stasophobia, or fear of standing. The stasophobia had a number of predictable repercussions and sequelae; for instance, once stasophobia set in, she quickly progressed to kinetophobia, or fear of movement. Then came acute shortness of breath and general fat paralysis, resulting in the inability to transport a 350-pound payload of flab into the kitchen, where it could be nourished. Before long, true hysterical panic took over; Orca found the telephone and called the hospital before it was too late ... for lunch.

Within hours she was back in the ICU, her belly soaring up above the bed like a mushroom cloud from some kind of atomic blubber bomb. Only the bed rails rendered a semblance of form to the rolling tiers of billow and bloat. Her massive stomach changed colors to match her breathing patterns: sometimes pink, sometimes blue, sometimes as white as the belly of a porpoise, but with none of the porpoise's graceful lines. Her color and her bulk gave her a decidedly aquatic look, because her ICU name had stuck, as if Adam himself had named her along with all the other beasts. "From this day forth you shall be called Orca, and Orca shall be your name."

This trip, Orca's first surgical procedure had been a gallbladder operation. After they got the gallbladder out, she developed methicillin-resistant staph aureus sepsis, and the pulmonologists could not get her off the ventilator. Pancreatitis sent her back in for an exploratory laparotomy, and the surgeons found abscesses, requiring incision and drainage. Next came the gastrostomy and a tube to drain the abscesses. Then followed bowel obstructions, adhesions, a colostomy, and finally a tracheostomy and another stint on the ventilator. Cleaning the tracheostomy was a major ordeal, because two nurses had to part the rolls of flab around her neck to get at the tube. The most recent prognostic indicator was renal failure.

Stella touched Werner's shoulder.

"She wants a doctor," Stella said with a nod toward Bed Six. "They're trying to wean her from the vent. She's got a talky trach in."

"Hi there," Werner said, approaching Orca with the same deference he would have for a public monument. "I'm Dr. Ernst. Dr. Butz asked me to see you. Can I get you to sit up for me?"

Orca stared up at him with small eyes sunk in whorls of fat.

"Can you sit up for me?" Werner repeated, "so I can take a look at you and listen to your lungs?"

Orca reached up and searched the flab around her neck for the button of her talky trach. "I don't set," she said, moving the ring finger of her left hand, a faint purple scar where a ring used to be.

"I beg your pardon?" Werner said.

"I don't set," Orca repeated.

"She don't set, Wiener!" Stella yelled into the cubicle from the console.

"If I helped you," Werner offered, "do you think you could sit up for me?"

"I don't set," she said. "I cain't git my breath."

"I see," Werner said. "Is that why you asked for me?"

"No," she said, fingering the button. "I thought I'd just visit with you." She scowled, her jowls wobbling with rage.

"OK," Werner said, "I'm just going to check you over, and then they'll be in to draw some blood for some tests, OK?"

"They won't git no blood, less'n I say it's OK," Orca said. " 'Formed consent. That's my right."

"Well," Stella said, appearing at Werner's elbow, "if you don't say it's OK, we'll ship you back home. Would you like that?"

Orca stared hard at Stella, trying to turn the nurse into a pig with her thoughts. "Move my arm," she said. "It don't feel right."

Stella hoisted the dimpled and wobbly limb out from between the bed rails. "Where do you want it?"

"Just set it back on that pillow," Orca commanded. "That's it."

Back out at the console, Werner jotted a few things in Orca's chart.

"I'm going to try to get a nap in a little bit, Stan," Werner said. "If it's OK with you, that is."

The Hippoblimp appeared at Werner's elbow.

"What did we get in Bed Six?" Martha asked.

Werner clicked the clicker in and out on his ball-point pen. "In Bed Six," Werner said, "we have the legacy of one of the four pillars of modern medicine."

"What are the four pillars of modern medicine?" Stan asked, playing straight woman and pretending she had not already heard this speech a dozen times before.

"The four pillars of the medical industry in America: cigarettes, ethyl alcohol, old age, and fat. All self-inflicted."

"Now just a minute"—Stan giggled—"how do you figure old age is self-inflicted?"

"Anybody over seventy-two who consents to an ICU admission is guilty of inflicting old age on themselves," Werner said.

"Any orders on her?" Stella asked.

"Yeah," Werner said. "A block and tackle, a winch, a crane, a flatbed truck, and some high-test suspension cables. Also, if you discover that blood is not flowing to any part of the continent, place that portion below the level of the heart, if possible. Otherwise keep her on a thousand calories a day, and check her vital signs every hour."

Chapter

4

The next day, she was waiting for him in the lobby at six o'clock. His first thought was that he had fallen asleep on the elevator and was dreaming. She wore a floral sundress in impressionistic pastels, and her lipstick, nail polish, and eye shadow each picked up a different theme from the dress. Her skin was a shade darker than the day before. She wanted to talk. Not in the hospital. Not where Connie could come busting in again. Would he like a cup of coffee or a glass of wine? Werner had a six-pack of cold beer and ten hours of sleep in mind, but he could have a glass of wine as an aperitif.

The sun hurt his eyes, and the warm bath of July humidity made him instantly sleepy. Would she be insulted if he just nodded off until they got to her car?

"Nice car," Werner remarked, climbing into a new-looking Porsche, which she had parked in the hospital parking lot, right across two spaces marked "Reserved for the Handicapped."

She wetted a finger with the tip of her tongue and erased a water spot on the hood before getting in. His ears popped when his copilot slammed the door of the pressurized cockpit.

She revved it up to the accompaniment of several beeps and

flashes from the console. Werner snuggled into his seat, glancing about the Porsche's interiors, wondering how in the hell he had wound up in this car commercial. He waited for her to slither around on the leather upholstery, caress the stick shift with her manicured hand, fondle a wild jungle cat or two, sigh breathlessly, shiver on the verge of a climax, and tell him how many miles per gallon she got on the highway.

Instead, she snapped the sunroof shut and got preoccupied with the rearview mirror. Just when he thought she was going to back up, she reached up and deftly tweezered an eyelash between her thumb and forefinger to remove a bit of mascara. Werner marveled that she could bring her fingers that close to her eyes without blinking.

Werner stared, then closed his mouth.

"Anyway," she said, "what kind of car do you drive?"

Werner cleared his throat. "I don't."

"You don't drive?"

"I don't have a car," Werner said, studying the curvature of her calf as her candy pink high heel worked the pedals.

"Abnormality," she said, zooming through a caution yellow with a lurch. "I thought you were a doctor."

"I'm an abnormal doctor."

"Whoever heard of a doctor with no car?"

"Well," Werner replied, grabbing the handle over the glove compartment, "I have several serious philosophical and environmental objections to owning a car. Think about it! As much as ninety-eight percent of our air pollution doesn't come from factories; it comes from automobiles. I just don't think I could, in good conscience, own a car . . . unless I could afford to buy one."

"Oh," she said, with no expression. She jabbed a button on the console and released a crescendo of electric guitars and the jubilant refrain of a toothpaste commercial.

Werner studied the breast nearest him as it bobbled with the Porsche's suspension. "That was a joke," he said.

"I know that," she said. "You think I'd fall for that? Who would fall for a doctor not having a car?"

"No," he said, "I really don't own a car, I meant . . ."

"Get out of my town," she said. "Try that slug in another video game. No car. Right."

Werner watched the familiar skyline through the tinted windows of Felicia's leather-upholstered bullet. He decided against telling her how little medical residents get paid. She punched a button and unleashed a blast of arctic air from the dash.

"Sorry about your father," he shouted over the radio.

Felicia shrugged, setting up another brave vibration each way free. "It's not your fault," she said, pressing the cigarette lighter in. "I think he ate too much red meat."

They hurtled down a four-lane street doing a flagrant sixty-five, looking for a place called the Luxury Hour Lounge. She poked a different button, activating a compact disk player; an obscene riff from a bass guitar reverberated in Werner's testicles.

"It's the weekend," she said, adding volume.

"It is?" Werner asked.

"Sure," she said, drumming her painted nails across the leather-upholstered dashboard, "it's Friday."

"Is it?" asked Werner.

She hit the brakes hard in response to cautionary beeps from the fuzz buster. "See any Empire warships?" she asked him.

"What?" Werner said. Sleepless, squinting through the heavy pink eyes of a hibernating bear.

"Cops, cops . . ." she said impatiently. "Do you see any?"

"Oh," Werner said, getting his second wind at the thought of getting arrested. "Where? What's that beeping noise?"

She rolled her eyeballs hard. "Forget about it, Chewbacca. Go back to sleep."

Touchdown at the Luxury Hour Lounge, a pricey joint fitted out with plenty of mirrors, brass railings, and stained glass lampshades; merry clusters of social drinkers (nothing but savory characters) in designer exercise togs, sipping on pastel drinks with pieces of fruit and paper umbrellas sticking out of them. Werner remembered the low-ceilinged haunts of his undergraduate years, dives with pool tables in the back room, sticky tables and floors, and vinyl upholstery cured by decades of cigarette smoke.

Werner and Felicia sat across from each other in the deep cushions of an oak booth, under a bower of ferns, scheffleras, and dieffenbachias.

"Very nice," she said.

A quick check in the mirrors assured Werner he was still awake, though the cushions were beckoning.

"I love Tiffany lampshades," she said, sipping on a tropical affair. "It's so nice having a nice drink in a nice place like this. Some guys take you to those totally gross places that smell."

"Atmosphere is of the utmost importance," Werner observed. "If it weren't for atmosphere, we'd have no oxygen, and if we had no oxygen ... Well, we wouldn't be able to drink beer, would we?" He held up his glass for a toast.

Was that funny? Her eyes said no. She twirled a swizzle stick in her mai tai. Seeing sleep nowhere on the horizon, his brain was probably reluctant to waste energy on anything so superfluous as wit.

A waiter appeared and left again. Felicia fanned her fingernails out on a white napkin and inspected them for flaws.

"You must be real smart if you're anything like the doctors on TV," she said. "What's it like being a real doctor?"

He was too tired to tell her what she wanted to hear; the truth was shorter. "It's like being a waiter in a really expensive and complicated restaurant," he explained. "Only if you serve people the wrong thing, they die, instead of just getting mad."

"Gosh," she said.

"And of course, you have to deal with incompetence all day long," he complained. "It's always such a pain in the ass to work with stupid, incompetent staff."

She took a sip of her drink and smiled. "I guess you probably wish they were all as smart and competent as you, huh?" she said innocently.

"What's that mean?" Werner asked.

"Well," she said with a shrug, "if everybody was as smart as you, you'd be average, right?"

Werner searched her face for traces of a malevolent sense of humor at work and found none.

She blinked and smiled and began trying to hook the two ends of her cocktail straw together. "I read an article on stress, and it said that being a doctor was like the worst for that. Is that true?"

"No," Werner said. "It's boring." He wondered if she could see his eyes watering and his lids fluttering. "There's a lot of math involved. When you haven't slept for two days, sometimes the numbers come out wrong. But it must be stressful for some people, because in school they kept warning us that the rates of suicide, alcoholism, and drug addiction are higher for physicians than for the members of any other profession."

"Well," she said, her nails getting in the way of her work on the cocktail straw, "I'm not real curious about suicide or drug addiction, but if you wanna experiment with alcoholism, just to get an idea of what you're up against, I'll go along for the ride."

Another cold beer, and another pink mai tai.

"Doctors are so important," she said. "And people need you so much. And just because you know so much, you can cure them. I mean, what's more important than someone's health?"

Sleep, Werner thought.

"I saw a sign once that said: HEALTH IS A CROWN THAT EVERY HEALTHY MAN WEARS, BUT ONLY THE SICK MAN CAN SEE IT. That's so true," she said. "All the money in the world won't help you if you don't feel well."

Feel good, Werner thought, *or is it the other way around?* Sleep.

"I had a spastic colon several times," she said, "and the whole time I was sick, I kept realizing how much I had taken my health for granted." She looked up suddenly from her work on the straw. "You probably think a spastic colon is no big deal, because you're always working on brain tumors and stuff like that."

I'm glad you said it, Werner thought. "I wouldn't say that," he said.

She began describing her symptoms. Werner remembered a lecture given by Dr. Butz on gastrointestinal disorders to Werner's second-year medical school class. Dr. Butz, the now-senile author of *The Fundamentals of Internal Medicine,* called spastic colon, or irritable bowel syndrome, Fruitcake's Disease. "Although this syndrome represents probably half of all GI referrals," Butz had said, "all you need to know about this so-called disease is that three fourths of the patients who get it are women and no anatomic cause can be found." The women in the class had raised holy hell after the lecture, but as always, Butz's untouchable credentials and his senility had protected him.

"Did you work things out with your sister?" he ventured, figuring the booze had softened her up enough to talk about the hard stuff.

"Seeing her is the worst part of this thing," she said. "I see Dad every day, because I have to be there when he goes, but her I can't stand."

"What happened between you?" Werner asked.

"She's a hippocritter," Felicia blurted. "I'm selfish, right? I'm

selfish, she tells me"—the sarcasm with a pH of less than 1. "I
don't care about anybody but myself. So I tell her, 'Look, Connie,
who's not selfish, OK? Jesus Christ, maybe. Maybe He wasn't
selfish.' I don't know, I wasn't born six million years ago in Beth-
lehem or Nazareth or Jerusalem or whatever," she said, "and
neither was Connie."

The sudden character assassination surprised him, so he reflex-
ively came to the moon-faced sister's defense. "If she cared for
your father during a long illness, she probably resents you because
she feels that she had to bear that alone. That's not uncommon."

"Yeah, and I'll tell you why she took care of him. Because she
got off on it, that's why. Until he got sick, she had nothing to do.
She was so bored she was probably thinking about killing herself.
You know what her so-called job was? She was a volunteer in
some hospital. A *volunteer*. She couldn't even find a job where
somebody would pay her a wage, much less a salary. She couldn't
even feed herself. She's what, thirty-seven? No guy has ever looked
twice at her. You've seen her. She's fat and ugly, and she wears
clothes that make her look even worse. What does she have to do
all day? Nothing. So, when my father got sick, her prayers were
answered, and she had something to do with her life. And it wasn't
enough just to take care of him. What fun is that? No, she had to
tell everybody how much work it was to take care of him, how
hard it was on her. And I'm supposed to cover myself in shame
because I *work,* and I can't stand around being selfless all day?"

Werner could feel the beer diluting his professionalism. "She
said she took care of your father for a long time before he came
into the hospital. That's hard on a family member, especially a son
or a daughter. On top of that, the usual fear and guilt of losing a
parent are going to make you both suffer."

She drew the dregs of a mai tai up through a new straw with a
slurp. "I don't know why you're standing up for her. She's only
keeping him alive so she'll have something to do besides gain
weight. She's a superfish, and if it wasn't for her, Daddy would be
out of his misery by now, instead of tied up to those machines."

"Super what?" Werner interrupted. "Hippocritter" had slid by
unchallenged, but he was not about to let "superfish" by without
an explanation.

"Superfish," she repeated. "You know, superficial. She goes

around pretending like she's not selfish, like she cares about other people more than she cares about herself. But really, she's no different than everybody else, because the only reason she acts like she cares about everybody is because she gets off on it when everybody tells her what a great person she is for being so goddamn selfless. So really, she's just trying to make herself popular so she can feel good, which is the same thing everybody else does, so what's the difference? I don't get off on being selfless, so I don't walk around trying to lord it over everybody else by pretending I am."

Mmm. Werner's initial instinct was to take her to task over the structure of her arguments, but he quickly apprehended that, to do that, he would first have to drain the swamp of her assumptions, then he would have to build a bridge connecting the two halves of her brain. He would have to explain to her that "superficial" is not a synonym for "hypocritical" and that he could not stand by and leave the English language defenseless while she worked it over with a food processor. On the other hand, if he did that, she might think he was being pedantic or stuffy, and she might be less inclined to do anything but talk to him, and that would be unbearable.

There was lots more. Connie did not take care of her body. She'd let herself go to hell in a fat basket, and now she was happy only when everybody else was miserable. Connie especially liked to make beautiful, skinny people miserable whenever possible, because she was jealous of them. Felicia took care of herself and did not indulge in anything to excess. She jogged three miles every day. Well, she used to jog three miles every day; now she jogged three miles every other day when she could. Sometimes she could not jog because of health problems, but she used to run 10 K races all the time. She smoked ten low-tar and -nicotine cigarettes a day, and each of them had only 3 milligrams of tar and 0.1 milligrams of nicotine apiece, which was the equivalent of smoking only two regular cigarettes a day. Becoming too much of a fanatic about your health was not good for you. Becoming too much of a fanatic about your health could endanger your health, so exercise should always be moderate exercise, to avoid straining yourself or stressing your body's natural resources. A doctor told her that. He also told her that the stress and tension you alleviated by smoking two or three cigarettes a day would probably count for more in the way of longevity than having spotlessly clean, sterile lungs. The doctor was a light, conscientious smoker himself, and he knew of several studies that supported his claims.

"None of it probably matters anyway," she said, blowing smoke into the Tiffany lampshade. "I mean, in the long run it's all the same, isn't it? We all end up in the same place, don't we?"

"That's true," Werner agreed. "But do you want the pathologist who does your autopsy to dictate in the postmortem notes that your lungs are plump, ripe, well-vesseled organs anybody would be proud of? Or do you want him to say: 'Lungs—stiff, black, fibrotic, and severely compromising the diaphragm'? You can't overestimate the importance of a good last impression."

Was that funny? Her eyes said no. She went to work on a chain of cocktail straws.

She loved clothes. She hated dogs. Loved cats. Felt sorry for ugly people. Felt very, very sorry for ugly people. She would kill herself if she were forced to live in an ugly body or behind an ugly face. She would definitely kill herself if she had to live in a body as fat and ugly as Connie's. She loved to watch television. She belonged to an organization of TV fanatics called the Couch Tomatoes (the female contingent of the Couch Potatoes). It was the duty of Couch Potatoes and Couch Tomatoes always and everywhere to flaunt their appreciation of television, especially when Desk Eggs (intellectuals or "pseuds") tried to put down TV viewing. After all, had these people ever stopped to consider what life would be like without any television? For a long time, she did not believe in marriage, but her father's illness had made her realize how short life can be and had made her think about the really important things in life. She was a fashion model. Photos of her had appeared in advertisements, mostly advertisements for sales on women's clothing at local department stores. She had been hired to do a series of auto shows. She was going to be in a national magazine advertisement for lip gloss.

Werner stared past her animated chatter and disported himself in the contours of her face, so smooth and without blemish, it could have been carved by a sculptor in the Golden Age, except that the white marble had been irradiated by cosmetic pinks and suntan bronzes. His imagination soared in inverse proportion to the conversation (she was talking about her codependency group, how she had not even known she was codependent until she had joined up, and how lucky it was that she had found out in time to do something about it, before it was too late).

He imagined she was Galatea, the statue of a woman of perfect beauty sculpted by the ancient Greek Pygmalion. No sooner did Pygmalion finish the statue than he fell madly in love with his own creation. He then beseeched the gods to bring the statue to life, to make flesh and blood his marble goddess.

Werner felt like old Pygmalion sitting on a stool, kneading his dusty, calloused hands, wild-eyed from sleepless nights of frenetic creation, bits of stone under his fingernails, unfinished limbs underfoot, plaster motes in his hair, his heart beating a hole between his ribs, as he watched the breath of the gods fill the stone he had so lovingly rubbed and polished, whose every dimple and bevel he had kneaded into being. He gasped with awe as the limbs became flesh and stirred in the moonlight, and the marble pores breathed forth warmth and fragrance. "Galatea!" he shouted, when he saw her breasts rise with her first breath. Tears formed in the dusty cracks around his eyes, as he watched her incline her delicately molded head. Her eyes moved. Her slender fingers brushed a forelock of real hair back from her temple, where a moonbeam shone on a sheen of fresh perspiration. Then she reached into the folds of her Doric chiton and fetched out a Marlboro Light: "Hey, Mac! Gotta light?"

"Gotta light?" Felicia repeated, one of her breasts nuzzling the glass tabletop through her sundress; her lips etched in cinnamon-colored wet-look lipstick; the dark hollow of her clavicle, where a stray ringlet had abandoned itself; her rounded, supple haunch swelling in the pleats beneath the crimped, elastic waistline of the sundress. She held the cigarette between them, a miniature hearth drawing them closer together.

"I need your help," she said.

This was new. She was talking to him, instead of emoting into the ambience of the booth.

He lit a match, and the sulfur flare scattered firelight and shadows into the tinted hollows of her uplifted face. She lit the cigarette; he snuffed the guttering flame.

She gave him a long look over a brand-new pink drink. "Will you help me stop my father's suffering?"

Was she artfully showing him the tip of her tongue or just tasting the smoke?

"Ah-uhm," he rumbled, casting about in his drunkenness and exhaustion for an articulation, his mind still accustomed to disengaging itself from her conversation. "How would I help you do that?"

"I have to get a lawyer to stop Connie and the hospital from putting in the feeding tube. It's called an end junction."

"Injunction," Werner said.

"Whatever," she said. "The lawyer told me that if I don't go to court now, before they put the tube in, that it might be too late. That the hospital could keep my father alive for months, maybe even years, and I wouldn't be able to stop them. He also said I need two doctors to testify that my father is in a permanent coma before the court will stop them from putting the feeding tube in."

"Tell me about your father," Werner said. "What do you think he would have wanted?"

"I don't have to think," she said. "I know. He told me several times that he would never want to be kept alive by machines. One time, we were watching the news, and they had somebody on who was in a coma and was hooked up to machines. And the family was going to court to get the machines turned off. And he said, as clear as I'm saying to you, 'Felicia, I don't want to die that way. If that ever happens to me, I want you to tell them I don't want to be kept alive by a bunch of machines.' Then he held my hand, and he said, 'Promise?'

"Also, my mom told me that when Dad was in the Navy, he was a signalman on a ship in the South Pacific. He almost died once in an explosion at sea. And he wrote my mom a letter afterwards telling her that if anything ever happened to him, then he wanted to go quickly. He didn't want to hang around paralyzed or comatose. He wrote that to her in a letter."

So she inherited her good medical instincts, Werner thought.

"Did your father ever make what they call a living will, where he put down in writing what he wanted done about his medical care if he was ever incapacitated?"

"If he did," she said, "I don't know where it is. Connie may have gotten to it first. She went through all the papers after my mom died. See, first my father married Connie's mom. I never met her, because she left before I was born. Then he married my mom, and it was one of those things where he was a lot older than her.

But she didn't marry him for his money, because she had plenty of her own money. They were both philanderers."

"Philanthropists?"

"Whatever."

"How did your mother die?"

"Cancer."

Killed by one terrorist cell, Werner thought. Werner did not want to know what kind. What if it had been breast cancer? He could not bear the thought of increased risk to such specimens.

"I'm sorry," he said.

"It wasn't your fault," she said. "It just happened."

He snagged on the eyes in their delicately feather-brushed and painted settings, her irises shining crystal blue against her tanned complexion. He remembered her hair as being light brown, but upon closer examination it proved to be a wide variety of colors, all brown, but every strand a different shade.

Staring at him intently, she slowly lowered her forehead, until her brow cast a lunar shadow over her eyes, and she was looking up at him through a silver mist, smiling with her cinnamon-colored lips, looking shy and unsure of herself.

"Do you think you could help me if we had to go to court?"

Werner was still hooked into the eyes, wondering if he tipped her back, would the doll lids close.

"I'll have to think about it," he said. "And I'll have to talk to Dr. Butz and maybe some of the other doctors."

It was the end. He was sinking into the lagoon of his subconscious. His brain exhibited the five cardinal signs of infection, especially heat and swelling. He felt warm slumber oozing out around his eyeballs. He dropped off between phrases without losing track of things. He wandered out to the car, dozing, while she steered him along, giggling and holding him up whenever he dropped off. It was all right. He was just an overworked young doctor. He just needed his alcohol and his sleep. Wouldn't any other young, intelligent, ambitious overachiever do the same?

Before he passed out, they settled on her place for drinks. He dropped off en route, and the car nap did wonders for him. He woke up in a condo parking lot landscaped with footlights and ornamental shrubs.

Once inside, Werner exclaimed, "Nice place!" though he had

no taste for interior designs and did not usually notice things until other people pointed them out to him. But he did notice things, despite his drunkenness: the soft, swollen salmon-colored sofas, chairs, and pillows, all members of a carefully matched set; a vaulted, cathedral ceiling with rosy stained glass skylights veined in reds; the pink walls; the deep red floor cushions. Plenty of woodwork; he'd been told wood was important, so he was careful to say, "Nice woodwork!"

"Solid rosewood," she said, drumming her painted nails on a carved mantelpiece.

He noticed even more when he followed his bladder into the half bathroom. A huge mirror hung over a fluted seashell-shaped marble sink, antique brass water taps, expensive-looking wallpaper, little baskets and bowls of ornamental soaps, decorative hand towels with so many designs, inscriptions, and ribbons on them that even a lout like Werner knew they were not to be used for wiping your hands.

All in all, it was the most elegant, carefully designed little bathroom he had ever peed in, and it was obvious that a human being standing (or sitting) in here was meant to feel a sense of place, the way those Renaissance chapels were supposed to make you feel good about being the center of the universe, midway between God in heaven and the animals of the earth. Felicia's bathroom was the same way, and Werner, the humanist, felt just great holding himself up with one hand on the wall, midway between the shitter and the ceiling, peeing a crystal-clear stream of kidney-filtered beer. He had found his place in the music of the spheres.

Everything went too smoothly. Music, amaretto, lips, tongues, off the sofa and onto a rose-petal shag carpet, so soft it was slick. Friendly, magnificent breasts nuzzled the palms of his hands. Her hair spilled over his face in a fragrant, enchanted tapestry.

They paused for a silent, breathless journey upstairs. Werner felt his pulse pounding in his eyeballs. Off came the high heels and the pastel sundress.

Under the sheets, flesh A and flesh B, heat applied to the mixture, speeding the reaction along to its critical temperature . . .

"I can't," she said, a two-word thunderclap that broke the momentum.

Werner rolled onto an elbow and into a holding pattern.

"I can't," she repeated.

"Why not?" Werner asked, as pleasantly as a TV doctor.

She sighed a long sigh in the dark. "I don't think I can talk about it right now," she said.

She went to the bathroom, and upon returning, she touched his arm and said, "Can we just sleep together?"

"Sure," Werner said. *But what am I supposed to do to relieve the peripheral vascular congestion in my corpora cavernosa?*

She took a deep breath and tucked a few stray tresses behind her ears. "Sometimes it hurts, and I can tell when it's going to hurt. I'm not a virgin or anything, and I'm not frigid. It's just that sometimes it doesn't feel right, and I know it's going to hurt. Even though I know I'd enjoy it with you. Except that it would hurt."

"Lubrication," Dr. Ernst said.

"I've tried that," she said. "Then, instead of hurting, it burns."

"But you probably used a petroleum-based lubricant," the doctor said. "Those don't work. You need a water-soluble lubricant. We use water-soluble lubricants for everything in the hospital, inserting catheters, nasal suctioning, rectal exams. . . ."

She moaned, wrapping the pillow around her head.

Werner slid back under the covers, exhausted and booze-weary. He had done his duty as a warm-blooded drunken male and protested; now he could forget about it and fall asleep.

"Maybe you have an infection or something?" he murmured.

"My doctor says it's not an infection," she said. "I had a bladder infection," she explained. "I went back to him three times, and he tried to tell me the pills he gave me had gotten rid of my problem, when I could tell the pills hadn't worked. Would you prescribe tetracycline for a bladder infection?"

Werner roused himself. "I don't know anything about young, healthy people and urinary tract infections," he explained. "All I know how to do is keep old people in total body failure alive for extended periods of time."

"I think I had it when I went back to see him," she said, "but it was still in its early stages. I think the germs were growing; they were just right below the number where the lab people say, 'Oh, this is an infection.' Other people might get small infections without even noticing that they're going to the bathroom more or that it feels different when they do go. They don't listen to their bodies, until something major goes wrong, and then it's too late. A person could go for years having minor infections, never noticing them, never going to the doctor, until the infection spreads all the way up to their liver, and that's very serious."

"Kidneys." Werner interrupted without thinking, then kicked himself for not staying out of it. "Severe urinary tract infections, or UTIs, sometimes spread to your kidneys, not your liver. It would take some doing on the part of a bunch of single-minded bacteria for them to entertain designs on your liver if they were operating out of your bladder."

"Oh, I meant kidneys," she said. "Of course, because that's what happened to my girl friend's sister. She had a bladder infection that spread to her kidneys, and she had to have a kidney transplant. All because she probably didn't listen to her body giving her the early-warning signs that she had an infection."

"Uh-huh," Werner said, wondering if he should send the bill directly to her insurance carrier.

Their heads nodded together in a doze and drifted in the fairy world between alcohol and sleep. He reached down toward his waist to turn off the beeper and woke up beeperless and out of the hospital. She mumbled in her sleep. Werner propped his chin up in the palm of his hand and studied her breasts, marveling at the tautness of her Cooper's suspensory ligaments, idly wondering, as he looked on, if somewhere inside those tender bosoms there was one wicked cell lying dormant, waiting for its chance to mass-produce and start a tumor.

He dropped off into an alcoholic slumber atwitch with nightmares. He was in the physician's on call room at the Med Center. He exited the room into a close, luminous corridor lit by one blue bulb, the source of which was lost somewhere in the upper recesses of the passage, but which still cast a soft, lunar glow down the length of the hallway, where the doors of chambers and water closets alternated with the openings of dark passages, branching and forking like the tunnels of a large rabbit warren.

Werner quietly closed his door behind him and fitted a large iron key into the rusty tumblers. Then he heard a door open at the other end of the hallway and saw emerge the silhouette of a man, who quietly closed his door behind him and, glancing down the long hallway at Werner, fitted his key into the lock on his door.

They passed each other in the hallway, two morticians who had been working together in the same morgue for twenty years.

"What'd'ya have tonight?"

"Couple John Does from the loony bin," Werner said. "How 'bout you?"

"Guy named Ernst. Werner Ernst. He was a doctor upstairs. Heart attack, I think. Good lungs, though."

Werner followed the man into a laboratory, where another man in a black rubber apron and sterile gloves was sewing the gums of a body shut.

"Hey, Gilmore, what's shakin'?" the man said. "Workin' on dead people or what?"

"Naw," Werner's companion said, "just lookin' for one. You got an old heart in here by the name of Ernst? Werner Ernst, some kinda doctor?"

"Young or old?" the man asked, jamming the two-foot trocar in just below the ribs and running it up to the hilt.

"Young, sixty-nine or so, croaked upstairs when they was doing an echo on him."

"Oh, right," the man in rubber said. "I think he's in E-nine. They sucked everything out of him yesterday. All you have to do is squirt him up with plastic foam and get his face painted."

Chapter

------ - - - --

5

While Werner slept the restless sleep of the wicked, Stella worked the graveyard shift in the Death Lab. She preferred nights, because there were fewer doctors around, giving her that much more authority and making it easier for her to keep zealous technicians away from her patients. She had been in this business long enough to know that, dead or alive, what these patients really wanted was sleep, not medical care. She was partial to trauma patients and people with congenital diseases, expert at calming panicking open hearts, hard on chronic lungers, drug and alcohol abusers, and suicides, hated whiners and moaners. She did not smile much anymore, unless she thought it would calm somebody who was about to make work for her by going into V-tach.

She left a clutch of monitor technicians and residents in the med room and slipped into Bed Two to do her hourlies. She closed the door of the pod, drew the blinds, dimmed the heat lamps, and left all the big science behind her at the console. Here, in the artificial twilight, she could be alone with her patient and maybe turn into a person for just a few private minutes.

She made a secret practice of compassion, even though it did not produce consistent, measurable results. If compassion, or kindness, or, God forbid, prayers produced any miracles, the results could not be duplicated; therefore, science had absolutely no use for them. Results might be interesting, provocative, sensational, miraculous, or astounding, but if they could not be duplicated by other scientists in a controlled setting, they were, by definition, useless to science and to the medical profession.

Bed Two was awake and running a fever that hovered somewhere just below the flash point of human flesh. Stella could not remember the last time she had a patient with a 105 axillary temp. He was making a run at the record books. If it went any higher, maybe he would simply combust in a blaze of spontaneous cremation.

Stella busied herself with adjustments to the cooling blanket, a plastic mattress filled with water and hooked up to a pump with a thermostat, designed to act as a heat sink for the joules radiating from Bed Two. She punched a button on the Swan-Ganz monitor, putting it into a self-test mode, and prepared to do a cardiac output on Bed Two. She copied information from the digital readouts onto standardized forms. She checked Bed Two's medication changes, took his vital signs, and tidied up the place.

She untied the bony orange hands and held one of them. Bed Two's palm was hot and dry as baked leather and glazed with urea crystals, left over from the sweat of days gone by. She loosened the cuffs on the wrist restraints and remembered her first day of orientation in the ICU. How disturbed she had been that the patients were restrained—tied down in bed. She and every other student nurse had asked the instructor, "Why do they have their hands and feet tied down?" The perfectly logical response: "To keep them from pulling out their tubes." The answer seemed to satisfy everyone. Nobody ever asked the next question—namely, "Why do they keep pulling out their tubes?"

Later someone had told her that lawsuits had tied the patients down in their beds, because every time a patient brought off a successful extubation—making it out of the ICU and into the cemetery—Family sued the doctors and convinced the jury that a reasonable doctor would have foreseen the possibility of grandma's self-extubation, and therefore, the patient should have been restrained.

"I wanna die," Bed Two said, curling into a ball and then

suddenly whipping his spine into a violent arch; he reminded Stella of a strip of cold squid hitting a hot griddle.

"I know you do," Stella said.

"I'm not kidding," Bed Two said, following her on her tour of the machinery surrounding his bed.

"I know you're not kidding," Stella said.

She had a soft spot for Bed Two. Most of her patients were suffering and dying, but most of them were also tubed and in gomerland, so they could not complain about what was happening to them. Even if they could talk, it would be in vegetablese and would make sense only to other rutabagas.

Bed Two had already been tubed twice; but each time his pulmonary functions had improved, and the pulmonologists had extubated him. Now he was heading for another intubation, and when he was not hallucinating, he was just with it enough to bitch about it.

"I don't want to go back on that fucking ventilator, understand?" he told Stella. "You tell those fucking doctors *they* can get on the fucking ventilator. I don't want it."

"I'll put that in your chart," Stella promised, "but I don't think it will do any good."

"Why not?" Bed Two demanded.

"Your family," Stella said. "You have to think about them, too, you know. They don't want you to die. They love you. Your fiancée, your father, especially . . . If there's a chance, they want to save you."

"Fuck my father," Bed Two said. "What does he know about dying? He's only tried it from the neck up. What do they know about death? Wait until their time comes, and it's all over them like stink on shit!"

Stella heard Bed Two's voice crack and felt her soft spot expanding. If he had any spare fluids, he would probably be crying. She held his hand and looked tenderly into his hot orange face.

"I'm on fire," Bed Two said. "I'm sweating gasoline here. Can't you give me some pills or turn off these goddamn machines? Just end it, OK? It's over. I got sick and died, OK? What's the big motherfucking deal? People have been getting sick and dying for five million years. Now my number comes up, and you wanna change the rules?"

Stella looked Bed Two over from stem to stern, and entertained options. There was always the Slow Code. She could let him arrest and perhaps have trouble remembering what exactly she was supposed to do in a Code. For instance, she might make a very common mistake and hook compressed air up to the ambu bag instead of oxygen. In all the excitement, she might forget to call the hospital operator, until it was too late. She might give him too much potassium, by mistake, of course, an error that usually would not show up during the autopsy of a kidney patient. Wacky electrolytes in a kidney patient had all the significance of clouds in stormy weather. Maybe somebody could forget to flush the formaldehyde out of his dialysis machine before running his blood through it? Bed Two also recently had been switched over from tube feedings to total parenteral nutrition, which could cause him to run a high blood sugar, which in turn would call for insulin—an overdose of which would also be difficult to detect by autopsy.

"I'll put all this in the chart," Stella said. "And tomorrow, when your doctor comes, you tell him what you've told me."

Stella's soft spot was retrosternal and just to the left of midline. She could feel it swelling with the desire to help Bed Two. She wondered again if the spot had appeared because of the remodeling they had done on her three years ago, after she had discovered a lump in her left breast.

She had asked one of the docs to check the lump out. "Don't worry," the residents had told her, "it's probably just fibrocystic disease. You can get lumps from lots of things besides cancer."

Three days later her oncologist had leaned across the table and said: "The sample we examined was malignant."

The word "malignant" wound itself like a tentacle around her throat. One sentence had transformed her into a patient. She cried and thrashed around just like a patient. She begged for some reassurance that perhaps a mistake had been made, just the way patients and Family do. No sooner had she regained some of her composure than the oncologist leaned over at her again and added, "The surgeon is especially concerned about the axilla. You have palpable lymph nodes."

In response to the obvious questions about percentages, prognosis, and life expectancy, the answers were not good.

"My job is to convey information to the patient," the oncologist said briskly. "I must do that whether it's good news or bad news. Then I help the patient make decisions based upon the available options. Let me show you where you appear on a chart, which was compiled from a study done on two thousand women with your type of cancer," he had said, producing a photocopy of a bar graph.

"I put you about here," the oncologist said, indicating the twentieth percentile. "That means your chances of living five years are approximately twenty percent. The surgeon was less optimistic."

"Is that five years of living?" she had asked. "Or is that five years of producing vital signs?"

She had walked out of his office and onto the surface of another planet. It was far bigger, brighter, and more impersonal than earth. Instead of the gravitational disturbances she had come to expect from watching men walk on the moon, it was time, not gravity, that had warped. Instead of weighing one sixth of her earth weight, time passed at one sixth its normal speed. Eternity assumed abbreviated, five-year proportions, and seconds became large rooms for her to sit in and realize that she was dying.

She could not sleep, because every time she got into bed, she smelled flowers and saw herself dead in a coffin, heard people talking about her in the past tense.

The specialists ran the usual gamut of scans on her to see if the cancer had already spread. The tests were usually performed on a Friday, so she could spend the weekend waiting to hear about the results. Then she had to wait a week before she could get into surgery, sitting around wondering if the surgeons would open her up and find her "full of it," as they say in the trade, wondering if they would simply sew her back up and tell her to go home and put her affairs in order.

But it had not spread yet. The surgeons had tried to get it all, but there was no way they could be sure. Only time—moving at one sixth its normal rate—would tell. It could reappear anywhere in her body, at any time, and it would be five years (or thirty years, depending on one's perspective) before she knew whether she had achieved the five-year survival mark. Even after five years, it could still erupt one day, announcing itself with a seizure or a dry cough, abdominal pain, lethargy, another lump, or a headache.

Her first day home from the hospital, she spent the entire day watching the sunlight in her four-year-old's hair, unable to decide whether she wanted Tammy to miss her desperately or forget all about her. She imagined Tammy asking her new guardian between mouthfuls of cornflakes, "Is my mommy in heaven?"

Simple advertising jingles and the cassette tapes of children's songs she played for her daughter were filled with pathos and tragedy. "Rockabye, Baby" brought tears to her eyes; she had sung it, listened to it, and played it for decades, without ever hearing the part about the bough breaking and the cradle falling.

That night her evening walk had lasted about six months. Clouds sailed through vistas of color, and nature held itself in a trance for her to look at for the first and last time.

For the next two years, whenever she got sick or felt a twinge of pain somewhere in her body, she thought it was a new tumor growing. She read books about where it was most likely to reappear—her lungs, her liver, her bones, her brain—and what kind of death was in store for her in each case. Every night, she felt the breast they had not taken and swore she felt lumps deep inside.

She took to watching candles burn. And when she watched them, alone, at night, she asked herself: *What if this is the last time I watch a candle burn? What if this is the last spring? What if this is the last Christmas?*

Now, at the three-year mark, she told herself she was in no worse shape than anyone else on the planet; they all could die tomorrow. The only thing different about her was her soft spot, a place inside her, where she knew that she, too, could wake up, tubed and tied down in a roomful of strangers wearing white lab coats.

A resident in a pink polo shirt and a snowy white lab coat came into Bed Two's pod. "Hey, Stan," the resident said, "is this guy getting ready to crump on us again?"

As nearly as Bed Two could tell, he was tied down in outer space, out past Pluto, hidden behind radar interference and static from sunspots, tucked safely in the shadow of a white dwarf. He was being held captive in a space station, which had been colonized long ago by renegade scientists, who had slowly evolved into a mutant strain of human beings. Governments on earth and the press there did not even know about the place, because it had been kept secret by the elite fraternity of scientists who had founded it.

Bed Two was part of an important top secret experiment to determine the medical feasibility of eternal life. Preliminary studies had shown that—when nutrition and ventilation remain constant —relentless suffering has a rejuvenating effect on diseased vertebrates. Some lucky Nobel Prizewinner discovered that pain stimulates the cells through some as yet unknown physiological process and induces a cellular mitogenic response that cancels the aging process. It might be possible to live for hundreds, or even thousands, of years, as long as the vertebrate is maintained in a steady state of suffering. Fascinating. The medical implications are limitless.

So Bed Two was wide-awake and suffering. The centuries unfolded before him. He petitioned for the right to die after 1,000 years, but the request takes 150 years to process. It has to be sent back to earth and approved by three generations of scientific committees and an appellate court.

Fever. Before crumping, Bed Two got so hot he melted the plastic seams of his cooling blanket and the steam rose around him. He panted for air, heat and nausea rolling through him in unbearable waves.

"Anything but three more fevers! Anything!" he screamed at the space matron who turned him in his bed.

The fevers always came in threes. Up and down, three times. Thrice. The number of times Peter denied Christ. The number of "so thens' " in a bad joke, the last one being the punch line. The number of personages in the Blessed Trinity. The number of "beings" in Bed Two's room right now—that is, if . . .

Oh-oh. Just what he was afraid of. Over there, sitting on the window ledge. It was . . . Bed Two dared not speak the name; he dared not think the name. Certain African tribes never call a snake by its name for fear it will answer the call and reappear. The Hebrews would not speak God's name, and Bed Two instinctively knew not to utter you-know-who's name. He could not help looking at it out of the corner of his eye, though, just out of curiosity.

The Thing with No Name was all goat below the waist, a shaggy pelt of evil-smelling hair, bent faun legs, a Sperry Top-Sider on one foot and a cloven hoof on the other. Above the waist, the torso was human in shape, but the skin was reptilian or crustacean, consisting of crusty red lobster shells and charred scales. Most annoying of all were the orange eyes, with deep, black, grimy circles under them, peering out over a beard of charbroiled steel wool, full of soot and ashes.

The Thing wore a hot pink polo shirt and horn-rimmed glasses, which perfectly matched the goaty horns sticking out of its head. A pointy, muscular tail bobbed around behind its back.

Bed Two squirmed into the fetal position, his joints glowing with fever and itching, inside where he could not scratch them.

"Hi," the creature said. "I'm the Furnaceman. I've been sent to explain a few things to you."

"I wanna die," Bed Two said. "That is . . . if I'm not already dead."

The Furnaceman chuckled softly and took a seat, punctiliously crossing his goatish legs at the knee.

"Are you employed by these mortuary technicians?" Bed Two asked. "Or do you work for someone else?"

"I wouldn't trouble myself with complexities in your state," the Furnaceman suggested. "Let's start off with the basics, and maybe we can get into employment relationships later."

The Furnaceman reached behind him and pulled his tail up front, stroking it gently as he talked with Bed Two. "You're having trouble communicating your wishes to others, is that right?"

"How did you know?" asked Bed Two.

"I know everything," the Furnaceman said, referring to a smudged metal clipboard. "Now then," he said, riffling through a bundle of receipts and carbon copies, "your background is . . . Catholic. Status . . . inactive." He made a notation on a piece of paper. "That makes things easy."

"It does?" Bed Two asked.

"Yes," the Furnaceman said. "You can understand these people when they talk to you, but they can't understand you. That's because you're in purgatory, and they aren't."

"What does being Catholic have to do with it?"

"Everything," the Furnaceman said, the orange eyes sparkling with amusement. "Only Catholics go to purgatory because only Catholics *believe* in purgatory. It's like those African tribes that don't have a word for 'no.' They don't know what 'no' means, because they don't have a word for it."

"I see," Bed Two said. "Then I'm already dead."

"Actually, that's another term of art we'll be dealing with over the course of our . . . therapy, shall we say? It's quite possible to be in heaven, hell, or purgatory and still be alive, depending on how you define your terms."

"Oh," said Bed Two.

"Let me tell you what your biggest problem is," the Furnaceman offered. "Your illness has rendered you absolutely useless to others. From here on out, you are a burden on the living. Other people have absolutely nothing to gain by being nice to you. You and your disease represent only unpleasant work to be done, preferably by others. Your loved ones may, out of a certain emotional inertia, continue to display a subhuman, instinctual affection for you as a stricken member of the brood, but even they will ultimately shun you."

Tears spilled onto Bed Two's cheeks and surprised him; he didn't think he had any moisture left in him.

"Let me put it this way," the Furnaceman continued, "when you were healthy and out chasing money and women, how much time did you spend trying to comfort dying people? Not much, I'll warrant, and I can tell you why. It's depressing, disturbing, and thankless work. And what do you expect from your friends? What are they supposed to do? Bring you cards that say, 'Get well soon'? 'Hope you're feeling better'? Or maybe some funny ones? 'Hope the doctors took care of that swelling in your wallet' or 'We hear you have a pain that radiates to your doctor's neck.' "

The Furnaceman laughed good-naturedly, showing Bed Two a row of black and gold teeth and a swollen tongue glistening with bloody saliva. "You simply have nothing to offer anyone. Nothing. Except for one thing."

"What's that?" Bed Two asked.

"Health insurance," the Furnaceman said, laughing uproariously. "Get it? You still have health insurance."

"Go away," Bed Two said feebly.

The Furnaceman looked up from his clipboard and smiled at Bed Two. "It's particularly excruciating, isn't it? Suffering the way you are suffering and for no apparent reason? I mean, here you are, tied down in this place, undergoing one hour of torture after another, and for no reason. Have you thought about your friends? They're not here! They're healthy. They're attorneys, insurance agents, stockbrokers. They're out comparing the virtues of propane grills over charcoal grills. They're trying to decide whether to get a trash smasher or a dishwasher. They're expecting children. They're making monthly payments on cars. They're trying new and more expensive bottles of wine, while you sit in here suffering, and for what? So you can suffer some more tomorrow!"

"Get out," Bed Two said.

"The thing that really gets me," the Furnaceman added, smiling broadly and suppressing an outright laugh, "is how *unfair* the whole thing is. Why did all this happen to you? How come your kidneys gave out and not someone else's? Do you realize that for a white male of your age group, the odds of coming down with Goodpasture's syndrome is approximately one in one point four million? Do you know what that means? It means there are one point four million guys out there, just like you, and they *don't* have Goodpasture's syndrome. What's more, they never will have Goodpasture's syndrome. They are not in purgatory, suffering and dying like a common hamster. They are not burning up with fevers and being experimented on in space laboratories. Most of those guys are going to die in their sleep at age seventy-two."

Bed Two reached for a small metal emesis basin and halfheartedly vomited, spilling some here and there, but getting most of it into the kidney bowl. Nurse Stella Stanley entered with a warm washrag and a syringe.

"You're getting pretty good there with that emesis basin, Maynard. Thanks for not making a mess. I owe you one."

"Water," Bed Two begged.

"I'm sorry," Stella said. "Really I am. You can't have any water because your kidneys don't work. I can swab out your mouth for you."

"With vinegar?" Bed Two asked, alarmed.

"With water, Chumley." Stella chuckled. "Do you think I'm the Wicked Witch of the West or what?"

"I thought you were with him," Bed Two said, gesturing at the Furnaceman.

"That's Dr. Hansen," Stella said.

"I'm still here," the Furnaceman interrupted in a malicious singsong. "Don't tell her, but I make a pretty wicked order of barbecued ribs. What do you say to an order of country-style ribs with some of my special sauce?"

Bed Two belched sulfur and choked back another shudder of nausea. He felt his feeble body gearing up for the high fevers again, panting faster and faster, trying to blow off heat. Fire. If they came in here and cracked his skull open with a hammer and a scalpel, serpents and hot lava would spill out all over his pillow.

"Oh, God," Bed Two cried, "please, just let me die!"

Bed Two felt the Furnaceman scorch his forehead with a touch of his scaly hand. He looked up from his hot bed of pain and fever and saw the glazed lizard skin, the blasted red shingles, realizing with a prickle of horror that each of the shining ruby scales held a reflection of him on his deathbed.

"I hate to tell you this," the Furnaceman said, "but you're already dead. And after death, the fever just gets worse."

"Get him out of here," Bed Two yelled.

"I'm calling Anesthesia," the resident told Stella. "He's not going to make it until morning without the ventilator."

After the reintubation, Stella washed Bed Two with a warm, soapy white washcloth, taking particular care to rinse the raw rectum and grease it with some soothing lotion. She turned him gently from side to side, rolling him this way and that, like a yellowed glassine envelope of dry bones. She was looking for angry red patches, which heralded the onset of bed sores.

Once the tube had gone back in, Bed Two's eyes went blank, his pupils moist and dilated, seeing through air with the liquid eyes of a dying fish. No matter how she turned him, his eyes remained transfixed on the ceiling, the focal point of the dying.

After bathing him, Stella rubbed special bath oil all over Bed Two to soothe the itching caused by the uremic frost on his yellow leather skin. With the lights dimmed and the blinds drawn, she got lost in the rhythms of her caresses, and for a few minutes Bed Two's body became her body. She examined it with the same intensity, the same tender vigilance that she used to bathe herself or to feel for new lumps in her lymph nodes.

She felt another episode coming on, something that had been occurring with pernicious regularity for the last year or so. She guessed the best description for it would be idiopathic fits of tearfulness. Crying, some might call it, if they were just looking at her from the outside. She had been in this business so long that nothing got to her. Her hands had been in everything from septic wounds to open incisions; she had seen everything from end-stage toxic shock to AIDS, to unspeakable burns, tertiary syphilis, gas gangrene, necrotic bowels, and back again. She had seen things that had left bruises under her eyes. But for some reason, after decades of trench warfare, these strange . . . eruptions began occurring. Crying without feeling anything. The tears usually came as a complete surprise, not at particularly stressful times and not usually because of any particular trauma to herself or her patient, not at "touching" moments, not at shocking moments, just random attacks of tearfulness during the normal day-to-day business of being an ICU nurse. Inside, she felt nothing. She moistened Bed Two's dry lips with lemon swabs and rubbed him with cool lotions.

On the inside, she might as well have been eating a ham sandwich or looking at a pair of sevens in a blackjack game. (Should she split the sevens? Take a hit?) She felt nothing. But outside, she was attending to Bed Two, holding one bony, orange hand in hers, smoothing Bed Two's brow, being kind to Bed Two for no good reason . . . and crying.

Chapter
---- --- - -
6

The next morning, Werner was late getting to the hospital. Felicia refused to believe that anybody had to start work at 6:00 A.M.

The sun rose, and the real doctors—thoracic surgeons, neurologists, nephrologists, pulmonologists, oncologists, radiologists, chiefs of this, and heads of that—began arriving between six and seven, medical luminaries briskly passing one another in the hallways, each doing his or her damnedest to outluster the other. During the daytime, Werner had to take his place among the lesser lights in the medical hierarchy, a mere reflection of the brilliance shining down from above. During the daytime, he had to take orders before he gave them, get yelled at before he could yell at others. He wiped the smirk off his face, wore real shoes, a tie, and dress pants.

Refreshed by a solid eight hours of sleep in houses protected by burglar alarms, the real doctors arrived, cranked up on caffeine and ready for another fast-paced day of Money and Medicine. They called their answering services on their new cordless phones, checked their beepers, grabbed their stethoscopes out of their glove compartments. They parked their luxury sedans right outside the

Emergency Room doors in privileged parking places. It had been calculated that this simple expedient saved each doctor almost fifteen minutes a day, during which he or she did not have to drive around and look for a parking place, resulting in hours of additional quality patient care.

At about 6:30 A.M., Werner met with Roy Hansen in the cafeteria, and the two of them took report from the House Officer of the night before. Hansen was Werner's "Three," or the third-year resident immediately above Werner. Hansen supposedly oversaw Werner's work in much the same way that Werner oversaw the work of two interns below him, each rung in the medical ladder having a year's more seniority and combat experience.

Ideally the Three was the medical big brother, or big sister, to the second-year resident, known as a Two. A good Three let the Two learn by making mistakes. A good Three let the Two think the patient was in respiratory acidosis, until the blood gases came back and indicated it was metabolic. A good Three let the Two lose it in a Code Blue and give too much bicarbonate, before the Two really knew what was going on with the patient. A good Three smiled when the Two ordered Isuprel, even though the rest of the Code Blue team knew the Two should have given atropine. A good Three let the Two misread EKGs, order the wrong dosages for vasopressors, and panic in emergencies.

A good Three knew that there was no such thing as an emergency, that the worst that could happen was that the patient would die, and since most of these patients were doing their best to do just that, it was no emergency if they eventually succeeded. A good Three knew that, if the patient got what he was after, the most important thing was to be sure that it was nobody's fault but the patient's, to make sure that anyone reading the dead patient's chart would come away with the unmistakable impression that the Three and the Two had done everything in their power to deny the patient any purchase on his bid for the afterlife.

If something suddenly went haywire with a patient who was only halfheartedly trying to die, and the word got out around the hospital that somebody had messed up so badly that no amount of clever documentation could disguise the blunder, then the Two, the Three, and everybody under them got a double O after their names, as in .007: the license to kill. The derision of their peers followed them through the remainder of their training, until they redeemed themselves by making a stunning diagnosis, or by executing a difficult procedure under pressure, with an audience to testify.

The Three was somebody a Two could call when it was the middle of the graveyard shift, and the ICU was a witches' Sabbath, with goblins and demons screaming just out of range of the human ear, shrieking in frequencies higher than bat sonars and dog whistles; when Death pushed its ugly snout up against the glass of the cubicles; when Family clawed at the sleeve of the Two's lab coat, and the mutilated bodies summoned the Two to their bedsides by sounding the alarms on their monitors; when it was the night of the living dead, only instead of walking out of open graves, the stiffs were ripping out their IVs and pulling out all their tubes, so they could lie down in their coffins and go to sleep once and for all. When the Two had tried all the science he knew, and it only made things worse, then he got on the phone and called his Three at home.

The assumption was that the Three knew more than the Two, an assumption unfortunate for Werner, because Werner could put everything Hansen knew about internal medicine into a sputum cup. Hansen did not like practicing medicine; he just liked being a doctor. Hansen had everything he wanted as soon as he got out of medical school: He could walk up to a blonde in any bar and tell her he was a doctor. He kept his class rank to himself.

Once out of school, Hansen realized he was but one more novice in a field swarming with massive egos and high-powered intellects. He also saw that if he were going to distinguish himself from the rest of them by knowing more than the other guys, he would have the next twenty years of his life cut out for him. Hard work was out of the question, but he could not bear simple mediocrity. So instead of learning anything about medicine, he simply developed a colorful, dashing personality, an image that set him apart from all the other doctors. He wore cowboy boots and western shirts, chewed tobacco, chased women, and went in with three other docs to buy a racehorse. Werner could tell that Hansen thought the down-home, ranch hand image provided an intriguing counterpoint to the traditional image of the learned physician. Trouble was, when Werner talked to Hansen, he saw nothing of the learned physician; he saw a cowboy.

When Werner was alone on the Unit, knee-deep in blood and

barf, he knew it would do him no good to call Hansen, because Werner knew that once Hansen went home and got into bed, the cowboy doctor was capable of making only one diagnosis, and it was always the same diagnosis, no matter what was going on with the patient. This dangerous state of affairs was not apparent to Werner, until he got himself in a few jams and called his Three for help.

The first time Werner called Hansen, it was 4:00 A.M. Werner had a seventy-four-year-old open heart from a few days back, who suddenly started talking utter gibberish. This was not the usual goofiness you see with CO_2 retention, Sundown syndrome, or general ICU psychosis; the guy was not imagining he was one of the disciples on the road to Emmaus, nor was he hollering for Jeb to bring the John Deere 'round front of the barn. That kind of daffiness came with the territory. ICU patients rarely made any sense, because they never got any sleep; somebody was always doing something to them: giving them treatments, baths, starting IVs, taking their blood pressures, drawing blood samples, turning them, checking the alarms on their machines, performing hourly calibrations on the machines—as if general busyness could keep the patient from Sleep and from Sleep's big brother, Death.

But along with not making sense, this patient seemed unable to form intelligible words. Every time he tried to say something, he invented a new language as he went along. When Werner listened closely, he could sometimes make out syllables, as if the words were getting chopped in half somewhere inside the patient's head, then getting mismatched before they came out his mouth in meaningless hybrids, known in the trade as word salad. Very bizarre. Werner got on the phone to Hansen and gave him all the information, the blood gases, the lab values, the scan results, the EEG report. Hansen yawned and said, "Jeez, I don't know, Werner. It sounds to me like the guy threw a PE."

This struck Werner as a plausible hypothesis, because a PE, pulmonary embolus, or a blood clot in the lung, could happen to just about anybody in the hospital, and it could present with any number of symptoms and cause many other things to go wrong; so much so, that if everything was going wrong, it was a safe bet that a PE happened before, during, or after whatever else was going on.

The next time Werner called Hansen, the patient was a thirty-three-year-old male with Hodgkin's disease, who was hemorrhaging fore and aft, port and starboard, and Werner was desperate for ideas on how to keep blood in his patient. Radiation and chemo had killed off most of the patient's platelets, and once the bleed got going, it seemed there were not enough cells to make a clot and stop it.

"I've already poured twenty units of platelets, five units of fresh frozen plasma, and twenty milligrams of vitamin K into the guy," Werner told Hansen, "and he's still bleeding from everywhere."

Hansen grumbled something to somebody on the other end. "Golly, I don't know, Werner," he said, "I'd be thinking PE about now if I were you."

Considering the magnitude of the other things going on with the patient, Werner felt a PE was about as pertinent as a busted headlight in a head-on collision. Furthermore, because the patient seemed incapable of forming any clots anywhere, let alone in his lungs, the suggestion struck Werner as ludicrous at best, so he hung up and decided to wing it on his own.

The final time Werner called Hansen, the patient was a cerebral aneurysm complaining of severe abdominal pain. Hansen told Werner to hold on while he had a look at his *Merck Manual.* Two minutes later, he was back. "I bet he's having referred pain from a PE," Hansen said in all seriousness.

That was the demise of Werner's working relationship with Hansen. Thereafter, Werner was all alone in the Ninth-Floor ICU, carrying the heavy weight of eight bodies through his nights on call.

But the two residents had to face each other every morning in the cafeteria, Hansen using cream and sugar, Werner taking his black. The two of them usually managed to insult each other at least once while going over the events of the previous night, making no attempt to compromise their widely divergent ideas about medicine.

At six forty-five, Hansen and Werner met with Dr. Paul Marlowe, the Head Resident, a tall, dorky-looking guy who looked like the John Lennon of the house husband years. Every resident Werner had ever spoken to on the matter said that Marlowe was the most brilliant medical mind ever to land the Head Resident job at the University Medical Center, but Werner never had a chance to talk to Marlowe about medicine, so he had no way of knowing how much Marlowe knew. Marlowe drank tea, not coffee, and somebody told Werner that it was a mystical thing; that Marlowe was a Zen adept who had lived in India, passed through enlightenment years ago, and then discovered that above and beyond Satori there was Medicine.

Marlowe joined them at the table without bothering to look at them. He pulled a journal article on hemodynamics out of a pile of photocopies and began scanning. "Go ahead," he said, between slurps of tea. Werner and Hansen gave him a rundown on what had happened overnight. Marlowe continued reading, interrupting them every so often with terse questions, like, "What did you say his prothrombin time was?" or "How much nitroprusside did they give him?" This went on until Marlowe finished the article. Then he squeezed his tea bag into the Styrofoam cup, laid it in the ashtray, and said, "Don't fuck up! If you fuck up, call me right away!" which was what he said every morning.

Werner exited the cafeteria and rounded the corner balancing a Styrofoam cup of coffee, his black bag of tools, and a packet of drug company pamphlets. At the service elevators, he hit the up button and wondered if anything else had gone wrong with the ghouls upstairs in the Death Lab. The chimes sounded, the up arrow glowed overhead, the doors began to cycle open, and Werner fell into a persistently recurring daydream: One day he would be waiting for an elevator, here or in another plain-label hospital, a normal, dull, medical night or day; a normal elevator, slow in coming, stopping on every floor; the normal raft of patients waiting to be seen; the normal, tiresome drugs, numbers, symptoms, and lab results going through his head. . . . The elevator doors would open to reveal a fresh corpse, or a Martian, a man in a bowler hat standing upside down, or a white unicorn, a leprechaun, or a blob of plasma from another galaxy, the head of St. John the Baptist, a crystal ball, a disemboweled dragon smoldering on a pile of fiery gems, a necromancer in a wizard's cap, Abraham, Moses, and Elijah . . . the Beatles, alive and well, or the young Peter Werner Ernst hunched over a game of marbles . . . some guy who died three days ago on the table, asking Werner to place his hands in the steaming wounds . . . something unquestionably beyond the pale, and impossible to process without denying everything he had ever learned, something that would allow him to walk out of the hospital and forget about science forever.

Instead, standing in the elevator was the tall, angular figure of Dr. Richard Hofstader, the most real of all the real doctors.

"Good morning, Dr. Hofstader," Werner said, gulping at the prospect of riding in the elevator alone with the Chief of Internal Medicine.

Dr. Hofstader glanced at Werner and parted his lips, as if he meant to acknowledge Werner's presence or bestow a reciprocal salutation on him, but then, the Chief of Internal Medicine thought better of it, raised his right hand, and spoke into a palm-size microcassette recorder: "Gladys, letter to Dr. Kohn, re the subdural bleed in Seven ICU, Bed Four, the name is on the cover of the file, Dr. Kohn, colon. . . ."

While politely listening to Dr. Hofstader's letter to Dr. Kohn, Werner pondered the perfect geometric figurines formed by the facial hair of Dr. Hofstader: the parabolic mustache, the rectangular termination of a sideburn in profile (the inferior border exactly parallel to the base of the chin and the floor of the hospital). Both Werner and Hofstader knew that Werner was supposed to be up on the ninth floor preparing to go on teaching rounds with Dr. Hofstader. Werner was not supposed to show up cold and tag along for the ride. Although he was dictating a letter, Dr. Hofstader was probably recalling that when he was a young resident, he had always arrived two hours before rounds began, so he could read all the charts twice before the Chief of Internal Medicine arrived.

As the ninth floor approached, Dr. Hofstader slipped the microcassette recorder into his long, spotless lab coat—nothing short of a starched, white raiment, with the initials RLH embroidered in gold at the sleeve—and pulled out a slim black appointment book.

"What have you and Dr. Butz been doing with the young Goodpasture's syndrome?" Dr. Hofstader asked, without lifting his eyes from the appointment book.

Werner realistically coughed and swallowed. "We're having some success with the increased dosages of steroids. We're more on top of his fluids, now that we have the central line in, but the dialysis still isn't producing the results we'd hoped for."

"I see," Dr. Hofstader said. "And what are your plans for Bed Five. Legal tells me that a family member is resisting the gastrostomy."

"Yes," Werner stammered. "A daughter. I've spoken with her ... several times, but she is resisting placement of the tube."

"You should be able to move her off that," Hofstader said. "He's late sixties, isn't he?"

"Sixty-nine," Werner said.

"An adolescent," Hofstader said. "He could be home in a couple of months, if you'd just get him off that ninth floor." He smiled distantly.

Werner ran this high-priority stuff through his circuits one more time, then dared go in search of elaboration.

"You mean, you think he should be moved to the pulmonary ICU?" Werner asked.

"No," Dr. Hofstader said. "I think you should get him off the ninth floor. Nine is an unlucky number."

The doors opened at the eighth floor, and Dr. Hofstader stepped off. "Someday," he said, without looking back, "you'll understand what I mean."

Werner was left alone to ponder the pronouncements of the Oracle. The elevator ride had turned out to be a visit to the Cave of Trophonius, filling him with terror and confusion. What was Legal doing calling Hofstader about Bed Five? And what was all that about the number nine? Somebody had once told him that Hofstader was superstitious, but this was his first inkling that it might be true.

If Hofstader approved of the gastrostomy, then the gastrostomy was unquestionably indicated, because Dr. Hofstader knew more about internal medicine than any other human being living within five hundred miles of the Medical Center. How could Werner break this news to Felicia?

Hofstader's opinion could not be challenged by mere medical experts. If he thought the tube was indicated, it was going in, lawyers or no. He was a medical visionary. He had stopped seeing or touching patients in the traditional office setting years ago. His time was far too valuable to be squandered in seeing patients one at a time. Every so often, he dabbled in examining an unusual case with the lingering affection one has for a childhood hobby, probably something like old Beethoven tinkering around in the basement with a harpsichord, while the notes for the Ninth Symphony were upstairs on the writing desk.

Instead of bothering with patients, Dr. Hofstader had surrounded himself with a staff of highly trained, servile technicians, computers by the roomful, and the best in diagnostic instruments —all of which answered to him. He was the central macroprocessor in a vast information processing system. He was hooked up to his subordinates and his computers in much the same way a brain is connected to a nervous system, or a heart to a circulatory system, and from his formidable brain pure medical knowledge flowed out into the veins and capillaries of the medical community, carrying the rush of pure knowledge out to the ignorant tissues.

From his office in the Medical Center, Dr. Hofstader was hooked up to forty hospitals in five states. When all the head honchos and Chiefs of Internal Medicine at all those small-town operations were baffled and befuddled, when their machines and monitors and technicians strained at the limits of their capabilities, they called Dr. Hofstader. They hooked up the smart modems of their computers to the smarter modems of Dr. Hofstader's computers.

A devoted H technician made the necessary arrangements for the transfer of the raw data and later packaged the information, according to His instructions, in a format called the file. The file contained every conceivable lab test and result, X rays, Swan-Ganz monitoring results, ultrasound, echographs, CAT scans, sleep studies, steady state studies, perfusion studies, oximetry results, anything ending in "scan," "gram," or "graph," and dozens upon dozens of values, numbers telling him what was going on inside a patient who was probably three hundred miles away. The results were indexed in black binders according to organ systems and disease processes.

Actually seeing a patient was a waste of time and might even interfere with the objectivity needed for an accurate diagnosis. What the patient said about his pain or his symptoms, his psychological profile, and the gross examination of him, were matters best left to lower-level physicians, who could then edit and compress the information into a page or two.

Dr. Hofstader was a being who appeared every morning, and every morning a clutch of unworthy, devoted residents waited at the doors of the ICU, eager to witness the reincarnation of Knowledge.

Werner could see the endless journey unfold before him, the eightfold path of the medical specialist, the rites of passage and pain. Werner could learn at least a third of what Dr. Hofstader knew, if he just worked hard at it and went to bed every other day for four hours. That was conceivable. It could be done. It might even be intellectually stimulating, but how good would it feel? After a life of bitter struggle, self-denial, and ruthless discipline, he would have to go to bed every night knowing that he had acquired about one third of the knowledge stored in Dr. Hofstader's sensorium. Why bother?

Werner pushed the lighted panel switch to the automatic doors and held his breath. The daytime machinery was up and running in the Ninth-Floor ICU. Clone time. Werner brought up the rear in a procession of residents (R2's and R3's), interns (R1's), and medical students (M3's and M4's)—devout altar boys and girls in white vestments and surplices; acolytes, deacons, and deaconesses, waiting in hushed anticipation for Dr. Hofstader, the High Priest of Internal Medicine.

When Hofstader passed through the automatic doors, another procession of ministers and minions streamed in behind him. *Introibo ad altare dei.* The entire procession filed into Bed Two's cubicle and arranged themselves around the bed rails, forming a semicircle of young, well-educated heads—each head packed with upwards of a hundred thousand dollars' worth of medical knowledge. The heads intoned Latin back and forth and spun extravagant, medical conceptualizations; each head developed a slightly different variation on the theme developed by the heads before him, then passed it along, so other heads could feed and thrive.

Werner slid into place, another white lab coat in a congregation of long white lab coats, each of them fitted out with Captain Kangaroo—size side pockets, bulging with manuals and handbooks, quickie recipe books put out by the pharmaceutical companies, instruments, otoscopes, ophthalmoscopes, rubber hammers, calculators, beepers, and medical supply company penlights, for shining in the eyes of dead people, whose pupils were fixed and dilated (F & D).

Bed Two's skin had darkened a hue or two since Werner had last seen him, and he had been placed back on the ventilator, for the third and, perhaps, final time. Dazed and exhausted, frail and wasted, Bed Two floated on a cooling blanket, his hands tied to the bed frame with cotton restraints, orange NG tube down one nostril, ET tube taped in place, wrists and elbows bruised and bloody from lab sticks and continuous arterial blood gas sampling. The ventilator at the head of the bed was connected to Bed Two by a long arch of corrugated plastic tubing held aloft by an adjustable support arm. Bottles and bags of fluids dangled from ceiling hooks, dripping food, medicine, and fluids into Bed Two. Bed Two no longer ranted about outer space or what God had done to him; he had been silenced by the ET tube and the ventilator. He no longer ate, drank, or peed; the overgrowth of tubes took care of that for him.

Dr. Hofstader glanced from monitor to monitor to monitor in Bed Two's cubicle, then strode over to the patient for a cursory appraisal of the chart. He spoke in short, succinct, crisply enunciated sentences, reviewing the latest vicissitudes in Bed Two's treatment, the pertinent complications and system failures attending the imminent demise of Bed Two: his increasing bacterial count, his declining major medical insurance coverage.

"The patient presented eight weeks ago with pulmonary hemorrhage, severe hemoptysis, dyspnea, and hematuria," he said.

The pens clicked out and went to their clipboards.

"Kidney biopsy shows linear deposition of immunoglobulin and complement in the glomerular basement membrane. Chest X rays show migratory, bilateral, fluffy densities. Blood cultures show rapid growths of staph aureus and pseudomonas. Lab values continue to show progressive, severe renal failure, with rising blood urea nitrogen and rising creatinine, as well as increasing metabolic acidosis. Congestive heart failure caused by fluid retention and the pericarditis we frequently see resulting from uremia. The patient's EEG shows decreased amplitude and slowing of wave forms indicative of encephalopathy."

The clone brigade scribbled in unison, desperately trying not to miss a syllable.

Werner drew a small spiral notebook from his vest pocket, filled in the date at the top of the page, and wrote: "Rounds, 9 ICU." A little farther down the page, he wrote: "Bed 2—Pickled Cabbage."

Dr. Hofstader continued with a rundown of the current meds. "We've got 250 milligrams of Solu-Medrol Q six hours. Cefobid 2 grams BID dobutamine 10 micrograms per kilogram per minute. Two amps of sodium bicarb per liter of normal saline. Aminophylline 30 milligrams per hour continuous drip. Mercaptopurine. Ferrous sulfate 300 milligrams TID. . . ."

Werner surveyed an attractive M3. Sweet. Tight curves. Friendly, aimless smile. He wrote, "See about poking Sabrina Romple," copying the name off her UMC ID badge.

Bed Two rattled the bed rails, clawed at his restraints, and made a motion an M3 recognized as a request for a pencil and paper. Dr. Hofstader faced the clone brigade and held forth on the relative virtues of corticosteroids, azathioprine, and mercaptopurine. The M3 motioned for Bed Two's nurse. The nurse untied the right wrist restraint and held a pad for Bed Two. Bed Two scrawled in huge, wobbly, barely legible letters: "W A T E R."

An M4 showed the scrawl to Dr. Hofstader.

Everyone smiled at the medical impossibility of Bed Two's request. Everyone knew that Bed Two could not have any water. Everyone except Bed Two.

"Tell the patient that fluids by mouth are out of the question," Dr. Hofstader said to the M4.

"Fluids by mouth are out of the question," the M4 told Bed Two.

Bed Two opened his mouth, his lips and tongue trying to make words around his ET tube, the tube buckling against the gag of tape, crusty with blood and dry adhesive. Sores in the corners of Bed Two's mouth broke open and pleaded for water. A string of premature ventricular contractions appeared on the three-lead EKG monitor over his bed. He spazzed out momentarily, rattling the bed rails with his bony orange arms; the irises of his eyes were a wild, shallow blue, staring so hard the jaundiced whites bulged.

"You might suspect hypocalcemia," Dr. Hofstader explained, removing a gold fountain pen from his lab coat and using it to indicate Bed Two's spastic fingers.

Bed Two writhed in the cotton restraints, motioning with his head for the return of the pad and pencil. He scrawled another message for them, this time a slanted squiggle of pencil lead that said: "D I E."

The nurse showed it to the M4, who in turn showed it to Dr. Hofstader.

Dr. Hofstader read it and passed it back to them without so much as a ripple in his instructor's demeanor.

"The patient's confusion is probably the result of hypertensive encephalopathy."

Werner studied the bosomy fullness of Sabrina Romple's lab-coat. Very nice. Large, but taut and well formed. He made eye contact, then eye-breast contact, deliberately performing a gross examination of her well-formed compound alveolar glands.

Not funny, she said with a sour look.

DC that one, Werner thought. Another M3 subclone.

An R1 clone asked Dr. Hofstader an abstruse question about nonanion gap acidoses and endocrine disorders, going out of his way to talk about carbonic anhydrase, renal tubular acidosis, plasma phoresis, and everything else he could remember reading about the night before.

The rest of the house staff exchanged split-second glances, confirming their suspicions that the clone knew nothing about kidneys.

Much to everyone's disappointment, Dr. Hofstader spared the R1 the humiliation he deserved. Instead, the Chief of Internal Medicine took up each of the discrete topics, reviewed them in a brief, orderly fashion, and closed with a short summary displaying their proper relationship to one another, as if he'd just sorted and batched a collection of rudimentary geometric shapes that had gotten all jumbled up inside a toy box.

Next, Dr. Hofstader indicated the coffee-ground appearance of the old blood that had been sucked out of the orange tube in Bed Two's nostril.

"The nasogastric drainage could be either GI ulcerations or the result of upper GI trauma," he said. "The urine is pink-tinged with sediments and mucous shreds. Also, note the prominent uremic frost on the skin," Dr. Hofstader advised, pointing out the delicate scales covering the orange skin of Bed Two, giving him the look of a glazed doughnut.

"If the patient were not restrained, you would probably observe scratching and other signs of severe pruritus, as the toxins being excreted through the skin cause painful itching."

Werner inserted a comma after "Pickled Cabbage," and wrote, "Auschwitz."

Dr. Hofstader lifted his stethoscope to his ears and gracefully bowed over the bed rails, moving the gold bell of the scope over the bony, orange washboard of Bed Two's thorax.

"There is an impressive pericardial friction rub at the fourth intercostal space over the midclavicular line."

The clones took turns listening to the impressive pericardial friction rub. Wow, and what a pericardial friction rub it was! It sounded just like the pericardial friction rubs they all had read about in their textbooks.

"Impressive," said an R1.

"Very impressive," said an R2.

Dr. Hofstader continued lecturing, never quite looking at anyone—especially not at Bed Two—always looking just above or below the eyeline of his audience, gazing off in the throes of some abstraction, which none of them could possibly understand. The minor strain of these lesser, teaching ideas caused him to frown slightly, as if lecturing were a conditioned reflex monitored by his brainstem, leaving the other parts of his mind free for more important tasks.

"Treatment with Solu-Medrol has caused immunosuppression, resulting in sepsis and compounding bacterial endocarditis. Intra-alveolar hemorrhaging has caused severe respiratory failure and anemia. . . ."

Every so often, Dr. Hofstader paused to get his breath, and the group collectively inhaled a short silent gasp, afraid that he was about to ask someone to interpret some lab results or suggest a prognosis other than certain death, afraid that they would be forced to shine their forty-watt intellects into the sunburst of knowledge itself.

"So, what are your options with this patient?" Dr. Hofstader asked.

Everyone noted the "your" of "your options" because everyone knew that Bed Two was once a patient in the care of Dr. Hofstader but now was no longer his, in the clinical sense. The patient was no longer of any clinical interest because of the dismal and simple prognosis. If Bed Two still had a chance, Dr. Hofstader would have asked about "our options," not "your options." Dr. Hofstader was implicitly telling the residents to go ahead and exercise their feeble skills on Bed Two, go ahead and blunder all over themselves, and maybe they could obtain some primitive understanding of clinical end-stage Goodpasture's syndrome.

Werner's beeper activated. Dr. Hofstader paused.

Before Werner could get to the volume control, the hospital operator shouted in staticky singsong, "Call the switchboard for an outside call. Please call the switchboard for an outside call."

The beeper was supposed to say things like "Call Seven ICU for blood gas results," or "Call X ray stat." One's beeper was not supposed to say, "Call the switchboard for an outside call," especially when one was on teaching rounds with the Divinity.

Werner made for the door of Bed Two's pod. Dr. Hofstader resumed lecturing.

The beeper cycled again. Werner realized too late that he had mistakenly turned the volume up, not down. He felt a dozen split-second glances of disbelief, as the hospital operator broadcast to the group that the call would be transferred to extension 9909, the phone at Werner's elbow.

"Dr. Ernst," he said, hoping this was medical business.

"It's me," she said with a giggle. "Did I make you late this morning?"

The creature between his legs stirred and told him it was Felicia. Werner went numb, looking around the Death Lab and trying to integrate the sound of her voice, not knowing how to tell her that she should not under any circumstances call him during the day, especially not when he was in the Ninth-Floor ICU doing rounds with Dr. Hofstader. He wanted to say he could not talk, but then everyone would know that he had received a personal call. But wait, this was not a personal call, was it? No, it was a call from Family.

"Let me check," he said, pulling out his appointment book. "I won't have any time until four-thirty, can we discuss it then?"

"Is somebody there? I just wanted to tell you I'm sorry if I made you late."

"Yes. No. That's OK," Werner said, hearing the drone of Dr. Hofstader's voice talking about glomerulonephritis and immuno-fluorescent staining.

"I . . . enjoyed myself," she said. "And I wanted to thank you."

I almost enjoyed myself, Werner thought.

"I thought about your advice," she said.

"In what regard?" Werner said, a strain of impatience rising in his voice.

"About your recommendation," she said.

"Regarding your father's care?" Werner asked, confident that he sounded as if he were conducting medical business.

"No," she said with a missy sigh of exasperation, "about the lubrication. I think we should try that water stuff you were talking about."

Werner gathered his lab coat in front of him. "Yes," he said through a dry throat. "I agree with you. I think that would be the best procedure, and we should promptly obtain an opening for the treatment."

"Is that Dr. Butz guy there?"

Werner skipped a beat going from lubrication to Dr. Butz.

"No," Werner said, "Dr. Butz is not on the Unit right now, though we expect him shortly."

"I just wondered if you had a chance to talk to him about my dad yet. And I wanted to warn you that—"

Out of the corner of his eye, Werner noticed Dr. Hofstader looking straight at him over the heads of the fawning gaggle of white lab coats.

"I'll schedule the procedure as soon as possible, and I'll get back to you with available dates. I have your service's number."

When the receiver hit the cradle, Dr. Hofstader called out, "Dr. Ernst, Dr. Romple has asked me if there are any other disorders presenting with both pulmonary hemorrhage and renal failure that can be mistaken for Goodpasture's syndrome. Would you give us the benefit of your expertise?"

"Certainly," Werner replied, reading "expertise" as a dig intended to remind him and the other residents that Werner had originally misdiagnosed Bed Two as having idiopathic pulmonary hemosiderosis.

Werner faced Dr. Romple, performed another eye-breast exam in a nanosecond, waited to be sure that she had seen him do it and that no one else had, then said, "Certain collagen vascular diseases, acute glomerulonephritis with circulatory congestion, bacterial endocarditis, and idiopathic pulmonary hemosiderosis may all present with symptoms of pulmonary hemorrhage and renal failure, but they can usually be ruled out by renal biopsy and the other distinguishing features of the diseases."

Werner punctuated his finale with another eye-breast exam. Sabrina flushed and started to give him another sour look, but chickened out in the interest of remaining inconspicuous.

"You didn't mention Wegener's granulomatosis," Dr. Hofstader said, "a generalized necrotizing granulomatous vasculitis involving the upper and lower respiratory tracts, the skin, the lungs, and the kidneys."

"I said, certain collagen vascular diseases," Werner said. "Wegener's granulomatosis is a collagen vascular disease."

Silence. Throats cleared.

"Dr. Ernst," said Dr. Hofstader, "you're on your back under the car in your driveway, and you need a three-quarter-inch hexagonal wrench. Are you going to ask me to hand you a wrench, or are you going to ask me to hand you a three-quarter-inch hexagonal wrench?"

"Neither," Werner said. "I'm going to ask you to call me a mechanic."

Scattered giggling, quickly suppressed.

"I thought you wanted to be *called* a doctor," Hofstader said. "But if you wish to be *called* a mechanic, Dr. Ernst, I'll *call* you a mechanic, and then I'll *get* you a doctor to help you distinguish Wegener's granulomatosis from the other collagen vascular diseases."

"Ew," someone said.

Hofstader closed Bed Two's chart. "Precision," he said. "Some of you may recall that our mechanic, Dr. Ernst, originally misdiagnosed this patient. The symptoms suggested two choices: It was either Goodpasture's syndrome, an uncommon Type Two hypersensitivity disorder, or it was idiopathic pulmonary hemosiderosis, an extremely rare disease of unknown etiology, most commonly seen in young children and seldom seen in adults. Our mechanic chose the latter diagnosis. He ignored something I've told you all before: When you hear hoofbeats, think horse, not zebra."

Werner's beeper cycled again. This time the volume was turned down low enough so that only the clones standing closest to him heard the operator advise him that he had received yet another outside call. The clones visibly moved away from him, so as not to be associated with a resident who received two outside calls and mouthed off during teaching rounds with Dr. Hofstader.

Werner headed out to the console and dialed the operator before she could send the call to Bed Two's pod.

"Dr. Ernst," the male voice said, "my name is Sheldon Hatchett, and I am an attorney for Ms. Felicia Potter. She told me I could reach you at work."

"I can't talk now," Werner said briskly. "I am extremely busy."

"May I leave you a phone number then?" the voice said. "As you may know, we will be seeking an injunction in a matter of days, and we would like to have your testimony, if possible."

"I don't think I can do that," Werner said.

"Ms. Potter wishes to discontinue all invasive procedures and to enjoin any further surgical procedures, including the scheduled gastrostomy, which under the circumstances will do little but prolong Mr. Potter's suffering."

Your basic one-dimensional attorney, Werner thought. *Only lawyers have the luxury of examining complex problems from a single point of view.*

"It's not that simple," Werner said, arguing more with himself than with the lawyer. "It's not clear that further medical treatment will prove absolutely fruitless."

"Well, then, let's say it will prove relatively fruitless," the lawyer said. "Let's say that the odds of a recovery are slim indeed and are not worth the suffering Mr. Potter must endure to keep the hospital's tidy ethical concerns in order."

"This is easy for you," Werner objected. "You have one client. I have a patient and two daughters who want different things."

"Constance Potter is a diagnosed nut case," the lawyer said. "Come to the hearing and see for yourself. She has some kind of hysterical personality disorder with religious delusions, denial, guilt, and I don't know what all. I'll let you tell me what it all means."

"She appears to be closer to the patient than your client," Werner said.

"Just give us your honest opinion," the lawyer begged, "not the company line we'll get from all those other docs. We need your testimony to help this man and his daughter put an end to their suffering. Under state law, we must have two doctors testify that the patient is in a persistent vegetative state, with no hope of regaining cognitive, sapient thought."

"I like your vocabulary," Werner said.

"Shall I tell Ms. Potter that you'll help us?" the lawyer asked.

"I need more time," Werner said.

"As you probably know, we will be seeking a temporary restraining order, a TRO, within the next forty-eight hours, or else your friend Dr. Butz is going to have that tube in. Once it goes in, it will take months of legal maneuvering to get it out, especially in this state. Depending upon what happens at the application for the TRO, there could be a hearing on the preliminary injunction within ten days."

Werner saw the entourage come out of Bed Two and move over to Bed Three.

"I really don't have any more time," Werner said.

"Miss Potter or I will call you again within the next forty-eight hours. She would really appreciate your help in this matter, and so would I."

"Good-bye," Werner said.

Werner slipped back into the rear of the crowd in Bed Three Dr. Hofstader took a phone call at the console. No sooner was Hofstader safely out of earshot than Hansen, the cowboy doctor, tried to step in and fill the knowledge vacuum by giving a short dissertation on what the proctosigmoidoscopy of Bed Three would show tomorrow, the percentages associated with diverticulosis as opposed to carcinoma as described in several recent studies. Marlowe, the Head Resident, promptly rained a hail of counterstatistics on Hansen's parade, citing a raft of studies that directly contradicted Hansen's right to exist.

A wombat touched Werner's elbow and handed him a phone. "Call for you on oh-one. And Family is waiting for you in Bed Five."

Werner put the receiver to his ear and covered the mouthpiece with his hand. "The fat one?" he asked.

The nurse nodded.

"Dr. Ernst, this is Wilson down in Legal," the phone said. "I'm calling all the docs writing orders on Bed Five, Nine ICU, patient named Potter. Guy's been in about nine months or so. Patient of Dr. Butz. We have received two state court subpoenas requesting all medical records on him. I talked to one of the lawyers, and it looks like they've been hired by the patient's family to fight over some kind of restraining order against further invasive procedures. If anybody under you is writing any orders, you might tell them to keep their noses clean."

Chapter 7

Werner found Constance Potter standing over the flesh-fallen frame of Bed Five, reading aloud from a book, her back to Werner and the entrance to the pod:

> *Their idols are silver and gold,*
>   *the handiwork of men.*
> *They have mouths but speak not;*
>   *they have eyes but see not;*
> *They have ears but hear not;*
>   *they have noses but smell not;*
> *They have hands but feel not;*
>   *they have feet but walk not;*
>   *they utter no sound from their throat.*
> *Their makers shall be like them,*
>   *everyone that trusts in them.*

Werner promptly ruled out steroids as the cause of Constance Potter's fat face and concluded that the puffiness was caused by psychiatric medication, probably one of the phenothiazine group.

That would also explain why she was reading the Bible out loud to a comatoid.

"Shall I come back later?" he asked, as humbly as possible, making a mental note to refer Constance to Pastoral Care for a theology consult.

"No," she said, placing a Bible on the nightstand. "I asked to see you."

She pushed the patient tray out of the way and shimmied her bulk through a forest of IV poles overgrown with tubing and bags of solutions.

"This has been changed," she said, pointing at the bellows of the spirometer as it filled with air from the collapsing lungs of Bed Five.

The ventilator cycled again, filling the lungs of Bed Five and causing the bones of his thorax to creak. The bellows rose and fell in a clear plastic sleeve calibrated in cubic centimeters.

"One of the technicians told me that this measures the air that my father exhales," she said.

"Almost," Werner said. "Actually it measures the air that the machine delivers into your father's lungs, as well as the air that the machine pumps into all these tubes."

Werner used a pencil to trace the path of the air from the ventilator, through the humidifiers and one-way valves, into Bed Five, and out to the bellows of the spirometer.

"To figure out what the patient is actually getting," he continued, "we have to subtract the amount of air in the tubes, or what we call dead space. That usually amounts to about one hundred fifty cc's. So, even though this spirometer reads about six hundred fifty, he's actually getting about five hundred."

Werner refrained from adding that Bed Five's lungs were probably dead space, too.

"But this marker doesn't go up as high as it did yesterday," she said. "Yesterday it was going up to seven hundred fifty."

"That's because we changed his tidal volume," Werner patiently explained. "To put it as simply as possible, he's still getting the same amount of air, but he's getting ten small breaths per minute, instead of eight big ones."

"I see," she said. "I thought perhaps someone had changed one of the dials or bumped it."

"No," Werner said. "That's possible but very unlikely. The

respiratory therapists check all the dials on the machines every hour. In between times, if a change in volume occurs, the alarms go off."

Werner pushed the test button on the spirometer alarm, and a piercing beep filled the pod.

"But what if the alarm doesn't work?" she asked.

"There are two alarms," Werner explained, "the spirometer alarm and the ventilator alarm." He pushed the alarm test button on the ventilator, releasing a different high-pitched beep.

Her eyes followed the ventilator tubing back to Bed Five. Suddenly she lurched back through the thicket of IV poles and grasped the flaccid hand of Bed Five.

"It's OK, Daddy. The doctor was just checking the alarms on your machines."

Werner steadied a swinging bag of 5 percent dextrose in water and stared at his shoes to keep from rolling his eyes.

"We were just testing the alarms on your machines," she repeated, squeezing his hand. "Everything is working the way it's supposed to."

If Bed Five took any solace from this bit of information, he kept it to himself. He looked like any other septuagenarian who had endured seven surgical procedures in as many months, was crucified, died, was buried, descended into hell, and on the third day was coded again, strapped down in bed, and seated at the right hand of a Bennett MA-2 ventilator.

"Can the alarms be turned off by accident?" she asked in a loud whisper.

"Not likely," Werner said. "The alarm disabling switches are on the back of the machine, under a metal guard."

"Can they be turned off intentionally?" she asked, her eyes narrowing.

"Yes," Werner said, "but only when the patient expires, or when the doctor has written an order to disconnect the ventilator."

She looked at him sharply and raised her finger to her lips, then angrily motioned him out of the pod.

Werner followed her out, slapping his feet like a schoolboy following his principal to the office for a scolding.

Outside the pod, the ICU was a pinball machine of flashing lights, buzzing alarms, ringing telephones, shrieking beepers, and personnel bouncing from pod to pod.

"Are you people trained to be inhumane?" she asked, raising her voice so he could hear her over the noise. "I've been reading books on healing and holistic medicine."

Holistic, meaning full of holes, Werner thought.

"As you know," she continued, "people in comas or under anesthesia can subconsciously hear every word that is being said by those in attendance. Negative comments, especially by physicians, can dramatically affect the course of a patient's illness."

Werner knew there was no arguing with Family about the validity of the latest medical best seller. Forget about practicing medicine according to studies published in reputable medical journals; those data had been contaminated by conspiracies of science in the medical establishment. Family wanted its doctor to be enlightened and to practice medicine according to the bibble-babble found in its self-help books. He could see it in her eyes. She was about to tell him that if they could teach Bed Five to think positively, he could grow a new leg and climb out of bed with the vital signs of a pro basketball player.

"What did I say?" he protested.

"Look," she commanded, pointing into Bed Five's pod, "a human being is recovering from a life-threatening illness in there. My father and your patient."

Werner followed her finger through the pod window and saw a seventy-five-pound, inflatable turnip strapped to the bed rails.

"Imagine you were dependent on a machine for your every breath," she said, her voice cracking with anger, "and you heard your doctor casually talking about disconnecting it? Would you let someone make those comments if it was your father in there?"

Werner tried to imagine himself tied down in Bed Five and found it much like trying to imagine he was a fence post or a doorstop. Next, he tried to imagine his father tied down in Bed Five and was equally unsuccessful, because he would never bring his father to a place like this. Talk about inhumane? Checking your father into an ICU? Now that would be inhumane.

Someone laughed in one of the other pods and called out: "This guy's chewing up his tube again. Will somebody bring me an airway and some tape?"

Constance stared him down with a look of disgust. "This is structural evil," she said. "Do any of these people remember how to cry, or pray, or feel compassion for the sick? Or is it all sneers and laughter?"

Werner spied another opportunity to consign a menial, non-medical problem to subordinate, ancillary personnel. "Have you spoken with any of the chaplains or nuns in our Pastoral Care program?" Werner asked.

"I have," Constance said. "They are wonderful people. But there aren't enough of them."

Werner pulled a drug company ball-point pen out of his lab coat pocket and clicked the clicker in and out a few dozen times.

"You look at suffering all day, but you don't see it anymore, do you?" she said.

"Medicine is only a profession," Werner said. "You're asking the impossible. You want us to love your father as much as you do and still practice good medicine. You've heard of the doctor who had a fool for a patient because he treated himself? The same goes for the doctor who tries to treat his family or anyone else he cares too much about. Objectivity is essential."

"Laughing at sick people is objectivity?" she asked. "Giggling over TV programs while people are dying in the same room, is that objectivity?"

"No," Werner said. "That's human nature. You can't spend twelve hours a day, every day, dejected because you're working with the terminally ill."

"How many of your patients recover after you tell them they are terminally ill?" she retorted. "My father is not terminally ill. He is convalescing."

Werner's beeper intervened with an instruction to call Dr. Butz.

"Two days ago, Dr. Butz told me we would be going forward with surgery to put the feeding tube in within forty-eight hours," she said. "Maybe, when you see him, you can review a little math with him."

"He's probably calling to tell me it's been scheduled for surgery," Werner said, wishing he could write an order in the chart forbidding Family from talking with Butz after twelve noon; either that, or write an order requiring Buttface to submit to a Breathalyzer before allowing him to meet with Family.

"A few days won't make any difference in the ultimate outcome ... of the procedure," he added.

"Really?" she said. "Dr. Butz told me that it was essential that my father begin receiving appropriate nutrition as soon as possible."

Maybe the thing to do was come clean and choose up sides in this dispute. He could stand by the lovely Felicia and tell the truth about Bed Five, and Buttface could team up with the fat-faced Connie and her Bible. Maybe it was time to suggest that Bed Five did not have to worry about flossing regularly anymore.

Constance looked past him into Bed Five. Her lips quivered, and tears appeared. "I don't mean to be like this," she said. "I don't mean to be . . . angry."

"Forget about it," Werner said. "I don't mean to be inhumane."

"I know you don't," she said. "We are all sinners. But God loves sinners."

Werner was relieved to hear the good news.

Randolph Hiram Butz, M.D., Ph.D., AA, was sitting behind a desk stacked with leaning towers of medical journals, computer printouts, patient charts, correspondence, and gift notepads from pharmaceutical companies. Wedged between the towers were glass Med Center ashtrays brimming with rancid cigar butts. A speaker-phone was jammed into an open drawer. Styrofoam coffee cups dotted the landscape of the desk. His walls were covered with framed degrees and certificates of merit, most notably his medical school diploma, magna cum laude, Yale Medical School.

He was a gaunt, jaundiced man with bags sagging from the bones of his face and a paunch that barely crept over a silver and turquoise belt buckle. When he grinned, his teeth eerily matched his yellow skin, and black fillings in his rear quadrants showed the ravages of sixty-five years of horrendous oral hygiene.

"My favorite resident," Butz hollered, slapping his hand on his thigh. He kicked back in his stuffed recliner and puffed on a cigar. "What can I do for you?" Butz asked, lifting some papers off his lap and examining them.

"You beeped me," Werner said.

"Now cut that out." Butz laughed. "You're always pulling my leg. I didn't page you." Butz held up the papers, which had the state seal engraved across the top and showed them to Werner. "But as long as you're here, have a look at this piece of catshit."

"What is it?" Werner asked.

Butz picked a bit of tobacco from between his teeth and spit into a wastebasket. "Two years ago, those muttonheads from the state medical board accused me of being an alcoholic, remember that?"

"There was a rumor to that effect," Werner said.

"You understand the difference between drinking and being an alcoholic, don't you?" Butz said.

"Of course," Werner said.

"Well, none of those administrative morons can control their drinking, so they think that anyone who drinks regularly is an alcoholic."

"Oh," said Werner.

"Take me, for instance," Butz continued. "I worked hard my entire life. I graduated magna cum laude from the Yale Medical School, and I helped write *The Fundamentals of Internal Medicine*. You've read it. Hell, everybody's read it. I wrote it twenty years ago, before I started drinking, and chasing women, and enjoying life. The publisher pays roomfuls of assistant editors to update the blasted thing every five years."

Butz took a deep breath, clasped his hands behind his gray head, and settled back into his recliner. "Now, I'm sixty-five years old, and I'm entitled to relax and enjoy myself. I usually have a scotch or two instead of lunch, and then I'll have another taste or two as the afternoon wears on, and maybe one or two of an evening after I get home. I go to bed every night at eight o'clock sharp, and I'm up at four the next morning. If you figure that out, you'll realize I spend less than a third of each day drinking. I never get drunk, and when I'm drinking, I don't perform any surgical procedures or make any important medical decisions; I perform only mundane tasks, paper work and so on, or talking to you, for instance. You hear me?"

"Yes," Werner said.

"Well, now this infernal medical licensing board is coming after me with a pack of rattlesnake lawyers!" Butz yelled, loudly enough to be heard at least four offices down the hallway, where other physicians had waiting rooms filled with patients.

"Somebody filed another goddamned complaint!" he shouted. "And look at this"—he jabbed his finger at the papers—"this time they're not just accusing me of being an alcoholic. No, this time they're saying I'm a *chronic, severe* alcoholic. Can you believe that?"

"Yes, I can," Werner said.

"So, now some bureaucrat sends me a notice and a request for information, and right here they ask me: 'Do you now have, or have you ever had, a problem with alcohol dependency?' Does that make any monkey-fucking sense? If I was an alcoholic, I'd deny it, wouldn't I? Because denial is a symptom of alcoholism. Am I right?"

"Right," Werner said.

"Of course, I'm kidding," Butz said. "I would never intentionally tell a lie. But guess what? If I was a chronic, severe alcoholic, I'd have Wernicke's encephalopathy and Korsakoff's syndrome, wouldn't I? And I wouldn't be able to remember whether I was an alcoholic. Am I right?"

"Correct," Werner declared. "Chronic alcoholism can cause Korsakoff's syndrome, which in turn usually results in almost total short-term memory loss."

"And what's another classic symptom of Korsakoff's syndrome?" Butz asked.

"Confabulation?" Werner suggested.

"Precisely," Butz shouted, banging his desktop and beaming with pride at his protégé's command of internal medicine.

Butz rooted through the slanted piles of charts and journals on his desk and pulled out his *Merck Manual.* "Here we are." He ran his finger around in the index, then opened it and read aloud: " '*Korsakoff's Syndrome*. An amnesic state in which the inability to record new memory traces may lead to confabulation and a seemingly paradoxic situation in which the patient can carry out complex tasks learned before his illness but cannot learn the simplest new skills.' Blah, blah, blah . . . Here's more: 'Since memory for new information is affected but memories for distant events are not, the patient's previous experience is available to guide his actions; there may be little apparent intellectual loss.' "

Butz paused, looking up from the *Manual.* "This could easily be me, couldn't it? I mean, I carry out complex tasks all the time, and I also show little apparent intellectual loss."

"It could be you," Werner agreed.

"Of course, I'm kidding; it's not me. But OK, now on to confabulation," Butz said, returning to his reading. " 'Confabulation is a striking feature that frequently occurs during the early course of the illness in association with the defect in recent memory. . . .

The bewildered patient substitutes imaginary or confused experiences for those he cannot recall. Convincing confabulations may deceive the doctor into seeing the patient's mental state as normal.'

"See what I mean?" Butz said, looking up again.

"See what?" Werner asked.

"Well," Butz said, "these people have sent me a notice and request for information accusing me of being not just an alcoholic but a *chronic, severe* alcoholic."

"Yes," Werner said.

"If what they say is true," Butz argued, "then, as you and I have discussed, I probably have Wernicke's encephalopathy and Korsakoff's syndrome."

"So?" said Werner.

"So," the old doc continued, "I am bewildered, and I will substitute imaginary or confused experiences for those I cannot recall. That's why I'm going to write these bureaucratic herd animals back and tell them that there was a death in my family, and I was under a physician's care for depression for a period of time, but I have since recovered completely. In the meantime, I can go on drinking as much as I want, because I can still carry out all the complex tasks I learned before my illness, and because I have little apparent intellectual loss."

"I see," Werner said.

"Of course, I'm kidding," Butz continued. "But hell's fire, I'll be better for it if I keep drinking, because I used to know plenty before I came to this godforsaken place. If I could erase all the short-term crap my head has soaked up in this hellhole over the last ten years, I'd be a genius again," he yelled, and yanked his thumb over his shoulder toward his Yale diploma.

"Now then," Butz said, closing the *Manual*. "What can I do for you?"

"You asked to see me," Werner said. "You paged me."

"Bullshit," Butz said. "You brought this *Manual* in here and asked me about priapism."

Werner shook his head. "No, I didn't."

"Sure you did," Butz said, showing him the *Manual*. "Have a look. It's even open to the page you were reading. See?"

"I did not ask you about priapism," Werner said.

"Right there," Butz said, his finger shaking slightly. " '*Priapism.* Painful, persistent, and abnormal penile erection, unaccompanied by sexual desire or excitation.' " Butz sat back in his chair. "I had priapism once," he said.

"You did?" Werner asked.

"Sure. Ten years ago, a nurse sued me for sexual harassment," he explained, "and come to find out, it was all caused by priapism. *Atypical* priapism was the final diagnosis, I think, because in my case it was a pain*less*, persistent, and normal penile erection, *accompanied* by sexual desire. But never mind me, what can I do for you?"

Werner took a deep breath. "You paged me."

"Listen, rapscallion," Butz said, shaking his finger at him,"you may be a goddamned rocket scientist, but you won't get too far in this place if you can't remember what you're doing from one minute to the next. I don't even know how the goddamn paging system works around here, so how in the name of Jesus H. Christ would I page your shabby carcass?"

"OK," Werner said, heaving a sigh, "I came to see you about Bed Five, Nine ICU."

"Bed Five?" Butz sputtered. "What's wrong with Bed Five?" Butz pulled a manila folder out of a rack and instantly peeled off two onionskin sheets. "He's paid up. He's got three insurance companies paying his bills monthly. He's as regular as a Swiss watch."

Werner's beeper sounded, instructing him to call the emergency room, stat.

"I'll get it," Butz said, engaging the speakerphone and jabbing the button marked "ER."

"Butz here," he said to the female ER voice. "I'm with Dr. Ernst. What do you want with him?"

"Dr. Hansen told us to call Dr. Ernst," said the woman in the ER, "because we are stacked up down here and we have a nineteen-year-old with a potentially severe head injury who was turned away from the County ER because they couldn't get to him soon enough."

"Does the patient have insurance?" Butz demanded.

"Excuse me?" the woman in the ER said.

"Insurance, health insurance!" Butz yelled, banging the speakerphone. "Does the patient have health insurance?"

"I'll check," the woman said, putting Butz on hold.

Butz pushed the mute button and said to Werner, "That's a tomato for you, she doesn't even ask about insurance. I can tell you right now the guy's bare as a baby's ass."

"Dr. Butz?" the ER said.

"Yes," Butz said in singsong.

"The patient does not have health insurance," she said. "The ambulance service is still here. They originally took him to County, but the County ER was full."

"What a surprise," Butz said to the voice. "I bet you thought the County Hospital dumped only patients with premium health insurance on us, didn't you?"

"I'm sorry, Dr. Butz, I—"

"Never mind!" Butz shouted. "Dr. Ernst and I are extremely busy at the moment, and I'll send him down as soon as I can spare him; but it will probably be at least half an hour before he is available. In the meantime, if the ambulance service receives word of an opening at another facility, they should obviously transport."

The ER voice became agitated. "But Dr. Hansen said—"

"Tell Dr. Hansen his skull is full of horseshit," Butz advised, "and if he says it ain't so, you tell him to call me. Good afternoon."

Butz switched off the speakerphone. Werner hopped out of his chair and took a step for the door.

"I can go take care of it," Werner offered.

Butz banged his fist on his desk. "Get your bones back in that chair before I beat the stuffing out of you! Have you lost your mind, boy? Are you silly enough to work for nothing? Even if you are silly enough, I'm not, and you work for me. If you work for nothing when you're working for me, that means *I'm* working for nothing, too."

"But they said it was a potentially severe head injury," Werner protested.

"Head injury?" Butz shouted. "How many times have I told you to listen! You young bucks can talk until the cows come home, but you never learn to listen! They said it was potentially severe abdominal pain. And there's the catch. If it was really severe, they would have said so, but they didn't, did they? No, they said *potentially* severe, because they're trying to hoodwink you into working for nothing. Head injury? Sure, if it was a head injury, I'd say go ahead. That could be serious. But potentially severe chest pain in a ninety-year-old? Wait and see what your chest feels like if you make it to ninety!"

Werner buried his face in his hands.

"How much money did you have to borrow to get through that place you call a medical school?" Butz crowed, relighting his cigar butt and settling back into his chair. "A hundred grand? And how much didn't you make while you were going to school for four years? Another two hundred K? OK, you're not as smart as I am, but you probably could have made at least ten bucks an hour doing something. Let's call it another eighty K. You start off a hundred and eighty thousand dollars in the hole, and now you want to go downstairs and work on Leroy Washington's gallbladder for nothing?"

Werner took a deep breath, slowly and carefully enunciating his words: "It's a nine*teen*-year-old with a potentially severe head injury. Nobody said a thing about a gallbladder."

Butz shook his head. "You're wrong. But let's pretend you're right, OK? He's nineteen, he's got no health insurance, he's got a head wound, and his name is Leroy Washington. Now. What do you suppose would happen if I drove over to Leroy's house on a Sunday afternoon and hollered at him, 'Hey, Leroy, my grass needs cutting and I don't have a lawn mower. I don't have any money either, but bring your mower on over to my place and cut my grass. If I ever get some extra money, I'll pay you. Really, just send me a bill, Leroy."

Werner banged his fist on the desk with considerably less authority than Butz. "But cutting grass is different from emergency medical care," he argued.

"Sure it's different," Butz yelled, "like a dog and a hound are different. This is a service economy. Time was we had factories, and time was we produced useful things like missiles to keep peace in the world. Now, they changed all that. Now, it's a service economy. You want services, you pay for them. If you give away services for nothing in a service economy, you could destroy the entire country!"

Werner raised his hand. "But—"

"But nothing!" Butz said. "If you sew Leroy Washington's head up for nothing every time his girl friend cracks him in the skull with a frying pan, you're going to be as broke as a toad with no warts! Not only that, you'll be running the country into the shitter besides!"

Werner put his elbow on the front of Butz's desk and held his head in his hand.

Butz moved a stack of papers to another corner of his desk. "Maybe you've got all day to bump your gums about cuts in the defense programs, but I don't. Let's get down to business. What can I do for you?"

Werner rubbed his palms into his eye sockets. "Bed Five," he groaned through clenched teeth.

"Bed Five?" Butz sputtered. "What's wrong with Bed Five?" He pulled the same manila folder out of the rack and peeled off the same onionskin sheets. "He's current. He's got three premier carriers paying his bills on time. He's as regular as a spastic colon greased with laxatives."

Werner bit his lip. "He's supposed to be scheduled for a gastrostomy, but the Family won't consent to it."

"So what?" Butz rejoindered. "We're the doctors, and Bed Five's the patient. I don't give a good goddamn what his wife thinks. I went to Yale. Where did she go to medical school?"

"It's not his wife," Werner said. "It's his daughter. There are two daughters. One of them is somewhat heavyset, and the other is . . . attractive."

"Let's get the attractive one in here," Butz said, "I can convince her to go ahead with the tracheostomy."

"Gastrostomy," Werner said, correcting him.

"You said tracheostomy before," Butz protested. "I was sitting right here, I heard you."

"I've already spoken to her at some length about the gastrostomy," Werner explained.

"If she's a morsel, I'll bet you had some length in her," Butz said. "Sniffing around like a bloodhound, I've seen you." He spit into a wastebasket and relit his cigar.

"And after I spoke with her," Werner continued, "I started thinking that maybe she was right, I mean, about not proceeding with the gastrostomy."

Butz's mouth fell open.

"She's got a point," Werner hurriedly explained. "Why should we feed him if he's not going to get better?"

"You've got the point, boy," Butz thundered, "and it's in your pants. That's your pecker talking for you. I'm assuming the man needs a tube put in because he can't eat, am I right?"

"Yes," Werner admitted, "but aren't we just prolonging the inevitable by putting the tube in?"

Butz appeared on the verge of apoplexy. "You want to starve a man to death, just because he might die soon? Hell's bells and pork pies! I'm gonna take the last call any day myself! You wanna take my feedbag off me, too? Why should any of us eat? We're all gonna die! Why turn good food into shit while we're waiting for Judgment Day?"

"I was just postulating—"

"You were *copulating*," Butz interrupted. "Being a doctor isn't good enough for you. Now you want to be God Almighty on the Day of Wrath! Kill them all and let God sort them out, is that it?"

"But if there's no reasonable prospect of a cure, why should we proceed?" Werner begged.

Butz tried to bang his desk and missed. "Where have you been in life, you mooncalf? It's called *revenue*!" Butz again referred to the onionskin sheets in the manila folder. "The guy has catastrophic health insurance, long-term care insurance, the works! And you want to yank his tubes? This is money. This is not one of those heists where the hospital ends up taking a second mortgage on the homestead. This is a bird in hand. Revenue! Cash money! Of course, I'm kidding. But still."

Werner shook his head. "What difference does insurance make?"

"Hold it right there," Butz said. "I'll get my secretary in here with the documentation." Butz jabbed a button on the speakerphone, and a woman answered.

"This is Gwen."

"Gwen?" Butz asked querulously. "Where's Doris?"

Gwen sighed into the speakerphone. "Doris quit two years ago."

"Horse feathers," Butz said. "I'll go to hell and stay there if she wasn't here yesterday."

Werner heard the secretary cross her fingers at the other end of the line.

"Bring me the last bill we sent out to Bed Five, Nine ICU," Butz said.

"What's the patient's name?" asked Gwen.

"Name?" Butz yelled. Butz pressed the mute button and said to Werner, "I could have gotten a Nobel Prize if I'd done a study on this kind of female incompetence. It's all caused by the ovaries; they secrete some kind of hormone." He released the mute button and said to the secretary, "Susan, how in Sam Hill am I supposed to know what his name is? Get me the last bill the hospital sent to Bed Three, Seven ICU."

"Bed Five, Nine ICU," Werner shouted. "The name's Potter."

"Never mind bringing the bill, Dolores," Butz hollered. "Just give us the bottom line."

Gwen emphatically placed Werner and Butz on hold.

Butz put Bed Five's manila folder back in the rack. "Did you want to see me about something?" he asked. "What can I do for you?"

Gwen came back on the speakerphone. "The total of the last bill, which was for the month of May only, was sixty-seven thousand nine hundred and seventy-three dollars and thirty-two cents."

"Bill?" Butz screamed. "What bill? I'm in conference in here! Who says I owe them sixty-seven thousand dollars?"

Gwen hung up.

"Hello!" Butz hollered, poking several buttons and prompting a busy signal from the speakerphone. "Can you believe it? The worst goddamn secretary I've ever had. Useless! Tits on a bull!"

"Bed Five, Nine ICU," Werner said.

"Bed Five?" Butz sputtered, grabbing the manila folder again.

"I know he's paid up," Werner said. "He's comatose. We're supposed to schedule him for a gastrostomy."

"Do it!" Butz said, examining the folder. "I get a cut of the money that comes in for every test and procedure done on the guy. He's got catastrophic health insurance; he's as prompt as an undertaker at a funeral."

"My question is," Werner said, "if you were comatose, would you want to be kept alive for months by machines?"

Butz sat bolt upright and gave Werner a stupefied look. "Hell, no!" he retorted. "Do you think I want to die tied down in a roomful of strangers? I'm going to die at home in my own bed with a bottle of scotch and a cold beer."

"Well then?" Werner said, throwing out his hands for an explanation.

"Well, then, what?" Butz said irritably.

"Well, why is it OK for us to tie down Bed Five and allow strangers to torture him if it's wrong? You said yourself, you wouldn't want any part of it. Can we at least make him a No Code?"

Butz gave Werner a look of utter perplexity. "This must be the generation gap. You don't know your ankles from your elbows, do you? I'm going to explain this entire matter to you, and I don't want to be interrupted until I'm finished. Do you understand?"

"Yes," Werner said.

"You're a doctor, right?"

"Right," Werner said.

"I'm a doctor, right?"

Well, Werner thought. "Right," he said.

"Now, doctors get paid piles of money to keep people alive, right?" Butz explained. "Are you still with me? That's revenue. Money. Lots of money, paid to us, you and me, for keeping people alive. Got it?"

"Got it," Werner said, "but—"

"Stay with me, you helpless gawp!" Butz screamed. "See this," he said, holding up the onionskin papers from the manila folder. "According to these records, this fellow in Bed Five purchased three different health insurance policies that pay us wheelbarrows full of cash for keeping him alive. If we don't keep him alive, we don't get paid, understand?"

"Yes," Werner said, "but—"

"Quiet!" Butz bellowed. "Let me put it another way, just so there's no mistake about it," he said, calming himself. "As soon as he dies, the insurance companies stop paying us millions of dollars."

"I know," Werner interrupted, "but you—"

"I'm getting to me," he howled. "I don't sneeze because someone else has taken snuff. I don't want to be tied down in bed and tortured before I die," Butz explained. "I want to die on my back porch with my feet up and my belly full of barbecued ribs. That's why I don't have any catastrophic health insurance. In fact, I don't have *any* health insurance."

"Really?" Werner said.

"Of course," Butz said. "And all my assets are in trust accounts that strictly forbid anyone from using the money to pay for my health care."

"But what if you get sick?" Werner asked.

"If I get sick," Butz replied, "I guarantee you no doctor on the planet will come near me. Any country bumpkin can figure that out. You've heard of these goddamn living wills? You don't need one of them. Just make sure there's no money there, and you'll die in your own bed with a smile on your face."

Butz selected a cigar butt from one of the glass ashtrays and lit it, puffing luxuriously. "This poor bugger in Bed Five didn't load up on catastrophic health insurance so he could go gently into the good night. He wanted us to put up a fight for him, and he wanted us to be paid in cash money to do the job right. Otherwise, he wouldn't have bought the policies in the first place."

Butz's phone rang. He took the call using the handset, said hello, and listened for half a minute. "Does the patient have insurance? I see. He *had* insurance, but it expired. I'll tell you what. Hold on a second."

Butz engaged the mute button. "Does this Hansen fellow work for me?"

"No," Werner said.

"Hello?" Butz said. "I'm tied up at the minute. Would you page Dr. Hansen and tell him to see the patient as soon as possible? Very good, thank you."

"Now then," Butz said, "you came in here looking for some season tickets to the ball game, didn't you?"

"No," Werner said wearily. "No, I didn't."

"You need more sleep," Butz said. "Were you on call last night? You told me not two minutes ago that you wanted tickets for Saturday night, loge reserve, for the seven-thirty game."

"No," Werner said. "I did not."

"Be that way," Butz said with a shrug. "Well then, what can I do for you?"

Werner took his splitting headache with him when he left Butz's office. He rode the elevator to the Ninth-Floor ICU and wrote an order in the chart scheduling Bed Five for a gastrostomy, ASAP.

After writing the order, he went into Bed Five, where Stella was changing IV tubing.

Stella held up a package of IV tubing containing two lengths of clear, slender tubes, about twelve feet long. "Fifty-six bucks for a pair of these," she said loudly. "I know a tropical fish store where

I can buy the same tubing for aquarium pumps at a dollar and a half."

Werner stood over Bed Five and studied the skull under the skin. A coarse tremor caused the fingers on Bed Five's right hand to tap against the bed rails, making a soft pinging sound. He coughed, and dark secretions gurgled in his trach tube.

Stella snapped on a pair of rubber gloves and unwrapped a suction catheter from a sterile bag. "These cost fifteen bucks apiece," she said, holding up the catheter, "and he gets suctioned hourly. That's three hundred and fifty bucks' worth of suction catheters a day. Just think what a living person could do with that money. I could take three days off and drink cold beer."

"What's your assessment of this patient?" Werner asked Stella.

"TAX ASSESSOR, WHAT?" yelled Stella. "MY HEARING AID'S IN THE SHOP."

"I SAID, WHAT'S YOUR ASSESSMENT OF THIS PATIENT?" Werner said.

"HIM?" Stella said. "Don't be a comedian." She squirted a 5 cc vial of half-normal saline down Bed Five's trach tube and into his lungs, causing him to cough violently. The suction catheter filled with brown mucus.

"They don't call it pulmonary toilet for nothing," she remarked, skillfully twirling the catheter and suctioning down the left main stem bronchus.

"HAVE YOU EVER ASKED HIM TO SQUEEZE YOUR HAND?" Werner asked, studying Bed Five's coarse tremors.

"Him?" She laughed. "WHAT FOR?"

Werner watched a new bout of tetany ripple through Bed Five's flaccid muscles.

"As long as we're on the subject, Dr. Sausage," Stella yammered, "could somebody please tell me why we're dripping a thousand bucks a day worth of total parenteral nutrition and meds into this summer squash when the country is full of unvaccinated kids? Vaccinations run, what? Two bucks a pop? We could vaccinate Brooklyn on this guy's tab alone."

"Fear of death," replied Werner. "Old people are no different from the rest of us; they're afraid to die. They'd rather pay us to keep them in suspended animation. I believe it's called AAFLAB."

"A WHAT?" Stella shouted.

"AAFLAB," Werner shouted back. "The American Association

of Fat Lazy Aged Bodies. They know how to do two things: play golf and vote for members of Congress who send them money, instead of wasting it on little kids who can't vote."

On the way out of Bed Five, Werner ran into the Hippoblimp. She was smiling broadly and beaming over an open chart.

"Remember that No Code order you gave on Bed Seven the other night," she asked.

"Vaguely," Werner replied.

"I believe your verbal order was 'Corpse. No Code,' " she said. "Does that sound familiar? And I asked you if you had cleared that with Dr. Butz?"

"Is there a point to this?" Werner asked.

"Dr. Butz wrote an order making Bed Seven a Full Code today," she said. She showed Werner a totally illegible scribble in Bed Seven's chart.

"I'll be sure to make you a Full Code someday, too," Werner said.

The hospital operator handed him three messages on his way out of the hospital. One was from Sheldon Hatchett: "Seeking temporary restraining order tomorrow." One was from Mr. Wilson in the Medical Center's Legal Department: "Opposing TRO tomorrow. Meet with me at 8:30 A.M. My office." One was from Felicia Potter: "Can we obtain an opening for the treatment tonight? I have your address."

Chapter

8

Werner rolled into his apartment just before eight (1945, medico-military time), another fourteen-hour day of internal medicine behind him. He waded through the wrack and ruin of his apartment, a single, large room filled with dirty dishes, beer bottles, wads of dirty clothes, wads of clean clothes, stacks of textbooks, papers, and medical journals, a white takeout bag bulging with the Styrofoam debris of his last meal at home, a University Medical Center coffee mug with tiny lily pads of mold adrift in a pond of instant coffee.

It was a studio with a kitchenette and a bathroom, but it was cheap, and there were no patients or cockroaches.

He had scrawled her number on a pharmaceutical unit conversion table, which was lost somewhere in his lab coat. After rooting around for five minutes in the vast interiors of the kangaroo pockets, he found her number in the hip pocket of his pants. No answer. Maybe she had given up on him. Maybe she was in the ICU with Bed Five.

He flipped through his mail—medical journals, bills, one-time-only low, low offers for life insurance, auto insurance, malpractice insurance, renters' insurance, and major medical insurance. The bills went into the base of a horizontally transected human skull (stolen from the pathology lab), which was full of other unopened bills. The one-time-only low, low insurance bargains went into a loose trash bag on the floor.

He assessed his sleep status: Was it exhaustion of the usual profound variety, calling for immediate sleep, or was it moderate exhaustion, which could often be modulated with alcohol to produce exhaustion of the recreational variety, which, in turn, with careful attention to dosages, could sometimes progress to a feeling of normal wakefulness or even euphoria?

He took two beers out of the refrigerator and put them in the freezer. Four ice cubes in a tall glass, four fingers of scotch, no water. He went over to a tall cabinet in the corner, turned on the stereo, and sifted through a laundry basket full of cassettes, searching for something loud and mindless, something with a good beat, something he was familiar with, but not too familiar with, something . . .

He called her again without getting an answer.

He pulled down the Murphy bed, wadded up a pillow into a prop, and cracked open a glossy medical journal. Nothing like a good read. He belched and tore into the lead article: "Inhibited Gastric Secretion of HCL in Patients Receiving Prostaglandins (PGE1, PGE2, PGA1) and Their 16, 16-dimethyl Analogs."

Midway through the arcane journey into the effects of prostaglandins, Werner wondered if she might have just stepped out for some groceries. He tried her again. No answer. At footnote twenty-five, he polished off the glass of scotch and went after a cold beer.

It was absolutely essential that they schedule an opening for the treatment as soon as possible. He flipped through the journal to see if there were any recent articles on dyspareunia (pain during intercourse causing sexual dysfunction and inhibited orgasmic response in the female). She could easily develop into one of the most important clinical experiences of his career. He wanted to rule out vaginismus, vaginitis, suburethral diverticulum, and pelvic inflammatory disease and get on with the business of getting laid. He tried to think of a way to sneak in a pelvic exam, or get a swab specimen for a culture and Gram stain, in case she had picked up something contagious.

He dialed the number again—just another pigeon experiencing

extinction in a Skinner box, pecking the colored dispenser buttons, even though the grain pellets had stopped coming hours ago. He had to watch himself; he could be coming down with a touch of the old love-at-first-sight virus, or LAFS, as he had called it when he had suffered from it a dozen times in med school. It was characterized by acute dementia, erotomania, and hysteria libidinosa. A florid case of LAFS could mean unnecessary downtime for his formidable information processing systems.

He fetched beer number two. Life was good. He was out of the hospital. As long as he kept his beeper on him, he was free to forage for food, go in search of a mate, and even—the most forbidden of all pleasures—sleep. He picked up the phone and tried to call a twenty-five-year-old Caucasian female in apparent good health, oriented times three, cranial nerves I–XII intact, breasts symmetric and without masses or discharge, heart sounds normal, regular rate and rhythm, respirations 12, pulse 72, blood pressure 120/80, skin warm, dry, and pink. . . .

Life was simple and pure. If he worked hard, the money would come in. And when the money came in, he could spend it. If he wanted, he could buy a big house and even settle down with a twenty-five-year-old Caucasian female in apparent good health. She was dull, simple, and shallow, but who wanted drama, complexity, and depth after sixteen hours in the ICU? It might be pleasant to come home to a lovely simpleton.

Maybe one more beer to celebrate. Work hard, play hard. Buttface was a harmless, kind, old, grandfatherly racist, sexist, greedy, senile bastard, but he was old and could not help it. Live and let live. The Bed Five thing would probably just work itself out. Constance was a flake, but she meant well. Felicia was . . . gorgeous. Werner was an industrious, young physician doing his best to make his way in the world, and God smiled down on all of them from above, if God was still there.

In college, he had read that God was dead. In medical school, he learned that God was not dead; He was just very sick. The first reports of God's death had been circulated over one hundred years ago, and God knows how little they knew about brain death and cardiopulmonary resuscitation back then. God was probably pronounced dead prematurely. Instead of dying or being found murdered, God may have just slipped into a coma or had an attack of transient global amnesia (TGA), during which time He simply forgot He was God and left the universe to its own devices. Instead of announcing his debility to the world, maybe God just went into seclusion, the way ailing Russian premiers do, leaving the masses to speculate on the particulars of His absence during a long convalescence.

The scenario was easy enough to imagine. God was probably out slumming in some clip joint on the wrong side of purgatory, carousing with sinners and archangels alike, refreshing His familiarity with all things human and divine. God went over to the bar to get some change for the pinball machines and video games. Having had a few too many, He dropped a quarter on the floor, so He got down on all fours, lit a match, and poked around in the sawdust and peanut shells until he found the coin. On the way back up, He whacked the bejesus out of his skull on the underside of a barstool and gave Himself a royal concussion, a cerebral contusion, or a subdural hematoma. Retrograde amnesia and post-traumatic cerebral edema set in, and He forgot He was God.

In the meantime, planet Earth fell apart. Nietzsche's books got published, Archduke Ferdinand was assassinated, and World War I began. By the time God got to a decent emergency room, Hitler was in power and World War II was in full career. Before the right specialist could be reached at home, the A-bomb was invented.

Things look bad for the world, but why jump to conclusions and pronounce God dead, when He probably just needs to be transferred to a crackerjack ICU equipped with the proper technology? Miracle drugs could keep His blood pressure up and straighten out His electrolyte imbalances. It may be that God is in critical condition and waiting for ten units of platelets or three units of whole blood. The lab could be having the devil's own time typing and cross-matching Him.

Medicine advances at such a furious pace the newest breakthroughs might not be available up there yet, forcing God to make do with outdated equipment and physicians who are hopelessly uninformed. One can only hope that the deceased medical personnel already in heaven can effectively manage what little life support technology is available to them and keep God's vital signs in the pink, until the Chief of Internal Medicine from the Mayo Clinic or a specialist from Sloan-Kettering can make it up there with a little know-how, take over as God's attending physician, put God on a ventilator, get a cardiac catheter in Him for some hard-core central venous pressure monitoring, and call Radiology in for a complete body scan.

Once God gets to feeling better, He can go back to thinking of Himself as a doctor, in much the same way that doctors think of themselves as God. Maybe God knows what it feels like to be on call all the time and never to get enough sleep. Maybe God is sick to death of incurable diseases and random catastrophes, of stillbirths and venereal disease, of bowel obstructions and dissecting aortic aneurysms. Maybe God wears a long white lab coat and pores over everyone's charts, constantly chewing the end of His ball-point pen and clicking the clicker in and out, desperately trying to decide whether to let Bed Two expire or make him hold on for another two weeks of dialysis. Maybe He was frantic over whether and when to take the eighty-two-year-old liver in Bed Six. What if God has to sit up all night, trying to decide whether to take the cystic fibrosis patients before age twelve or let them live into early adulthood? Is a life of constant suffering worth a few wedding receptions and sunrises? Is it better to take sickly infants in the cradle or to let them live through one tragedy after another, on the off chance that they will discover a few scattered moments of intense rapture, or maybe even learn the mysterious trick of transforming their sufferings into joys?

Werner returned to the article on prostaglandins. There was barely enough time to learn the hard sciences and no time at all to frolic about in the enchanted forests of speculation. The important questions in life were usually nothing more than medical questions in disguise. Religion dealt with final questions, which assumed primary importance only after all the medical alternatives had failed. Most people intuitively knew this, even though they could not really understand it.

Werner heard a quiet, powerful engine arrive out on his parking lot, sounding more like a Stealth bomber than a car. The engine stopped, followed by the whir of headlights retracting and a muffled, precision clunk, like someone dropping the lid of an expensive coffin. He heard the sexy ticktock of high heels on the pavement, on the fire escape, on the landing outside his door.

The patient had arrived.

"Dr. Ernst?" she called shyly through the screen door. "Are you home?"

He let her in and kissed her. *Family must be just like nurses,* he thought. *They keep calling you Doctor, even when you are about to slip it in.*

She teetered in on white, sling-back, stiletto high heels. Her hair sprouted aloft in a profusion of twirled topknots, sprays, and beribboned ponytails. White earrings the size of wind chimes swagged against her neck. She giggled and blushed and took a turn for him, swirling the hem of a sheer white cotton-mesh dress and rattling a wristful of white bangles.

She had a portable home entertainment center and a bulging overnight bag.

"You told me you didn't have a TV," she said, "so I brought one over for us.

"You like?" she asked, pulling the dress up above her knees and extending an ankle braceleted with a gold chain. "I bought it today."

She rocked back on her high heels. "How's my tan look against all this white stuff?" she wanted to know, presenting a sun-bronzed shoulder and a strap for inspection.

Werner held her and touched the smooth brown skin with his lips, tasting warm coconut oil and feeling the heat left over from the day's dedicated tanning. The dress was so slinky it moved with his hands, and he could feel the bands and bows and embroidery on her panties underneath.

She broke away and fanned her face with her hands. "Ick!" she squealed. "It's totally muggy in this joint. I'm pitting out already. Don't you have an air conditioner?"

"I have a number of serious moral and philosophical objections to owning an air conditioner," Werner said. "Think about it—"

"Put a sock in it," she said. "Those must be the same objections you had to owning a car, right? When do they start paying you the money?"

"As soon as they are absolutely sure you're too old to have any fun with it," he said.

She kissed him, then went into her overnight bag and came out with a pack of cigarettes and a can of diet soda. "Will you open this for me?" she asked, handing him the can of soda and fanning her nails at him. "I'll set up the TV."

They relocated to the couch. She was in no apparent hurry to get on with the treatment. Werner watched her brown skin peeking through pores in the delicate weave of the summery fabric as she set up the TV. Instead of hanging on her, the stuff seemed to float around her, draping itself here and there over the curves and swells of her supple body. The puffed-out pleats of the bodice stirred with her curiously mobile breasts, both of which were unmuzzled and roaming free, an observation that colored Werner's thoughts a tactile pink, as he watched the nipples being abraded by the fabric.

She lit a cigarette and clicked on the set, using a remote control. "I hope I wasn't bothering you when I called this morning," she said, flopping from one channel to the next, sampling each of them momentarily.

"I was in teaching rounds with the Chief of Internal Medicine," Werner said. "Never call me before noon. Never. Mornings are out of the question. I told you that, but you didn't listen," he said, catching himself before he slipped all the way over to the tone he used on wombats.

"I'm sorry," she said. "I felt like the evening had turned out all wrong or something. And I wanted to talk to you about it. I didn't want you to be upset or anything."

"I never get upset," Werner told her. "If I get upset, all I have to do is go to sleep . . . assuming I'm not on call."

"Well," she said, looking down at the remote control, "I hope you're telling the truth, because I don't want you to be upset. I liked sleeping with you. It was very intimate, even though we didn't . . ."

Werner took his cue and moved in for a closer look.

"I also wanted to warn you that the lawyer would be calling," she said. "I told him not to, but he insisted on it."

"I talked to him," Werner said. "I also spoke with the other doctors." He took a deep breath. "I don't think I can help you people."

Tears appeared, staining the perfect cheeks, racing one another down her chin. "I didn't think so," she said, her eyes settling vacantly on a microwave popcorn commercial.

He took her hand. "I feel what you feel," he said, leaning into her line of sight and holding her eyes with his. "But I can't testify against my superiors. I'm just a resident."

"In other words," she said, "you think I'm right, but you can't testify about it in court."

"Let's don't talk about it anymore," he said, taking both her hands in his. "Let's talk about ourselves."

She tapped the ashes of her cigarette into the diet soda can. "OK," she said, still sobbing. "My name's Felicia Potter. My dad's been in a coma for months in the Intensive Care Unit, and I'm always afraid to leave him alone, because I can't stand the thought of him dying and me not being there. OK," she said, "that's me. What's your name?"

"This is a complete mess," Werner complained. "It's the uncertainty principle. If you study the problem, you disturb it, and it changes into something else. There are no black or whites; it's nothing but gray. One specialist says do it; the other says what for?"

"My lawyer said you were the Editor in Chief of the University's *Journal of Medicine*," she said. "He said a judge might listen to a resident who was the editor of a medical journal."

"Why?" Werner said. "That's just a lot of busywork. That doesn't have a thing to do with practicing medicine. That's academics."

"I go to the hospital, and I stare at him for hours," she said. "But I don't see my father. My father was full of life. He liked to run, bike, play basketball, swim. He was active. He hated doctors, and he hated hospitals. Now look at him. One time he told me, 'I don't want anything to do with nursing homes, understand? I want to be remembered as the old guy who took you out dancing, not the guy who asked you to change his diapers.' "

"I wish I could help you," Werner said, "but I can't testify for you. I'd get kicked out of the program."

"You don't have to testify," she interrupted. "My lawyer hired two medical experts to testify for us."

This was good news, Werner thought. Now maybe they could concentrate on more important things.

She put out the pretty cigarette, then lit another. "He said you would be a better witness," she added, "but we could get by without you."

"That's great," Werner said. "And you're going to court tomorrow?"

"He said it's a small hearing tomorrow. Kind of an emergency hearing to temporarily stop them from putting the tube in. Then,

ten days from tomorrow, there will be a big hearing, and the judge
will decide whether we can permanently stop them from putting
the tube in."

"You'll probably do better without me," Werner urged. "Do
you understand that I would testify for you if I could?"

"There are other ways you can help me," she said, looking at
him levelly.

Nothing came to mind. Nothing ethical anyway.

"For instance, you could begin by telling me if I'm doing the
right thing," she begged. "Maybe then I could sleep at night."

"You're doing the right thing," he said. "Don't ask me to explain it. Just take my word for it."

"Explain it to me," she said, resting her hand on the lateral
aspect of his thigh. "Just tell me why I'm doing the right thing. For
my own peace of mind, so I can sleep at night."

"It's too complicated," Werner said. "Just take my word for it.
He's in what we call a persistent vegetative state."

When she touched him, the pressure receptors in his skin set up
an electrical brush fire that swept through his parasympathetic
nervous system and redirected blood flow to the pelvis (a phenom-
enon that might be called true genital shunt).

"I have to ask you something else," she said. "I hope you don't
think this is weird of me, or whatever. I mean, it's a favor for a girl
friend of mine. She had an abortion once, and she got really sick
afterwards, I mean, like for three days. Sick, like she couldn't even
get out of bed . . . that type sick."

As opposed to another type sick, Werner thought. *Now I know
what you mean.*

"And after that she kept having health problems. She had attacks, you know. They said it was like anxiety attacks or something, but she had lung problems, too, like asthma or something.
And she's worried that the abortion caused blood clots to clog
up her lungs. Or maybe it was birth control pills, she said.
Doesn't the pill cause some people to have blood clots? Could
that make you have lung problems, like not being able to get
your breath and so on?"

"Not usually," Werner said, watching her closely, as she exhaled, smoke curling around her nostrils. She trimmed the ash of
her cigarette four different ways on the lip of the diet soda can and

took another puff, tasting the smoke with her lips and tongue, as if she had just inhaled a wad of cotton candy.

"Different kinds of abortions have different complications," Werner explained. "Besides, what does a guy like me know about abortions? I know how to keep dying people alive, that's all. What kind of abortion are we talking about? Vacuum aspiration, dilation and curettage, dilation and evacuation, saline injection? They all have different risks, ranging from nausea and vomiting to sudden death."

"You can die from having an abortion?" she asked in disbelief.

"Sure," Werner said. "You can die from eating a tuna fish sandwich, but not very many people do. I think the odds are something like one in one hundred thousand for a first-trimester vacuum aspiration, and it goes up from there. See? Practically negligible."

"OK, how about the pill?" she asked. "Could that cause her to have blood clots in her lungs?"

"Oral contraceptives may contribute to the formation of thrombi, or clots, which usually form in the arms or legs. When clots break off and float through the bloodstream, they are called emboli. Other things can be emboli, too: air, fat, foreign objects. Clots in the arms and legs send emboli to the lungs. Clots in the heart send emboli to the brain," he said, pausing and looking straight through her skull, almost seeing the squiggling convolutions of gray matter afloat in the bubble of spinal fluid, "in which case, they cause you to have what's commonly referred to as a stroke, or a cerebral vascular accident, a CVA," he said.

He drank the last of his beer and recalled the brain samples he had worked with in anatomy—the cerebellum of a John Doe who had died of a ruptured berry aneurysm—a blob of veiny, gray brain tissue with a black, cauliflower-shaped explosion of blood, right at the bifurcation in the circle of Willis.

"When emboli or floating clots get caught in your lungs," Werner continued matter-of-factly, "they block off part of your lung and make you suddenly short of breath."

She was pale and quiet.

"But we're talking about stuff that's very, very rare," he said. "It's just that it's less rare, or more common, in women who take the pill, especially if they are also heavy smokers," he added, careful not to emphasize any of it.

She dropped the cigarette through the slot in the soda can.

"Very low odds, though," he said again, "especially in a young person. Odds that are four or five times greater are still low odds when you begin with a risk of less than one percent. But then, four or five percent is four or five percent," he said. "Besides, a blood clot in your lung would cause a permanent problem, not something that comes and goes. You said you were having episodes, or attacks, didn't you?"

"No," she said. "It's a friend of mine. A girl friend."

"Oh, come on," Werner scoffed. "What kind of abortion did you have?"

"Really," she said. "It was my friend. She had a saline abortion, and she got really sick afterwards. Now she has attacks."

"OK," Werner said with a shrug, reading from the script she wrote for him.

She got up and took the soda can to the counter of the kitchenette, the dress clinging to her hips in locomotion, nicely delineating her gluteals.

"If you had a blood clot in your brain, could that cause you to get splitting headaches?"

"Maybe," Werner replied. "Probably just one sudden splitting headache. Then you'd either die or have a stroke. Chronic headaches are caused by a thousand and one things. Everything from a brain tumor to eating Chinese food. Headaches are like ringing in the ears. Do you know how useless it is to have someone tell you they have ringing in the ears? It's like somebody telling you they get sleepy after eating a big meal."

"My ears ring sometimes," she said.

"See what I mean," he said, throwing up his hands.

"It's so complicated," she said. "I don't know how you can keep track of it all."

She returned to the couch, breasts asway, bent over him, and gave him a big, wet kiss.

Werner ran his hands under her dress and up the back of her cool, smooth legs, his pulse causing water hammer in his ears.

"You did say that your friend was on the pill, didn't you?" he asked, without ever really ending the kiss.

"Yeah," she said. "That's why I was asking you all those questions. Why, is there something else it does to you?"

"Never mind," he said, nuzzling the breasts, which were dangling like blood-warm clumps of grapes, just above his nose.

"I want to make love to you," he said to the breasts.

She rubbed them against his lips, moaning softly, "I want to make love to you, too," pausing to swish the inside of his mouth with her tongue, "and that's exactly what I'm going to do," she murmured, "when I get out of the shower."

"No showers," Werner said, pulling her down on top of him with a lurch that started out passionate and wound up authoritarian. "How 'bout showering later . . . afterwards?"

"It's totally gross in here," she whined. "I smell. I'm all sticky." She pecked him once on the neck.

"I can't smell you," Werner said, going for a spot of comic relief by trying to lick her armpit, "and if I could, the smell would probably drive me nuts."

"What about me, though?" she said. "I don't like to smell. And when I'm fresh and clean, I feel good." She kissed him again. "And when I'm fresh and clean, I feel sexy. Did you bring the water stuff?"

Werner went blank, then panicked. How did he forget it? The most important thing he had had to do today, and he had completely forgotten it. "I . . ."

"You forgot it," she said. "Oh, well, maybe it won't matter." She jumped up, grabbed the overnight bag, and disappeared into the bathroom. "I'm locking the door, so don't try any surprise attacks."

Round two, Werner thought, kicking himself for not thinking to grab some jelly packets after he had got her message at the hospital. He poured another finger of scotch into his glass and tossed it off.

He tore through his lab coat again, hoping he had a spare packet on him left over from an intubation or a rectal exam. "Damn!"

The phone rang. "Damn again!" He weighed the risks of not answering it, then picked it up. He ventured a quiet hello and resolved to hang up if he didn't immediately recognize the voice.

"Wiener? This is Stella. Your man in Bed Five is putting in a bid to buy the farm."

Werner covered the mouthpiece. "Damn!" he said. He held the phone up in the air and shook his fists.

"Are you still there?" Stella said.

The shower continued running in the bathroom. "Yeah," Werner said, "I'm here."

"We're still getting pacemaker spikes, but they're not capturing," she said. "He's having sinus pauses, runs of V-tach. He's blocked down a couple of times. His CO_2 is creeping up, and his pH is dropping," she continued in a monotonous tone. "I bolused him with lidocaine. He's had a couple amps of bicarb, and I've been giving him atropine whenever he blocks."

"I tried to make him a No Code today," Werner said, "and Buttface wouldn't budge."

"Yeah," she said. "Well, we called Buttface at home, and you can imagine how that went. Dr. Slurred Speech. He ordered a heart and lung transplant, and he said he'd come in tomorrow and do it himself."

"Damn," Werner said, listening again for the shower. "This guy would sink like a stone if we could just leave him alone."

"Yeah," she said. "Unfortunately, we can't. The fat Bible beater's here going hysterical on us. We had to call in a couple hit men from Pastoral Care. We can't reach the other daughter, the Playboy Bunny? There's a note in the chart that she wants to be informed immediately of any changes. The Code Blue team is here waiting. Hansen's here ready to take care of any pulmonary emboli. . . ."

The shower turned off.

Werner felt his chest tighten. He put his hand over the mouthpiece. Damn.

"Whoops," Stella said, "there goes another run of V-tach. I'll get back to you."

She hung up. *Great,* Werner thought. *Just great. Damn!* He went to the kitchen counter and threw back another finger of scotch. He listened to her humming in the bathroom. Another bout of true genital shunt set in.

She came out wearing a magic, high-luster teddy that changed colors every time she breathed. The neckline dipped gracefully into a rounded V, throwing her breasts into high relief under the slippery satin. One side of her head was smooth and slick, her hair pulled up and held on top and behind with a decorative arrangement of combs that steered it over to the other side, where a freshet of loose curls, ringlets, and tendrils burst forth. The one lone, dainty, scrubbed ear left behind was pale and naked, a small, intricate ornament cast in skin and cartilage, the lobe pierced and dangling a gold teardrop earring.

"How did you do that so quickly?" the doctor wanted to know, weak-kneed at the sheer artistry of what she had achieved.

"I'm a model," she said, touching the corner of her wet-look lips. "You learn to look good fast in my line of work." She sauntered over to him and gave him a profile.

He kissed her neck, tasting lotions and perfumes. The forty-watt bulb cast a soft orange glow from the bathroom.

"Isn't this better than being all sticky and smelly?" she asked.

"You're the most beautiful woman I've ever seen," Werner said, kissing her neck again and holding the pendulous breasts against him.

"Promise?" she said.

"Absolutely," Werner said.

"What about on TV, though?" she said.

"What?" Werner said, rousing himself from his flesh feast.

"Am I the most beautiful woman you've seen anywhere? Or just in real life? Did you see somebody that looked better than this on TV or in a movie?"

"No," he said. "I haven't."

"Good," she said. "Because that's my competition. I need national airtime, preferably in a cosmetic ad."

Werner kissed her and got the teddy off, along with his own encumbrances. Once they were squirming on the Murphy bed, he began to formulate a regimen of foreplay to remedy the recurring, idiopathic dyspareunia.

He followed his mouth around on an oral expedition, osculating the dual pink nodes with tongue and lips, lavishing extra care on the finer aspects of the nipple treatment. They went erectile, but she subtly shrugged, steering him away from them and pulling him up to kiss her mouth. A silent kiss, technically erotic, but without the hunger of Werner's own prehensile lip work. He explored her neck and ears for erogenous zones.

He held himself up for a final, lingering examination, her parted lips, her body spread before him like a valley of warm, bellying curves. She reached over and snapped off the cord switch on the bedside lamp, abruptly ending the video display. Undaunted, Werner went right back to work, conscientiously staying away from his ultimate destination.

She had probably been manhandled by a caveman, he hypothesized. Someone had hurt her, because he had failed to prepare his materials before performing the procedure. Werner planned to take all the time he needed. He planned to turn her into a blob of warm, wet clay on a potter's wheel. He would warm her with the friction of his hands, knead the skin and the muscle, press her into a well-wrought receptacle with his fingers, fashion a warm, smooth urn with beveled lips and flowing ovals, mold her with one hand inside her, and the other tracing the external contours, draw her up and out, open her, and tenderly pour himself into her, filling the smooth, slick chambers with pleasure.

He roused himself from his fantasy and kissed her again. Had she moved? Yes, her arms had moved. She had definitely embraced him with her arms. However, he could not remember her moving her legs. He reared up again into the command position and worked her legs apart by spreading his knees slightly.

"Kiss me," she said, moving her legs perceptibly closer together and undoing everything he had just accomplished.

After another ten minutes of kissing and massaging, of breathing in her ear and telling her how beautiful she was, he gingerly sent his hand down for some exploratory palpation, feeling in the darkness for the warm, wet rosepetal flaps of skin, so unlike anything the physician sees or feels in the clinical setting. . . . Instead, his fingertips located membranes. Mucous membranes as cool and dry as a surgeon's sterile glove. Nothing. Not a drop of transmission fluid. Not a glimmer of the miraculous essence that transforms an organ into a sex organ.

"What's wrong?" she asked nervously. "Is something wrong?"

"No," Werner said, "nothing's wrong," losing the penile pulse he had been monitoring on himself. "Does it bother you when I touch you?"

"No," she said, stiffening somewhat, "I like it."

Werner touched her for a while, trying the three or four procedures he had picked up in the course of his training as a male animal. He kissed her, pressing what was left of himself up against her, hoping things would take off automatically.

"Something's wrong, isn't it?" she said.

"Nothing's wrong," Dr. Ernst assured her, wondering if indirect stimulation of the clitoris, inferior to the prepuce, by way of the labia minor, might be the answer.

"You can't do it, can you?" she said in a disappointed tone of voice.

"Now wait a second," Werner blurted.

"It's not hard anymore, is it?" she said, gently shifting him off center with a thigh. "See, it's not just me, is it? It's you, too."

Chapter

9

At 6:30 the next morning, Werner watched dawn break in the Death Lab, sitting with a cola, four aspirin, and a headache. He had pulled the rack of patient charts up next to him at the console, intending to review them before teaching rounds with Dr. Hofstader. Among other things, the clone brigade was going to observe a colonoscopy on the eighty-three-year-old bowel obstruction in Bed Three at 7:30 A.M. After his last encounter with Dr. Hofstader, Werner thought it might be prudent to know everything in Bed Three's chart, just in case Hofstader was still in the mood for some more intellectual sadism.

But Werner had been in the Death Lab since six and had not as yet touched a chart. Spread before him on the console was the American Psychiatric Association's *Diagnostic and Statistical Manual of Mental Disorders*, third edition, open to the chapter on the etiology and diagnosis of psychosexual disorders. He also had the *Merck Manual of Diagnosis and Therapy*, specifically, section 171, "Disorders of Sexual Function," wherein it stated: "Proper sexual functioning in men and women depends on an anticipatory mental 'set' (the sexual motive state) or state of desire, effective vasocongestive arousal (erection in the male; *lubrication* in the female), and orgasm [Werner's emphasis]."

Ha! Should he call her at home? he wondered. Or should he simply photocopy the page and mail it to her? So much for her insinuation that it was not just her doing. Ha! *His* anticipatory mental set began at age twelve and reached a new peak last night. He was normal. The *Manual* specifically stated the missing ingredient was her responsibility.

As for the etiology and diagnosis of her intervening neurosis, there were several hypotheses. One was that she perceived their anatomies to be incompatible. This was not as farfetched as it might seem to a layperson. It is not uncommon for patients to seek medical help after initial sexual encounters are unsatisfactory because of organ incompatibility. More likely than not, Werner's mighty phallus struck fear into her heart when it reared its noble head. Any woman would cower before the majesty of such an organ. He went straight to the trusty *Merck Manual* to check on just that. Aha! "Psychologic factors include anger directed toward the partner, fear of the partner's genitals, or of intimacy, or of losing control, dependency. . . ."

Or maybe it was his intellect she feared. Maybe she could not relax around him, because she was afraid he might think she was simple or stupid. That had happened before: nurses who could not relax during sex, because they were afraid they might make a mistake, afraid that Dr. Ernst would yell at them. No, you moron! What kind of technique is that? I said faster, not harder. I'm talking about frequency, not intensity. Understand? I don't mind you temporarily assuming the control position, but follow instructions, please!

Werner stared at Bed Five's rhythm on the monitor and pulled the chart. The new Physician's Orders took up three pages. The Medical Center was accumulating evidence to combat the temporary restraining order. Butz had ordered another nuclear magnetic resonance imaging (MRI) scan and another PET scan to determine the extent of Bed Five's cerebral atrophy, with the notation that the results of each test were to be forwarded to Dr. Hofstader and to two consulting neurologists. This month's bill was going to be a lalapalooza.

The Death Lab bustled with morning chores. Patients had to be

weighed by being rolled onto stretchers, which were then hoisted
with a winch and crane up onto bed scales. While they were hanging up in the air, the sheets and absorbent pads were stripped from
their beds and replaced. Baths had to be given. New meds had to
be hung in bottles and bags. The relentless cranial checks had to be
done.

"Can you tell me what day it is?"

"It's the day before yesterday. And payday is every other Friday. Bring me my goddamn pants."

"Do you know where you are?"

"Of course. I'm at the soda fountain in Woolworth's in Yank-
ton, South Dakota. Where are you?"

"Who's the President of the United States?"

"The Fair Deal man, Harry Truman. I know that. Ask me a
hard one, would ya?"

If cranial checks served no other purpose, they at least got the
patients all warmed up for the pearly gates. Nobody gets past St.
Peter unless he or she can name the President of the United States.

Every morning the nurses also changed yards and yards of tubing that connected the machines to the patients. The respiratory
therapists changed all the components on the ventilators. The lab
technicians drew new blood from arterial lines and IVs. Other
technicians calibrated and tested all the machines, checked the
alarms, inspected the maintenance records, and replaced any dis-
posable parts. Afterward the environmental technicians came
around and collected massive trash bags bulging with the refuse
generated by twenty-four hours of intensive care medicine.

Werner thought of one of his classmates who had been seized
by humanitarian delusions in her fourth year of medical school
and had signed up with a nun who operated hospitals in India.
When the eager young medical resident arrived, she was shown
into a cavernous warehouse in Calcutta stacked with hundreds of
starving, sick people lying on wooden pallets. Families of the
wealthier patients brought medications to the hospital daily and
administered them to the patients. Otherwise no medications were
available.

In the first five minutes, Werner's friend had seen a dozen or so
patients who were at death's door, so she turned to her guides and
asked, "Where's the critical care unit?" The question was trans-

lated for the nun, who promptly showed the woman her hands: "These we use for critical care."

Werner sneaked into Bed Five's pod, while the nurses were busy loading Bed Two onto the bed scale. Bed Five's brush with the Code Blue Team had left him none the worse for wear. His white head still shuddered against the pillow, and the coarse tremors in his tethered right arm still set off a muted tintinnabulation in the steel bed rails. Yesterday's battery of tests had probably worn him down and had sent him into heart block last night. Now he was a warm skeleton lying in state.

Werner peeked out of the pod to be sure no one was looking; then he untied Bed Five's right hand.

"Squeeze my hand," he commanded.

Bed Five's bony fingers continued twitching.

"Sir? If you can hear me, squeeze my hand."

Nobody here but us passive tremors, Werner thought. He looked forward to seeing the newest PET scan and MRI report. Progressive cerebral atrophy no doubt. His brain was slowly turning to porridge.

Felicia and her lawyer were probably right. If Bed Five were his father, Werner would object to the gastrostomy and the ventilator, but then he would be objecting as a family member, not as a physician. It could be argued that as a physician he should simply deliver health care and let the lawyers and ethicians decide when and where medicine should stop.

It was one thing to walk around the Death Lab thinking that most of these cabbages would be better off dead and quite another actually to take the stand and testify under oath that an individual person should be tagged and transported. What if the law acted on his testimony? Withholding medical treatment was one thing, but food? Water? If Bed Five was still feeling anything, how would it feel to starve slowly to death? And all that said nothing about the ultimate questions, like, How much more treatment will Bed Five's insurance cover?

Clones began arriving in groups of two and three, eager for the opportunity to do something other than histories and physicals. Hofstader and his entourage appeared at about seven-fifteen, and the clone brigade relocated to the Gastrointestinal Lab for the colonoscopy on Bed Three.

Bed Three was an obese eighty-three-year-old Caucasian female with recurrent bowel obstructions and heart failure. She had been NPO (nothing by mouth) for twenty-four hours. This morning, in the twilight of her golden years, she had been roused at four, given an enema, bathed, and weighed, because she had to leave for the GI lab at six-thirty. Throughout the early-morning ordeal, she kept calling for her dog to stop digging in the neighbor's flower garden.

"Smoky! I told you to stay out of Mr. Mulligan's flower garden. Now come on over here and be a good boy. Mr. Mulligan is calling the dogcatcher again, Smoky. I'm going to spank you."

At seven-fifteen two technicians bent her over a tilt table and cranked her ponderous rear end up four feet into the air, turning her into a rack of old flab hanging upside down. When the clone brigade showed up, they saw two round cheeks of moon jelly shot through with pink starbursts of exploded veins, cellulite, and stretch marks.

Hofstader would be otherwise occupied, he explained, so he introduced Dr. Thea Hallorhan, a slender redhead doing a fellowship in Gastroenterology, whom Werner had resented as soon as he had heard she was married. She was well known and well liked for not standing on ceremony or pulling rank on clones.

Eight or nine R1's, M3's, and M4's gathered in a half circle around the eighty-three-year-old derriere. It occurred to Werner that Bed Three had probably not had this much attention in twenty years, until she developed bowel obstructions. She probably would have been glad for the company, except that she was naked and hanging upside down.

"Smoky, you come on over here."

Dr. Hallorhan showed them all the fiberoptic endoscope, a black rubber hose the width of a broomstick, fitted out with a light source, biopsy forceps, and lines for flushing with normal saline or air. The saline solution allowed the physician to wash the membrane walls during the procedure to get a better look at the disease processes underneath. Inflating the bowel by running compressed air through the line—a process called insufflation—was a form of artificial farting, allowing the physicians to distend the crowded landscape of the bowel and examine it with the scope. The endoscope had also been fitted out with a teaching scope, meaning the clones could take turns looking through the extra scope during the procedure.

   Patient history: deaf, senile, and bowel-obstructed three times
over. Her toes had been amputated because of creeping diabetes.
AV-sequential pacemaker was in place, Swan-Ganz heart catheter
and introducer, arterial line, telemetry monitor strung up overhead on an IV pole. Thanks to modern medical science, this
deaf, senile, diabetic, bowel-obstructed, and heart-diseased
eighty-three-old coot might soon be fitted out with a colostomy
bag and transferred to the rehabilitation unit for six months of
intensive prodding and pushing at three hundred dollars a day,
then discharged for another three weeks of the best outpatient
care available, before she told everyone to leave her alone please
and died in her sleep.
   They had some trouble getting the consent to treatment forms
straightened out. Apparently one of the rookie nurses got a bit too
enthusiastic in the interest of thorough patient teaching and actually showed the old grimalkin the rubber fiberoptic scope, then
told her where it was going. In a sudden relapse of alertness, Bed
Three refused to sign anything. They had to soften her up with
some Xanax and calm reassurances, convincing her that getting to
the bottom of these recurrent bowel obstructions was in her best
interest.
   An M4 gingerly spread Bed Three's dimpled cheeks, while an
R1 greased the better part of a six-foot scope with lubricating jelly
and slid it up the eighty-three-year-old asshole, into the large in-
testine. Werner surreptitiously slipped six or seven packets of
water-soluble lubricating jelly into his lab coat.
   Dr. Hallorhan hiked her skirt up above her knees, leaned forward on the stool, and took the controls of the scope in hand.
Werner studied the lines of her calves as she hooked her heels over
the metal ring at the base of the stool. *Nice wheels, Dr. Hallorhan.*
He wondered if, instead of looking up assholes all day, Dr. Hallorhan might be interested in going away with him to Tibet. There
was probably not a fiberoptic endoscope anywhere in the Hima-
layas.
   "Now we are distending the lumen of the bowel with the air
insufflator," Hallorhan said, working the compressed air button
with a slender, pale finger.
   She let the gallery of baby clones peek through the teaching
scope at the vistas of eighty-three-year-old bowel lying before them
like the surface of an unexplored planet.

The conversation included party anecdotes, baseball scores, differential diagnoses of bowel disorders, a rundown of neoplastic diseases of the colon, a plot synopsis of a prime-time TV drama, hospital scandal, and carcinoembryonic antigen test results.

"Note the proliferation of diverticuli," Hallorhan advised, pushing the rubber hose in another couple of inches, "and the decreased motility of the bowel."

"I think we should go out," an R3 said to the beautiful Hallorhan. "Is your divorce final?"

"Get a piece of that," Hallorhan said, working the air insufflator with her thumb, operating the forceps with her index finger, and giggling in the putter of escaping artificial farts.

"You fail to see the adenocarcinoma," she explained, "and you fail to see that I don't want to go out with you. I am eliminating all possible complications from my personal life."

"But I'm not the least bit complicated," the R3 protested. "I want only one thing."

"Put that in fixative and send it down for cytology," Hallorhan said with a giggle. "Have somebody check it for lymphoid hyperplasia."

Aha. If Werner heard that right, there was hope. Another marriage sacrificed to the Moloch of medicine. He and Dr. Hallorhan could possibly use each other: She could help him survive the remaining years of the siege known as the Internal Medicine Residency; he could help her remember how to date.

"Take the teaching scope," Hallorhan said, "and tell me when we get to the appendix."

Very cute, Werner noticed again, and she had a sick sense of humor anybody would be proud of.

Every now and again, a nurse came in, held Bed Three's hand, and asked her who was President of the United States.

"No treats for you, Smoky. I told you not to dig over there."

At eight-thirty, Werner took the elevator to the mezzanine and found Wilson's office tucked away in the administrative catacombs of the Legal Department.

Wilson was short and pudgy. He showed Werner into an office the size of an ICU pod and took a seat behind a metal desk with pictures of himself and his family on a fishing trip at an overdeveloped resort. His see-through, short-sleeved polyester shirt had black and blue marks above the shirt pocket where he had inserted his uncapped ball-point pens. His dark blue machine-cut suit coat hung on a clothes tree next to Werner's chair; when Werner put his elbows on the armrest, he could feel the welted polyester rubbing against him.

"First things first," Wilson said, his stubby fingers sorting piles of documents.

Werner declined his offer of a stick of gum.

"Here's your copies of these," Wilson said, handing Werner several documents the thickness of college term papers.

At the top of each cover sheet it said: "FELICIA E. POTTER, for herself, and on behalf of her father, JOSEPH F. POTTER, PLAINTIFFS versus . . ." Werner's eyes skipped down the list of names to where his name leaped off the page, "PETER WERNER ERNST, M.D.," and at the bottom of the list, "DEFENDANTS."

"Why did they put my name on this?" Werner asked, feeling his face flush with the new sensation of litigation. "I thought they were suing the Medical Center."

Wilson craned his fat neck and pulled at his collar, showing the prongs of a clip-on tie. "I can see you've been around," he said with a laugh. "If you're going to spend good money having this stuff drafted up," he said, showing Werner the heft of the papers in his hand, "you might as well sue everybody you can think of, and let the judge sort them out. Besides, they want to make sure that everybody treating the guy will be bound by any order the court issues."

"But I haven't done anything," Werner protested.

"You and thousands of other people who get sued every day," Wilson said. "You think they have somebody sitting up at the courthouse checking to make sure that nobody files a petition against Werner Ernst, unless Werner Ernst really did something?"

"But why me individually?" Werner whined. "Does this mean that I could end up having to pay part of a judgment to . . . these people?"

"There's no action for damages," Wilson said. "Not yet anyway. But there could be. It's a new cause of action. The patient's family sues the doctors for keeping the patient alive too long; then they try to recoup the cost of the medical care, damages for negligent and intentional infliction of emotional distress, battery, fraud. . . . Like I said, they haven't done that yet, but they probably will."

"But you mean me *personally?*" Werner repeated, having difficulty swallowing.

"Don't worry," Wilson said, "the Medical Center will protect your interests. We're getting outside counsel to take care of this. Our big firm people. It will be done right."

"Do I need my own lawyer?" Werner asked.

"Watch it." Wilson chuckled. "That's kind of like asking a barber if you need a haircut."

"Pardon me," Werner interrupted, "if I'm not amused. I've just been sued."

"Lighten up," Wilson said. "Like I said, the Med Center will protect you. Have you ever heard of Mitchell Payne?"

"No," Werner said. "Who's that?"

"Our outside counsel in this case," Wilson said. "He was a county prosecutor, then a U.S. attorney, *the* U.S. Attorney. They wanted to make him a federal judge, but he turned it down. I heard it was because he was used to a steady diet of fresh red meat, and he wasn't ready to watch the hunt yet. He's a good lawyer at the biggest firm in town, and he's your lawyer, too, if you want him."

"Sounds good to me," Werner said.

Wilson grabbed another document. "But just as a formality, you must sign this joint representation agreement, which states that the Medical Center agrees to provide you with legal counsel, and that you agree to such representation. It also states that we reserve the right to cease representing you at any time if, in the sole discretion of our attorneys, your interests become adverse to those of the Medical Center, at which point you will be responsible for obtaining your own lawyer."

"Why does it say that?" Werner asked suspiciously, feeling his hackles standing up on the back of his neck.

"Lighten up," Wilson said. "It's a form agreement. Every doctor on this list will have to sign it. It just gives the Medical Center the right to cut you loose if they find out you went around committing intentional torts."

"Such as?" Werner asked.

"I don't know," Wilson said, "such as intentional battery, or fraud, or something. I don't know. Lighten up, would ya? Man! These residents they send down here. What do they do to you guys in medical school? Some of these assholes are so tight you couldn't get a knitting needle up there if you dipped it in axle grease first.

Sign the goddamn agreement," Wilson said. "Or go out and get your own lawyer to the tune of a hundred and ninety bucks an hour."

Werner read the agreement and signed it.

"Now then," Wilson said, "I'll bring you up-to-date on this thing. The one daughter, what's her name?" Wilson asked, grabbing one of the documents. "Miss Felicia Potter. Do you know her?"

"Yes," Werner said, "from seeing her on the Unit," he added. "I don't know her any other way. I mean, I didn't know her before I met her on the Unit."

"OK," Wilson said. "She's seeking injunctive relief. She wants to stop us from putting the feeding tube in. She also wants to have all invasive treatments and procedures discontinued, including the ventilator, the blood pressure meds, everything.

"The other daughter," Wilson said, referring to the papers again, "Constance, I guess. She wants us to go ahead and do everything we can to keep the old guy alive."

"OK," Werner said.

"From what I can gather in talking to the lawyers," Wilson said, "these women despise each other. This is going to be a bloody mess by the time it's over, because they've each retained big firms and good lawyers to make paper."

"Great," Werner said. "And Bed Five's caught in the middle."

"That ain't all," Wilson said, reviewing papers from another pile. "Our lawyers did a litigation search and found another family lawsuit filed two years ago. Apparently these two are half sisters. The guy in Bed Five is the father, but he had two different wives. The second wife set up a testamentary trust when she died, a big trust created in her will, which presently contains over two million bucks. Anyway, two years ago one of the daughters filed a lawsuit trying to anticipate her interest in the trust principal."

"I'm a linguistics major who went straight to medical school," Werner said. "How does one anticipate a trust principal? Wait, first, exactly what is a trust?"

"A trust is a way of giving away a big pile of money without losing control over it," Wilson explained. "Instead of giving the money away outright to a specific person or charity, you create a trust account at a bank, and the trust owns the money. Before you put the money in the account, you draw up a long list of specific

instructions called *provisions,* telling the bank what you want
done with the money. You put all the provisions and contingencies
in a trust instrument—a document—which simply tells the trustees
at the bank what to do with the money if X, Y, and Z happen or
don't happen. The instrument usually tells the bank what to do
with the *principal,* the pile of money itself, as well as the income
earned from investing the big pile of money. You could say, for
instance, 'I want the income generated by the trust to be used for
my son's education, but once he turns twenty-one, I want it to go
to my daughter if she is still living and, if not, then to Aunt Hilda,
especially if she needs it,' and so on. At some point, the trust
terminates, and all the money is distributed according to the final
instructions in the instrument."

"Where does Bed Five come in?" Werner said.

"The daughters and the guy in Bed Five are beneficiaries," Wilson said, "meaning that in certain circumstances, the trustees at
the bank are supposed to pay either the money itself or the income
from the money to them. A beneficiary anticipates her interest in
the trust by trying to get at the money before the provisions say she
can have it. That's what one of the daughters did."

"So, two years ago, they tried to get the money, and the court
said no?" Werner asked.

"That's right," Wilson said.

"So who gets the money now?" Werner asked.

"Bed Five gets all of it," Wilson said, "but only if he lives to be
seventy years old and remains unmarried, which will happen in
about a month."

"You're kidding," Werner said. "Why would the wife put a
crazy provision like that in there?"

"That's a very common provision," said Wilson, "especially in
a trust set up by a will. It's a convenient way of ending the trust or
turning the money over to the other spouse, so that he can either
give it away or make a new set of instructions appropriate to the
circumstances of the family, but only if he remains faithful to the
decedent."

"But he's a veg," Werner objected.

"Careful," Wilson said. "He may be in a persistent vegetative
state."

"Call it what you will," Werner said. "He's certainly not going
to know if he gets two million dollars."

"That's right," Wilson said. "He's incompetent, which means that the money is going to become part of his estate, and it will pass according to the residuary clause of his will."

"What kind of clause?" Werner interrupted.

"The residuary clause," Wilson said. "The clause in a will that disposes of everything left in your estate that you didn't specifically give away in another provision of the will. That's where this kind of money usually ends up, because the testator doesn't own it at the time he makes his will, so he can't specifically give it away."

"What if he dies before he turns seventy?" Werner asked.

"Now you're thinking like a lawyer," Wilson said. "That's what we all want to know. A trust instrument is not a public document; that's one of the reasons a lot of wealthy people prefer trusts over wills. As soon as you die, your will becomes a public document, and if you leave your mistress the farm in Connecticut, the whole world knows about it. Excerpts of the trust instrument were attached to the pleadings in the two-year-old lawsuit. We can tell from those excerpts that if Bed Five dies or remarries before age seventy, the trust terminates and all the money is distributed outright. But we don't know who gets it. The excerpts did not include the names of the contingent beneficiaries or their respective shares."

"Contingent beneficiaries?" Werner asked.

"The people who get the money if Bed Five doesn't make it to seventy," Wilson said.

Werner stared at the picture of Wilson and his family. "This is pretty complicated," he observed.

"It might be nothing more than an innocent disagreement about whether to pull the plug," Wilson said. "It might be something else, too." He looked at Werner and lifted his eyebrows.

"You're not suggesting that either one of them would manipulate the timing of her father's death?" Werner asked.

Wilson gave a who-knows shrug. "Suppose the second wife, the one who set up the trust, liked one daughter a lot and didn't like the other one so much. Let's pretend that she may have preferred her natural daughter to her stepdaughter. She may have provided that if Bed Five dies before age seventy, the trust terminates and the money goes to her natural daughter, or more of it goes to her natural daughter. If I was that daughter, I might think about how nice it would be if Dad could just take the last ferry before he turned seventy."

"That's terrible," Werner said.

"On the other hand," Wilson said, "suppose Bed Five preferred one daughter over the other. Suppose his will leaves each of them certain gifts, but the residuary clause leaves the rest to only one of them. Then all that money is going to come out of trust, go into Bed Five's estate, and then out, through the residuary clause of his will, to only one daughter, the one he liked or trusted the most. If I was that daughter, I might think about how nice it would be if Dad could hold on for another month."

Werner was receiving too much nonmedical information at once. Felicia was the natural daughter of the second wife who had set up the trust. If Connie was to be believed, Bed Five and Felicia had not seen eye to eye in the years preceding his illness.

"It's impossible to assign any funny motives until we see both the trust instrument and Bed Five's will," said Wilson. "As I've explained to you, the trust instrument is a private document, so is the will, until he dies. But now that this lawsuit's been filed, we can probably obtain copies of those by way of discovery."

"When?" Werner asked.

"Soon," said Wilson. "We are in equity, and the judge will probably order expedited discovery."

"I see," said Werner.

"Don't get me wrong," Wilson said. "These big firm lawyers are paid to be thorough. Many times they end up chasing bugbears that aren't there. It could very well be that these two banshees come out the same whether Bed Five dies now or later, but the lawyers are suspicious."

Wilson flipped to the last page of one of the documents. "Has an attorney named Sheldon Hatchett or Gregory Mace contacted you?"

"Hatchett called me," Werner said.

"What did he want and what did you tell him?" Wilson said, getting out a notepad and pulling an uncapped pen out of his shirt pocket.

"He asked me to testify that Bed Five was in an irreversible coma or a persistent vegetative state and that further medical treatment would be pointless. I told him that things weren't that black and white and that I couldn't testify for him."

Werner peeked to see what Wilson was writing. Wilson settled back in his chair and put the pad up in his lap.

"OK," Wilson said. "New rule. Don't talk to anybody about the case. Don't talk to the lawyers. Don't talk to the other residents. Don't talk to the other doctors. If you wanna talk or if you have a question, ask me. If I can't answer your question, I'll hook you up with our lawyers. Understand?"

"Why?" Werner asked.

"Above all, don't talk to the family," Wilson warned.

"How am I supposed to not talk to the family?" Werner objected. "What if they ask me a question?"

"Keep it straight and narrow," Wilson said. "Incontrovertible facts. No opinions. Don't speculate about the probability of recovery. Don't discuss treatment plans. If you have to, say that during the pendency of the litigation you have been instructed not to discuss the case, except when absolutely necessary for the welfare of the patient."

"That strikes me as being overly cautious," Werner remarked.

Wilson reached across his desk and tapped his fingernail on the metal to get Werner's attention.

"Hey, Doctor, I've done this before, OK? I'll tell you what's going to happen here. No matter what we do, one of these women is going to sue us. If we keep this guy alive, this Miss Felicia is going to sue us for unauthorized medical treatment, battery, the cost of his care, and the rest. And if we let him die, dear Constance is going to sue us for medical malpractice. No matter what you say to them, you're going to be supplying one of them with evidence. So keep your mouth shut, understand? Remember, if your interests become adverse to our interests, you have to pay for your own lawyer. Now does it seem overly cautious?"

"No," Werner said.

"This morning, Miss Felicia's lawyer is going for a temporary restraining order, a TRO, and he'll probably get it. That means the judge will temporarily stop us from doing anything new, until we have a full-blown preliminary injunction hearing. That's the big one."

"Since I've been sued, does that mean I have to testify?" Werner asked.

"You mean, do you *get* to testify?" Wilson suggested. "Probably not," he said. "We don't need you, because we've got Hof-

stader and other experts who've been through this kind of thing
before. We'll also have an outside expert. We'll have to put Butz
on for as short a time as possible. And then we'll have somebody
from the ethics committee get up and testify about the Medical
Center's policies and the procedures we follow when there is no
living will. The other side won't want you, because they won't
know what you'll say, unless they take a deposition first, and they
probably won't spend that kind of money to get testimony out of
a resident."

"So, if they have a deposition hearing," Werner said, "then I'd
have to testify?"

"*Get, get* to testify," Wilson said. "Think of this as a learning
experience. A deposition is not a hearing," Wilson said. "I wish
they would start teaching a course on litigation in medical school.
A deposition is two lawyers and a court reporter sitting in a room
with a witness asking him questions. They never show depositions
on TV because they're deadly dull, and even an excerpt from one
would put a prime-time audience soundly to sleep. Look at this as
an opportunity to watch a lawsuit while you're still just a bit
player. In the unlikely event they want to depose you, we'll prepare
you first. As I said, they won't."

"Oh," Werner said.

"Any more questions?" Wilson asked.

"Not right now," Werner said, absorbed again in staring at his
name on the document entitled: "PETITION FOR INJUNCTIVE
RELIEF AND DECLARATORY JUDGMENT."

"Good," Wilson said. "I'll send you a copy of the signed joint
representation agreement. Here's my card if you have any more
questions. And if the firm lawyers want to talk to you, I'll call you
first. Don't talk to anybody else."

Still feeling the sting of love turning into litigation, Werner rode
the elevators back to the unit. They were practically having a
relationship, and she had violated him with a lawsuit. She had not
even warned him it was coming.

When he got back up to the Death Lab, he heard Hofstader in
Bed Seven giving a lecture to M3's and M4's on mechanical ventilation. It was a class for subclones, with no residents. Werner
watched from the console, reviewing the morning orders that Butz
and Hofstader had written.

Bed Seven's seventy-nine-year-old limbs were curled up in contractures, and his eyes were locked on the ceiling in oculogyric crises, as if he had decided many weeks ago that he could no longer bear the sight of anything except a ceiling. His jaw flapped open and closed around an ET tube that was planted like a plastic sapling in his throat, taped in place with a rubber airway. His bound hands and fingers exhibited the characteristic pill-rolling tremors of Parkinson's disease.

Dr. Hofstader faced the semicircle of subclones over Bed Seven's torso.

"When one or more disease processes severely debilitate the organism, the single most demanding activity becomes breathing. Breathing is hard work. It burns calories, especially when the lungs are diseased and the accessory muscles come into play."

Dr. Hofstader walked around the bed and placed his hand on a new ventilator.

"Before ventilators were invented, the gram-positive pneumonias and the sheer work of breathing used to kill elderly patients off in three or four days. Pneumonia was called the old man's friend. The root *pneuma* means 'air' or 'wind,' but for the Greeks the word also meant an 'ethereal fire' or 'spirit,' which was the life-giving or cosmic principle, the world soul, or the spirit of God. In Genesis, before there was light, there was only a formless wasteland and a dark abyss, but wind swept over the waters. The Holy Spirit visited the apostles in the form of a great wind. When someone dies, we still say they *expire,* or exhale their spirit. Certain African tribes say of dying men and their increased respiratory rate: 'He is climbing the mountain of his death.' Thus, when we talk about mechanical ventilation and proper management of the airway, we are talking about the management of life itself."

The disciples were in awe. Was there ever a more articulate Renaissance man of the healing arts?

Werner remembered hearing the same lecture word for word three years ago. Hofstader seized every opportunity to prove he was more than just a scientist.

Werner's beeper signaled an outside call, and he took it at the console. It was Felicia again, sobbing into the phone. He was glad this was a phone conversation, because things sounded very wet and hysterical at the other end.

"I know you said not to call in the mornings," she said. "But I got a message on my machine when I got home. My father almost died last night, and I didn't even know about it."

Werner watched Dr. Hofstader lift the cover of the ventilator and lecture on the use of positive end expiratory pressure with synchronized intermittent mandatory ventilation.

"I just found out myself," Werner said. "I think he's stable now, but I don't have the details. I'll have to review the chart and get back to you."

"And they are having that stupid hearing today," she said, "in an hour, as a matter of fact. This is such an ordeal," she groaned, more lamentation pouring in his ear. "Don't they realize how I feel? I have to beg them to let my father die."

"I can't talk," he said. "I'll have to call you back." *If this keeps up*, he thought, *he would be making an appointment for Felicia in Pastoral Care.*

"Will anything happen to him today?" she asked. "I want to be there if anything happens."

"In his condition," Werner said, "it is impossible to predict when or if anything might happen. Impossible."

"I have to show my portfolio to a bunch of ad people this afternoon," she said. "I guess I'll just call in and check my machine whenever I can. I left my bag at your apartment. What time will you be home?"

"Probably seven-thirty," Werner said. "I want to talk to you, too," he said, looking down at the wad of papers her lawyer had filed.

"I'll be thinking about you," she said.

Werner handed the phone back to a wombat and looked again at Bed Five's rhythm on the monitor.

Out of the corner of his eye, Werner caught sight of a patient's untethered white arm pointing at the ceiling and trailing a cotton wrist restraint. It was the eighty-seven-year-old bird woman in Bed Four with bird claws for hands and feet. She was moving out onto the medical-surgical floor today. And if all went well, she would make it to a nursing home.

Werner left the console and went into her pod.

Bed Four's bent, mottled fingers were pointing at the ceiling, where she had been staring for weeks. She moved her bare gums and looked at Werner without lowering her hand.

"Good morning," said Dr. Ernst.

She smiled and pointed. Werner turned for her in an exaggerated manner and showed her he was looking where she was pointing.

"What are you pointing at?" he asked her.

"My grandma," the woman said.

"Your grandma?" Werner said, unable to contain a chuckle. "That would be something."

"She's come for me," the woman said. "I have to go with her."

Werner came around the bed and took Bed Four's hand in both of his. He pressed her fingernail and watched it blanch, then turn a healthy pink.

"You're getting better," he said. "You're going to be moving out of here."

Werner tried to release her hand, but she clutched his hand in a firm, palsied grip.

"Sit with me, young man," she said. "Just sit with me a little while before I go."

Werner looked at his watch and held her hand.

The Unit secretary stuck her head in the door and told him the Unit was receiving a new admission in Bed Eight.

His beeper signaled, giving him the message, and telling him that the results of a set of Bed Seven's clotting studies were ready. He pushed the reset button and promptly got another message that the stat labwork he had ordered on Bed Two showed dangerously abnormal values.

Werner patted Bed Four's hand.

"Just sit with me for a little while," she said, refusing to let go of his hand, desperation creeping into her voice.

Werner grabbed the call light that was pinned to Bed Four's gown and pressed the button. Thirty seconds later, Marie Something came into the pod and stood next to Werner.

"Just a little while, young man," Bed Four said. "Please?"

Werner pried himself free of Bed Four's claw and placed it in Marie's soft hands.

"See what this patient wants," he said.

Chapter

10

Back in his apartment, Werner put three beers in the freezer and the scotch up in a tall cupboard, out of the striking range of impulse.

It was time to simplify his life. He went to the couch and settled into his wishing chair, resolving to shut out the world until he decided what to do about Bed Five. He would concentrate and systematically attack the problem, just as he would handle any other medical problem.

Step one, eliminate irrelevant considerations. Connie, Felicia, Wilson, Connie's lawyers, Felicia's lawyers, the hospital lawyers: None of them were relevant. Bed Five was Werner's patient. Not exactly. Bed Five was a patient of Dr. Butz, and Werner worked for Butz. The new teaching, which the authorities had drummed into his head in medical school, was patient autonomy. Informed consent. The patient had to be given enough information to decide properly whether to accept the physician's recommended treatment. But his patient was in a persistent vegetative state. His eyes might open from time to time, he might squeeze people's hands, but he had no idea what he was doing. He certainly was in no condition to make decisions about his medical care. If he could make such decisions, what would he want? Ask the family. No luck there. They were in total disagreement.

Maybe a courtroom was the best place to decide what Bed Five would have wanted in the way of medical care, especially with these trusts and wills lurking in the background. Maybe every human life—no matter how diseased and debilitated—is precious.

This all sounded logical, but deep in Werner's heart a small voice told him that Bed Five would never recover. He would never leave the ICU; he would certainly never leave the hospital. Bed Five's "life" would consist of a few more months of Code Blues, of having his ribs broken during cardiopulmonary resuscitation, of having raw, gaping bed sores, of never sleeping in any normal sense of the word, of being stuck with needles six or seven times a day, of poking, prodding, turning, suctioning. . . . For what? Werner was kidding himself if he thought that anyone would choose such an existence. Useless treatment was useless treatment, no matter what the motives of the family, the doctors, and the lawyers.

But if quality of life was the decisive standard, then why not simply execute everyone afflicted with chronic, incurable diseases?

Werner fetched a cold one from the freezer, closed his eyes, and tried to slip inside the mind of Bed Five. He was floating in a bed with steel railings in a sea of bright, white gelatin. A cold, dense fog fell. Spotlights were mounted above and below the bed. People dressed in white came through the isinglass fog and spoke foreign languages to one another. They seemed to be discussing mathematics in Latin. Sometimes he recognized them; sometimes they were total strangers, laughing and telling him jokes he could not understand. His family also came through the fog; their faces were drawn in fright masks of grief. One of his daughters came in, and he evaporated in the warmth of her presence, rising and disintegrating at the vapor barrier, where the surface of the jelly dissolved into light. Sight, smell, taste, and touch fell away from him, leaving only sound, which passed under him in waves of inverted thunder.

Enemy cells had crossed the Rubicon and were taking over his vital functions. His heartbeat had become a precarious, arrhythmic flutter. The blood no longer reached his hands and feet. He felt the weight of his flesh leaching away like mud. His senses shut down, one by one, but in mute horror, he realized that each loss of bodily power gave rise to a corresponding surge of inner clarity, as if all energy, all metabolic products were being shunted to the mind, where each thought passed with the clarity of a shriek. Every mental image was far too clear—dreams, memories, hallucinations—all shining brilliantly against the stark white movie screen of death.

Thoughts screamed in vacant echo chambers. Just as he was given the most frightful, ecstatic intuitions, revelations, visions, he found himself left with only the most passive sense. He could hear. He was receiving everything and transmitting nothing. He could not even tell them that there was something sharp digging into his side; he had to wait until one of them came in and found it. He labored away quietly at the mental effort of death. He could fall asleep forever so easily, if they would only let him. The pain, the exhaustion, the labor of letting the machine breathe for him were like working a rock pile in a prison camp.

Werner looked up into the blinding spotlights and saw two pretty young female astronauts he had never seen before in his life standing on either side of his bed. Both were dressed in white spacesuits. He could smell their perfume and the minty odors of their chewing gum.

One of them giggled and said, "You think that one's bad, listen to this. What do you call a kid with no arms and legs who is hanging on the wall?"

"I give up," the other one said.

"Art," she said, giggling hysterically.

"That's terrible," the other one said with a laugh.

While Werner watched, one of the women put on a pair of sterile gloves. The other one threw back his bed sheet and pulled up his flimsy half gown, exposing his genitals.

"OK, then. What do you call a kid with no arms and legs who's lying on the floor?"

The woman with the sterile gloves took hold of Werner's penis. She poured orange disinfectant all over it and scrubbed it with gauze.

"What?" she asked, pulling the foreskin back and reaming out the tip of the urethra with a cotton swab.

"Matt."

They both giggled uncontrollably.

"Shit, we are punchy, aren't we?"

The woman poured more orange fluid on Werner's penis and scrotum. Then she picked up a long rubber tube and showed it to Werner.

"See this?" she said. "This is what we call a catheter. We have to poke this tube into your penis and run it up to your bladder so you can pee through it, OK?"

Werner vigorously shook his head no and tried to say something around his ET tube.

"Stop trying to talk around that tube," the lady astronaut said, "and listen to me. The only reason we have to keep sticking this tube into your penis is that *you* keep pulling it out, understand? And that's why tying your hands down isn't good enough for the likes of you. So now you know what we have to do? We have to tie your hands down, and then we have to wrap your hands in bath towels and tape them with adhesive tape, understand? All because of *you*. Yesterday you pulled out your IV, and the day before that you pulled out your chest tube. . . ."

Werner shook his head no.

"Save your breath," said the woman wearing the sterile gloves, "he's out of his fucking gourd."

Werner watched as the tube went in the end of his penis and all the way up to his bladder. He tried to stop the woman, but he had been handcuffed, spread-eagled under the blinding spotlights.

"Good afternoon," another astronaut said. "My name is Dr. Slaughter. You may remember me from a few days ago. Dr. Butz asked me to do a few tests on you."

Werner looked Dr. Slaughter up and down a time or two. It was the man who told Werner to hold still while he stuck a needle in his spine.

"The results of the tests we've done are not encouraging," Dr. Slaughter said. "We've discovered malignancies."

"Does that mean I get to die now?" Werner asked, miraculously talking around his ET tube.

"No," Slaughter said. "We are going to give you and the tumors a lot of poison and see which one of you dies first. Sometimes that works. Since you're so much bigger than the tumors, you've got a better chance of surviving."

"I see," said Werner. "Anything else?"

"We'll do the same thing with radiation," Slaughter said. "We will nuke the two of you a couple of times a month and see if the cancer flees in terror of a nuclear accident, while you stay behind and fend off the blast."

"Is that all?" Werner asked.

"Not quite," Slaughter said, brightening somewhat. "Some major breakthroughs have been made in this area, thanks to extensive research. There's a new treatment that may offer some hope, but it's still in the experimental stages."

"Oh," said Werner. "What is it?"

"Well," Slaughter explained, "what we do is cut off your arms at the elbows and your legs at the knees."

"Why?" Werner asked, terrified at the thought.

"It's simple," Slaughter explained. "Research has shown that if we cut off your limbs, all the blood, oxygen, and nutrients that previously went to supporting your limbs will instead be available for fighting the tumors. As I said, it still hasn't been thoroughly researched using human subjects, but they've had documented successes with rodents."

The room was suddenly crowded with figures hooded in white. They slit Werner's belly open and rummaged around inside him.

A pretty young nurse pulled out his pancreas and stuck a needle in it. Then she smiled at him and said, "That's a microsensitive radioactive needle thermometer. We have to implant it into your pancreas in order to get an accurate pancreatic temperature."

"Do we have a pancreatic temp yet?" a technician called from across the room.

The pretty nurse turned and punched a button on a monitor. "P temp is 41.46573 degrees Centigrade," she said.

"41.46573," the technician repeated, writing the number on a clipboard.

In came a six-foot lizard dressed in surgical scrubs and wearing a stethoscope, a beeper tucked into the pocket of a lab coat. The lizard examined Werner through the eye holes of a hollowed-out goat's head muzzled by a surgical mask. The lizard pried Werner's chest open with a sterile crowbar and extracted one of his lungs by main force.

"This organ is full of some of the worst-looking pus I've ever seen," the lizard called over his shoulder, tossing the heavy lung into a lined wastebasket.

Lately, when they asked him to squeeze their hands, he desperately tried to hold still, hoping they would think he was dead and leave him alone. But they would never leave him alone. For some hellish, twisted reason, they would not let him die. Death was against their religion. He sank back onto his pillow in a morphine stupor, praying with every cell in his body, trying to kill himself by an act of sheer will.

He could hear his family calling his name.

"Werner?" his daughter called. "Werner?"

He dared not move, for fear they would perform another procedure on him.

Werner opened his eyes and found Felicia wearing a bathing suit cover-up and standing over him with another vinyl bag, her hair moussed, blown dry, and teased out into an outrageous mane.

"We got our temporary detaining order," she said, "and guess what else?"

"Restraining order," Werner said. "What else?" he asked, jiggling his empty beer can.

"I'm going to Los Angeles tomorrow for Renée Feral Cosmetics. If I get the job, I'll be on national TV, and not just my face either. You wanna see?"

"I guess," he said with a yawn.

"What's wrong?" she asked. "This is big. This is like a super-celebration spectacular."

Werner turned his head. "I guess I'd be more excited if I wasn't a defendant in a lawsuit."

She tossed her bag on the Murphy bed. "I told you we didn't need you to testify. I thought we weren't going to talk about it anymore," she said. "Wasn't that your idea?"

"How can I not talk about it?" he protested. "You sued me."

"I didn't sue you," she said. "My lawyer did. He said it would look awfully suspicious if we listed everybody except you."

Werner pouted.

"Don't let that get in the way of this," she said, hugging herself. She threw back her head and shook her hair. "Close your eyes, and I'll show you what I'm doing tomorrow."

"I never turn down an opportunity to close my eyes," he said.

Werner heard ligaments cracking and clothing sliding off. "OK," she said after a few moments.

She had peeled off the cover-up and was slithering around his apartment in a tangerine urethane maillot swimsuit that sent out sparks. The cut of the hip holes rode up above her waist to somewhere around her rib cage. The tangerine borders converged on her flat stomach, dipped into a skinny V at the pelvis in front, and articulated the firm curvature of her cheeks behind. Her hips bloomed in brown ovals and tapered into the long, wicked lines of her legs—legs that put Werner at their mercy, sending his eyes down one lean curve after the next, all the way to pointed toes and painted tangerine nails. The straps of her matching tangerine high heels were tied in big bows, like presents waiting to be opened.

Werner's eyes traveled back up the flexures of sun-basted leg to the main dish of the haunch.

"Watch this," she said. She bowed her head, then threw it back and smiled broadly, a preformed wave dipping racily over one eye. "I don't trust my skin to any moisturizer. I insist on Renée Feral." She laughed. "Did you see that? What do you think?"

"Where can I get some Renée Feral moisturizer?" Werner said.

She giggled and hummed and flounced around the apartment.

"I spent the whole day shooting with them, and they want me in L.A. for a week, starting tomorrow. They threw in the heels and the suit, too. Are these peg walkers a turn-on, or what?"

She slowly pointed and rotated a spiked heel by way of illustration. *The proverbial well-turned ankle,* Werner thought, realizing that if such an ankle had been glimpsed a hundred years ago in the swirling crinoline of a lifted hoopskirt, it would have touched off heart attacks.

"How about this suit?" she said, splaying matching tangerine nails across her abdomen, cocking her elbows and throwing him a side view. "What do you think of it? Is it spectack?"

"It's super," Werner said, a smile slipping loose.

"I've got work to do before tomorrow," she said. "The first thing I have to do is test-drive a new face. You can watch if you want."

"You're going to what?"

"Face," she repeated, going into the bag and coming out with a palette of pastel eye shadows and a clutch of brushes. "I'm going to try on a new one. You can watch if you want."

He thought it was forbidden to see how it was all done, the same way an audience should never expect a good magician to reveal the technical sleight of hand involved in her best tricks. You had to trust the magician to protect you from yourself, so that instead of going home bored and cynical about a few gimmicky tricks, you could go away bewitched and enchanted by magic.

"May I?" he asked.

She went into the bag and came out with a portrait-size makeup mirror bordered with light bulbs behind tinted panels.

She clicked on the TV with the remote and cleared the top of his desk into a laundry basket.

"I need space," she explained, pulling up a chair and setting up the makeup mirror.

"Watch this commercial," she said, "it's great."

"I hate commercials," Werner said.

"That's because you have no imagination," she said. "Commercials are the funnest of all the fun things on TV, but you have to use your imagination. You can get the symbolism and all that junk. Like you know they're just trying to sell you toilet paper, or whatever, but you go beyond that and use your imagination, start thinking about stuff like psychology, or try to see if you recognize the people in the commercials, and see if you can name all the other commercials they've ever been in. If I really use my imagination, even talking to you can be fun." She snickered, pinching him in the butt. "Know what I mean?"

As usual, he somehow knew precisely what she meant, even though she spoke gibberish. Her mouth made noises, not really words. The pitch and inflection of the sounds conveyed her likes and dislikes. She had no use for words.

Werner switched off the blaring TV with the remote, before he could hear more about diet soda, oat bran, and low-calorie mayonnaise, which would make every woman in the country look like Felicia. She grabbed six or seven plastic bottles from the overnight bag and headed for the bathroom.

"I'm going to totally beautifulize my face," she said, "but first, I'm getting in the shower."

While she was in the shower, Werner got out the jelly packets and placed them in the drawer of the table next to the Murphy bed. He fetched beer number two and took a seat, ringside, at the makeup mirror.

She emerged, smelling of lemon cream rinse and scented soaps, wearing two purple towels, one tucked into a sarong under her armpits, the other turbaned on top of her head in a leaning tower of wet hair. Werner got up and followed her over to the overnight bag for another taste of skin, freshly steamed to a fragrant, warm plumpness.

"Watch it, monster mouth," she said, squirming away from him and squirting pink lotion into the palms of her hands. "Scented emollient cream," she explained, rubbing the stuff all over her arms and legs.

"What's that?" Werner said, pointing at a large dial on the makeup mirror.

"Light selector," she said, turning the dial and causing different tinted panels to slide into place over the bulbs.

Werner turned the dial and watched as the names of each selection appeared on the dial: Daytime Office, Daytime Sunlight, Daytime Indoors, Twilight, Candlelight, Nighttime Indoors.

"C'mon," Werner said. "Tell me it really makes a difference."

"Men," she muttered, the picture of exasperation. "Light changes everything. You probably think a woman puts on makeup once a day. Go ahead, admit it!"

"I . . ."

"You're an ultra nerd," she moaned. "You don't appreciate what goes into a state-of-the-art face."

Werner took a slug of cold beer and shrugged his shoulders.

"Let's say you work in an office," she said, dialing in "Daytime Office." "OK, you've got a lot of harsh fluorescent light to deal with, so you want soft colors, subtle stuff—peaches, corals, citrons, and junk like that. Your main concern is to soften the face with white-toned foundations and sheer peach or lemon yellow highlights. Understand?"

Werner bobbed his head.

"OK," she continued. "Then you go out to eat that night. Now you're talking twilight or candlelight," she said, dialing each of them up on the mirror in succession. "Now you've got a lot less light, so you want all your colors deeper. Plus candlelight takes all the natural reds out of your face, and your day face is going to look like a funeral mask, unless you get some reds back into it. So you want to think about stuff like tipping your eyelashes with the new red mascaras, after you've done them in basic black, or even rimming your eyes with a little red, after you've lined them in black. You want blush, lots of it. You want bold, shiny eye colors and lots of stunning highlighters. You want to extend the eye shadow, extend the brow, extend the cheekbone. . . ." She rolled her eyes. "Maybe it would be easier if you just watched."

She dialed in "Twilight" and went back into her bag, laying out eyebrow pencils, cotton balls, brushes in four or five sizes, eyelash curlers, lip pencils, lip brushes, eyeliner pencils, eyebrow pencils, concealer stick, more color palettes, powder compacts, and an array of little bottles, jars, and vials.

"You're looking at about a thousand bucks' worth of tools and materials," she said. "All these brushes are made out of real sable. And Renée Feral goes at twice the price of her competitors' stuff because it's quality. It doesn't smudge, crumble, or fade on you," she said, dabbing dots of lotion at strategically important points of her face, then going back and blending each of them into the skin with light, sweeping finger strokes. "And it stands up under hot lights. That was moisturizer," she said.

She turned her face this way and that, dabbing and spot rubbing. "OK, skin tone corrector and liquid foundation," she said, rubbing creamy pink lotion into her face with a damp cosmetic sponge.

She dipped a cotton ball into a powder compact.

"What are you doing now?" he asked.

"I'm blotting the foundation with translucent powder," she explained, dabbing the cotton ball all over her face, "and then I buff off the loose stuff with this," she said, showing him a large sable fan brush.

She yanked the purple towel off her head and swung long tresses of wet, fragrant hair over her shoulders.

"The lawyer said the temporary detaining order was no problem at all," she said.

"Temporary restraining order," Werner said.

"Right," she said. "He thinks we might even win the final end junction."

"Injunction," Werner said.

"Right," she said. "He says the hospital is only keeping my father alive because they're making two or three thousand dollars a day just for having him hooked up to those machines in that room."

She gave him a look out of the corner of her eye and shook her wet hair.

"Sounds like something a lawyer would say," Werner observed.

"Well?" she said. "What do you say? You never tell me what you think. Is that why they don't let people die, because they make so much money off them?"

"Of course not," Werner said. "Lawyers are the reason they don't let people die. The doctors and the hospital don't want to get sued for malpractice."

She teased her eyebrow with a pencil. "I think some Russian guy named Chekhov said that doctors are just the same as lawyers; the only difference is that lawyers merely rob you, whereas doctors rob you and kill you, too."

Werner momentarily lost his balance in his chair. "Since when do you quote Chekhov?"

She dabbed at the corner of her eyes with a sable brush. "I went to college, too, you know," she said vacantly. "But as soon as I learned enough to make a decent living, I quit reading and started watching TV."

Werner tried to crane his neck around for a look into her eyes.

"Concealer stick," she said, rubbing what looked like white lipstick under her eyes. "It takes out the dark circles I get from thinking about my dad."

She tilted her head and looked down her nose, bringing one of the sable paintbrushes to her eyelid. "Eye shadows are what separate the amateurs from the pros," she said. "Rookies put one or two colors on. Depending on the job, models can put four or five different shadows on."

She raised her eyebrow and painted a slash of silver glitter below the brow. "Silver Mist on the outside," she said. "Coral Satin and Coral Umber in the middle"—she raised her eyebrows again—"and Silver Satin on the inside," she said, trailing silver glitter. "You can really make these new metallic eye shadows stand up and shimmer if you go after them with a wet brush."

She rimmed her eyelids with a soft-toned charcoal eyeliner. Werner winced the entire time at seeing a pencil point so close to the bare white of an eyeball. Felicia was as steady as an ophthalmologist, her naked eyes never so much as blinking under the point. She curled the lashes with a pair of clamps ("eyelash curlers," she explained, "not clamps, dorkmeyer"). She tweezered, plucked, and penciled in the eyebrows. She combed mascara into the eyelashes, separating each of the lashes with a straight pin. She streaked pink and white highlighter above the eye shadow, hit the top of her cheekbones with blush, buffing it up and around the temples with the sable fan brush. A pink pencil etched in the contours of her lips; then she puckered them and painstakingly filled every crease and crinkle of lip with pink.

"That's lipstick, right?" Werner said.

"Lip color," she said impatiently. "Nobody uses lipstick anymore, dippo." She applied the lip color with a brush, blending the pencil and lip color in a seamless topcoat. She went back into the bag and finished off with a sprinkle of glitter dust, to make it look as if the fairy godmother had done it all.

She touched up her nails, then ducked back into the bathroom and got back into the suit.

After a few more minutes of humming in the bathroom, she returned to the mirror and discussed possible hair designs. Werner studied the nipples straining against tangerine urethane.

Had he noticed that her hair had been highlighted with henna? Did he want it out and wildly free-flowing or up and elegantly arranged?

Dusk fell while she was working at the mirror, and gradually the apartment became darker, until the mirror was the only source of light, and her face became a breathtaking sunset of colors and shadows, a silver mist clinging to her skin.

She flipped the mirror over, dialed in "Daylight Indoors" and reexamined her work under magnification.

"Do you think I took the eyeliner out too far?" she asked him, teasing the line out another millimeter or two. "Space it. What do you know?

"It's finished," she said, thrusting her chin at herself in the mirror. "Now all I need is some bruises and a spiked dog collar, and we're all set."

She dialed in "Twilight" again. "See that face?" she said. "Every woman who sees that face is going to be saying, 'I've got to have Renée Feral cosmetics.' And every guy who sees it will say, 'Wow!' "

"Wow," Werner said.

She studied her craftsmanship in the mirror.

"It's all perfect," she said, still staring into the mirror. "Except that when I'm out at Renée Feral's in L.A., my dad will still be back here . . . suffering. When I'm eating lunch with the ad people, he'll be getting suctioned. When I'm shooting, he'll be getting stuck with needles. When I go back to my hotel at night, he'll still be hooked up to the ventilator."

Her shoulders sagged, ushering forth a long sigh. Her hair fell off her shoulders and formed garlands of curls around her breasts.

She looked at him in the blue twilight and sniffled. "Will you help me?" she whispered.

Werner moved closer and touched her thigh. "You got the restraining order," he said. "How can I help?"

"My lawyer told me the facts of life today," she said quietly. "Even if we win this thing in front of this judge, the hospital or Connie could appeal. He said cases like this almost always are appealed. It could take months before anything actually happens, and then it will be too late."

"Too late for what?" asked Werner, watching her closely.

"Too late to save him from six more months of torture," she said. "My lawyer said most patients die before the court can get around to making up its mind."

Werner hugged her and smoothed her hair with his hand. "Now that all this has happened," he said, "the hospital is not going to agree to any withdrawal of life support without a court order. It's too dangerous. You've got a lawyer, Connie's got a lawyer—"

"I know," she said, suddenly looking straight into his eyes at close range. "I know all that. That's why, if there's a way," she said, "I'm asking you to end my father's life."

Werner tried to look away and saw her face in the makeup mirror, her eyes shining like gems in painted wounds.

"You mean, kill him?" Werner said.

"It's not killing," she said. "It's letting him die. Just let him die. Turn off the machines for an hour. Do something. I'm sure you know a hundred different ways to do it."

She zipped open the overnight bag and grabbed another pretty cigarette. She flicked a lighter, and an orange tip of flame appeared for a split second, just where she wanted it, just long enough to light the cigarette and deliver the first breath of blue smoke. Her lungs made an eager baby's pant.

Werner watched the high-gloss suit shimmer with the ripples and surges of her torso when she inhaled. He pulled himself up next to her, smoothed a dark lock of hair, and kissed her shoulder.

"I don't think you know what you're saying," he said. "Why is this so important to you? You're obsessed by it."

Her forehead darkened, threatening rain.

"It's my father," she said, breaking down into an unseemly display of tears. "He asked me to do this for him if he ever ended up like this, and I haven't done my job, have I?"

She is Hamlet, Werner thought. *Her father is haunting her with his request for a peaceful death.* "I am thy father's spirit,/Doom'd for a certain term to walk the night,/And for the day confined to fast in fires,/Till the foul crimes done in my days of nature/Are burnt and purged away." And Werner must be Claudius, the perpetrator of the evil deed. She must *act,* but all action involves her in evil, like asking him to pour henbane in Bed Five's ear.

"We have to do something," she said.

Werner noted the reckless way she used the most fearsome of pronouns. We?

"There's no other reason, is there?" Werner asked. "I mean, let's just pretend that the lawyers and the judges looked at all the documents and heard all the witnesses in this case? There wouldn't be anything that would make them think you were doing this for some other reason, would there? Because it seems to me that might be troublesome."

She caught his eye again in the makeup mirror. "You've been talking to Connie," she said with a sniffle.

"She talks to me," Werner admitted. "I'm the doctor, remember."

"She told you about the trust then?" Felicia said.

Werner shrugged, affecting nonchalance. "All I can remember is it has something to do with your father living to age seventy?"

"Yeah," Felicia said. "If my father dies before he turns seventy, a large trust fund, set up by my mom, gets paid out to me and Connie. I get half; she gets half. My mom didn't play favorites, even though she could have."

"OK," Werner said. "And what happens if your father lives to be seventy?"

"Then the trust goes to him," she said. "All of it."

Werner held her hand. "Now I'm not suggesting anything. I don't want you to get upset. But don't you think a lawyer or a judge might suspect you have a motive for wanting your father to die before he's seventy?"

She blew smoke into the mirror, then turned to him and said, "You think I'd go through all this just for money?"

"I said someone else might think that," Werner protested.

"You've been talking to Connie," Felicia said. "She thinks she can win this lottery if she plays her cards right."

"How so?" Werner asked.

By now the room was in total darkness, except for the twilight from the makeup mirror. Her face was a veil of shadows glinting with streaks of color and glitter.

"If my dad lives to be seventy and gets the trust," she explained, "then all the money in the trust will get disposed of by his will, or so my lawyer tells me."

"And?" Werner said.

"Connie has a will my father made five years ago. Five years ago, my father and I weren't getting along. Connie probably told you that, too."

"She mentioned that you and your father had a falling-out for a period of time," Werner said.

"He didn't approve of the way I was living," she explained. "He left me some money in the will, but only in trust accounts. He left everything else to Connie, which would include the trust money if he lived to be seventy, even though it wasn't specifically mentioned in the will."

Werner paused and waited to see if she understood what she was saying.

"So, if your father lives to be seventy," Werner said, "Connie gets all the money from the trust set up by your mom."

"That's what the will says," Felicia said. "That's why Connie is killing herself to get the feeding tube in and to keep the ventilator going, because she thinks she's going to be a big winner."

"How do you know that's why she's doing it?" Werner asked.

"Easy. Two years ago Dad was in the hospital with his first stroke. Then Connie was begging them not to make him suffer unnecessarily. She specifically said she did not want any extraordinary measures taken, blah, blah, blah," she said. "That was before her lawyer explained the trust and the will to her. After that, she got religion and started telling them that God was going to cure him, but that God wanted everything done, just in case."

Felicia leaned back on her elbows, gently blowing a plume of

smoke through pursed lips. Werner watched the swirling forma-
tions of blue smoke drift away into the invisible.

"What Connie doesn't know is that there's another will," Felicia said. "The one she has is no good."

"Another will?" asked Werner.

"Before my dad got sick, he gave me a key to a safety-deposit
box and told me that the box was in my name, too, in case anything ever happened. Right after he got sick, I emptied the deposit
box and found another will. The new will treats Connie and me
exactly the same. She gets half; I get half. The new will also re-
vokes the old one. Wait till she finds out about that."

"But why don't you just tell her?" Werner asked.

She took a deep breath and tapped her ashes into an empty beer
can. "Right about the time I found the new will, I heard Connie
had gone to see her lawyer. So I took all the papers from the
deposit box to my lawyer. My lawyer told me not to talk to
Connie about any of this stuff, or she could use it against me in
court. He said she might try and say that the later will was invalid
or that I had tricked my dad into making the second will. See, he
knows Connie. She can be pretty funny without making you laugh,
if you know what I mean."

"And I guess the will wouldn't be any of her business until your
father died," Werner added.

"I don't talk to her," Felicia said. "But she's going to find out
soon enough, because my lawyer says the court is going to make
the lawyers give each other all the documents having to do with
the trust or my father's will."

Her painted lips closed around the filter of the cigarette. "I'd
like to see her face when she reads the new will."

"This thing could turn into a complete legal mess," Werner
said. "I guess you know that."

"That's why I'm asking you for help," she said. "My sister is
trying to keep my dad alive, because she thinks she's going to take
the whole trust with her when he goes. I'm only trying to do what
he asked me to do."

Werner took her hands in his. "I can't do something like that,"
he said. "It's too . . ."

"Risky, right?" she said. "In other words, you know it's *right*.
It's just risky. I know you feel the same way I do," she said. "You

told me that. You said it was the right thing to do. You know as well as I do that my father is not going to get better. Why can't you just say it?"

"We're trained not to say it," Werner said. "You can't say, 'Oh, this patient is a hopeless case, so let's just shut the machines down.' Six months later a lawyer will come around with three medical experts who will say you were wrong. No. The safest thing to do is to continue treating the patient, unless the family goes to court and gets an order. Then, if a mistake is made, it's the court's mistake, not ours."

"But people like my father spend months, years even, suffering, while the lawyers argue in court and appeal the thing up and down. And look at the medical bills you run up in the process. It's a crime. I know you think it's a crime. I can see it in your face when you're walking around in that ICU. You don't believe in what you're doing. Why can't you just help me do what we both know is right?"

It could be done, Werner thought, *and easily done.*

"I have to think about it," Werner said.

"Great," she said, gathering her hair at the nape of her neck and lifting the mass of curls off her shoulders. "In the meantime, will you help me out of this suit?"

Desire was slowly driving him past exhaustion, beyond frustration and into hysteria. He peeled the suit off her and watched her walk over and slip into a silk robe. How much longer could he stand this? His unconscious was taking over.

He took her in his arms and nuzzled a warm, perfumy nest of curls in her clavicle.

He wanted to crawl inside and build a fire, paint pictures of bisons and hunting parties on the walls. He looked at the light from the makeup mirror and dreamed he fell asleep. In his dreams, he sent his hoary head down to the underworld, into the vaulted cathedrals of the nether regions. No stained glass, no light, only darkness of venous blood gorging the interiors, and the silence of nerves firing.

The phone rang, and they both jumped out of their skins. "Damn!" he said.

He was on call; he had to answer it.

"Wiener," said Stella Stanley, "we've been coding your man in Bed Five for the last hour and a half."

"Oh," Werner said, holding the phone tightly against his ear. "What happened?"

"I was in Bed Seven because Bed Seven was getting ready to code, too," she hurriedly explained. "Butz made Seven a Full Code, too."

"I know, I know," Werner said.

"When I got back out to the console, I looked up at the cardiac monitors and Bed Five was in V-fib. So I told the unit clerk to call a Code and ran in there. He was as purple as an eggplant, and his monitor was nothing but V-fib."

"Is he gone?" Werner asked.

"We got him back," Stella said. "Nothing special. We zapped him a couple times with the paddle electrodes. We did the epinephrine, the bicarb, the atropine. Just a standard Code, but he came around."

"Yeah," Werner said, watching Felicia putting her tools away. "Everything's all right now?"

Felicia hummed and drifted back into the bathroom.

"Like I said, he's an eggplant, but he's got a sinus rhythm now, and he's probably still got a brainstem," Stella said. "Harold's cruising around with his gurney, but I don't think it's time . . . yet."

"Who ran it?" Werner asked.

"Marlowe," Stella said. "Too bad it didn't happen last night while Hansen was here; he would have gone all the way down the tubes for sure."

"Keep me posted," Werner said, and quietly hung up the phone.

She was smoking another cigarette on the edge of the bed. "Do you have to go to the hospital?" she asked.

"Nah," Werner said. "It wasn't important."

He put his arms around her and tried to kiss her. She turned her head aside and took a puff.

He kissed her neck and whispered, "I brought everything we need for the treatment."

"Not tonight," she said, turning her face away for another puff.

"But . . ." Werner began.

"I don't want to talk about it," she said. "We just can't do that tonight."

Werner dropped his hands in his lap and felt rage surging up through his carotids and into his skull. *Maybe this is how aneu-*

rysms happen, he thought. He went back into the kitchen and pulled down the scotch, went to the freezer, and got two ice cubes. Two ice cubes, two fingers.

"I've got to call the hospital back," he said, grabbing the phone. He turned his back to her, lifted the receiver, and kept his finger on the button in the cradle. He punched seven buttons on the phone and placed the silent receiver to his ear.

"Yes, this is Dr. Ernst. Any messages?" He paused. "Could you transfer me to Nine ICU? I had a call a short while ago regarding the patient in Bed Seven." Another pause. "Thank you. Yes, this is Dr. Ernst. How are things with Bed Seven?" He paused again. "Oh. Oh, no. When? What happened?" Werner asked, speaking into the telephone and pausing and then continuing. "No. My God." He waited several more seconds. "Is he all right? Dr. Marlowe's there then? OK, I'll keep in touch. Has Dr. Butz been notified? Call me if anything else happens."

Werner hung up the phone and switched on the light next to the Murphy bed. She crawled behind a loose sheet and stared at him.

"What's wrong?" she asked, her lip trembling.

"Your father had a cardiac arrest," Werner said.

She sat up stiffly and slowly and sat on the edge of the bed. Her face turned white behind the makeup. She looked at Werner and soundlessly mouthed, "Papa. My papa." She began rocking in slow, wide arcs, mouthing "Papa" and weeping.

"They resuscitated him," Werner said. "He's still got a rhythm for now, but it was very close."

She leaned forward onto the nightstand and took three or four massive breaths.

"Easy," Werner said, sitting next to her and putting his arm around her, but she shrugged him off.

"Air," she said, pushing him away from her face. "Air." She clawed at his arm.

Within twenty seconds, she was at thirty-six breaths per minute, using her accessory muscles to breathe, leaning forward from the waist and gasping with air hunger. He had seen it a hundred times if he had seen it once, everything from the prolonged expiratory phase to the anxiety screaming in her eyeballs. Acute shortness of breath. SOB. Tachypnea. Respiratory distress.

Without realizing it, Werner fell into the old Emergency Room routine.

"Do you have asthma?"

She shook her head no. "I'm dizzy. I'm spinning."

"Are you taking any medications?" he asked her.

No again. Then she thought better of it and pointed at a pouch on the overnight bag.

Werner zipped open the pouch and turned the bag upside down and five vials tumbled out, all prescription drugs: Tagamet, Xanax, Lomotil, Compazine, phenobarbital, and Maalox; trade names for antacids, tranquilizers, anticholinergics, antiemetics, and sedatives; prescriptions for "nerves," excess stomach acid, nausea, vomiting and diarrhea. She and her doctor took this spastic colon business very seriously indeed.

"Did you take any one of these for the first time today?"

She shook her head.

He clocked her pulse at 140.

"Has this ever happened before?"

No, the head said.

"I'm taking you to the Emergency Room," Werner said. "I can't do anything for you here."

She shook her head no again and ran to his window. She knelt, threw up the sash, and put her head out into the night.

"This isn't normal everyday-type stuff, you know," Werner said. "You're wheezing. For all I know, you could be going into anaphylactic shock. I think we should go to the ER and find out what's happening."

He got her by the shoulders and gently tried to shake some sense into her.

"There's no lab here," he explained. "We can't do a chest X ray on you. We can't draw arterial blood gases and find out what the partial pressure of carbon dioxide is in your blood."

"Is he dead?" she moaned.

"No," Werner said. "I told you, they resuscitated him. He's not dead. He's back on the ventilator. I'd feel better if we went to the ER," he repeated.

"We don't have to go," she said, dropping her respirations to the twenty mark. "I've had this before. It will go away. For a minute I thought he was dead."

"So, you *have* had this before," Werner said. "Why didn't you tell me? Did you go to the doctor?"

"Yes," she said.

"And, *and,*" Werner said, wishing he could just yell for some-body to bring him her chart, "what did the doctor say? Did they think it was asthma, or what?"

"I had to go to another doctor," she said. "They couldn't figure out what it was. They said maybe it was asthma."

"So you went to a pulmonologist, right?" he said.

"I don't know," she said. "Leave me alone."

"But what did the *tests* show?" Werner fairly shouted, nearing complete exasperation. "Did they do any tests on you? Pre- and postbronchodilator pulmonary functions? Blood gases? Allergy tests? Are you allergic to anything? People don't just up and present with acute shortness of breath for no goddamn reason."

"I can't remember what they said," she moaned, sagging onto the windowsill. "Just leave me alone, I'll be OK."

"I'm sorry," Werner said, touching her shoulder. "I'm just try-ing to figure this out. It's unusual to just up and go into respiratory distress when you've never had it before."

"I'm unusual," she said. "I can't stand the thought of him living like this, but the thought of him actually dying is worse," she said.

"It will be for the best," Werner said, touching her shoulder.

"But then what?" she said. "Is he just dead then? I can't think about it. I hate the sound of the word. Death," she said, crying out the window.

"It will be for the best," Werner said.

"Best for him," she said. "Not for me. I can't call him and tell him I'm sorry. It's too late for that. I can't sit with him on the porch and spend the day with him. I had the chance; but I had other things to do, and there was always time."

"Don't do this to yourself," Werner said. "It's over. You did the right thing."

"They'll put him in the ground," she said, staring out into the night. "In a cold coffin. The water will leak in on him. His finger-nails and toenails will keep growing, even though he's dead."

She leaned farther out the window, talking into the night air.

"When my mother got cancer," she said, crying quietly, "she turned into a skeleton right before she died. She had a paper hairnet on her head, and the bones of her face stuck out. My mother looked at me and said, 'I am going to the black, disordered land where darkness is the only light.' "

"Come back inside," Werner said.

"Connie said that was from the Bible," Felicia whispered. "I've never forgotten that. She said she was going to the black, disordered land where darkness is the only light. Now Papa's going there. Someday I'll go there, too. I'll be in a coffin, too. My furniture, the photographs of me, those will still be here, but I'll be gone. It doesn't make any sense that a piece of furniture should last longer than a person."

Werner put his hands on her shoulders again and tried to bring her back inside.

"What does it mean?" she asked, looking out into the night. "I'll bet you're glad they kept him alive for this. Did they beat on his chest? Did they stick him with needles and shock him with electricity?"

"Stop it," Werner said. "Don't do this."

"My grandmother told me that after you die, you can see inside everybody you left behind. You can look right into their head and see their thoughts. What if that's the way it is? What if dead people can see inside of us?"

"Don't think about it," Werner said.

"I have to throw up," she said. "Then I'm going to the hospital."

She got up, wrapped her robe around herself, and went to the bathroom. "Don't follow me," she said.

Chapter

11

Stella left Dr. Marlowe and Poindexter in Bed Five arguing about the proper fuel mix to drip into the post Code. She went into Bed Two's pod, where the young Goodpasture's syndrome was getting ready to give the machines the slip.

Bed Two's head rolled toward her on the pillow, and his eyeballs listed in their sockets. He made a claw with one of his restrained hands and motioned for a pencil and paper.

Stella tucked the notepad under her arm. "You don't have to write it out again," she said. "I know what you want."

Bed Two managed half of a palms-up so-how-about-it? gesture with his restrained hands.

Stella looked out at the central console, where a lone monitor technician sat dozing in front of the bank of eight cardiac monitors.

In the corner of her eye, she saw a bizarre, sinister-looking arrhythmia squiggle across the monitor over Bed Two's head. She studied the rhythm for a few seconds, then pushed a button and printed a strip of it. She hustled back into Bed Five's pod, interrupted Poindexter and Marlowe, and asked Poindexter if he could help her turn Bed Two.

Poindexter came out of Bed Five with two piggyback IV bags

slung over his shoulders, a fistful of vials and ampoules, and a syringe stuck into a stoppered vial. Multicolored syringe caps bristled from his teeth like candy cigarette butts.

"Can't this wait?" Poindexter said. "I'm mixing cocktails."

"I don't want to turn him," Stella said, indicating the monitor. "I just wanted you to take a gander at this rhythm."

Poindexter pushed his glasses up the bridge of his nose with the back of his latex-gloved hand and watched the monitor.

"Torsades," he said, naming the arrhythmia. "I haven't seen torsades in five years. I'd like to get a twelve-lead EKG of that."

"That's what I thought it was," Stella said. "Do you think Dr. Marlowe will order a twelve-lead for us?"

"Just call down to EKG and order it yourself," Poindexter advised. "If Marlowe won't sign off on it, we'll have Dr. Wisenheimer do it tomorrow."

"Torsades," Stella said. "Unbelievable."

"Torsade de pointes," Poindexter elaborated. "A particularly malignant and extremely rare arrhythmia. I think I've seen it twice."

"He's going down in flames," Stella said. "He's a Full Code, too."

"Who made him that?" Poindexter asked through syringe caps and clenched teeth. He deftly pulled the syringe out of the stoppered vial and brought the needle point first toward his face, sticking it back into one of the caps between his teeth in a single fluid motion. "Family?"

"I hate it when you do that," Stella said, cringing as the bare needle went safely into the cap between Poindexter's lips.

"You're just jealous," Poindexter said. "Ew," he said, frowning at the monitor. "Look at that."

"Ultra torsades," Stella said.

"This Syracuse Orangeman is headed down the tubes," Poindexter said. "And my money says he's gonna do it tonight, right behind flotsam in Bed Five and jetsam in Bed Seven. They've both been circling the drain since start of shift."

"How do you feel about slow coding this one, Poin?" Stella asked.

"I don't know," he said, playfully squirting epinephrine in the port on the IV bag. "The Hippoblimp's here, and with all the activity tonight, staffing has planted a tech out at the console to watch the heart monitors. It might be tough to pull one off. The tech is going to scream bloody murder if she sees a fatal arrhythmia. She'll call the Code, and we'll be in here looking like a couple of LPNs."

"She's new, and I don't think she's seen torsades before," Stella said, nodding toward the dozing monitor tech. "She'll think it's an artifact caused by the patient's movements."

"Maybe we can tell her that torsades is a delicate French pastry," Poindexter said, ambling back out to the console, the IV bags swagging against his shoulder blades.

"I might have an idea a little later about what to do," Stella said, stopping him on his way out.

Poindexter shot a parting glance at the emaciated orange frame of Bed Two. "Let me know what you wanna do," he said. "No fucking way that guy should be coded."

Bed Two either woke up or fell asleep and found the Furnaceman leaning over his bed. The sooty reptilian hands left charcoal streaks on the bed rails. The white lab coat accentuated the charred shingles of the torso. The orange eyes twinkled as he consulted his metal clipboard.

"Go away," said Bed Two. "I'm sick."

"Sick ain't half your trouble, bub," said the Furnaceman, scratching his steel wool beard. "Wait until you leave that bag of bones you call a body. I'll show you some sick."

"What do you want?" Bed Two moaned. "I'm dying. I'm finally dying. I can feel it. So just go away and leave me alone."

"I know you're dying," the Furnaceman said. "That's why I'm here. We need to talk about the important things. Death, eternal life, your soul. Soon you will make a number of crucial decisions with lasting repercussions. I'm here to advise you in that regard. I bill by the hour, and you don't have any choice about whether to accept my services."

"So there is a God," Bed Two said, "and an afterlife? Is that what you're telling me?"

The Furnaceman settled back on the window ledge next to the bed and folded his hands.

"This is the very best part of my job," he said, beaming with satisfaction. "I get to talk to people who, at long last, know what's important. The living make such meaningless distinctions. Especially in your country. In America, the living worry about whether they have too much high-density lipoproteins or low-density lipoproteins. Entire careers are squandered predicting what the Federal Reserve will do with interest rates. Or they get hung up on the difference between a two-door sedan and a four-door wagon. Or a shovel and a home computer. Or a birth control device, as opposed to, say, a stapler. A stereo sound system as opposed to a tool bench. All meaningless distinctions among silly little inert objects. Why do humans waste their brains on widgets, thingumajigs, doohickeys, gizmos, and whatchamajiggers? I mean, the same brain that creates a symphony gets up the next morning and spends the entire day trying to figure out the difference between an adjustment to gross income and a tax deduction."

"I don't care about any of that stuff," Bed Two said.

"Precisely," the Furnaceman said, clapping his scaly hands. "Isn't it beautiful out here in deep space! Out here, the earth is just a tiny speck of light. The two-door car, the four-door car, the shovel, the home computer, the birth control device, the stapler, the high- and low-density lipoproteins, the Federal Reserve Board, all are just a tiny, tiny speck of light, off somewhere in a distant galaxy. And the big and small moments, the long years, the people you knew and loved, the products you consumed, your commodity fetishes, all just a teeny pinpoint of light out the pod bay window. One thing indistinguishable from another.

"That leaves just you and me to talk about your future," the Furnaceman continued. "You had an engineering degree, didn't you? What was it you wanted to be? A missile systems expert? No doubt that was because you wanted to help people, am I right?"

"Yes," Bed Two said. "Keep the country strong and raise a family on a good salary, what's wrong with that?"

"Hey," the Furnaceman said, "don't get touchy. I'm the last one to pass judgment on anybody. I think you made an excellent career choice. Too bad it was cut so short. But let's not dwell on what might have been. Let's talk about your future."

"Am I going to heaven?" Bed Two asked. "Will I see God the Father?"

"Two different questions," the Furnaceman said with a giggle. "I'll take the second one first, because if I took the first one first, or the second one second, you'd probably get bewildered or frightened. Whereas, if I take the first one second and the second one first, you'll probably come to a better understanding of what's in store for you. And don't worry if you get confused. I have video-tapes and cassette tapes and other learning modules, which I can leave with you to help you understand all this, OK?"

"I was asking about God," Bed Two feebly repeated.

"God is dead," the Furnaceman said. "I can tell you for a fact that God died. The rumors are true. He died from a broken heart. It was very sad. He was immortal, omnipotent, omniscient, every-thing. But He had an Achilles' heel. Kind of like Superman and green kryptonite. Nothing in the entire universe could harm Him, except man's inhumanity to man. In the end, relentless human cruelty weakened Him. It made Him sick to death, gave Him chest pains, raised His blood pressure, gave Him fevers. All the wicked things people did to each other—especially what people did to children—He felt them all, and He felt them on a cosmic scale. Finally, it drove Him insane. He did Himself in. He couldn't stand the anguish anymore."

"That doesn't make any sense," Bed Two protested. "God is almighty and everlasting. He can't die."

"Correct premise," the Furnaceman said. "Faulty conclusion. He *was* almighty and capable of all things. But by definition, being almighty and capable of *all* things meant He was also capable of taking His own life, which He did. I think He did it the day after they invented commercial television. That was the end. He stag-gered into bed and pulled the blinds for the last time."

"I don't believe you," Bed Two said, shedding a few stray tears and chewing on his ET tube. "You're talking utter nonsense."

"Have it your way," the Furnaceman snapped. "God is a tall, muscular middle-aged white male with long white hair and a beard. Blood type I, for ichor. He owns seven candy-colored Mer-cedes four-fifty SLs—one for each day of the week. And in heaven, you can get down and party out of bounds. The drugs have no side effects. Twenty-four-hour tanning parlors, heated swimming pools. The sex never stops. You can soak your head in endorphins and cop a buzz without a finger's worth of exercise. If you're an ascetic dimwit, you can assume the lotus position and sit around in transports of mystical jubilation. Every day you can wake up and get struck dumb with ecstasy at the sound of God's voice. If you're feeling self-righteous, you can agitate for permission to view the sufferings of the damned. Sometimes it's permitted, and it satisfies those virtuous types who are happy only when everybody else is miserable. Feel better now?"

"I don't want to talk to you anymore," Bed Two said.

"Sure," the Furnaceman said. "You'd rather stick your head in the sand. I'll tell you something: Where you're going, nothing changes. It's still every man for himself. I'm here to prepare you for the proceedings. If you wish, I can represent you at the hearings as your advocate. As you've probably realized by now, you no longer command the mental clarity necessary to argue your own innocence."

"What kind of proceedings?" asked Bed Two.

"How old are you?" the Furnaceman asked in exasperation and disbelief. "What do you mean, 'What kind of proceedings?' " he said sarcastically. "Judgment Day, you gaumless bosthoon. You've heard of that, haven't you? Did you think it was a fairy tale, or what? You've seen what a jury of twelve looks like? Pretty imposing, don't you think? Greater than the sum of its parts and all that rot, right? Well, you're going to be judged by a jury of *billions*. And every encounter you had with a member of the human race is going to be examined by committees of thousands. And each committee is going to be headed up by a person you fucked over in the interest of satisfying your own appetites."

Bed Two writhed under the sheets and tried to lift his hands.

"Don't say it," the Furnaceman said, stopping him with a gesture. "You're probably thinking, *That's impossible. How could they go through that kind of procedure for every single human being who dies?* Ha! They've got nothing but time on their hands! Mountains will disappear from sparrows sharpening their beaks on them, and they will have just begun processing your case."

"But I didn't do anything," Bed Two protested. "I committed no mortal sins. If anything, I committed a few little sins, *venial* sins, I think we used to call them, that's all. Other than those, I didn't do anything."

"That's right," the Furnaceman said with a savage laugh. "You didn't do a *fucking* thing! This sin analysis of yours is a little out of date. It doesn't come close to cutting it anymore. You must have stopped going to church before Vatican Two, or maybe sometime before the Last Supper. You're stuck back in the days of arcane statutory construction. Are you worried about whether you committed a mortal sin when you didn't go to church because you had a chest cold? Those days are gone. The regulatory language was abolished and the guidelines were simplified. You were supposed to love God and love your neighbor. You didn't do either. You got your degree in missile systems engineering, and then you fell in love with a beautiful, pleasant young woman. How *selfless* of you. You loved your mom and dad. So do spider monkeys! You didn't comfort the sick, or feed the hungry, or give alms to the poor, did you? No. You loved only people who were useful or entertaining, or sometimes you went the extra mile for a blood relative. Big fucking deal. Even spotted hyenas share the kill with other members of the pack.

"Now, because you didn't do what was expected of you, you're looking at doing some *hard time,* unless you come up with a plausible defense to explain your behavior."

"But I wasn't *evil* or anything," Bed Two argued. "I didn't hurt anybody."

"Am I talking to a tire iron here?" the Furnaceman replied. "You're missing the point. Let me show you what I mean. If you'll just take a moment and look back over your life. Here, if you like, I can run it by for you, frame by frame, on the monitor here. On the other hand, why bother? We both know what your life looks like. It's a chronicle of you satisfying your appetites and, in your spare time, helping out a few others who will be most likely to return the favor. Also, you've got to disabuse yourself of your notions of earthly justice, where people look at what you *did,* your actions. Divine justice is based upon an examination of that dark conglomeration of thought and action we call *being.*"

The Furnaceman paused and polished the scales on the back of his fingernails, peeling off a burned one and throwing it into the wastebasket.

"I bet you can tell I used to be a philosophy teacher," he said, batting his singed eyelashes. "But never mind me," he continued, "divine judgments are, pardon the pun, infinitely more complex than earthly ones, where the verdict comes in after two glib and oily-tongued lawyers give soap opera speeches for an hour or two. The committees will examine every nanosecond of your existence. They'll blow up each frame and project them on massive screens. They'll hold caucuses to determine why you stepped over the homeless on your way to the convenience store."

"I was young," Bed Two said. "Hell, I'm twenty-three. I never had the benefit of an epiphany or a spiritual awakening. I just got out of school when all this happened. Give me a break!"

"Save your eloquence for the tribunals," the Furnaceman said, picking soot out from under his fingernails with a scalpel. "And come up with a different theory of the case. Reason dawns at age seven, and you haven't done shit for anybody but yourself since you learned your multiplication tables. You are going to be one fucked phantom doughnut if that's all you've got for an excuse."

"They'll understand, won't they?" Bed Two whimpered. "I'll explain it to them myself. I don't want you talking for me. I'll do my own talking."

"Have it your way," the Furnaceman said in a pleasant singsong. "Go galloping in there on a camel and try to ride it through the eye of a needle. See if I care!"

The Furnaceman laughed uproariously, his pointy tail wagging merrily behind him.

"Excuse me," the Furnaceman said, producing a stethoscope from a heap of glowing coals on Bed Two's nightstand. The metal parts of the stethoscope glowed red under the heat lamps. "I just want to have one listen."

The Furnaceman placed the bell of the stethoscope on Bed Two's chest, and Bed Two felt the metal ring burn its brand into his chest.

"You have an impressive pericardial friction rub at the fourth intercostal space over the midclavicular line," the Furnaceman said. "I just wanted to hear it for myself. Would you like to hear it?"

Bed Two shook his head.

"Here," the Furnaceman said. "Have a listen."

He placed the prongs of the stethoscope in Bed Two's ears and again pressed the red-hot bell into Bed Two's chest.

"Hear that," the Furnaceman said with a jolly laugh, his voice suddenly booming inside the echo chamber of Bed Two's dry ribs. "THAT'S AN IMPRESSIVE PERICARDIAL FRICTION RUB AT THE FOURTH INTERCOSTAL SPACE OVER THE MIDCLAVICULAR LINE. WHAT DO YOU THINK OF THAT? IMPRESSIVE, ISN'T IT?"

Stella watched a new flurry of torsades scatter across Bed Two's monitor at the console. This time the malignant rhythm persisted. The monitor tech was on the phone with a romantic interest, but she had one eye on Bed Two's monitor. Stella sensed the tech was preparing to get off the phone and tell somebody, like the Hippo-blimp or a doctor, about Bed Two's bizarre rhythm.

Stella slipped into Bed Two and drew the blinds, leaving a crack through which she could view the monitor tech on the phone. She was a few minutes early for her hourlies, but not conspicuously early.

Bed Two had his eyes wide open in their bony orange sockets, staring straight up into the heat lamps and the black hole of eternity overhead.

Stella opened a new package of EKG electrodes, unbuttoned her blouse, and pasted the electrodes in a triangle over her surgical scars. She attached the leads to the electrodes on her chest, buttoned up her blouse, and drew the wires out through an opening between the buttons at her waist.

"I'm redoing his leads," she hollered out to the tech, silencing the alarm, and watching through the blinds as the tech held up a thumb-and-finger OK.

She unhooked Bed Two from the monitor. In a split second, Stella had the leads hooked up to the electrodes on her chest, and she was watching her own rhythm on the monitor over Bed Two's head.

"Not bad," she said. Maybe an elevated T wave, here or there, but otherwise she looked damn good on the monitor.

Bed Two's head shuddered against his pillow. Stella untied his hands and held them.

"I love you," she said. "You can go home now. After you get there, shut the door behind you. When it's too late for them to bring you back, I'll hook you back up and call the Code."

The lights went out, and the Furnaceman grabbed Bed Two's arm. "Hold on, Orville," he said, "it's a rough flight!"

A hurricane blew Bed Two and the Furnaceman up into a dark corrugated tunnel. Bed Two was buffeted back and forth in an ass-over-elbows ascent, up through some kind of dark gullet, or passage. When he tried to stop himself by clawing at the walls of the passage, his hands slid over warm, sticky muscular walls ribbed with cartilage or ligaments.

Gales blew him along inside the tunnel.

"Where are we?" Bed Two shouted over the wind.

"It's either the asshole or the birth canal," the Furnaceman yelled. "You won't know until you come out the other end. If it's the asshole, I guess I don't have to tell you what you'll be, you worthless piece of shit."

Bed Two and the Furnaceman were dumped out into a red cavity; the walls were dark with mucus and venous blood.

"This is your last chance," the Furnaceman said, panting to catch his breath. "In a minute this place is going to implode, and you'll be pushed out into the courtroom, where you'll spend the rest of eternity with all those slobs you didn't give a shit about the whole time you were alive. Or you can come with me and relax in a stress-free environment, free of guilt and with no obligations of any kind. It's entirely your decision. Once you're dead, you get to do whatever you want."

"I want to see my Father," Bed Two said.

"Yeah," the Furnaceman said. "And if you think back over all the wonderful things you did for Him and His children, you can imagine for yourself how thrilled He'll be to see you. My son, the missile systems expert! You don't have to submit to judgment. You can avoid the whole thing by fleeing the jurisdiction."

The cavity shook with the rumblings of an earthquake.

"Don't say I didn't warn you," the Furnaceman hollered over his shoulder. "Every son of a bitch you fucked over during the course of your whole miserable life is waiting for you at the other end for the chance to fuck you back. Come with me, and you'll never even have to lay eyes on them. It's your choice."

The muscles in the walls of the room contracted, closing around Bed Two and squashing the wind out of him. He slithered through an orifice and came out a bald, blue little Samson, into a hall filled with blinding light. Fluid sluiced out of his ears, leaving his auditory nerves naked in the wind. Symphonies sounded in the new medium, followed by the round sounds of new and wonderful words. The thrumming vocal cords of magnificent beings. Wind chilled his spastic maiden-pink lungs, and with his first breath, he sang songs of joy with lungfuls of all the gases in the universe. His pain became an ecstatic mutant with wings, and he rose, borne aloft by his own intense yearning, soaring on the crescendos of an overture, a thrilling, gentle ascent toward the light.

Chapter

12

Night shift. Werner was back at the controls in the Death Lab. The R2's and R3's had some good laughs before they left, speculating about what was in store for the luckless drudge on call. Cowboy Hansen handed him a stack of histories and physicals and two new admissions, with a packet of lubricating jelly stapled to the upper-left-hand corner of the top sheet—a token of affection from the departing Nazi vaudeville team of Hansen and Marlowe, complete with the scrawled instruction, "Bend over, and have a good night on call." Four appalling gorks, three trench wounds, two curdled gomes, and a CABBAGE in Bed Three. Werner found a mock memo taped to the console. He recognized the dot matrix printing of Poindexter's laptop computer on official Med Center letterhead, complete with a photocopied signature of Dr. Hofstader, addressed to all Medical Center ICU personnel.

To: Staff Physicians
From: Doctor Richard Hofstader, M.D., Ph.D.
Re: The Four Pillars of Modern Medicine

The United States Government and the Health Insurance Industry have advised the Medical Center that they will no longer reimburse intensive medical care for the following groups of patients:

1. Cigarette smokers
2. Chronic alcoholics
3. Patients over seventy-two years of age
4. Patients more than thirty pounds overweight

Henceforth, intensive care medical treatment of any patient in one or more of the above categories will be provided only on a pay-as-you-go basis. Thank you for your cooperation in enforcing these new guidelines.

Any inquiries should be directed to Dr. Weimaraner von Wisenheimer.

The memo provided the only chuckle of the night. It went precipitously downhill from there.

First on the agenda was Family. Two or three large ones—most notably Bed Seven's Family—were waiting in the family room to talk to the resident on call. Werner considered speed reading the histories and physicals and reviewing a stack of new and old charts, but knew he would be unable to concentrate until he got the Family business out of the way. It would be at least two hours before he could strap himself into the control tower and work without interruptions.

He took a cup of coffee with him for company and headed for the Visitors' Lounge, where dozens of grieving, weary family members wore blue and gray faces and huddled together in clusters, like small tribes of anxious primates. As he passed, he could hear them pointing him out and whispering, urging one another to approach the doctor and ask him for more information. Werner felt as if he were walking into a humid jungle clearing, waiting for Family tribesmen to fling the toils of their clammy emotions all over him like wet hunting nets.

Werner motioned Bed Seven's family into a conference room, resolving to get the worst of it out of the way first.

Bed Seven's middle-aged son was a stoic, take-charge kind of guy who had vowed to remain strong and to get to the bottom of just why his dad had been admitted as a dignified, silver-haired gentleman complaining of stomach pain, only to turn into a gork on a ventilator. Bed Seven's son had a reputation for trying to find out everything about the ICU and the Med Center, and he frequently thought he was getting tough with the right people. He spent a lot of time in a phone booth, conferring with several medical specialists who were friends of his. Then the son of Bed Seven would confirm or question every move Werner made in the treatment of his father.

Bed Seven's son never lost an opportunity to emphasize that his father was staying here only until he could be transferred to the Mayo Clinic; he knew the right people, and it was only a matter of time.

The son of Bed Seven addressed Werner as if the young resident were a rude, incompetent waiter in a cheap steakhouse.

"I guess I'm asking you why, after over six weeks in the Intensive Care Unit, you still haven't made any progress," Mr. Bed Seven's son said.

Werner recalled the two kinds of chronic lung patient: barrel-chested emphysemics, usually called "pink puffers," who get shorter and shorter of breath and skinnier and skinnier from the work of breathing, until they fall over dead, and the overweight chronic bronchitics, or the "blue bloaters," who get fatter and bluer until they drop dead of cardiovascular accident. Noble deaths one and all, but clinically distinguishable.

Bed Seven's son was well into the blue bloater classification, Werner thought. Bed Seven was a gork, and Bed Seven's middle-aged son was an apprentice gork. Fat-clogged veins stood out on the son of Bed Seven's neck, and the cold blue of cyanosis had seeped into the pink beef of his hands and face. His plumbing vasculature was all backed up with steak and booze and the best of everything else. The ripeness of early edema had set in.

Werner slipped into one of his favorite space age daydreams— namely, that someday, in the thoroughly state-of-the-art future, everybody will have a panel installed in his chest with a digital display of his blood gases and electrolytes and a running video of his three-lead EKG. The implications for health care would be breathtaking. "Open your shirt, there. Let's get a look at your monitor." People could be diagnosed at a glance. It was not a new idea. Momus, the sleepy, cantankerous god of the Greeks—son of Nyx, the goddess of Night—believed that Zeus ought to have made men with windows in their breasts, whereby their real thoughts might be revealed.

But who cares about thoughts, if the window could be used to display a running three-lead EKG?

"Have there been any new developments?" asked the son of Bed Seven.

"His pH is better," Werner said.

"What is the pH right now?" the mesomorph asked, pulling an appointment calendar out of his suit and producing the requisite gold pen. Twenty-four carat. The kind everybody loses.

"It's seven-point-two-four at the moment," Werner said. "I can refer to the chart if you need it to the third digit."

"I'm a businessman, Dr. Resident," Bed Seven's son said, apparently detecting the undercurrent of Werner's bad attitude and making forceful eye contact in an effort to confront it, doing his best to look like the kind of guy you do not mess with. Werner saw only sebaceous glands sweating forth a sheen of oil on the bluish forehead.

Mr. son of Bed Seven's porky face went stern and red with the gravity and import of the situation, warming to his role as the mover and shaker, even though he had nothing to look forward to in life except right-sided heart failure.

"And being a businessman," Mr. Bed Seven's son continued, "I'm not accustomed to paying this kind of money without seeing some results. My concern is that we try the right approaches."

I am so glad you are here, Werner thought. *Until I ran into you, I was all set to try the wrong approaches.*

Dr. Resident. Did he really say that? He did, Werner thought, *and he got away with it.* Werner took it in the face, stubbornly holding on to the knowledge that, as long as he did not call attention to himself or his treatment of Bed Seven, he could manage Bed Seven's illnesses any way he liked.

"Dr. Hofstader was here today, wasn't he?" asked Bloat. "I want to know what he had to say about all this."

Werner became the earnest, young, and humble resident. He fed Mr. Bed Seven's son the we-are-all-in-close-consultation line of shit, secure in the knowledge that it was a solid, medical fiction that Hofstader and any doctor would back him up on.

Bed Seven's son did not like Werner's evasiveness one bit, and Werner was overjoyed. The women family members had womanly concerns. The blue bloater tactically stalled, then waved them on Werner like a general signaling his right flank.

"Is he in pain?" Bed Seven's daughter asked. "Is he feeling all this?"

"The pain medications should prevent that," Werner replied, waiting for B-squared-over-blue to ask him about the dosages.

The women seemed truly deserving of gentleness and compassion. The only solution here was to take the daughters and wives off to the side and console them in their sorrow. That done, Werner could hustle Bloat into a private consultation room and slap him around with the hard facts. Mr. Family, your father is a rutabaga. Your father is an acorn squash, a turnip, a Mr. Potato, gomerland, a gork, a chunk on a slab, a veg, a stiff, lunch meat, a carcass, hamburger, fertilizer, a box lunch for worms. Wake up, come to, back off, and get lost.

What Werner found most unseemly was the way the fat man thought he could jump right in and start mixing it up with something as terrifying as Death. Truly a revolting sin of pride. A mere businessman trying to muscle up to all the death professionals and get some action. First-degree Nimrod on the loose.

He questioned Werner closely on the vasopressor dosages and the central venous pressure line readings.

Werner gauged the fragility of the man's skull and eyed a fire extinguisher hanging on the wall.

Dangerous, Werner thought, trapped in close, well-lit quarters with another savage intellect, the two of them baring their fangs like hyenas, without so much as a snarl betraying their mutual desires. Bed Seven's son wished he could sue Werner so hard the young doctor would never practice again; Werner vividly imagined the clinical delights, the procedural ease of ripping the man's fatty jugulars out of his neck without using any instruments.

After a few more rounds with Mr. Bed Seven's son, Werner explained the results of Bed Three's colonoscopy to Bed Three's Family, which consisted of septuagenarian brothers and sisters, old and fat and waiting for their turn in the ICU, sharing their sister's congenital deafness and as dumb as oxen when it came to understanding anything medical.

After them, there was Bed Eight's Family. Bed Eight was a brainstem infarct. She had been complaining to a store clerk in a mall about a bottle of cream rinse conditioner she had purchased the day before when she grasped the back of her neck and fell to the floor, taking a display of fingernail polish bottles with her. Something squeezed off blood to the medulla, probably a clot or a thrombosis. Every organ in her body was in tiptop shape, except her brain. The only sensible thing to do was harvest those organs and give them to other people.

The papers were all drawn up, the autopsy forms, transport, everything was ready to go when the family called it off. They got together and started freaking each other out about the autopsy and the donor procedures. They started thinking about how it would be, standing around at the wake, telling themselves that Bed Eight had been gutted like a fish and stuffed full of sawdust and plastic, and would she still look all right in an open casket, without any eyeballs, or kidneys, or heart, or liver inside her? So they talked it over for three or four days and brought in a SWAT team of Roman Catholic priests to help out the house staff. They mulled over all the moral, ethical, religious, and fiscal aspects of the deal, until the bottom fell right out of Bed Eight's blood pressure, and she headed down the tubes so fast that her attending physician could not say for sure whether they got her back in time . . . to preserve the integrity of her organs, that is.

Halfway into that mess, the beeper called him downstairs, where the R1 had gotten in over his head. Bed Four in the Eighth-Floor ICU had extubated himself again.

Werner scrubbed down at the sink in the Eighth-Floor ICU, his tennis shoes in blue surgical booties deftly working the hot- and cold-water pedals, soaping up and scrubbing down, getting ready to go in and do another piece-of-shit intubation on Bed fucking Four.

"Didn't we just go through this *twice* last time I was on call?" Werner asked the same jackass wombats who had let Bed Four extubate himself twice the day before yesterday.

The goddamn respiratory therapists and the dumb-ass nurses apparently could not keep Bed fucking Four's hands tied down. If the motherfucks had simply taped the tube in real tight, like good

boys and girls, then tied the goozer's hands down and snowed him
with the PRN drug cocktails that were written all over the chart,
everything would be fine. But no, they tried to be nice about it.
They untied the guy's hand because he made like he wanted to
scratch his balls, and pop! he got the tube out again. *How many
times are these pig-ignorant drones gonna fall for it? Someday,*
Werner thought, *they will train rhesus monkeys to be respiratory
therapists and nurses,* and then he would not have all this interference.

And now that they had lost the airway, he could see them inside
Bed Four's cubicle, screaming commands at one another, yelling
for suction, dropping things. Three or four nurses bumped into
one another in their search for an ambu bag and an O_2 nipple
connector. Consequently, with all of them trying as hard as they
did, the place looked like a hospital Intensive Care Unit, people
running back and forth in a frenzy of inefficiency and poor procedural technique.

This kind of thing never happened in the Ninth-Floor Intensive
Care Unit, because Stella and Poindexter worked there. On the
other floors, the nurses and even some of the residents were so
afraid that they might make a mistake and kill a dead person that
they usually made a mistake and killed a dead person. On top of
it all, the patient often died before change of shift. Real medical
misfits.

The Ninth-Floor ICU got busy but never frantic. Stella and
Poindexter knew too much ever to hurry. Hurrying was a pain in
the ass and had no place in the critical care setting. Contrary to the
impression some of these critical care personnel got of themselves
from watching their TV role models, there was no such thing as an
emergency. Emergencies happen in pediatrics, not in adult critical
care. The idea that every second is critical in a medical emergency
is a dramatic device used to fuel prime-time potboilers about hospitals. Two or three seconds or even two or three minutes or hours
usually do not matter in the treatment of an old gaffer who has
already acquired momentum, a falling body drawn down to the
gravity of the grave.

Werner swore violently throughout the entire procedure, insulted everyone in the Eighth-Floor ICU, and then returned to the
Ninth-Floor ICU, where Stella Stanley had a cup of coffee waiting
for him.

"Good morning, Dr. Ernst," Martha Henderson sang out, as Werner shambled through the automatic doors, holding his breath.

Werner noted the time, confirming his hypothesis that the Hippoblimp's nightly spasms of good cheer usually coincided with the 2:00 A.M. opening of the Med Center's cafeteria. Every night, at precisely 1:45 A.M., one of the Head Nurse's parablimps took everyone's order and came back a half an hour later pushing a cart laden with white takeout bags.

Werner found the usual sloth of big-butted wombats feeding out of Styrofoam troughs in front of the cardiac monitors, where they could blissfully gorge and still keep an eye on the electrical conduction of their patients' hearts. In his present frame of mind Werner thought the Hippoblimp and the other full-figured gals in her brood looked like the Venus of Willendorf flanked by the wives of Java Man, Peking Man, Piltdown Man, and Australopithecus—all gathered around a giraffe carcass for a grease and protein orgy.

His nostrils filled with the smell of fried deep fat, as he watched them bolus themselves on beef tallow and chicken parts, fries and onion rings. He could see fat settling in their butts like gobbets of hog lard sinking in a vat of cold water; he could see globules of lard collecting in their coronary arteries and the yellow Jell-O of adipose tissue filling the ponderous rolls around their midriffs.

They stared at the monitors and put fried pieces of dead animals in their mouths. One day, the heiferettes would rise from their stools, clutch at their throats, stagger into empty pods, and paste electrodes on their chests, just in time to watch their own heart attacks on the monitors over their beds.

"Stella," Werner said, pulling a stack of charts out of the carousel in the middle of the ICU, "I love you, my darling. Why don't you marry me and take me away from all this?"

Stella hung a plastic bag of fluid on a med hook and spiked it with a Soluset.

"Hey, Poindexter," Stella said.

"What?" Poindexter said from the half-light of Bed Five.

"Come on out here. Dr. Megalosperm is about to propose to me."

Werner glanced at Bed Five's monitor. *It could be done, and easily done,* he thought. He could simply turn down Bed Five's dopamine drip, for instance. The bottom would fall out of his blood pressure within an hour and ... Perfectly natural. A guy who coded just a few nights ago would quite naturally code again. He could dial down his FIO_2, or fraction of inspired oxygen, from 70 percent oxygen to room air, 21 percent, without triggering the spirometer alarms. The spirometer measured the *volume* of exhaled gases, not the *content*.

"Who would marry you?" Stella asked, breaking in on Werner's scheming thoughts. "I'd have to wait until the money rolled in, thank you very much. But right about the time the money rolls in, you'll go in for an upper GI, and they'll find a string of bleeding ulcers. You'll start having chest pains. Then you'll realize you're going to bite it one day, just like your patients. You'll panic and realize how short life is. Then you'll buy a sports car and start running around with twenty-year-old nurses. Hey, I know doctors even better than I know patients."

"But I love you, Stella," Werner said. "I could make you happy. Did you see this guy's clotting studies?"

"Whose?" she asked, a stream of tiny bubbles rising in the chamber of IV solution.

"Bed Seven's," he said, with a Mr. Science chuckle of amazement. They were some of the worst clotting studies he had ever seen. So bad they were laughably bad, as well as devilishly intriguing, for there was no good medical reason they should be so terrible.

"Diffuse intravascular coagulation," he said, still snickering in disbelief. "The guy was a sieve; now his blood's turning into cottage cheese. But that's neither here nor there. The important thing is what I feel for you. Deep down inside."

"He's still a Full Code, you know," Stella said.

"I thought he was a Slow Code," Werner replied.

Stella poked her head around to be sure the gorging wombats were out of earshot.

"Hey, Poindexter," she whispered hoarsely. "Dr. Wienerschnitzel von Ernst, the spermoblastic and spermoplasmic expert on vaginomania, has just modified the code status of Bed Seven."

"And not a minute too soon," Poindexter said. "Have you seen his blood gases?"

"If we're lucky, we can Slow Code Bed Five tonight, too," Werner observed.

"Too many lawyers sniffing around there," Stella warned.

"They had an outside neurology expert in here on days. Apparently the guy was hired by one of the daughters. He was trying to tell us that Bed Five's tremors were purposeful attempts at communication."

Werner got up from the console and marched into Bed Five. He pulled up at bedside and looked down at the skull wrapped in mauve skin. Werner heard the soft pinging of Bed Five's fingers on the bed rails.

"Sir?" Werner hollered, taking Bed Five's tethered hand in his. "We have to know whether you can hear us. Will you squeeze my hand if you can hear me? I'm your doctor."

The lids of Bed Five's eyes opened, and empty blues stared up at the ceiling. He lifted his skull off the pillow for a split second, then closed his eyes and went back to gomerland.

"Stella!" Werner yelled.

"What?" she said.

"He just opened his eyes and lifted his head off the pillow," Werner said.

"So what?" she said. "He's done that before. That doesn't mean anything."

"Yeah," Werner said vacantly. "Yeah, you're right. I guess I forgot he had done that before."

"Go take a nap," Stella said. "You're a spook."

"You're right," Werner said. "The MRI scan and PET scan showed blood flow and metabolism in the cerebral cortex are about half that of a normal brain."

"Yeah," Stella said. "Of course, that's what your MRI scan would show, too, and you went to medical school."

"Squeeze my hand," Werner said.

The spastic fingers trembled and partially closed. It was not purposeful grasping in any normal sense, but what if Bed Five's tremors were *intention* tremors, meaning they accompanied purposeful movement and prevented Bed Five from simply grasping and holding the hand?

"Relax, would you?" Stella said. "Another hired neurologist came in right after that and said the guy's cerebral cortex was tofu, and the tremors were patterns of disturbance caused by neurological deficits."

"I want both those reports," Werner said.

"You can't have them," Stella said. "They were done by hired medical experts. They said they were making reports to their lawyers, so they could testify at the upcoming hearing."

"Our lawyers will get them," Werner said. "I'll review them then."

"At any rate," Stella said, "no Slow Code for this boy. Too many lawyers are reading that chart."

Full Code status meant that when the patient stopped breathing, or his heart stopped beating, everything had to be done to save him. The patient was *coded*. "To code" was a transitive verb meaning to assault at the exact moment of death. It usually entailed a full-scale production on the order of a trained assault team securing a bridgehead, except a Full Code Blue cost more than a bridgehead. Medical drama, advanced technology, wonder drugs, the best young minds trained at the best institutions. It was so exciting, for the interns anyway.

Nobody ever survived a Full Code and made it out of the hospital, but that did not seem to matter. The patient was dying anyway, the reasoning went; why not at least try to resuscitate? Relentless medical logic in the face of eternity. The physicians stubbornly clung to the notion that death was the worst thing that could happen to someone, even after they had broken the ribs of eighty-five-year-olds and zapped them with paddle electrodes in Code Blues.

Chemical Codes were more humane. Those entailed no physical assault on the patient, except the insertion of IVs in order to give cardiac stimulants, bicarbonate, and vasopressors. No cracked ribs or electrocution.

Werner's favorite was the No Code status, which meant that nobody was allowed to do anything. It was not often he could secure a No Code order, especially from the likes of Buttface, because it was unprofitable: A dead patient could be billed only for services rendered before he or she was pronounced dead. A Code Blue was one way of delivering a maximum amount of services in the shortest possible time, resulting in a scrupulously itemized charge for a rescue attempt. After that, the physician stepped back and declared the patient dead and unbillable. At that point, the funeral home took over the billing process.

No Codes were also hard to come by, because nobody wanted to stand around with hands in pockets when Death was afoot. The impulse was to do something, anything at all, preferably something medical. Then there was Family, and there was guilt. Who among us could agree to let our loved ones succumb to death without putting up a fight? Even a senseless, expensive assault was better than nothing.

Then there were lawsuits. It was not uncommon for Family to agree to a No Code Status only to be consumed by guilt after the patient died, whereupon they got on the phone to a good lawyer, who sued the hospital and the doctors for not trying to save the patient.

The last category was the Slow Code, which cannot be found in any medical textbook or manual of Medical Center procedures. A Slow Code meant that the patient's physician or Family, or both, insisted on making a helpless, aged, dead person a Full Code, but when the patient arrested, the nurses and the residents had trouble remembering the number they were supposed to call to inform the hospital operator of the Code Blue. Was it "0" for operator? Was it "S" for switchboard? Was it 911? Was it an outside call? "Do we have to dial nine first?" Bed Seven was up for a Slow Code, but only if the Hippoblimp was not on the Unit when he put in his bid.

Werner snagged one of a dozen drug company ball-point pens out of his lab coat and clicked it in and out a few times. He jotted down meds and dosages, as Stella rattled them off to him. He went to the computer console and stuck his head back into Bed Seven's lab work, giving the ball-point pen a good clicking over, flicking the point in and out so fast that the individual clicks slurred into a continuous buzz of high-frequency ball-point pen clicking, a sound almost resonant and expressive, like the sound of Werner's nerves firing, a kazoo of ball-point pen clicks, humming a dirge called the "Death of Bed Seven." Werner flip-flopped his way through the pages of Bed Seven's chart, and the ball-point pen clicking grew steadily faster. Poindexter maintained that if you could plot the frequency of the clicks on one leg of an X/Y axis and Werner's cranial pressure on the other, the graph would show a direct relationship between the two, and from there you could practically use it as a diagnostic tool if you included the inverse relationship between Werner's cranial pressure and the status of any given patient in the ICU, meaning that when a patient started to bottom out, Werner blew his top.

Stella stuck her head into Bed Four and hissed at Werner, motioning for him to follow her into the pod.

"This is the new one we got on evenings," Stella said. "She's a subdural bleed. Her CO_2 is 50, and her cranial pressure is 120."

"Age?" Werner said.

"Eighty," Stella said. "A top-of-the-line Cabbage Patcher."

"Is she responding?" Werner asked.

"Oh, sure," Stella said. "Come on in."

The new Bed Four was in reverse Trendelenburg (forty-five-degree angle with the head elevated to reduce cranial pressure). Her head was heavily bandaged, with a pressure monitor sticking out of her skull, looking like a meat thermometer stuck in a Christmas ham.

Stella grabbed a couple of tissues and wiped the drool from the patient's chin. She checked the IV for input and the Uro-meter for output.

"The doctor is here to see you," Stella said, in the singsong reserved for children and patients. "This is Dr. Wienerschnitzel von Ernst. He's your doctor whenever Dr. Butz isn't here. He's the doctor in charge of the Intensive Scare Unit."

"Pizza," said Bed Four, lurching somewhat with the effort of enunciation.

"Pizza?" Werner repeated.

"Wait," Stella said. "It gets better."

Werner and Stella stood on either side of the bed. Werner absentmindedly checked the woman's color.

"Tell Dr. Wienerschnitzel who you say your prayers to every night," Stella said.

"Pizza," said Bed Four, a clonic spasm rippling through her left leg.

"OK," Stella said. "Never mind the prayers. What's your favorite thing to eat on Saturday nights?"

"Jesus," Bed Four replied, punctuating her response with a rattle of the bed rails.

"Shall I perform cranial checks, Dr. Ernst?" Stella asked.

"Proceed, Nurse Stanley," Werner commanded, grabbing the nearest clipboard to record the results.

"Can you tell us where you are?"

"Jesus," Bed Four said.

"OK, can you tell us what day it is?"

"Pizza," said Bed Four.

"Now," Stella said, straightening the pull sheet and checking the restraints, "who is the President of the United States?"

"Jesus," Bed Four said, shaking her bandaged skull and tugging on the restraints, "Jesus."

Stella's Socratic method was interrupted by a flurry of activity and cries for help from Bed Three, where the obese eighty-three-year-old colonoscopy had hopped the bed rails and had ripped out all her tubes and catheters. Poindexter was propping her up on a chair in a puddle of shit, blood, piss, and IV solutions. Werner was amazed at the devastation the woman had accomplished in thirty seconds.

Twenty minutes later, the Death Lab was a madhouse of chimes, alarms, warning buzzers, flashing lights, video displays, and personnel in surgical scrubs bouncing from one cubicle to the next, cussing under their breaths when their paths crossed in the middle of the ICU. Poindexter and Marie Something were in Bed Eight, working on the cerebral aneurysm. A team of respiratory therapists ran in and out of Bed Six, trying to find a ventilator capable of inflating Orca's lungs. Bed Seven's monitor showed a string of some nasty-looking ventricular escape beats. The Hippoblimp was in Bed Three, hollering something about somebody's blood sugar. . . .

The nurse with square glasses and freckled flab appeared at Werner's elbow.

"We have a patient in Bed One with severe pulmonary hypertension who looks like she's headed for complete heart block. She's unresponsive. Her blood pressure is 70 with the Doppler. Her arterial blood gases are PO_2 55, PCO_2 79, pH 7.31. She had forty of Lasix an hour ago, and we've got an Isuprel drip running at 5 micrograms per minute. They're getting wedge pressures of 30 on her. Her serum potassium is 6, and her lungs are sounding very wet. There's a stat chest X ray from evenings and a lot of blood work."

Werner scanned Dr. Butz's admission scribbles, just to be sure there was nothing of any medical importance. He did find one valuable insight scrawled diagonally across three lines in the Physician's Notes: "Patient seems very sick and time at this ill."

Nice work, Buttface.

"Creatinine is at 3, blood urea nitrogen is at 50," the nurse continued, "her cardiac output is 2.1."

He went in to have a look for himself, not liking what he saw in Bed One: a chubby young naked female tied down in bed. Belly mottled pink and blue. Some wacky variation on the theme of tachycardia on the monitor overhead. Outrageous wave forms for a pulmonary artery pressure. A forest of IV pumps on poles, huddled around the bed like grieving relatives. The usual tape and gag affair held the endotracheal tube into her throat. The pressure gauge on the ventilator spun three quarters of the way around the dial every time it delivered a breath.

"Things aren't too goddamn whippy in here, Dr. Wienerschnitzel," Stella said, using a large bulb syringe to suck brown fluid out of the patient's nasogastric tube. "I was wondering when you'd show up. Her blood pressure is seventy over squat and falling, which wouldn't be too bad, except that her pulmonary pressures are rising, like they wanna burst."

"Primary pulmonary hypertension," Werner said.

"What's that?" Marie Something asked.

"Well," Werner explained, "It means the blood vessels in this woman's lungs are in a constant state of constriction. Pumping blood through them is like hooking your garden hose up to a drinking straw and turning it wide open. The blood backs up in the heart, making the heart work itself to death, and everything else goes wrong from there. 'Primary' simply means that it's not secondary to anything else, and nobody knows why it's happening. Meanwhile, on the other side of her heart, her blood pressure is too low. So that every time you give her a drug to lower the blood pressure in her lungs, it lowers the blood pressure everywhere else, too."

"What do we do?" Marie asked.

"A heart-lung transplant," Werner said. "But we have no donors, and the list of people waiting for donors is a long one indeed. Now, if you promise to keep it very hush-hush, we can tiptoe back into the coffee room, gas the Hippoblimp with some nitrous oxide, bust her chest on the coffee table, remove her heart and lungs, insert them into the patient, move the patient down to the Eighth-Floor ICU, and send the Blimp down to the morgue for a good slabbing."

"In the meantime," Stella said, "we give her dopamine to keep her blood pressure up and nitroprusside to try to get her pulmonary artery pressures down, which is like pouring gasoline and water on an Alaskan house fire, in hopes that the water will put out the house fire and the gasoline will keep the fireplace going."

Werner went back out to the console and into Bed One's chart.

"Shit," he muttered, feeling the sting of sweat leaving the glands in his armpits. "Where's the first set of blood gases they drew on her this afternoon? Where's her admitting lab work? Where's the fucking hemoglobin they were supposed to draw on her this afternoon?"

Nobody answered his questions; they were all in pods, tending machines. He wrote, paused for a blizzard of ball-point pen clicking, wrote, clicked, wrote.

"How in the hell do they expect me to practice medicine without any fucking lab results?"

Poindexter emerged from Bed Eight, trailing a ribbon of graph paper. All knurly knees and knotted elbows, he looked like Ichabod Crane wearing surgical scrubs. He tapped on Werner's shoulder, ignoring the Do Not Disturb sign that some practical joker had Scotch-taped to the back of Dr. Ernst's lab coat.

"Wiener," Poindexter said, "I know you're very busy with Bed One, but Bed Eight's blood pressure is fifty with the Doppler and the balloon pump is already going every beat."

Werner gave the pen another good clicking.

"Say, Poin, where do we get these pens anyway? Don't they come from the lab?"

"Yeah," Poindexter said. "Why?"

"Will you see if you can get me another one? This one's wearing out. I like a nice, responsive click when I hit the button. After a couple weeks or so the springs lose some of their tension, or whatever."

"I'll get right on it, Dr. Wiener."

At 4:00 A.M., Werner managed to sneak off to the residents' on call room for a nap. He fell into a deep sleep for three minutes, then woke to piercing screams. He was trapped in the lower bunk in the dimness of the on call room. Dark, sudden shadows beat him with their wings. Bats with human faces screeched and swarmed around his head, their white fangs going for his eyes. He swatted at them and yelped, waving his arms and trying to drive them away, until he realized the flock of winged demons was only his beeper screeching. It was the battery-operated electronic scavenger that hung out on his belt, sucking his blood night and day, shrieking at him: "Code Blue, Ninth-Floor ICU. Code Blue, Ninth-Floor ICU. Code Blue, Ninth-Floor ICU."

Werner swung his legs over to the floor and tried to get his bearings from the red eye of the beeper recharging unit glowing through darkness from the table in the corner. Then he made out the band of light shining under the door; from there he found the doorknob, and he was on his way.

The fluorescent lights blinded him in the hallway. *This better be important,* he thought. *This better be a patient, under seventy-two. If the patient is over seventy-two,* he thought, then Werner was going to hoof it down to Simon's twenty-four-hour Pawn and EZ-Loan Shop, buy a .357 magnum, and go up to the ICU in a frenzy of bloodlust. First, he would drill the Hippoblimp in the kneecaps; then he would empty a clip into anybody over seventy-two. He would give everybody in kidney failure lots of water to drink, and he would take all the chronic lungers off the ventilators and give them their cigarettes. Then, gun in hand, he would go from cubicle to cubicle—Werner, the Johnny Apple-seed of Death—asking the patients if they would prefer to die now or hang out in the ICU for three months first. Silence or the inability to answer would be interpreted as a request for execution.

In Greek mythology, the destinies of men were controlled by three old women called the Fates, daughters of the god of Night, who spun the thread of life and arbitrarily selected the birth and death of every person. They were Clotho, who held the distaff containing the flax or wool; Lachesis, who spun the thread of life and measured it out; and Atropos, who cut the thread with a pair of scissors when life was ended. They were called cruel because they disregarded each and every plea and wish. Even Zeus himself was subject to their decisions.

"What do you say, girls," Lachesis said, "shall we cut it?"

"Naw," said Clotho, feeding flax to her sister. "Let it go on a little longer and see if anything funny happens."

The Fates may have told Zeus what to do in Greece, but Werner called the shots in Nine ICU.

The automatic doors opened, and Werner strode into the Death Lab, filling his mighty lungs with the odor. He was the knight coolly undertaking another perilous journey through the dark horrors of the ICU, where nothing lit his way but the beacon of reason shining forth from his formidable intellect. His path was soaked in blood and gore, his bones weary, his brain fatigued.

Nine ICU had been invaded by the Code Blue Team, which was staffed by foreign nurses who ardently believed that the death of an octogenarian was a medical emergency. The place was a madhouse of bickering incompetence. Conniption fits. Teams of personnel in white raced down the hallway with carts and machines in tow.

The operator came over the intercom and announced the Code again.

"Where is it?" Werner asked.

"Bed Seven! He's in V-fib!"

Nurses and technicians converged on Bed Seven's pod, pulling monitors and equipment on wheels behind them. A dozen people with carts and machines surrounded the patient—an old man, skinny as a starving child, with sutures and tubes sticking in him every which way and an oozing seam of staples, wires, and black stitches running from his belly clear up to his throat.

Out came the stainless steel instruments, the needles, the scopes, the tubes, and paddle electrodes.

"Where's the resident?" shouted a rookie wombat on the Code Blue Team. "I tried to seal the cuff on his ET tube and it ruptured. The tube's out. He's not getting any oxygen!"

"Yeah," Werner said with a scowl, "and I'm not getting any sleep. Relax already, huh?"

Werner's hair was a slanted mass of matted curls; his eyes were bloodshot and asquint with sleep. He tied up the bottoms of his surgical scrubs and strolled into Bed Seven.

"Pour yourself a drink, if you have to," Werner said, "but relax. Is the O_2 hooked up to the bag?"

Someone at the head of the bed covered Bed Seven's bony face with a mask and black rubber bag, which a nurse squeezed, forcing pure oxygen into Bed Seven's windpipe.

A burly nurse from another ICU climbed on top of a stool and bore down on Bed Seven's chest with the meat of his fists, pumping on his stapled and sutured sternum.

"Whoa, Hoss," Werner told him, touching the man's arm. "Ease up, would ya? Hear that cracking sound? That's the xiphoid process breaking away from the gladiolus."

"Hey," the man said, "they busted his chest two days ago. You're going to hear bones crack no matter what."

"Right," Werner said sharply. "Just do what I tell you, OK?"

An older woman in surgical scrubs and a paper hairnet walked into the cubicle with a black bag and a collection of plastic pouches containing ET tubes.

"Is that Anesthesia?" Werner asked, without taking his eyes off the cardiac monitor.

"No," the nurse anesthetist said, coming up behind him, "it's Madonna. I'm here to sing a few songs for you."

"Let's get the tube back in him," Werner said with a laugh.

The nurse anesthetist moved to the head of the bed and cranked Bed Seven's head back, until his Adam's apple stuck up, his neck as skinny as a chicken's gullet.

"OK, cowboy," she said, sticking a metal scope with a handle on it down the patient's throat. "You just hold still for a sec." She followed the scope with a long plastic tube, as big around as a good-size middle finger.

"Piss on it"—she scowled—"he's biting down."

"Hey," she said, bowing over the patient's ear, "don't bite on that tube, understand?"

"Bang him with ten milligrams of Anectine," Werner said. "That'll knock out voluntary muscle control long enough to get the tube in. Let's get another line in, and some blood gases."

Needles went in at both arms, needles in his neck, more chest compressions. A needle with a glass syringe went in at his groin and pumped up with black blood.

"The Anectine is in."

"I've got a line."

The nurse anesthetist in the paper hairnet pried Bed Seven's jaws open with the metal scope and reinserted the tube.

"That should do it," she said. "Somebody listen for breath sounds."

The mask came off the black bag. The black bag was attached to the tube. Bed Seven's chest rose and fell with each squeeze of the bag.

A nurse grabbed two electric metal disks with handles and telephone cords attached to them. "How much?" she asked, looking up at Werner.

"Two hundred," Werner said, staring intently at the green-grid cardiac monitor. "Let's get this guy hooked up to a monitor that will give us some strips, for posterity's sake."

A technician placed two gel patches on Bed Seven's torso, one for each paddle electrode, to keep the paddles from scorching the skin.

"Everybody back!" the nurse shouted, touching the paddle electrodes to the gel patches on the patient's chest.

Bed Seven jerked like a pithed frog. They all paused and stared into the various computer screens to study the results of their handiwork. They apparently found the screen images deficient in some way, because the nurse made ready with the paddle electrodes again.

"Hold compressions," Werner said, touching the burly oaf's forearm and watching the monitor. "What's that? More coarse fib? OK, zap him again."

"Everybody back!" the nurse with the disks yelled again, apparently wanting none of whatever she was giving the patient. Skinny, old Bed Seven convulsed with electric shock.

"All right," Werner said, studying the green fluorescent blip zigzagging across the monitor, "let's see what we've got now. Hold compressions. Fucking spaghetti is what we've got. Continue compressions. OK, let's try another amp of bicarb, some more epinephrine, and maybe some atropine. Oh, yeah, and the corned beef on rye. Isn't this the gentleman who ordered the corned beef on rye with mayo and hot mustard?"

The cubicle erupted in laughter.

"Bicarb's in," said a nurse.

"Epi's in," someone else said.

"Did he barf before they got the tube in?" the nurse at the head of the bed asked.

"I don't know," one of the technicians said. "Why?"

"Because he's gonna now. Suction!"

Two or three personnel rolled Bed Seven onto his side, and Bed Seven vomited black tar around the plastic tube.

"Looks like old blood to me," Werner said, "unless you guys have been packing him with axle grease."

Werner lifted the sheet, exposing Bed Seven's frail torso, stapled and sutured and sprouting tubes.

"What do we have here? Sumps to his bowels?" Werner asked, lifting a pair of tubes stitched into Bed Seven's stomach. "OK,

Sheldon cannulas, all right. An arterial line. A Hickman catheter. Two chest tubes."

"Total body failure," someone said. "TBF."

"How old is he?" someone else asked.

"Seventy-nine."

After fifteen or twenty more minutes of beating, shocking, pounding, and needle sticks, of personnel running in and out of the room with X-ray machines and blood samples, of more good Code Blue jokes and bizarre wave forms on the monitors, things slowed down a bit, and Bed Seven's earlobes went from blue, to purple, to a rich mauve, to a nightshade as dark and surreal as the blue-smoking darkness of Lawrence's *Bavarian Gentians.*

A nurse at the central console answered the telephone, chin pinning the receiver to her collarbone while she rapidly spindled several yards of EKG strips.

"I have some lab results," she hollered, "PO_2 is 12, CO_2 is 94, pH is 7.03. Potassium is 7, sodium is . . ."

The numbers were so terrible that everyone laughed.

Werner held his hand out and said, "May I have a cardiac needle, please?"

A nurse prepared a syringe with a wicked nine-inch needle, gleaming in the light of the high-intensity lamps, sinister as the stinger of a stainless steel devil fish—the thing bobbing with the weight of itself, as she handed it to Werner.

Werner held it aloft and squirted a few drops into the air. Then he inserted the needle just below the rib cage and headed north by northwest for the heart. A trickle of dark blood appeared at the site.

"If this doesn't work," Werner said, "we'll call it."

It did not work, and Werner called the Code.

A nurse at the console called Harold in the morgue.

Laughter and the sound of departing machine carts. Somebody had tuned in all-star wrestling on Bed Seven's TV. More Code Blue jokes. The funniest kind.

A wombat touched Werner's elbow and told him Bed Seven's Family was waiting for him in the Visitors' Lounge.

"Who is it?" Werner asked.

"His wife," said the wombat. "His son went home, but he's on his way back in. The wife's waiting in Conference Room B."

Werner sauntered down the hallway, his brain bobbing in the

twilight blur of exhaustion, trying to work up some sympathy for Bed Seven's Family, trying to remember what regular people feel like when they get all distraught over losing a loved one. He could not remember. Death had become as normal as raking up the leaves and turning them under the compost heap every year in the fall. Why does everybody get so goddamned upset about it? Do they want to take something like Bed Seven home with them and have it lie around the house for years?

He rounded the corner and made his way purposefully through the dazed and exhausted families in the lobby, heading for Conference Room B. He opened the door and found an old woman alone, bent and kneeling on the bare tile floor, a rosary wrapped around her hands.

Eighties, Werner thought to himself. *Pitting edema of the ankles, obese, cataracts, hearing aid, TED support hose, corrective shoes, spider capillary explosions of the face, petechiae, possible goiter, iodine deficiency . . .*

"Please tell me you saved him," she begged, taking Werner's hand. "Tell me I'm not alone." She bit her hand, soaking it with tears. "Please, Doctor. Tell me I'm not alone."

Possible Bell's palsy, Werner thought, noting the sag of her left jaw, *maybe early Parkinson's.*

"Your husband has passed away," Werner told her. "There was nothing we could do." He touched her shoulder, feeling suddenly normal, as if he could actually sit down and cry with her, if he really put his mind to it.

She squeezed her hands into her face and broke down into a mound of flab and old bones on the floor. Werner lifted her up and into a hard-backed chair.

"Please, please, go back and save him, won't you?" she said, taking his hand and pressing it to her wet cheek. "You'll save my husband, won't you?"

"We did everything we could," Werner said softly. "A nurse will be with you in just a moment."

"Don't let God take him away from me. Don't let Him leave me alone."

After that, Werner staggered back onto the Unit to chart the details of the Code.

"The wife's pretty upset, huh?" Stella asked.

"You think she's upset now?" Werner said. "Wait until she gets the bill."

"You look like hell," Stella said. "Why don't you take a nap first and chart later?"

"Why sleep?" Werner grumbled. "It only makes you think."

"I'm serious," Stella said. "You look terrible. You're in no shape to be taking care of patients."

"On the contrary," Werner said. "It's precisely because I'm in such a state that I provide such excellent care! You probably subscribe to the notion that a physician who hasn't slept for two days is in no state to deliver quality health care. Ha! Do you think that the medical profession—one of the most powerful lobbies in the country—would sanction such treatment of its interns and residents if it did not make them better physicians? The medical profession *abhors* any behavior that does not contribute to the expertise of physicians. Think about it. It's so simple. Instead of hiring three doctors who will each work eight hours a day, hire one doctor and have him or her work twenty-four hours a day! Not only will revenue be generated, but for the last sixteen hours of a sleepless shift, such doctors will be *better* doctors, because they'll be able to think about only one thing: medicine!

"They keep us up for forty-eight hours until we go into hypnagogic stupor from lack of sleep and overwork. The stupor in turn results in the absence of all counterproductive amedical thoughts. If they keep you up every other night for, say, two or three years, the effects on long-term memory are even more conducive to medical training, because the physician will soon forget all the useless nonmedical knowledge that cluttered up his brain before he went to medical school."

"Go home," Stella said. "Go home and go to sleep before it's too late."

Werner clutched his screeching beeper, turning down the volume and obeying the summons to the Eighth-Floor ICU.

"I must go and exercise my art in accordance with the Hippocratic oath, with uprightness and honor, solely for the good of my patients."

"Yeah," she said, "only you forgot the part about first doing no harm."

Chapter

13

At daybreak, Werner started charting Bed Seven's failed Code. Later, Harold showed up with the false-bottomed gurney.

"I'm here," Harold said to Stella, taking the vinyl cover off the gurney and opening the stainless steel compartment. "Where's the patient without a temperature?"

"Bed Seven," Stella said.

"Suffer and die, suffer and die," Harold complained. "Can't anybody do something different for a change? Remember that guy a few years back who sat up and pulled out his ET tube after the doctor had already filled out the death certificate? Now that was different."

Stella finished printing the body tags and handed them to Harold.

"When it's your turn, Harold, you be sure to do something different for us," she said. "If you really want to make a name for yourself, wait three days after they fill out your death certificate, then do something."

Harold spit the first of his sunrise chew into the pocket-mounted Styrofoam cup.

"What was he in for?" Harold asked with a nod toward Bed Seven.

"Total body failure," Werner said, without looking up from his paper work. "TBF."

"How do you get that?" Harold asked.

"As soon as we clean up Bed Seven's mess," Stella said, "we'll put you in there and show you."

"Oh, no," Harold said. "No, thank you, ma'am. I've never been sick a day in my life. No suffering and dying for me just yet."

"Don't worry about never being sick," Werner said. "It takes only one time. It's not the sick that gets you; it's the not getting well. And dying never takes more than a day; it's the suffering part that varies."

Harold yanked Bed Seven's lines and tubes and threw them into garbage bags. He pulled the ET tube and closed the jaw. The wedding ring went into a yellow envelope. He pressed the eyelids down and aligned the body.

Werner looked through the pod window at the naked purple corpse and was momentarily jealous of Bed Seven's eternal rest. He skimmed back through the history and physical. Four months ago, Bed Seven and his wife owned the house free and clear. He came into the Med Center complaining of abdominal pain and of difficulty urinating. Now the Med Center owned his house, and he was leaving with his toe tagged.

Werner stared again through Bed Seven's window and wondered whether suicide would be worth the sleep he could get out of it. *Maybe the only difference between sleep and death,* he thought, *is that death kills you.* Maybe at some point Werner would become so exhausted that madness would climb up from his subconscious, seize him, and throw him in front of a bus or hurl him off a cliff: "I said we need sleep, understand?" Maybe this was instant karma. As punishment for not letting patients die, God would not let Werner sleep.

Werner stared at Bed Five's rhythm. Werner and Bed Five were beginning their regular workdays over again. Neither of them had gotten any sleep.

Without deciding to do the deed, Werner thought about how it could be done. The respiratory therapists checked the ventilators every hour, on the hour. Bed Five had a dopamine drip—medication by IV that constricted all the blood vessels in his body and artificially kept his blood pressure up. Without dopamine, Bed Five would quickly go into shock and cardiac arrest. Patients on dopamine had their blood pressure checked every half hour, on the half hour.

Day shift would be the best time, with plenty of witnesses that nothing out of the ordinary had occurred. Immediately after an on-the-hour ventilator check and blood pressure check, Werner could sneak in and dial down Bed Five's dopamine to a trickle. He could also turn the ventilator's oxygen mix from 70 percent to room air, without affecting the volume of air being delivered by the ventilator and without triggering any alarms. Then he would simply wait twenty-five minutes. If Bed Five did not Code, Werner could slip back in, return the dopamine to normal levels for the half-hourly blood pressure check, and then cut him off again when the nurse left the pod. Even if the drop in blood pressure was detected on the half hour, it would be too late to do anything about it; Bed Five would be well on his way to shock. Considering Bed Five's condition, the first half hour would probably do the trick.

The how was easy. The why was troublesome. If he was going to help Bed Five along to the next life, why not do the same for Bed Four, or Bed Three? Pretty soon, he would be the Antidoctor, sneaking around and snuffing patients, waiting for a prime-time news team to burst in on him and do a news documentary. Dr. Death Poisons Patients. Mortician Physician Strikes Again.

Was it physiological? Bed Five's dismal physiology, or the effect Felicia had on the doctor's physiology? It could be an ethical conundrum. Allowing Bed Five to die was the ethical thing to do, but Werner was not the proper actor. He had already assumed a role in life that was inconsistent with what needed to be done for Bed Five and for Felicia. He was not unlike a lawyer who owed a legal duty to his unsavory client, even though his client's adversary was an esteemed clergyman.

He was too tired to concoct the theories to justify his decision. He was a physician; he could not kill his patient. A good night's sleep would supply the rationalizations. He would tell her no when she got back from lala land.

The commotion of the day shift gradually rose to a din around the console, and the ICU got crowded with real doctors, Pastoral Care staff, lab techs, respiratory therapists, nurses, Family, and residents. A wombat reached through a conference of three residents in surgical scrubs and handed Werner a phone.

"This is Dr. Ernst," Werner said, studying the new orders in Bed Five's chart.

"Ernst. Wilson," the phone said. "Can you come down here . . . now?"

"Sure," said Werner. "What's up?"

"Nothing," Wilson said tersely. "Just go to the mezzanine receptionist and ask her for directions to the Legal Department's conference room."

Werner took another cup of black coffee with him and rode to the mezzanine in an elevator filled with people who had slept the night before. They chatted merrily about major-league baseball and where they were going on vacation. Werner felt his brain swelling from fatigue and dully wondered if the tone of Wilson's voice meant that the new lawsuit for damages had been filed.

At the mezzanine reception desk, a dour woman with blue hair directed Werner down a skylit corridor to a set of double wooden doors. Werner chugged the last of his coffee and tossed the cup into a stylish wastebasket. He turned a latch handle on the door and walked into a conference room, where Wilson, Dr. Hofstader, and a lean fortyish gentleman in steel-rimmed glasses and a dark gray suit were examining documents at a table. Werner's pulse doubled at the sight of Hofstader. What was he—?

Wilson and the man in the gray suit stood up.

"Dr. Ernst, this is Mitchell Payne," Wilson said, "the hospital's outside counsel in the Potter case."

"Good morning, Dr. Ernst," Payne said, taking Werner's hand in his cool, dry grasp and holding it too long for Werner's liking.

Payne was a trim six feet with salt-and-pepper hair that had been clipped to a uniform quarter-inch burr. The steel rims framed green eyes, which fastened inquisitively on Werner's.

"Please have a seat, Dr. Ernst," Payne said, indicating a chair directly across the table from Hofstader.

Not the seating arrangement Werner would have chosen. His heart quickened again, and he regretted the extra dose of caffeine.

Dr. Hofstader smiled through tight lips without looking up from the documents he was perusing.

Payne sat at the head of the table, immediately to Werner's right, and opened a thick black binder with tabs. Werner could

read the names of physicians neatly typed on each tab: Butz, Hofstader, Ernst . . . Payne selected Werner's tab and opened the notebook.

"As Mr. Wilson has told you," Payne said, "I represent the
Medical Center in litigation that has been initiated by the Potter
family over the treatment of a patient named Joseph F. Potter. I
also represent you," Payne said, "under the terms of the joint
representation agreement you signed."

"Yes," Werner said.

"But as the agreement indicates, my first loyalty must always be
to the Medical Center. If your interests at any time become adverse
to those of the Medical Center, we will insist that you obtain
separate counsel. And indeed, you are free to obtain separate counsel at any time, if you wish."

"I understand," Werner said, slowly realizing that this was going to be a long meeting and wondering if he had the stamina or
the nerves for it after the witches' Sabbath of his night on call.

"Mr. Wilson tells me the patient is under your care and under
the care of Dr. Butz, among others, in the Medical Center's Ninth-
Floor Intensive Care Unit, am I correct?"

"Correct," Werner said.

Payne spoke in crisp, complete sentences. Werner had the dis-
tinct impression that the last time the attorney had had a stray
thought or used an unnecessary word was probably well before he
had gone to law school. Werner could see the origin and insertion
of Payne's facial muscles, and the scalp rippled under the burr
haircut whenever he spoke.

The attorney glanced at Wilson and Hofstader and then faced
Werner over the binder, clasping his fingers loosely.

"As Mr. Wilson has probably already explained to you," Payne
began, "this case is turning into a potentially dangerous piece of
litigation for several reasons. Number one, it could easily become
either a major medical malpractice case or, more troublesome,
what is coming to be called a wrongful treatment case, in which
the hospital is sued for delivering allegedly unwanted medical
treatment to a patient in a persistent vegetative state. Number two,
the Supreme Court's decision in *Cruzan* versus *Missouri* has made
this issue very hot, and the newspapers in town would jump at the
chance to follow one of these cases at the local level. It could turn
into a media circus, with the Medical Center and the doctors

portrayed as heartless bureaucrats or, worse, as shameless profiteers making off with thousands of dollars a day for medical care that nobody wants. I've known Sheldon Hatchett a long time," Payne said, "and he will conduct the better part of his trial on the six o'clock news, not in the courtroom."

Payne's speech had the cadence of a man talking into a Dictaphone. He was apparently accustomed to having everything he said taken down verbatim. An appellate court reviewing the transcripts of Payne's and his wife's pillow talk would doubtless find flawless syntax and a thorough enunciation of the attorney's position. Werner decided the burr cut gave Payne the ascetic look of a monk, or maybe a warrior monk, whose needs in life were simple and few.

"I only tell you this," Payne said, leaning closer to Werner and staring straight into his eyes through the spotless lenses and the steel rims, "because it is essential for your own welfare and for the Medical Center's welfare that you understand the importance of this case."

"I do," Werner said, without looking away. He was glad that his parched, caffeine-astringent throat had not produced a cracked voice.

"I also tell you this," Payne continued, "because something quite strange has occurred in this case, which has puzzled me."

Payne paused and peered so closely into Werner's eyes that Werner could see his pupillary reflex.

"I've discussed my concerns with Mr. Wilson and with your superior, Dr. Hofstader," he said, nodding his head in Hofstader's direction without taking his eyes off Werner.

Werner glanced at Hofstader; the Chief of Internal Medicine stared back without expression.

"We've received a subpoena from the other side ordering you to appear and testify at the preliminary injunction hearing," Payne said.

Werner felt heat break out under his collar, surge up through his carotid arteries, and explode in his cheeks and ears. A wicked gremlin hiding in his thorax picked up a rubber hammer and started pounding on the left side of his rib cage, setting up a steady thumping that Werner was sure could be heard all around the table. The modern condition—a fight-or-flight response, with no one to attack and nowhere to run.

"That's not a problem," Werner quickly protested, unable to hide his agitation. "I've told them, as I told you," Werner said, looking to Wilson for support, "that I will not testify for them in court. They know that," Werner said again. "I've specifically told them that."

Payne gave a short, mirthless laugh and glanced at Wilson, who was holding his head in his hand.

"There's no requirement in the Rules of Civil Procedure that you must consent before you can be subpoenaed to testify," Payne said. "You can be subpoenaed to a hearing and be compelled to testify whether you like it or not. Not many witnesses would testify if they didn't have to."

Payne handed Werner a piece of paper with seals stamped on it and the same heading Werner had seen on the documents Wilson had given him. Werner read a short paragraph in the body of the document. "Comes now plaintiff, for herself and for her father, Joseph F. Potter, and requests defendant, Peter Werner Ernst, M.D., to appear and give testimony at the hearing of the above-captioned case on the 21st day of August of this year at 9:00 A.M. or as soon thereafter as plaintiff may be heard."

In the lower-left-hand corner the words "So Ordered" were typed, and next to it was an illegible signature.

"I don't understand," Werner said. "You mean they can make me testify even if I don't want to, and even if I will testify against them?"

"That's what troubles us," Payne said, studying Werner through the steel rims. "We don't believe Hatchett would subpoena you unless he had some reason to think that your testimony would help his case."

Payne paused, and Werner suddenly realized that Payne's pauses were for dramatic effect only, that Payne already knew exactly what he wanted to say and exactly how to climb inside Werner's head and have a look around.

Payne glanced at Hofstader and Wilson again, drawing them into collective scrutiny of the witness. "We'd like you to take a few moments and see if you can think of any reason, absolutely *any* reason, that Hatchett would want to call you as a witness in this case."

Werner glanced once at Hofstader and imagined for a split second the look that would appear on Hofstader's face if he knew that last week Bed Five's daughter had spent the night at Werner's apartment.

"Nothing comes to mind," Werner said.

Payne smiled. He leaned back in his chair.

"Have you been involved in litigation before, Dr. Ernst?"

"No," Werner said, his voice cracking.

"Well," Payne said, "let me explain a few things to you." He held up the court documents that Wilson had shown Werner several days before. "This is a petition for injunctive relief. We are in a court of equity. Things move very quickly in equity. Even if we obtain a continuance of this action, we could easily be at a hearing within fourteen days."

Werner was looking for something he could say from time to time, something inconspicuous that would show that he was not afraid to talk and that he had nothing to hide. He settled on "I understand." It was short and unobtrusive, and it indicated he was obediently listening.

"You are now going to be a witness," Payne said. "Our only question is for whom. Either you will be our witness, or you will be plaintiff's witness."

"I'm not cooperating with them," Werner protested. "My testimony is going to be that the gastrostomy is indicated and that we can't rule out a possible recovery until we see what effect proper nutrition has on the patient."

Werner glanced at Hofstader in search of at least a nod of approval. Hofstader was reading documents.

"In any event," Payne said, ignoring Werner's protestation, "we meet with all witnesses early in the litigation, and we begin preparing our witnesses to testify for the Medical Center. This is the beginning of a long process called trial preparation, but the ultimate goal is to get at the truth. After we know the truth, then we teach the witness to articulate the truth to advantage."

"I understand," Werner said.

"Good," Payne said. "You must understand that before we prepare the case and before we prepare the witnesses, we must know the truth. It is absolutely essential to the defense of the Medical Center and to the defense of all the named parties, including yourself, that we know the truth. Otherwise we can't make accurate decisions about how to conduct the case, whether to settle it, whether to countersue, whom to call as witnesses, et cetera."

"I understand," Werner said, noticing that his field of vision was now expanding and contracting in sync with his pulse. Maybe he was having grayout, a transient dimming or haziness of vision resulting from temporary impairment of cerebral circulation.

"Let's pretend for a moment that you are aware of certain facts that might reflect poorly on you or the Medical Center if you were called to testify. You might be reluctant to disclose those facts because you fear reprisal, either from the law or from your superiors at the Medical Center. That's why I invited Dr. Hofstader to this meeting. You must understand that in any litigation conducted by competent attorneys the truth will come out; it's only a matter of when. You must also understand that it is far better for both you and the Medical Center if the truth comes out sooner rather than later. If we uncover bad facts early in the case, we can marshal evidence to defuse those bad facts; we can explain them; we can present the other side of the story; if we must, we can settle the case, because we do not want those bad facts to come out in the courtroom. But we can't ameliorate bad facts unless we know about them."

"I understand," Werner said.

"Now, I'm sure Dr. Hofstader, Mr. Wilson, and you would probably all agree that I have done too much talking. We asked you down here, so we could hear what you have to say. Have you, perhaps, thought of anything else that might prompt Ms. Potter's attorney to call you as her witness?"

Payne pulled a clean notepad from the binder and readied his fountain pen.

Werner looked around the room as if he were sincerely trying to think of something. "I . . . just don't know what it could be. I've spoken several times to both family members, but I just can't think of anything I said that would help her in this case."

"She would be attempting to prove that the patient is in a persistent vegetative state and that further medical treatment would be useless," Payne coaxed. "And you can't think of anything you said to her that might help her prove that proposition?"

In his mind's eye, Werner saw her placing her hand on his thigh: "Just tell me why I'm doing the right thing," she had said, "for my own peace of mind so I can sleep at night."

"I can't think of anything," Werner said.

"I understand," Payne said with a faint smile.

Werner realized that Payne was mocking him. Payne had said, "I understand," only because he knew that Werner was nervously repeating the same thing.

Payne reached up and slowly and methodically scratched his earlobe, not because it itched, but because there was a dial in the earlobe that intensified the X-ray vision of his green eyes.

"Maybe I should point out something else," Payne said, adjusting the steel rims for more intense scrutiny of the victim. "Let's suppose that you may have said something that will support their case in court, but you have . . . forgotten," Payne said, affecting another deliberative pause. "You said something to her, but now you can't remember it," Payne repeated. "The Ronald Reagan defense. The I-think-I-don't-remember defense. Let's pretend that is the case."

Werner shrugged. "If I can't remember, then I wouldn't know—"

"Exactly," Payne said, "and the rules of hearsay might prohibit other witnesses from testifying about your forgotten statements."

Werner felt a sudden wave of relief well up inside him. Of course! She couldn't testify about anything he supposedly said. That would be hearsay.

"But there is an exception to the hearsay rule," Payne continued, relentlessly stripping every shred of hope from Werner's grasp. "You have been individually sued in this case. That means you are what we call a party. The statements of a party are considered admissions against interest, which means that others can testify about those statements, and you can be questioned about those statements, even though you contend you don't remember them."

Werner had reached his limits. Within a few minutes he would lose consciousness, or vomit, and that would confirm Payne's suspicion that Werner was concealing information. Payne peered at him through the steel rims. Werner forced himself to stare back. The pores on Payne's face began to breathe, and his facial hair started growing. The tight muscles on the attorney's jawbones rippled and surged whenever he paused to appraise Werner's responses. The muscles in the hands and face said: "These are the same muscles I used as a prosecutor when I sent professional liars to the gas chambers. Don't lie to me, or you will be making a big mistake."

"Like I said," Werner protested, "I can't remember anything."

"I understand," Payne said with another faint smile. "And I hope you will understand if, in the interest of being thorough, we just go through the conversations you had with the family members one by one. That way we can examine those conversations and be absolutely certain that there's nothing Hatchett could use against us at the hearing."

Two and a half hours later, Payne was still patiently asking Werner questions about his conversations, and Werner was still anxiously answering them. Wilson and Hofstader had gone. But Payne had gone on asking him crisp, probing questions. Werner had the impression that Payne was calmly waiting for him to have a nervous breakdown or a heart attack, so that a possibly unfavorable witness could be eliminated at the outset of the litigation.

Werner admitted to his conversations with Constance Potter but admitted to only two conversations with Felicia: one in Bed Five and one in the coffee room.

Each time Werner described a conversation with Felicia, Payne questioned him exhaustively about every detail. Then Payne asked, "Is there anything else about that conversation you remember that you haven't already told me? Was there anything else said by either you or Ms. Potter that you haven't already told me?"

Finally, Payne reviewed his notes, page by page. Then he fastened his green eyes on Werner and said, "We are nearing the end of our first preparation session. I think you will appreciate the importance of these sessions as we approach the hearing date, and as we get closer to the truth."

"I understand," Werner said wearily. He began wiping the sweaty palm of his right hand on his pants leg, because he knew he would have to shake Payne's hand again before this was all over.

"One other thing," Payne said, as if he could hear Werner's thoughts screaming, *No! What now?*

"I've stressed the importance of the truth, but I forgot to mention its most important attribute: The truth never changes. You said this was your first experience with litigation?"

"That's right," Werner said.

"I take it you have never testified before?"

"No," Werner said.

"Which means you've never been cross-examined." Payne

grinned and gave him a look that said, "I've been doing this for twenty-five years, and you've never even seen a courtroom."

"Cross-examination can be a very unpleasant experience, even for a witness who is telling the truth. Successfully telling lies is almost impossible," Payne said. "Lies change. The truth does not change. If the honest witness gets confused during questioning, he or she need only remember the truth and cling to it and give the same, consistent answers to every question, even questions for which the witness is unprepared. If the witness is not telling the truth, his or her story will change. A good lawyer will easily detect that change and will let the witness go on changing his story. Then the lawyer will confront the witness with each change and ask him to explain it. In his panic, the witness can't cling to the truth because he is lying under oath, which is a crime. More changes inevitably appear. Then, as you might imagine, things get worse. . . . It can be a humiliating experience."

"I understand," Werner said.

"The only other thing I forgot to mention is this: It appears that plaintiff intends to call you as a witness at the hearing. Under the procedural rules, you will be their witness, even though you are an employee of the Medical Center. That means Hatchett will ask you questions on direct examination," Payne said with a smile, "and I will be cross-examining you."

"I understand," Werner said, vividly imagining the green X-ray eyes bearing down on him in a courtroom. He wiped his hand again on his pants leg.

Payne gave him his card. "This card has my home phone number, my office phone number, and my car phone number. If you think of something you did not tell me, call me. Immediately."

"I will," Werner said.

"Let me thank you for your time and your patience," Payne said. "And let me thank you in advance for the time we must spend in further witness interviews to prepare for this important case."

"Certainly," Werner said.

"I will see what I can do on my end," Payne said. "I used to work with Hatchett in the circuit attorney's office, and maybe he'll give me some clues about why he wants to call you as a witness."

Payne rose and shook Werner's damp hand. Werner felt Payne's cool, dry hand linger again, as if the hand were collecting Werner's sweat, obtaining a sample for a polygraph examination.

"I'm sure you would be relieved if I could find out what Hatchett has in mind," Payne said, still clasping Werner's hand and watching him.

"Yes," Werner said, "I sure would."

"One way or another, we'll find out what's going on before the hearing," Payne said with a smile. "I've been doing this for twenty-five years now, and I've never been surprised in a courtroom. I know everything about my witnesses and about the case before the day of trial." The smile left Payne's face. "Accidents occur at opposing counsel's table, not at mine."

"I understand," Werner said.

Once he got out of the Legal Department's conference room, Werner went to the residents' on call room and stood in front of a fan in the bathroom. He leaned over a porcelain sink and looked into the mirror at his sleep-deprived pale face. His lips were blue. Sweat had seeped into his shirt in dark rings. He spotted an uneven patch of stubble under his chin, where he had missed shaving at six-thirty this morning, before going back to the Death Lab. He could see dark smudges spreading under the skin below his eyeballs. *I am dying,* he thought. *I am paying too high a price for the money I intend to get out of this profession.*

Vivid, sunlit hallucinations crowded with him into the elevator. At least ten or twelve other people were crammed with him into the hermetic space. They all silently competed for the same air and said nothing. He forgot all the science he knew and wanted only drunkenness and dreams.

Werner found a conference room with a phone and got an out line. He called Felicia's answering machine and left an urgent message, his name, and the hospital operator's number.

He was too tired to grasp the dimensions of his newborn legal problems. Maybe the subpoena was just another legal formality from her thorough attorney. Maybe he would not have to testify. Maybe if he did, nothing about their personal relationship would come out. Maybe he could lie his way through cross-examination. Payne was trying to take advantage of him. Wilson had doubtless told Payne that Werner had been on call all night, and Payne had seized the opportunity to try to crack him. After a good night's sleep, Werner thought, he could handle Payne.

He sagged into his seat at the console and rejoiced. He was back in the medical world.

"Family wants you in Bed Five," a wombat said.

Werner's heart surged, then sagged when he recalled she was in Los Angeles. It was Connie.

She was keeping Bed Five company; the patient's eyes were open in a coma vigil. She held his right hand and read aloud to him from a Bible: "Love from hatred man cannot tell; both appear equally vain, in that there is the same lot for all, for the just and the wicked, for the good and the bad, for the clean and the unclean, for him who offers sacrifice and him who does not. As it is for the good man, so it is for the sinner; as it is for him who swears rashly, so it is for him who fears an oath. Among all things that happen under the sun, this is the worst, that things turn out the same for all. Hence, the minds of men are filled with evil, and madness is in their hearts during life; and afterward they go to the dead."

She put the book aside and smiled grimly at Werner.

"You look very tired," she said. "You don't look well."

"Thank you," he said instinctively. *You never look well, but I don't rub it in.*

"I don't think you are happy," Connie said.

"I'm just tired," he said. "I was on call all night." *Eight hours of sleep will cure my problem,* he thought. *When I wake up tomorrow, I'll feel better; you will still be fat and crazy.*

She patted Bed Five's hand. "This is a very bad time for us, Doctor."

"I know," Werner said.

"We must be vigilant," Constance said. "All intentions and motives are suspect."

Werner's eyes went briefly to hers. Then he looked abruptly away. After his encounter with Payne, Werner was afraid even his looks could be used as evidence against him.

"Whose motives and intentions?" Werner asked, looking at Bed Five's white head on the pillow.

"Has she outsmarted you yet?" Connie asked.

Werner punched a button on a CO_2 monitor and recalibrated it, giving him a reason not to look at Connie.

"She thinks that my father's death will set her free," Constance said. "But her soul is smaller than her thoughts. She wants to kill him, but she can't drink up the sea. She can't wipe away the horizon with a sponge or unchain the earth from the sun. Once he's dead, she will feel the cold breath of empty space. She won't know which way is up. Her nights will be longer. She'll hear the gravediggers burying him and smell him decomposing. The games she will have to invent to escape her self-loathing, the festivals of self-deception."

Werner wondered if this was a psychotic break. He had seen patients after a break but had never actually seen one unravel right before his eyes.

"I am here to attend to the medical needs of this patient," Werner said, looking at her across the emaciated torso of Bed Five. "Did you have a question about the patient's care?"

"Will you wipe the blood off her, Dr. Ernst?" she asked. "When she wakes up at night with the cry of 'Murder!' ringing in her ears, will you tell her it isn't so?"

Werner left Bed Five and told Marie Something to call Pastoral Care and get a hand holder up to Nine ICU, stat. The last thing he needed was a conversation with Constance. Then her lawyer would subpoena him.

He spent the rest of the morning looking after a new patient, a seventy-five-year-old lunger in Bed Four. When he finished writing the orders on her, his beeper signaled an outside call.

He found a vacant conference room and called the operator. "Is my father OK?" she asked.

"Yeah, your father's OK," Werner said. "I'm the one who's dying now. Your lawyer sent the hospital a subpoena ordering me to testify at the hearing," Werner yelled. "I am in deep shit. You told me you guys didn't need my testimony, and I trusted you."

All the terror and panic of Payne's morning inquisition came back as rage.

"I was afraid this might happen," she said, sounding genuinely concerned. "My lawyer is going overboard. Just before I went out of town, I saw him again. He asked me about everything you had said, and before I could think about it, I told him the stuff you said about how it was the right thing, and that I should do it. He said he was going to subpoena you, just in case we needed your testimony. He said that everything you told me was evidence that could be used in court, and that I had a responsibility to my father to make sure the judge heard that evidence."

A cold mass formed under Werner's sternum and grew until he felt it crowding his heart and lungs. Cardiac tamponade.

"You can't let your lawyer bring our personal relationship into this," Werner said.

"That's exactly what I told him," she said. "He said I should be thinking about my father and not about you."

"You have to understand that a lawyer is just like an auto mechanic," Werner explained, keeping his voice steady and beyond the reach of terror and rage. "You tell him what to do, and if he won't do it, get another one."

"That's funny," she said. "My lawyer told me that doctors are just like auto mechanics, and that if I told you what to do and you wouldn't do it, I should just get another doctor."

"Your father is my patient," Werner said tersely. "He hasn't told me what to do yet."

"It's so weird," she said. "You guys sound exactly alike. My lawyer said that, until the court appoints some kind of guardian for my father, he is acting as the attorney for both me and my father. So he said he was going to issue the subpoena whether I wanted him to or not, because my father was his client, too, and he owed it to him to be sure you testified about what you really thought."

"You can't let him make me testify," Werner said, unsure whether to issue a desperate plea or a direct order. "You can't testify about us, and neither can I."

"You should be glad it was only a subpoena," she said in a strange tone. "My lawyer went absolutely nuts. He was telling me to sue you for trying to take advantage of me when I was so upset about my father being sick. He said if he told that story to a jury, he could get me a million bucks and your career would be over. Hold on a sec," she said.

Werner listened to her conversing with advertising people in Los Angeles. He imagined himself shackled to a table in front of a jury while Payne and Felicia's lawyer took turns pointing their fingers at him and calling him a monster.

She came back on the line.

"I gotta go in about three minutes," she said, "but I'll call you tonight."

"Just so I know what to expect," Werner said sadly, "you're going to continue using a lawyer who wants to sue me because I supposedly took advantage of you?"

"I tried to tell him how we felt about each other," she said, "but then I realized I wasn't sure myself. I mean, I know how I feel sometimes, but you . . . It's like I've always said, you never tell me what you think."

"But we've been . . . seeing each other," Werner said. "You said yourself it was intimacy. And I felt that, too," Werner said. "Intimacy is what you feel; it's not done with words."

"My lawyer told me it wasn't intimacy. He said that I was in a very vulnerable position, and that you were taking advantage of me."

"Me taking advantage of you?" Werner yelled. "Did you tell him what you'd asked me to do? How does he think that would play in front of a jury?"

"He said I only did that because I was distraught and at my wits' end about how to end my father's suffering. He said terrible things. He said you were not going to help me end my father's suffering unless I had sex with you first. He said that was a breach of your ethical obligation to my father and to me. I told him that wasn't the way it was, and he said I was too upset and too caught up in it to be objective. He still wants to sue you, and I keep telling him no, but it's hard."

"Hard? What do you mean it's hard?" Werner said, feeling his palm slick with sweat against the receiver. "Now you're thinking about letting him sue me and make all those ridiculous accusations?"

"I thought they were ridiculous, too," she said. "But my lawyer tells me things that make me think. For instance, let me ask you something. That night my father almost died, remember? And I was at your apartment? Not that Code thingy but the first night, when he had heart problems. Remember?"

"Yeah, yeah," Werner said, impatiently.

"Well, my lawyer gets updated copies of the charts every week. And he said that the nurse called you at home and told you that my father was very sick and that he was getting ready to have an arrest. He said that the nurse wrote in the chart that Dr. Butz and Dr. Ernst were notified."

Werner felt another heat rash explode across his chest.

"So I guess I want to know why you didn't tell me," she said.

"That's a mistake," Werner said, smelling his own sweat. "The only time they called me at home was the time I told you about the Code Blue."

She paused at the other end.

"They didn't call you the night he had the Code Blue," she said. "You called them, remember?"

"That's what I meant," he said. "The night I called them. That was the only time I talked to them."

"Maybe it is a mistake," she said. "I don't know. It's just another thing that my lawyer keeps harping on."

"I don't believe this is happening," Werner said. "I thought we felt something for each other. If we could just get these lawyers out of the way, you'd see it."

"I wish there was a way we could just make it all disappear," she said, sobbing into the phone, "the whole mess, my dad, the lawyers, the lawsuit, everything. I wish it would just vanish. Then we could start all over again."

Maybe he heard tenderness returning to her voice.

"I've really got to go this time," she said. "If you make me cry, I'll mess up the two-hour job they did on my face for the shooting. I'll call you. Maybe something will just happen. Maybe we won't have a hearing."

"Maybe you'll get a new lawyer," he said.

"I don't think I can," she said. "Don't think about it. Take your own advice."

Chapter

14

At 7:00 P.M., he went back to his apartment and waited for her call. At 9:00, he began calling her answering machine. At 10:00 he called long-distance information and got the number of Renèe Feral cosmetics. A machine answered Renèe Feral's number and told him to call back during business hours.

He tried to sleep and failed.

As he went along in his residency, he learned that sleepiness was a zone between two waking states. Most people pass from the well-rested waking state, to sleepiness in the evening, and then to bed. Thus the common misconception is that the longer one stays awake, the sleepier one gets. Medical residents quickly learn that sleepiness lasts only about eight hours. Then begins the other, unpleasant, wide-awake state of nervous exhaustion, the evil twin of wakefulness.

Werner's subconscious razzed him mercilessly: *Did I hear you say about twelve hours ago that you had to stay awake? Well, here we are. Do you have a deck of cards?*

Eventually scotch closed his eyes and submersed him in hypna-gogic torpor. Constance promptly appeared, dressed as one of the

Weird Sisters, and stirred him in a caldron of double trouble. "Sleep no more!" she roared. "Werner does murder sleep . . . the death of each day's life, sore labor's bath. . . . Sleep no more! Werner has murdered sleep, and therefore, the doctor shall sleep no more, Werner shall sleep no more! The doctor shall sleep no more!"

He woke up at 3:00 A.M. and went to the refrigerator. A two-liter bottle half full of old cola and a package of individually wrapped American cheese slices. He shook the cola without getting even a trace of a fizz. He tore open a cheese slice and poured himself a glass of brown sugar water.

It was just as well she had not called and just as well he had not reached her. He might have lost control in his sleepless anxiety and driven her into the arms of her waiting lawyers.

Sleep had cleared his head. The solution was to save Bed Five from the schemes of the attorneys and the zeal of the physicians. Sleep had shown him that Bed Five was nothing but a pawn in the war among the lawyers, the doctors, and his family. Werner peered into the future and saw three lawyers on one side of Bed Five's bed, and three doctors on the other. They bickered back and forth for days, weeks, months, the lawyers being paid by the hour, and the doctors being paid by the procedure.

It also occurred to him that the legal drama erupting around Bed Five was just the sort of intractable mess that called for a scapegoat. He could feel himself growing scape-horns and scape-hooves. The ceremony would take place at the hearing, where Hatchett and the other lawyers would crown Werner with the sins and desperate motives of what might be called the community of Bed Five; then Werner would be banished forever.

If the lawyers had their way, we would return to the primitive times of witch doctors and medicine men. In those glorious times, the community brought dying people to the medicine man's house. If the sick person got better, the medicine man received gifts of cattle and grain; if the sick person died, the medicine man was stoned to death and set adrift on a raft with two slaughtered chickens.

The choice was a simple one: Werner's career, which was just beginning, or the life of Bed Five, which was all but over. And nobody, not even Felicia, needed to know.

*   *   *

At 6:45 A.M., he was back at the console, watching Bed Five's rhythm on the monitor. He pulled the chart and found a printed report from Dr. Hofstader summarizing the reports of two neurologists who had been retained to testify as expert witnesses: one hired by the plaintiff, Felicia, and the other hired by the Medical Center.

Plaintiff's expert concluded that Bed Five was in a persistent vegetative state—a form of eyes-open, permanent unconsciousness. Even though Bed Five had periods of sleep-wake cycles, he was totally unaware of himself and his environment. Bed Five had a functioning brainstem but absolutely no cerebral cortical function. The capacity to chew and swallow had been lost because these require intact cerebral hemispheres. The metabolic rate for glucose in the cerebral cortex was not compatible with consciousness. Because Bed Five had been in a persistent vegetative state for a period of two months, there was a high degree of medical certainty that the condition would not change and that the insertion of a gastrostomy tube would provide no benefit to the patient or his family. The neurologist noted that his analysis was consistent with guidelines adopted by the Executive Board of the American Academy of Neurology.

The hospital's neurology expert concluded that the CAT scans, PET scans, and MRI scans were ambiguous and that the metabolic rate of glucose in the cerebral hemispheres, although diminished, did not conclusively indicate a total loss of cerebral cortical function. The patient often lifted his head in the presence of others in the room. The expert also noted a wide range of random or spontaneous movements, most notably the repeated tapping of the fingers of the right hand on the bed rails, which the expert concluded was Bed Five's primitive attempts to communicate with the world outside himself. The expert stated that he had personally moved Bed Five's right hand away from the bed rail on three occasions. Each time, according to the expert, Bed Five's right hand slowly returned to the rail and resumed purposeful tapping in an attempt to get the attention of those around him.

The hospital's expert admitted that Bed Five apparently could not consistently respond to commands to squeeze one's hand or lift his head, but the ability and desire to communicate could be erratic or intermittent. Under the expert's observation, Bed Five had responded to eight out of twelve requests to squeeze the speaker's hand and had lifted his head off the bed three out of five times upon request.

The hospital's expert concluded that two months was an insufficient amount of time to say with medical certainty that Bed Five had no reasonable chance of regaining cognitive, sapient thought. The expert also hypothesized that Bed Five's apparent neurological deficits and the reduced rate of glucose metabolism in the cerebral cortex could be caused by his debilitated condition and his poor nutrition. The expert recommended insertion of the gastrostomy tube, followed by at least four weeks of appropriate nutrition, at which time the CAT scans, PET scans, and MRI scans should be repeated.

Poindexter appeared at Werner's elbow. He was pale, even paler than he normally looked at the end of a graveyard shift.

"May I see you for a moment?" Poindexter asked. "In Bed Five."

"What is it?" Werner said, following Poindexter into the machine-filled pod.

Bed Five was as frail and blue as ever. Memories of the report sent Werner's eyes straight to the fingers pinging on the bed rails.

"I noticed you reading Hofstader's summaries of the neurology reports," Poindexter said. "I read them at start of shift last night."

Poindexter grimaced sheepishly, as if he were still deciding whether to tell Werner what was on his mind.

"Did you know this guy was a signalman in the Navy?" Poindexter asked.

"No," Werner said, instantly recalling Felicia's description of an accident at sea and Bed Five's desire not to be kept alive by machines if anything ever happened.

"Well, you've seen the fat one who comes in here with her Bible every day?"

"Constance Potter," Werner said.

"Right," Poindexter said. "She has a tendency to run off at the mouth, and that was one of the things she told me about him. He was a signalman."

"So what?" Werner said, studying Poindexter in this uncharacteristic state of agitation and uncertainty.

"Well," Poindexter said, "after I read that summary last night, I started thinking about the fingers tapping. And I started wondering. . . . What if the family's neurologist was right? What if the tapping was a purposeful attempt at communication?"

"Be serious," Werner said. "You need sleep."

"I kept thinking about how he was a signalman," Poindexter said, "because I was a ham radio operator for years. A signalman would know Morse code."

"I take it back," Werner said. "You don't need sleep; you're having transient ischemic attacks that are preventing blood flow to your brain."

Poindexter blushed. "Listen, if you could watch the fat one in here with him. She thinks she's having entire conversations with him. It just started me thinking. What if he really can hear us, or what if he really is trying to tell us something?"

"If he was trying to tell us something," Werner said, "he would squeeze your hand on command. After what we've done to him, he'd reach out and twist your balls off. He'd poke you in the ribs when you were doing your hourlies. Get serious, Poindexter. If he was with it enough to do Morse code for you, he'd sit up in bed and spit in your eye."

"I thought the same thing," Poindexter said. "Then I started wondering if maybe there wasn't some weird neurological deficit, or maybe his strokes knocked out all lines of communication except one. What about those stroke patients who can read and write but can't talk? What if it was a hemorrhage in Broca's area or some other clot in a weird spot? You know how neuro can be. I'm not saying he's doing Morse code. It was just a wild notion."

"Most wild," Werner said, watching the tremoring fingers pinging away.

"Anyway," Poindexter said, "about two-thirty in the morning I started watching his fingers and wondering, just for the hell of it, what he would be saying if he was sending code."

"I'm leaving," Werner said. "I won't tell anybody about this. You won't have to be embarrassed around anyone except me."

Poindexter laughed. "OK, then, it's a joke." He got out a pad of paper with dots and hash marks on it.

"I take it that this is the Gettysburg Address in Morse code," Werner said.

Poindexter laughed again. "Do you know how code works?"

"No," Werner said, "but that looks like fourscore and seven chimpanzees were locked in a room with a pencil and a pad of paper."

"Letters are made up of dots and dashes," Poindexter explained. "A dot is a brief depression of the telegraph key. A dash lasts three times as long as a dot. You probably learned in Boy Scouts that SOS is dot, dot, dot—dash, dash, dash—dot, dot, dot. Three dots, three dashes, and three dots. Letters are separated by pauses the length of one dash; words are separated by pauses the length of two dashes."

"What separates the walls of your skull?" Werner asked.

"Now," Poindexter said, walking over to the tremoring right hand, "just watch his fingers for a few minutes. Just pretend that his fingers are tapping on a big telegraph key instead of a bed rail. There are short taps and long ones, with pauses between."

"Yeah," Werner said. "And Santa Claus and the Easter Bunny visit every dwelling on the planet in a single twenty-four-hour period once a year."

Werner watched the spastic fingers tremoring against the bed rails.

"It doesn't look like three dots, three dashes, and three dots to me," Werner said.

"It's not," Poindexter said. "He's not sending an SOS. I simply used that as an example."

"I take it you've deciphered a message from all this, or you wouldn't have told me about it," Werner said.

"I did," Poindexter quietly said, and turned away from Werner.

"Well?" Werner asked. "Does he want somebody to bring him his pants so he can go out for a cheeseburger and an order of fries?"

"No," Poindexter said. "He says the same thing over and over. It never changes. Here."

Poindexter handed Werner the pad. The dots and dashes were arranged in groups on the page over their respective letters and the words "D-O Y-O-U L-O-V-E M-E."

Werner read the words and felt depression settling in. Why was the best nurse in the Med Center telling him something this ludicrous?

"So you're telling me he's saying, 'Do you love me' over and over, right?" Werner said. "Now you're going to tell me he's a

Beatles fan. He likes that song. Tomorrow he'll tap out 'I Wanna Hold Your Hand' for us."

Werner checked his anger, because Poindexter was a valuable nurse in a profession staffed with wombats.

"OK," Werner said. "Let's pretend you're on to something. Let's say he's lost all lines of communication except finger tapping. Why don't you just ask him a question and see if he types you a different message? For starters, how about asking him, 'Am I having brain fade, or are you sending Morse code?' and see what he says?"

"I tried that," Poindexter said.

"And?" Werner asked.

"He tapped out, 'Do you love me.' "

"Did you ask him anything else?"

"Yeah," Poindexter said. "I asked him if he could hear me. He tapped out, 'Do you love me.' "

"Poindexter," Werner said with a sigh, "vegetative patients characteristically have a narrow range of stereotyped movements that are repeated. They have startle reflexes, tremors, fasciculations, spasms, tetany, and contractions. What you're seeing is a damaged brain sending a pattern of impulses."

"I don't know," Poindexter said. "I don't understand it. I don't know why he would be sending the same thing over and over. I just know what it looks like he's doing. It looks like Morse code to me. And how would a brainstem send the same complex pattern over and over?"

"When this guy goes," Werner said, "the autopsy will show overwhelming bilateral damage to the cerebral hemispheres. You know it, and I know it. You could get more cognition out of a penlight battery in a bowl of tapioca pudding."

"I suppose," Poindexter said.

"Are you going to chart any of this?" Werner asked.

"I was going to talk to you first," Poindexter said.

"I'm not about to tell you what to chart," Werner said. "But if I were you, I wouldn't chart pure speculation, especially at the end of a night without sleep."

Poindexter put his pad away and held Bed Five's hand. "I think I'm going to chart that I detected possible attempts at purposeful communications in the movements of the patient's right hand, but that I could not verify those communications. My observations would be consistent with the Medical Center's position in this litigation."

Werner shrugged. "Would your observations be consistent with reality?"

"I've got hourly checks to do," Poindexter said, checking the Soluset on the dopamine drip.

"What's his FIO_2 these days?" Werner asked.

"Seventy-five percent," Poindexter replied.

Werner returned to the console and reread the summary of the neurology reports. Gray, gray, gray. Bed Five's skin color was gray. His hair was gray. His brain was gray. He was gray-faced. He was not alive or dead; he was gray. Werner went to the Nurses' Notes in Bed Five's charts. He had trouble finding them because, like most physicians, he did not waste precious time reading the professional opinions of nurses.

Just as he suspected, several wombats had also adopted the Medical Center's party line. Marie Something had recorded her observation of tears in the eyes of Bed Five, seen during visits from the patient's daughters. Marie went out of her way to point out that, in her learned estimation, the tears were much more copious than the secretions stimulated by the reflex eye blinking that keeps the conjunctiva of the eyes moist. Marie opined that Bed Five produced tears because he felt emotion.

The Hippoblimp had written that Bed Five had lifted his head off the pillow on command two out of three times and that she "sensed" that when she was in the room, the patient was aware of her. *Never mind the glucose metabolism rate,* Werner thought. *If Martha Henderson "senses" something, the tests must be flawed.*

Werner could see where this was going: to a trial. After the hearing on Bed Five's medical treatment was over, Felicia's lawyer would launch a hysterical inquest into Werner's attempted seduction of the patient's unstable daughter. He had seen enough TV to know what was waiting for him in court.

Ladies and gentlemen of the jury, this is the story of a doctor who abused his position of power and privilege and took advantage of a vulnerable, emotionally distraught woman. Felicia Potter's father was a patient of the defendant, Dr. Peter Werner Ernst. Mr. Potter had been terminally ill for months and had been kept alive, against his will and against the will of his daughter, by the machines in the intensive care unit. Felicia Potter tried to end her father's suffering, but the doctors said no.

When she was at her wits' end and crippled by desperation, she went to the defendant for help. Dr. Ernst took her into a room at the hospital and told her that she had no choice but to accept the continuing medical treatment of her father. Over a period of several weeks, while her father lay dying in the intensive care unit, Dr. Ernst met with Felicia Potter, once at her apartment and twice at his apartment, and tried to have sexual intercourse with her. She refused. And when she refused, he pressed her and coaxed her, even threatened her.

"Dr. Ernst," the lawyer would say, "on the night of August fourth, at approximately nine P.M., where were you?"

"I was at home in my apartment."

"Were you alone?"

"No. Felicia Potter came to visit me."

"Ask that the witness be instructed to simply answer the question.

"While you were with Miss Potter in your apartment, did you receive any phone calls from the hospital?"

"No."

"No? Do you know a nurse named Stella Stanley?"

"Yes."

"If Nurse Stella Stanley noted in the patient's chart that she called you on the night of August fourth and told you that your patient Mr. Potter was in heart block and was in a serious condition, then she must have made a mistake, is that right?"

"That's right."

That would never hold up. Constance, Dr. Hofstader, Payne, Wilson, maybe even Poindexter and Stella would take the stand against him. OK, he would admit it then.

"Yes, I did receive a phone call from Miss Stanley regarding the patient in Bed Five, Nine ICU."

"And the patient in Bed Five, Nine ICU, was Miss Potter's father, correct?"

"That's right."

"Did you tell Miss Potter that her father was in a serious condition?"

"No."

"Why not?"

"I thought it would upset her."

"Your testimony is that you thought her father's serious condition would upset her, so you didn't tell her?"

"That's right."

"Were you with Miss Potter again at your apartment, on the evening of August fifth?"

"Yes."

"Did you receive more information from the hospital about Miss Potter's father at that time?"

"Yes. When I called the hospital about another patient, I learned that Mr. Potter had suffered a cardiac arrest."

"Did you share that information with Miss Potter?"

"Yes."

"So you did not tell Miss Potter that her father was in a serious condition on August fourth, because you thought it might upset her. But on August fifth, twenty-four hours later, you freely told Miss Potter that her father had suffered a cardiac arrest and that he had been resuscitated. Perhaps you can explain, Dr. Ernst?"

He could not allow it to occur. It would be the end of his life. The end of six years of brutal work, of rote memorization, of sleepless nights and hallucinatory days, of struggle and self-denial. And it would end with him on the stand. He would have to get his own lawyer, at a cost of thousands of dollars. The litigation would go on for years.

"After receiving the phone call from Nurse Stanley on the night of August fourth and learning that Miss Potter's father was on the verge of a cardiac arrest and death, did you again attempt to have sexual intercourse with Miss Potter?"

"How many times did you attempt to have sexual intercourse with Miss Potter?"

"Did you ever suggest to Miss Potter that you would

'treat' her and provide her with medications that would make it easier for her to have sexual intercourse with you?"

"You must understand," Payne had said, "that in any litigation conducted by competent attorneys the truth will come out; it's only a matter of when."

The truth could not come out. There was one way to see that it did not. The hearing was going to occur because Felicia was seeking an injunction against further medical treatment of the patient. Without a patient, there would be no hearing.

Poindexter left and a day shift wombat took over in Bed Five. At 9:00 A.M. the wombat did her hourlies and hung a new dopamine drip. Lab techs stuck Bed Five for blood cultures, and an X-ray tech took a picture of his chest to see if the antibiotics were clearing out the pneumonia. The respiratory therapist checked the ventilator and left.

A gurney brought a new admission to Bed Seven, and a small crowd gathered as a nurse read the orders aloud from the chart to the technicians and therapists standing by with machines.

Werner ducked into Bed Five, dialed down the dopamine, and turned down the FIO_2 on the ventilator to room air. Twenty seconds later, he was back at the console. Just a wee bit out of breath, a few butterflies, but not much in the way of guilt. It was so easy! Just two mechanical adjustments on a couple of machines. He had done nothing to Bed Five. He had not even touched Bed Five. Werner was simply removing mechanical obstacles from Bed Five, so Bed Five could continue his peaceful descent. In half an hour, Bed Five would be eternally happy, Werner would be free of the hearing, all would be right with the vegetable world.

His only mistake had been trusting her when she was obviously not to be trusted.

At 9:15, Werner saw a pacer spike fail to capture on the monitor. It was starting already, he thought. He watched the other nurses congregating in Bed Seven with the new admission.

The unit clerk handed him a phone. "It's for you," she said. "In house. Mr. Wilson in the Legal Department."

"This is Dr. Ernst," Werner said, watching another spike miss on the monitor. The unit clerk got into a conversation with a nun from Pastoral Care.

"Ernst, we have our documents," Wilson said. "I thought you'd like to know."

"What documents?" Werner said, squirming at the prospect of a long telephone conversation, during which he might not be able to get back to Bed Five before the wombat returned for her half-hourly blood pressure check.

"The discovery from the other parties in this case," Wilson said irritably, "the will, the trust, everything."

Also, Werner had to be back in Bed Five to readjust the machines before Bed Five coded; otherwise the Code Blue team would find the ventilator delivering room air and the dopamine dialed off.

Werner's heart threw a premature ventricular contraction when he saw the unit clerk lead the nun from Pastoral Care into Bed Five's pod. What was she going in there for?

"Great," Werner said.

"Great?" Wilson said. "It's not great. It's just what we thought it was. This is a battle between the two daughters over the testamentary trust left by wife number two, Miss Felicia's mom."

"What do you mean?" Werner said, noticing a spurt of V-tach breaking across Bed Five's monitor and watching the nun through the glass. The rhythm returned to normal, paced sinus.

"I mean," Wilson said, becoming exasperated, "that we have the complete trust instrument, and we have Bed Five's will. The trust provides that if Bed Five dies before he's seventy, the entire trust, income, principal, everything, is distributed to Miss Felicia Potter. Two million bucks, free and clear of taxes and all liabilities."

Werner swallowed hard and stared through the glass of Bed Five. His stomach tightened and squirted digestive juices into his esophagus.

"Are you sure?" Werner said, swallowing the burning acid and eyeing the dopamine. He checked his watch at 9:22 and saw the nun hold Bed Five's right hand in hers.

"What do you mean, am I sure?" Wilson snapped. "I've got a certified copy of the trust instrument right in front of me, and the thing has already been combed over by the trust and estates lawyers in Payne's firm. Miss Felicia gets it all if Bed Five takes the long walk in the night within the next two weeks."

Another short run of V-tach on the monitor. A wombat glanced at the monitors and went back into Bed Seven. The nun closed her eyes. Was she praying?

"And guess what happens if he lives to see seventy? Old Constance will get the whole wad. She will take the entire trust under the residuary clause of the will. Miss Felicia gets a couple spendthrift trusts from the old man, but the whole testamentary trust set up by Felicia's natural mother will go straight to Constance. I think both of them are playing the same game."

"But—"

"But what?" Wilson said.

"I don't know," Werner said. "I thought they each got half. I thought that's what you said when we talked."

"No, sir," Wilson said. "I said we didn't know. Now, we know. Felicia Potter gets the whole kit and caboodle if the old man goes within the next two weeks. And if he doesn't, Constance gets it."

"Where did the will come from?" Werner asked.

"Let's see," Wilson said, riffling papers. "The will came from Miss Felicia's attorney. Apparently it was in a safety-deposit box."

"Is that the only will?" Werner asked, a chill sweeping through him.

"Of course, it's the only will," Wilson said. "These are good lawyers. They play by the rules. If either of these guys had another will, he'd have produced it. Believe me. This is expedited discovery under court supervision. If there was any sandbagging going on, the judge would cut off some fingers. What makes you think there's another will?" Wilson asked.

"Nothing," Werner said. "It was a TV program I saw once. I just thought maybe there was another will—"

"I gotta warn you," Wilson said. "Payne is convinced you know things you're not telling us. I keep telling him that you're just green and that you're not holding back. You see what's brewing here," Wilson said. "These broads are playing this guy's life like a stock option. This could get ugly for everybody. I see three or four pieces of litigation coming out of this thing, not to mention criminal charges if there's anything insidious going on. You want to be on the right side if any of this stuff goes to trial."

"I understand," Werner said.

Werner got off the phone and went into Bed Five. The nun opened her eyes and smiled.

"Excuse me," Werner said, momentarily flustered. "I just have a few . . . adjustments to make."

He dialed the dopamine back up and watched the nun close her eyes again. He stood across the bed from her and next to the ventilator, close enough to dial the oxygen back to 75 percent in less than a second if anything happened.

Used! Things were happening too fast. He had been used. But did it make a difference as far as his own plans for Bed Five? If he dialed the oxygen back up, he might be able to save him. Maybe he could prove that she had used him, that she had plotted the thing from the beginning. Then she would be on the hot seat. But could he prove it? Even if he could prove it, would he appear more or less foolish to Hofstader and the rest of the profession? He would certainly be cast adrift from the Med Center's attorneys, as punishment for lying to the mighty Payne, if not for another, better, legal reason.

And none of it made any difference to Bed Five. He still needed to die.

The nun had sandwiched Bed Five's twitching hand in both of hers. She wore a habit of coarse brown cloth that covered her head, with a rope at her waist, and a rosary necklace.

"Excuse me," Werner said.

She opened her eyes and smiled again.

"May I ask you something?" Werner said, standing across from her. "Have you had any indication from him that he is still . . . alert in any way?"

The nun shrugged her shoulders, looked down at Bed Five's death mask, and smiled.

"I'm not qualified to detect that sort of thing," she said. "That's probably your department, Doctor. I'm a sister. I pray."

Werner looked again at Bed Five's fingers twitching in the nun's hands. "I just wondered if you were perhaps comforting him because you had some indication that he was still . . . conscious?"

She smiled broadly again. "That's not so important, is it?" she said, patting Bed Five's hand. "I'm not even sure what that means. Prayers are made with small, simple words. 'Consciousness' is a big word. I'm sure 'consciousness' has medical and legal definitions that are beyond the powers of my poor brain. I would comfort him whether he was conscious or not."

Werner persisted. "But if he was unconscious, he wouldn't know you were comforting him, would he?"

"You are too clever," she said with a genuine smile. "I keep forgetting what can be done with words. Somebody once told me that God gave speech to man so he could hide his thoughts. I am constantly amazed at what people do with words."

She patted Bed Five's hand, then reached up and smoothed his forehead.

"I guess I'm asking you this," Werner blurted, deciding to plunge ahead in the interest of science. "What if he's already dead? You realize these machines," he said, with a sweep of his hand, "can keep people alive for a long time after they're already technically dead."

"It doesn't matter," she said. "I am praying for him, and I am present for him if he needs me. If he's dead, then my prayers and God the Father are with him. If he's not dead, then my prayers and God the Father are with him."

"But if he's dead," Werner said, staring again at Bed Five's hand and deciding to come to the point, "then he can't feel you holding his hand, right? He doesn't know you're holding his hand, any more than a—"

"Corpse," she said, catching Werner's eye. "Any more than a corpse would know?"

"I guess," Werner said, "Yeah, any more than a corpse would know."

"I think you give death more credit than it's due," she said. "It's an important event in your line of work. In my field, it's not so important. For us it is a joyful time, and we celebrate. It's like a big birthday or a silver wedding anniversary. But for the person who dies, almost nothing changes. I think of it as taking off our clothes. When we take off our clothes, we look different, but then we get into bed and think about the same things we thought about when we had our clothes on."

Werner watched Bed Five's failing rhythm.

"People like to think that death changes everything," she said. "They think of it as moving into a big magnificent house. But people who move into big, magnificent houses stay pretty much the same. If they were unhappy before they moved, they will be unhappy in the big, magnificent house. Death is the same way.

People like to think they live one way; then they will die and live a totally different life. Maybe they think they can spend their whole lives loving only the material things, certain that they will be able to forget about those things once they take off their clothes."

"But after we die," Werner said, "and eternity begins, we won't have our bodies, there won't be any material things. That's a big difference."

"Exactly," she said. "After death, we will be obsessed by the same things that obsessed us in life, but those things won't be there. If we loved only money in life, we will love it even more after death, and we will wander through eternity searching frantically for money. If we loved only power, or fame, or food, or any of the other idols, we will become like them. We will be obsessed only by them, in life and in death. But you made one mistake. You said, 'after we die and eternity begins,' which is the source of this confusion. Eternity has no beginning. It has no end. It is the now and forever. It is all time, and no time. Eternity cannot come after life; by definition it includes life. It cannot come after anything; it is everything. We make eternity every day, every hour, every second; we choose what our eternity will be."

Werner dialed up the oxygen on the ventilator.

"But what about these people?" Werner said, indicating the entire Unit with a jerk of his head. "Their life is nothing but suffering. Are you telling me they'll go on suffering forever?"

"We all suffer," she said. "Suffering teaches us to love each other. When we see others suffer, we love them, and we comfort them, because we, too, have suffered, and we remember what it is like to be suffering pain or loneliness and to have one cool hand touch our brow, to have a person love us for no reason."

Her voice paralyzed him. He felt goose bumps and wanted to rest his head in her hands.

"These machines. The building. You and me. This is all tissue paper," she said, with a sweep of her hand. "At the proper time, you'll be able to part it like a curtain."

"I guess we look at the world differently," Werner said.

"Do we?" she said. "A teacher once told me, 'Be careful how you look at the world, it *is* like that.' "

She smiled. "Take you, for instance," she said.

"Me?" Werner said. "What?"

"You probably love science, but you love it because you use it to heal and comfort people. If you loved science only for its own sake, it would be an idol, and you would be practicing idolatry, not medicine. You wouldn't do that."

"No," Werner said. "I wouldn't." He felt a tear break in the corner of his right eye and turned that side of his face away from her.

"The truth is, Sister, I don't love science. I don't know why I am here."

"Of course you do," she said. "You're here to help this man. He's suffering."

"But it's not that simple," Werner said. "It's complicated. Help according to whom? What does 'help' mean? What does 'mean' mean? People are using this man. I—I have used him. Other people have used me and used him."

"People have always used one another," she said, smiling for him. "But you don't want to go on using and being used, or you wouldn't be having this conversation with me, would you?"

"I guess not," Werner said, crying openly.

"Pray, listen to your heart, and trust God," she said. "You're trying to understand too much. Reason will always obscure what we wish to keep in shadows. This man is your father. You must love and comfort him. If you both were dead, and your clothes were off, would you embrace him, or would you turn away from him?"

Werner looked at Bed Five's purpling death's head. "I would be ashamed," Werner said, wiping tears from his cheeks.

"Because you used him and because you do not love him," she said. "But you can change. You can teach yourself to love what is important and what will still be there when you take off your clothes and lie down in the night."

"But according to you," Werner said, "no matter what we love, it won't be with us after we die. Our bodies, our minds, everything will be gone," Werner said, "except our souls, or something, and eternity, I guess."

"No," she said, looking across Bed Five and into Werner's eyes. "I will still be here, holding this man's hand and praying. You will still be here, asking me these important questions and struggling to love me, and to love this man, and to love yourself. God the Father will still be here, and everyone who ever lived will still be here, too. They will all still be watching us. And we will have this important conversation. Forever."

Werner heard the hospital operator announcing the Code.

"Sister," Werner said, his voice cracking and tears appearing again at the cracks of his eyes, "I must ask you to step outside, because a lot of people will be coming in here."

Werner pointed at the monitor. "His heart is stopping."